Zanoye
Zanoyean, Vahan,
The sacred sands : a novel /
$16.95   ocn992981080

WITHDRAWN

Sacred Sands

A NOVEL

VAHAN ZANOYAN

This book is a work of fiction. All names, organizations, events and places are the product of the author's imagination. Any resemblance of actual persons, places and events is coincidental.

Cover photo courtesy of Bruno Barbey and Magnum Photos
Author photo by Charlotte Zanoyan
Cover Design by Linda M. Ganjian

Copyright© 2016 by Vahan Zanoyan

ISBN: 0998392405
ISBN 13: 9780998392400

Library of Congress Control Number: 2016917524
gampr books
NewPort Beach, CA

For Maro and Papken
Without their devotion none of it could have happened

Also by Vahan Zanoyan

A Place Far Away

The Doves of Ohanavank

The
Sacred Sands

gampr
books

Terms and Acronyms

Al Nadwa	The Symposium: Secret organization of professionals in the Arabian Gulf States to promote civil society
Al Qaeda	The militant Islamic fundamentalist global organization founded by Osama bin Laden
AUB	American University of Beirut
BMA	Bahrain Monetary Agency
BP	British Petroleum
CENTCOM	United States Central Command, a combatant command of the U.S. Department of Defense, based in Tampa, Florida
Downstream	The refining and marketing sector of the petroleum industry
EBITDA	Earnings before interest, taxes, depreciation, and amortization
Fao	The reference is to the Fao Peninsula in Iraq
Forward months	Future trading months of a commodity
GAAP	Generally accepted accounting principles
GCC	Gulf Cooperation Council. Members: Saudi Arabia, Kuwait, the UAE, Oman, Qatar, and Bahrain
Going (selling) short	The sale of a security (or other financial instrument, including futures) not owned by the seller
JNOC	Japan National Oil Company
KPC	Kuwait Petroleum Corporation
Limit up or down	The maximum amount by which the price of a commodities futures contract may advance or decline in one trading day
MITI	Ministry of International Trade and Industry, Japan
Motouri	The Japanese refining and marketing industry

Neutral Zone	Zone in the Persian Gulf shared by Saudi Arabia and Kuwait
NOCs	National oil companies
NYMEX	New York Mercantile Exchange
OPEC	Organization of Petroleum Exporting Countries
PCG	Petroleum Consulting Group
Short position	Position created by selling short
SOMO	State Oil Marketing Organization, Iraq
Spot month	The nearest delivery month on a futures contract
Statoil	National Oil Company of Norway
Symposium (The)	"Al Nadwa" in Arabic, the name of the secret organization in the Arabian Gulf States to promote civil society
Upstream	The (crude oil) exploration and production sector of the petroleum industry

Cast of Characters

Americans

Aimi Kaysik	CIA operative who cooperates with James Blackburn
Andy Zeller	Oil trader and chief technical analyst at A. Nitzen
Chelsea Blackburn	James Blackburn's daughter
Don Underwood	Oil trader at Tafco Securities
Gene Theiss	Retired CIA operative, close family friend of James Blackburn
George Ackley	Oil trader at A. Nitzen
George Shultz	U.S. secretary of state
Henry Blackburn	James Blackburn's father, deceased Foreign Service officer
James Blackburn	Global energy consultant, based in Washington, DC. Main character.
James Schlesinger	Former head of the CIA, secretary of defense, and secretary of energy of the United States
Jan Gabriel	Financial officer at PCG
Jerry Fishbine	Financial advisor who structures the sale of PCG
Jim Purdy	Energy correspondent for *The Financial Times*
Joe Edwards	Energy correspondent for *The New York Times*
Jon Solomon	Oil trader at A. Nitzen
Linda Hays	James Blackburn's secretary
Martha Blackburn	James Blackburn's mother
Mike Goldberg	Oil trader at A. Nitzen
Patrick Hagan	James Blackburn's associate at PCG
Robert Russell	Partner and president of Wilks, Russell & Co., a large public relations firm based in Washington, DC

Sophie Myles	Employee at Wilks, Russell & Co., and James Blackburn's girlfriend
Stanley Simmons	Chief of oil trading group at A. Nitzen
Steve Summers	Oil trader at A. Nitzen
Tom Bricks	Oil trader at A. Nitzen
Tony	Broker executing clients' orders on NYMEX

Arabs

Abdulaziz bin Salman	Saudi Arabian official at the Ministry of Oil}
Ali Khalifa Al-Sabah	Minister of petroleum, Kuwait
Fahda	Daughter of Karim Suliman
Fatima	Maid of Princess Hassa Al Saud
Hassa Al-Saud	Saudi princess studying at the American University of Beirut
Hisham Nazer	Minister of oil, Saudi Arabia
Issam Al-Tikriti	Iraqi operative with close ties to both Baghdad and Washington
Jaber	The reference is to Sheikh Jaber Al Sabah, the emir (ruler) of Kuwait
Juhayman Al Oteibi	Leader of group of insurgents that organized the siege of the Grand Mosque of Mecca in November 1979
Kamal Ashkar	Official of the Saudi Oil Ministry and member of The Symposium
Karim Suliman	Former Saudi Secret Service official who joins The Symposium and oversees its security structure
Majed Al-Shammary	Soldier in the Saudi Arabian National Guard and member of The Symposium
Ramzi Amin	Naturalized Kuwaiti citizen, businessman and Oil Ministry official, founder and intellectual leader of The Symposium
Rashid Al-Awadi	Official at the Kuwaiti Ministry of Finance
Saqr Al-Khalifa	Official at the BMA
Steve Kudairi	Correspondent for *The Middle East Economic Digest*
Yousef Anis	Ramzi Amin's nephew

Japanese

Akiko	Masahiro Akiyama's wife
Akiyama, Masahiro	Official of Idemitsu Kosan, a Japanese oil company
Furukawa, Hiroshi	President of Japan National Oil Company
Hayashi	Official at the Agency of Natural Resources and Energy at MITI
Itai, Makoto	Director of the Petroleum Department of the Agency of Natural Resources and Energy
Kato, Suzuki	Head of Middle East operations of the Japanese trading firm C. Itoh
Kawasaki	Executive at Fuji Kosan Oil Company, assistant to Kiyoshi Kurai
Kobayashi	Resident housekeeper of Idemitsu Kosan's executive resort in Gora, Japan
Kurai, Kiyoshi	Chief executive of Fuji Kosan Oil Company
Kyoko	Kurai's concubine
Mariko	Japanese singer Blackburn meets in Tokyo
Miyazaki, Akio	Director general of MITI's Agency of Natural Resources and Energy
Nagayama	Chairman of Nippon Oil Company
Okada, Sadahiru	Chairman of Idemitsu Kosan
Sato, Noburo	Official of C. Itoh negotiating a deal with Fuji Kosan and KPC
Takao	C. Itoh's representative in Washington, DC
Yamata, Masaji	Person who replaces Akio Miyazaki

Europeans and Others

Anthony Kraus	Son of Stefan and Bianca Kraus
Bianca Kraus	Executive assistant at the OPEC Secretariat in Vienna, who has a multi-year affair with James Blackburn
Paul Templeton	Official of British Petroleum
Roberto	Bianca Kraus' Italian lover
Rulwanu Lukman	Minister of oil, Nigeria
Stefan Kraus	Banker in Vienna, Bianca's husband

Prologue

November mid-1980s

It was another tense OPEC meeting, the kind that could easily shake the oil market and possibly the world economy. It was in its tenth day, with no clear direction as to which way the final outcome might fall. The oil ministers, along with members of their delegations, were being uncharacteristically tight-mouthed. Hints and highlights of the deliberations, which normally would be leaked generously, had been rare. But rumors ran wild as always, causing equally wild swings in the price of oil. Traders, reporters, speculators, and even the ministers were exhausted.

The Marriott Hotel in Vienna had been fully booked for two weeks, as were the Intercontinental, the Hilton and the Imperial. But the action was at the Marriott. Bilateral talks between ministers, before and after the formal ministerial meetings, were being held at the suites of the Saudi Arabian and Nigerian oil ministers at the Marriott.

The twenty-four-hour armed guards at both entrances of the Marriott had been there for the past ten days. There were two at each gate, in dark-green army fatigues and black berets, machine guns hanging casually from their shoulders. The plainclothes security guards at the elevator lobby on every floor did not carry machine guns. But Ramzi Amin knew they were armed. He had inspected the guards that were to stay on the tenth floor where his minister and other members of the Kuwaiti delegation had their suites.

The main issue at this meeting was not the Iran-Iraq war, which had dominated OPEC meetings for two years. It was the bitter acrimony among the countries of the Persian Gulf, which seemed to have launched yet another market-share battle against each other.

It was the Wednesday before Thanksgiving weekend. If the meeting came to an end after the futures market closed in New York, traders with the wrong positions would be stuck with devastating losses on the following Monday. The outcome of the meeting could easily push oil prices up or down by 15 to 20 percent.

In the early evening, the secretariat declared a closed ministerial session. That meant only the thirteen OPEC oil ministers could be in attendance. No aides or secretaries were allowed in the large meeting room on the mezzanine level of the hotel. No one could even come in to deliver a message, without the prior knowledge and approval of all. No minister could leave the meeting room. It was understood that no one would make or receive a phone call on the landline in the meeting room without the approval of all thirteen ministers. Of course, strictly speaking, any minister could violate these rules, but no one did. No one wanted to create any grounds for being suspected in case of a leak.

The reason for the closed session was that the ministers had already concluded their deliberations and were determined to bring the meeting officially to a close that same evening. But they would announce the outcome after 9:10 p.m. in Vienna, 3:10 p.m. in New York, when the futures market on Wall Street closed for the long weekend.

A draft of the final communiqué, handwritten by the secretary general, was circulated, and the thirteen ministers had a chance to suggest edits. It was short, just half a page. It had the potential of wreaking havoc in global oil markets when it was finally released. But the ministers were in no rush. It had just turned 7 p.m. They still had over two hours to have the communiqué typed and ready for distribution to the press.

Every table at the Garten Café in the lobby of the Marriott was occupied, and the hallway in front of the elevators was full of people. Members of the delegations of every OPEC country, along with reporters from the major wire services, newspapers and specialized energy journals, plus representatives of around half a dozen oil companies, and energy consultants and observers—some 200 people in all—had spent all day and most of every night in the lobby, waiting for news, speculating, predicting. For some, it was the thrill of being there. For others, it was business development: seeing their contacts again and, just as important, *being* seen, were both good for business. Some traders and oil companies were there to negotiate new deals with the oil producing countries. The reporters, especially those from the wire services, were extremely competitive. Getting news of any breakthrough or deadlock a few seconds before anyone else got it was a matter of survival. There was no way to cover an OPEC meeting other than being there. But this meeting had been as dry as a bone.

Suddenly there was a commotion. Futures prices of crude oil on the New York Mercantile Exchange were crashing. It was 8:45 p.m., 2:45 in New York. Trading would continue for another twenty-five minutes. The spot month went down by $1.65 per barrel in less than twenty minutes. Most forward months were limit down, that is, down by $1 per barrel, the maximum movement allowed in one day. Clearly, there was a major wave of short selling, but no one had a clue as to why. The OPEC secretariat was as shocked as the reporters in the lobby. As a rule, they had to investigate any price move of over 5 percent during an OPEC meeting. This was substantially larger.

A young reporter from Reuters came up with the first clue. A. Nitzen & Co. and Tafco Securities were the major sellers, and there were about a half dozen other trading firms and oil companies shorting the market. Everyone in the lobby knew what that meant. Both A. Nitzen and Tafco were clients of James Blackburn. But where was Blackburn? What did he know that no one else—not even members of the OPEC delegation hanging around with the reporters in the hotel lobby—knew?

*   *   *

James Blackburn had not been in the lobby that evening, or anywhere near the meeting room on the mezzanine. He had spent the whole afternoon and evening in a suite on the eighth floor of the Marriott. He had read the final OPEC communiqué with some amazement. This was not what the most seasoned OPEC observers would have expected. It was 8:15 p.m. in Vienna, which meant there was plenty of time to call his major clients before the market closed in New York. He gave Bianca a kiss on her naked shoulder, and walked to the bedroom of the suite to use the telephone.

*   *   *

An hour earlier, at 7:10 p.m., Bianca Kraus had been stepping out of the shower when she heard the phone ring. She wrapped a long towel around her slender body and ran to the telephone on the desk, leaving wet footprints on the plush, tan carpet. Water dripped from her short, dark brown hair down into the folds of the towel. James Blackburn looked longingly at her glistening neck and shoulders, and followed her out of the shower. He dried himself quickly, put on the white terrycloth bathrobe hanging in the bathroom, and joined her in the living room.

Bianca grabbed the phone, squeezed the handset between her ear and shoulder, and started taking dictation in shorthand. Blackburn gently rubbed her shoulders as she wrote.

"Shall I read it back to you?" she asked the person on the other end of the line when the dictation stopped.

"No need, unless you're not sure about something," replied the heavily accented voice of her boss. The entire communiqué was just one long paragraph, with no complicated terms or numbers.

"Okay then," said Bianca. "All clear. You can send someone to pick it up in half an hour."

She rolled her chair to face the typewriter at the right corner of the desk, and started typing. When she finished, she pulled the sheet of paper out of the typewriter and, without turning around, handed it to Blackburn, who was still standing behind her, rubbing her shoulders. He had loosened the towel somewhat, letting it slip and uncover part of her breasts.

"Proofread this for me, would you?"

He could not see her face, but sensed her smile through the tone of her voice. Sweet, naughty Bianca; she knew exactly what she was doing.

Fifteen minutes later an armed guard from the hotel appeared at the door of the suite. He picked up a sealed envelope and took it to the ministers, who made multiple copies of its contents on the photocopier in the corner of the room. Then they waited, helping themselves to coffee and pastries spread on a long counter next to the conference table. It was too late to change the final outcome of ten long days of difficult deliberations, and besides, they were not about to allow the crash in the market to affect their final resolution.

PART ONE

1987

James Blackburn couldn't have guessed that the journey upon which he was about to embark would take him through the most dangerous and, at the same time, most fulfilling period of his life. It was difficult to realize that the world was going through a critical period in history. Some of the most stubborn norms, long established in geopolitics, were being transformed that year. But the process of change was too subtle to be noticed.

In two different worlds, two unrelated events took place that went totally unnoticed. One happened in Japan and the other in the Persian Gulf. It wasn't until later, much later, that the unintended consequences of these events shocked the world.

I

The Motouri Protocol

Within minutes of each other, twelve black sedans arrived at the executive resort outside the small village of Gora. It was a spectacular afternoon, the air crisp and the sky deep blue and spotless. The white peak of Mount Fuji, normally hidden from sight by clouds and fog, rose majestically on the horizon, dominating the fields, hills, lakes, and lesser mountains of the entire Hakone area. Several buses carrying tourists up the narrow, curvy road had stopped by the roadside, allowing the photograph-crazy Japanese to snap pictures of each other with Mount Fuji in the background. Even the villagers, who had lived their entire lives at the foot of the mountain, could not help staring at its breathtaking grandeur. Standing upright in the rice fields, they allowed themselves the rare luxury of a break from the backbreaking task of planting rice seedlings in the paddies, enthralled by a view they had seen countless times.

As the last car pulled into the front courtyard of the resort, the large wooden gate slowly opened and the resident housekeeper stepped out of the building. For the twelfth time that afternoon, he watched the choreographed movements of the driver as he got out of the car, walked hurriedly to the rear, and held the door open with a ceremonious bow of the head.

A small man emerged from the back seat of the sedan. The housekeeper stood motionless in front of the doorway, his face transformed into an expressionless mask that concealed his mounting anxiety as he waited for the man to step out of the car. Only a few minutes earlier, after the passenger of the previous car had been received, Mr. Okada, the chairman of Idemitsu Kosan Oil Company, had reminded the housekeeper that he expected one last guest. "Take special care of him," Okada had said. "He is the most important guest here."

The new guest was barely out of the black Toyota sedan when the housekeeper bowed low, bending not just his head, but the entire top half of his body at a perfect ninety-degree angle. The guest stood next to the car for a few minutes and breathed the fresh air deeply, oblivious to the presence of the driver and the housekeeper. He looked up to the sky, then to the flowers planted under the tall wall, and a hint of a smile appeared on his face. He was barely five feet tall and weighed no more than 100 pounds. He wore thick, black-rimmed eyeglasses and a navy blue suit. His hair was as white as the snow on Mount Fuji, combed straight back to expose his wide, wrinkle-free forehead, which made him look about fifteen years younger than his actual age of sixty-eight. Then he noticed and acknowledged the housekeeper with a nod and a bow of the head and proceeded toward the gate. Only then did the housekeeper straighten his back. He accepted the small handbag the driver fetched from the front passenger seat, bowed again, and led the guest inside. The driver got back into the car and drove to the nearby inn, where he and the other eleven drivers were to stay for the duration of their masters' meeting.

"Miyazaki-sama," said the housekeeper, "welcome to these humble accommodations. My name is Kobayashi. My wife and I are the resident keepers of this resort. We are at your service."

"Thank you, Kobayashi-san. Have the others arrived?"

"Yes, Miyazaki-sama. Some arrived early and went for a walk. The rest are still in the bath."

"Very good. I'd like to bathe now too."

Miyazaki took off his shoes, placed them neatly next to the row of the other visitors' shoes at the entrance, and stepped up onto the thick tatami mat.

The reception room was large and impeccable. In the best Japanese tradition, it was nearly empty, with only two priceless ornaments placed at either end. In the left corner, on a black marble pedestal near the large window, stood a 150-year-old bonsai tree. There was nothing else at the left side of the room to distract attention away from the bonsai. On the right wall, some thirty-five feet away, hung a framed 400-year-old silk kimono that had once adorned several generations of young brides during their wedding ceremonies.

Miyazaki took off his coat and approached the bonsai. It was one of the best-maintained trees he had seen. The solid silver pot where it was planted, a priceless antique in its own right, seemed too small for the tree, but that did not seem to have hindered its growth. It was only about a foot tall, with a trunk barely two inches in diameter, but it branched out in the most intricate designs to almost two feet across at its widest points, its branches kept in shape by bright copper wires wrapped around them. It will have to be re-potted in about four years, Miyazaki thought, wishing he could be present at the event.

He and Kobayashi crossed the reception room and came into a wide hallway. The wall on the right was made of glass, overlooking the immaculate Japanese gardens and the rolling hills of Gora. It linked the lower wing of the resort, which housed the bedrooms and the bathhouse, with the reception area and the dining room, and was designed to serve as a long sitting room. Large coffee tables were placed at regular intervals along the glass wall, each surrounded by four large leather armchairs. On each coffee table there was a stack of magazines and a neatly laid out mahjong game set.

The volcanic hills beyond the garden were dotted with columns of thick steam that gushed from the ground. Had Miyazaki not been so nearsighted, he would have been able to see the boiling puddles of water bubbling in the rocks next to patches of snow scattered around the hills. But he could see the carefully manicured garden outside the glass wall, with every pebble in place, every shrub trimmed just right, and every rock where it should be. All is not lost after all, he thought, feeling an undefined nostalgia for an undefined past. Perhaps harmony will prevail in the end.

At the end of the hallway they turned into a narrower corridor lined with several soji doors. Kobayashi went to the first door and slid it open.

"This will be your room, Miyazaki-sama. I hope it is adequate," Kobayashi said with a bow of the head, and followed him in with the hand luggage. Except for the low, black lacquer table in the center, the room was empty. Kobayashi opened the door of one of the closets that lined three of the four walls of the room, placed the bag in it, and slid the door closed. "I'll be outside until you get ready," he said, bowed low, and stepped out.

Miyazaki surveyed the empty room with satisfaction. Okada was right, he thought. This is the best place to hold the meeting; it certainly was wise to get the men out of Tokyo and into the calm surroundings of Gora. The fourth wall of the room had three windows overlooking the hills. He slid open the rice-paper panels of one of the windows and stared out for a few minutes, seeing the same view he'd had from the long hallway. He then reached into his inside coat pocket and retrieved a twice-folded sheet of paper. He unfolded it and read the list of twelve names.

His name was first, followed by Hiroshi Furukawa, president of the Japan National Oil Company, which was a governmental organization acting as a bank providing financing for some of the riskier projects undertaken by Japan's private oil companies. Under Furukawa's name was a dotted line, followed by the names of ten corporate chief executives. Miyazaki did not like the dotted line. Whoever had typed the list was not thinking correctly about this particular meeting. There was no need to emphasize the distinction between corporate and governmental Japan.

Miyazaki studied the list of ten corporate executives for the hundredth time, ranking, re-arranging and matching them in his mind. Then he stared out again at the rugged, volcanic hills, and the shrubs, snow, steam and puddles of boiling water rising from deep beneath the earth.

"Sometimes the obvious solution is the only solution," he said aloud to the hills of Gora. He was beginning to like the hills. They seemed to be staring back at him, wondering who he was. The jets of steam punctuating the hillside made the landscape look alive and responsive.

"It *is* the only solution," he repeated, as if the hills had challenged his assertion. But the hills did not challenge. They just spewed steam, which rose from the ground with great force and arrogance, only to dissolve in the breeze a few seconds later. "And it is the obvious solution," he added. "But will it be obvious to everybody else?"

He folded the piece of paper and put it back in his coat pocket. He would not think about it again until later that night. It was time to cleanse his mind and prepare for the meeting. Keeping the rice-paper windowpane open, he walked over to the closet that Kobayashi had used, opened it, and started to undress. He put on the light cotton kimono that was neatly folded in the closet and stepped out of the room. Kobayashi led him to the bathhouse.

At 8 p.m. the twelve men gathered in the large dining room. They all wore the same dark blue cotton kimonos provided by the resort, with white and blue striped yukatas underneath. They sat on small square cushions on the floor, around a low table, in two rows of six. Warm sake, beer, and green tea were served in abundance by the two housekeepers and five maids hired for the occasion. The tabletop was covered with small dishes of appetizers, consisting of rice, pickled vegetables, fried fish and vegetables; bowls of soup and steamed shrimp; and two large, boat-shaped dishes of sashimi. The service was impeccable, from the exquisite hand painted ceramic and china dishes that Okada had sent from Tokyo for the occasion, to the meticulous yet unobtrusive attentiveness of the servers. The men spent the first half-hour eating and commenting on the spectacular view of Mount Fuji, while the maids and housekeepers kept busy collecting empty dishes and re-filling sake cups and beer glasses.

After the men finished the first course and the dishes were removed, Miyazaki, the powerful director general of MITI's Agency of Natural Resources and Energy, raised his glass.

"Gentlemen," he said, looking at the freshly bathed and groomed faces around him. "First, I'd like to thank Okada-san for putting this beautiful resort at our disposal." They all nodded and raised their glasses to Sadahiru Okada, the balding chairman of Idemitsu Kosan, sitting at the end of the opposite row from Miyazaki. "I would also like to thank all of you for accepting my invitation to come to this meeting. Tonight, while we enjoy the generous hospitality of Okada-san, I'll outline the main purpose of this meeting and leave with you some questions that have been bothering both my minister and the prime minister of Japan. I kindly ask each one of you to think about these issues tonight. Tomorrow evening, we can discuss plans and solutions."

Miyazaki took a sip of sake and allowed one of the maids, sitting attentively behind him, to refill his cup. He looked at the expressionless faces of the eleven men around the table, emptied the full cup in one swallow, and continued.

"As you know, in the past forty years our nation has excelled in many fields. But there are three specific areas where we lag behind the rest of the industrialized world.

"One of these is agriculture. But our shortcomings in the agricultural sector do not worry us. They do not worry us because they are not a *failure*. Our land is not fit for agriculture. In fact, given the natural conditions we have to contend with, it is impressive that we produce most of our needs.

"The second area is that of military development. This also is a shortcoming, a grave one perhaps, but not a failure. As you know, that's an area where we have not been *permitted* to excel. Some would even consider that shortcoming a blessing. Having relinquished a military vocation for the nation, we can keep a peaceful posture while freeing our economic resources for more productive investments than military spending."

Miyazaki looked around the table again. Some had closed their eyes and looked as though they were in a trance. Others were smoking, eyes staring vaguely in his general direction.

"Finally," he continued, "there is oil."

After a pause, he added: "Here, we *have* failed."

The speech was not an easy one for Miyazaki to give. True, the oil industry had failed, but he had always viewed this as the government's failure.

"We have tried, and so far failed, to create a truly world class oil industry," he said to the expressionless masks. "Japan does not have an Exxon or a Shell. We produce a tiny percentage of what we need, and a negligible percentage of total world output." Miyazaki was aware that these men were being invited to accept the responsibility for, and later correct, a mistake they had inherited from years of government neglect. But that did not cause any hesitation in his voice. "As you are all keenly aware, Japan has always been, and continues to be, at the mercy of foreign countries and companies when it comes to our oil needs. This, honorable gentlemen, has always been true, and has always been of great concern to the government."

"Yes. It has always been of concern," Miyazaki repeated after a short pause. "But there are good reasons to address the issue again today. The most important reason, gentlemen, is that the government believes Japan is finally ready to remedy the situation. We're ready due to our financial situation, and because of the state of the world oil market. We are rich, and the market is in chaos. Now is the time to act."

He stopped and reached for his sake cup again. Okada looked across the room to the doorway of the kitchen where Kobayashi was waiting, and nodded. It was time for dinner to be served.

If the others felt any reaction to Miyazaki's short speech, they did not show it. Some were still nodding quietly, even though Miyazaki had stopped talking.

As they started to eat the finely sliced Kobe beef, Miyazaki turned to Okada. "I have asked two members of this group to present brief reports on different aspects of the Japanese oil industry and the world oil market in general," he said with exaggerated politeness. "Okada-san, would you please start with yours?"

Okada made a few nervous shifts on his cushion, bowed quickly toward Miyazaki, and then spoke.

"I was asked to comment on the current status of crude oil supplies to Japan's refining industry, the Motouri. Japan's entire oil business is primarily Motouri—that is, all of us here are mainly engaged in refining and marketing. The only crude oil production we have is part ownership in the Arabian Oil Company, which produces in the neutral zone between Saudi Arabia and Kuwait. Remember gentlemen, this agreement expires in thirteen years.

"In recent years, important changes have occurred in the way we do business. This is because the players have changed. Before, we used to import our crude oil almost exclusively from the large multinational oil companies—the so-called majors. Today, we buy almost exclusively from national oil companies, particularly those in the Middle East."

Okada's high-pitched tenor filled the dining room and, under different circumstances, would probably have alleviated some of the tension created by Miyazaki. But many in the room felt uncomfortable being hosted by one of their main competitors. It was no ordinary event to gather together the chief executives of the ten largest oil companies of Japan, especially in non-neutral territory. Even Miyazaki had resisted

Okada's suggestion at first for this same reason. It was bad politics. It could—in fact, it most certainly would—be interpreted as favoritism by MITI. But Okada's counter-argument had won the day. It was simple and to the point. "If we're going to address the *nation's* problems," he had said, "it should not matter to anybody where we meet. In fact, let's meet at my resort to reinforce the point that location is irrelevant."

Now Okada was busy citing a long series of statistics. "In 1970, 75 percent of Japan's oil needs were supplied by these majors. Today, the majors supply only 27 percent of our needs. In 1970, the national oil companies supplied only 4.5 percent of our crude oil imports. Today, they supply more than 60 percent." Some in the audience found it amazing that the chairman and chief executive of a large corporation had such details in his head.

Darkness had fallen. The mountain and surrounding hills were no longer visible, leaving the corporate executives feeling alone. They had grown accustomed to the mountain and the hills, as if drawing comfort from their presence as witnesses of what was unfolding at this fateful meeting.

Okada-san's tedious analysis continued for a while longer, full of facts and figures many found hard to remember. His main message, though, was hard to forget. He kept repeating that the players had changed. The governments that supplied most of Japan's oil had non-commercial considerations, he said, which the majors did not have. "They negotiate differently, they compete differently, they price their oil differently," he declared, as if expecting everyone to be shocked by the revelation.

Then Okada bowed his head to the group, indicating he had finally finished his recitation. There was no immediate reaction from anybody around the table. Miyazaki broke the silence. "Very interesting, Okada-san," he said, still deep in thought, as if wanting to indicate that there was more to Okada's statements than met the eye. "Obviously, the changes that Okada-san spoke of present both risks and opportunities for us. One of the areas where both the risks and opportunities come into play is the push into downstream investments that these countries are now engaged in. Kuwait and Venezuela have been buying refineries and distribution networks in Europe and the United States. We understand that Saudi Arabia is not far behind. It is negotiating with its former Aramco partners for similar acquisitions.

"As these countries buy refineries and retail outlets, they will be faced with less pressure to sell their oil in crude form. They may even face less competition among themselves to secure markets for their crude oil. Of course, this is a long time away, but we cannot ignore it. The question for us is how are the Japanese Motouri affected by this trend. Nagayama-san, would you like to comment on that?"

Nagayama, the chairman of Nippon Oil Co., Ltd., sat facing Miyazaki and had listened to the past two monologues with his eyes closed. He too stirred nervously on his cushion, opened his eyes long enough to thank Miyazaki, and then shut them again as he started to talk.

"I was asked to comment on how the Japanese Motouri view the downstream investments of oil producing countries," he said in a bored tone. "I'll be brief. There are two views on this trend. The positive one is that as the producing countries increase their investments in the consuming countries, they will act more responsibly because they will have a stake in the downstream oil market.

"The negative view, which I share, is based on more pragmatic considerations. We don't trust the producing countries. We trust neither their intentions nor their competence. If they try to manipulate the market for refined petroleum products like they've tried to manipulate crude oil, we can end up in extremely volatile and unpredictable conditions. Even the argument of increased security of crude oil supplies is not convincing. The national oil companies cannot provide us with the same degree of security as the majors, because, unlike the majors, they have access to only one source of crude oil—their own.

"So the Japanese Motouri do not need such investments. We already have easy access to crude oil and do not need foreign assistance in the technical or financial area. Already, affiliates of the major international companies in Japan—Shell, Mobil, Exxon, Caltex—account for more than 40 percent of our refining capacity."

Nagayama opened his eyes and bowed first toward Miyazaki, then to the men on each side of the table. Then he shut his eyes again, folded his arms on his ample belly, and appeared as though he went right to sleep.

"Most interesting, Nagayama-san," announced Miyazaki after a few moments of reflection. "I'm sure the government will continue to be responsive to the views you expressed. In spite of the deregulation of certain petroleum activities, we still do not provide an overly attractive investment environment to foreigners. As you know, Japanese law does not allow more than 50 percent foreign ownership of any refiner. Besides, most foreign investors are not interested in buying refining assets alone, without the distribution networks to market the products. Unlike in the United States and Europe, in Japan service stations are owned by independent dealers, not by the major refining companies. So by acquiring refineries, the foreign investor cannot acquire these dealer-owned service stations. This, I'm sure, will serve as an additional disincentive.

"In any case, we are far more concerned with increasing our upstream assets than with foreigners buying our downstream facilities. We can always pass legislation to control the refining and marketing industry inside Japan, but we cannot acquire crude oil by passing legislation."

It was not apparent whether Miyazaki had just supported Nagayama's views on foreign investments in Japan or dismissed them as irrelevant to the task at hand.

"The bottom line, gentlemen," continued Miyazaki, "is that the government of Japan considers it essential that Japanese companies increase their equity crude oil production. Today, Japanese companies own less than five percent of our consumption. By the year 2000, or in less than thirteen years, the government would like to see at least 25 percent of our needs produced by us. Of course, in thirteen years, our needs will be higher than today. The government believes that in the year 2000, Japan's oil consumption will increase to more than nine million barrels per day. This means the target is for Japanese companies to *own* at least 2.25 million barrels per day of crude oil production in various parts of the world. This is no easy task. As Furukawa-san can tell you, JNOC has been financing exploration projects to the tune of 1.2 trillion yen in the past twenty years, and all we have to show for it is a few hundred thousand barrels a day."

Hiroshi Furukawa, the president of Japan National Oil Company, was the only jovial and outgoing person in the group. With a permanent smile glued to his chubby cheeks, he radiated warmth in a way that few Japanese executives did. Sitting to Miyazaki's right, he nodded cheerfully and drank his sake.

"The problem we've had in the past has two parts," Miyazaki said after acknowledging Furukawa's almost frantic nods of agreement. "One is external, and one internal.

"The external part has to do with the global oil market. In the past fifteen years, crude oil has been so expensive that the majors have not allowed us to participate in promising exploration projects. They have guarded the good acreage around the world, letting Japanese companies in only the high-cost, frontier areas.

"But this problem has been mostly eliminated in recent years. Prices have crashed, exploration is down substantially, interest in good acreage for exploration is down, and costs of exploration and production are down. Many producing countries are now trying to attract foreign investment in exploration projects. We have to exploit this situation, because it may be our last opportunity in this century to reduce Japan's dependence on foreign oil companies.

"But we still have the internal problem. We have many small oil companies with too much competition among them, with the result that none of Japan's oil companies can generate enough profits to become players in the international exploration area.

"This problem, gentlemen, can be eliminated only through your active cooperation. And tonight, on behalf of the Japanese government, I formally ask for your cooperation."

The men all knew that a formal request made on behalf of MITI was as close as one could get to a military order. They also assumed that Miyazaki had already made up his mind as to how this "internal problem" was going to be resolved.

"I will therefore leave you to mull this over until tomorrow evening," Miyazaki said after a long pause, during which he inspected the ten anxious faces of the corporate executives staring back at him. "Please feel free to discuss it among yourselves as you see fit. If any of you would like to have a private meeting with me, I will be available during the day tomorrow.

"For the rest of our stay at this resort, I kindly ask you to forget that you are competitors. Please concentrate on what is in the long-term interests of Japan. For as has always been the case, what is not in the interest of Japan cannot possibly be beneficial to any of us."

With that, Miyazaki rose from his cushion, bowed deeply toward the table, and left the room.

The following morning, a dense fog descended over Hakone, merging the geysers of steam on the hills into one hazy mass. The mountain disappeared from sight. A melancholy transfused the peace and serenity of Gora and overwhelmed the twelve men inside the resort. They did not leave the resort all day. The ten corporate executives requested and were granted private meetings with Miyazaki, who patiently explained the MITI proposal to each man. Okada and Nagayama spent a few hours alone in Okada's room. Furukawa and Miyazaki had lunch alone in Miyazaki's room, while the ten executives lunched together in the dining room. But they didn't discuss the Miyazaki proposals. The little conversation they did have revolved around Gora's history and how it was chosen as a site for Idemitsu Kosan's executive resort. Okada did his best to play the perfect host by entertaining his guests with ancient stories about the region.

By midafternoon, the fog started to clear, but the men stayed indoors. At 5 p.m. they all went to the bathhouse, content with the opportunity to surrender their bodies, and the futures of their companies, to the hot sulfur springs of Gora.

Miyazaki and Furukawa were last to arrive at the bathhouse. They too entered the large, rectangular hall with a sense of resignation, ready to surrender their burdens to the hot springs of Gora. The bathhouse was the room that made the resort. It was not just a room. It was an institution. This was where all tensions and frictions were purged from their nerves, at least temporarily. Without the bathhouse, the resort would have been reduced to an ordinary building, spread out on the outskirts of a small town. The slanted ceiling, which was about eighteen feet high at the entrance and came down to eleven feet at the end of the hall, hosted a dozen sunken lights, their beams shooting down the steam-filled room like twelve narrow pillars. The white marble of its floor and walls was wet and gleaming.

At the far left corner was the pool. It measured eight by twelve feet, four feet deep at one end and over eight feet deep at the other. The roof and walls around the pool were made of glass. From the edge of the wall, where the marble ended and the glass began, a metal pipe protruded and water from the hot sulfur springs poured from it into the deepest side of the pool. The pipe was connected to one of the boiling puddles up in the hills and the earth-colored water flowed constantly, all year round. It drained from another pipe at the other side of the pool into the garden outside.

At the entrance, Miyazaki and Furukawa took off their cotton kimonos and hung them next to the others on the rack. A cloud of thick steam rose from the pool down the hall, and Miyazaki counted the silhouettes of ten heads floating on the surface, partially hidden by the mist. He took comfort in knowing they were all there. This communal bath was the final ceremony that sealed the Motouri Protocol.

He crossed the width of the room and sat on one of the low wooden stools that were placed at four-foot intervals, one opposite each faucet that protruded from the marble wall. Furukawa joined him on a similar stool two faucets down. They turned on the faucets, filled the small buckets, and emptied them on their heads. They shampooed with slow, leisurely strokes, then filled the buckets again and rinsed by pouring the water over their heads one more time. The timing of their movements was so well synchronized that they looked as if they had rehearsed this beforehand. They took the bar of soap from the container under the faucets, and lathered their bodies. Then they stood up almost simultaneously to lather their buttocks and genital areas. They poured three more buckets of water down their heads and walked to the pool. The others did not stir. Miyazaki and Furukawa stepped gently into the dark water, went down the few invisible steps, and sat down. The water was hot and smelled of sulfur. They closed their eyes and felt the heat unwind their muscles and nerves. After about fifteen minutes, the fatigue of the past nine hours of bargaining was washed away. They were so relaxed that they felt faint.

At dinner that evening Miyazaki repeated his plan and received the formal pledge of everyone to honor its terms. Then they dropped the subject and concentrated on their sake. It was in the small hours of the morning that the maids and housekeepers started to clean the dining room.

Several hours later, upon Okada's instructions, the housekeeper summoned the drivers from the nearby inn. By 10 a.m., to the housekeeper's great relief, all twelve men had left the resort, headed back to Tokyo.

*   *   *

Two days after the meeting in Gora, Miyazaki submitted his confidential report to the minister of international trade and industry. It was short and to the point. His mission, which could potentially eliminate the primary remaining economic vulnerability faced by Japan, had been accomplished in two short and beautiful days.

"Your Excellency:

"The Motouri meeting in Gora was a success. We secured a solemn understanding among the ten corporate executives in attendance. The understanding, which was dubbed 'The Motouri Protocol,' made the following provisions:

"First, during the next four years, the ten oil companies will make their top priority the acquisition of foreign upstream assets. Competition in the domestic refining sector will subside. For this to happen, we have to be selective in our current deregulation program. Although this is a major departure from our policy in other industries—where we encourage competition in the domestic market and discourage it abroad—I'm afraid it will be necessary in the case of petroleum.

"In this period, the companies will compete freely and openly in the international upstream market. They will be free to form joint ventures with national oil companies as well as the majors, as long as such ventures give them access to equity oil. JNOC will continue to support all reasonable projects without giving preferential treatment to any specific company.

"Second, in four years—in April 1991—three companies will be chosen to lead Japan's petroleum sector. The choice will be based, first, on the volume of existing and potential equity crude oil production held by each company, and second, on financial strength. The Petroleum Department of the Agency of Natural Resources and Energy and JNOC will be the final arbiters in making this choice, even though the companies will first be given the opportunity to elect themselves.

"Third, the three chosen companies will acquire all other oil companies, including the ones not represented at the meeting, in an orderly but expeditious manner. These acquisitions will be completed in two years, by April 1993. The Petroleum Department of the Agency of Natural Resources and Energy will oversee the acquisitions. The banking sector will be encouraged by MITI to give its full support to this effort. In six years, therefore, only three large Japanese oil companies will remain, with much larger assets than any single one that exists today. It will then be the responsibility of these three companies to meet the government's target, and they will have only seven years to achieve it.

"Obviously, many details still have to be worked out. I believe that some alliances will be formed and mergers will occur before 1991. We should encourage this. We should even anticipate a certain amount of foul play, but that is normal. Idemitsu Kosan and Nippon Oil Company are the two obvious candidates that I believe will survive the test. But it is not clear which company will emerge as the third survivor.

"I believe a good seed has been sown. All we can do now is ensure that it grows and bears fruit."

II

The Wealthy Slaves

As the Japanese executives were gathering at the Gora resort, Kamal Ashkar was driving over sand dunes. Ashkar loved to go to the desert. He often took long drives in his Range Rover, deep into the heart of the Arabian Peninsula, to cleanse his mind and soul. The vastness, the unfathomable enormity of the desert, was the only absolute he had ever experienced. The desert was all knowing and alive. It was harsh and cruel, but it neither judged nor offended. Whatever did not belong in it, could not survive in it. In the desert, Ashkar felt free—as a living part of an eternal whole, without pretense, without pressure, without constraints.

On these excursions he took neither alcohol nor fancy foods. He took only a little bread, a small sack of dates, and a few gallons of water. He tried to live as closely as possible to the way in which he imagined his father and grandfather had lived not too long ago. He meditated, even prayed a few times, to feel closer to a past that was supposed to have been more coherent and meaningful than the present. He felt a strong urge to go on these one or two day stays in the desert every three months or so.

Of course, the rest of the time, he remained the frivolous loudmouth that everybody knew and ignored.

But on that particular morning his drive into the desert was not for soul-searching. Ashkar was on his way to the fourth executive committee meeting of the top-secret political coalition in the Gulf known to its members in Arabic as "Al Nadwa," or "The Symposium." He was not driving south from Riyadh, but northeast, toward the point where Saudi Arabia, Kuwait and Iraq intersect.

The Symposium was an unlikely political coalition. Not only had it managed to bring together different nationalities from around the Arab world, but it had also grouped the disgruntled conservative factions, represented largely by the Islamic groups, together with the more liberal professionals from around the Gulf. In the 1980s this was still possible because these groups shared a common distaste for the corruption that ran rampant within the ruling families of the Gulf. They also felt nostalgic for a past that was remembered as cleaner, simpler, more just and, most important of all, more dignified.

Members of The Symposium implicitly accepted the political structures in the Gulf and the role the ruling families had once played in the region. But they rejected the specific regimes and practices the current rulers had instituted.

The most difficult aspect of forming the coalition had not been finding enough people who shared the same frustrations; rather, it had been screening the potential candidates to make sure they fit in the meticulous ideological and political platform laid out by the founders. One *could* be too liberal, too religious, too conservative, or too radical to belong in The Symposium.

The liberals, comprising mostly young professionals—bankers, lawyers, judges and business managers—had to screen out the extreme liberals, which included, ironically, some disgruntled members of the ruling families, who wanted to see an almost total transformation of the social and political system of the Gulf. Their aim was to free the average Gulf citizen from the straightjacket of his or her own backwardness.

The religious factions, on the other hand, had to screen out the zealous fanatics, who, ironically, also wanted a total transformation of the political structures, but with the aim of establishing strict Islamic rule in the Arabian Peninsula. They were more dangerous than the extreme liberals, simply because they had a widespread following in Saudi Arabia. The region was still in the shadow of the legacy of the 1979 siege of Islam's holiest shrine, when a zealot named Juhayman al-Oteibi led several hundred insurgents and seized the Grand Mosque in Mecca, calling for the overthrow of the House of Saud, declaring his brother-in-law as the Mahdi (Messiah), and demanding a total rejection of the West and expulsion of all non-Muslims from Arabia.

The event shocked the Muslim world, and particularly the Gulf. The siege lasted for two weeks. The insurgents were eventually overrun, and those who survived the assault were executed. But it came to light that they had the support of a large group of wealthy sympathizers, including members of the Saudi National Guard. Their demands had found resonance in a significant segment of the conservative society in the Gulf. Those same demands, almost verbatim, were later to become the ideological basis of Al Qaeda and the central thesis of Osama bin Laden.

As disconcerting for the members of The Symposium as these events were, the official Saudi reaction was even more disturbing. After defeating the insurgency, King Khaled of Saudi Arabia decided to fight religion with more religion. He gave much wider powers to the religious elite. Cinemas and music shops were shut down, photographs of women in newspapers were banned, gender segregation was intensified, and the religious police were given wide leeway to become yet more assertive.

King Fahd, who followed King Khaled only a few years after the insurgency, continued the policy of allowing the religious elite to dictate laws and behavior. Many more hours of religious studies were added to school curriculums, at the expense of other classes. The fact that the ringleaders of the insurgency were prominent members of Saudi society and graduates of religious schools did not seem to give the authorities pause as they granted broader powers to those schools and religious leaders.

Members of The Symposium were alarmed by the long-term implications of this trend. They saw their youth becoming increasingly radicalized, instead of learning useful skills. They saw the next generation brainwashed into Jihadists by the very system that had fought the radicalism of the siege of the Grand Mosque. This generation would never accept the minimum level of individual freedom espoused by

The Symposium, which was, in fact, the main ideological foundation on which the organization was based.

One of the most influential founding members of The Symposium was a naturalized Kuwaiti citizen called Ramzi Amin. Originally Syrian, Amin had moved to Kuwait with his family when he was a child. He was a successful businessman and senior member of the Kuwaiti Oil Ministry. He did much of the recruiting for The Symposium and established many of the ideological foundations of the movement. Although he did not disagree with all the views of the extreme liberals, he knew the majority of people in the Gulf region, especially in Saudi Arabia, were not ready for such a drastic change. The Symposium could not enjoy broad popular support in the Gulf if it advocated a radical political agenda.

Most Gulf Arabs did not want democracy—at least not the Western style they had seen in Europe and the United States. That style of democracy brought certain freedoms, but also took away the built-in protections provided by the age-old tribal system of the Gulf. The typical male could not accept what Western-style democracy would do to his rights vis-à-vis his wife and children. The same democracy that promised to liberate him from the chains of his tribal masters would also liberate those who were under his control and influence.

With the freedom of Western-style democracy came the burden of assuming responsibility for oneself. In the Gulf, the system supported the individual and expected obedience in return; in the West, the system left the individual alone and arguably free, but did not provide any of the unearned material perks and benefits that members of the tribal system enjoyed simply because they belonged in it. To the average male Gulf Arab, there was more to lose than to gain by abandoning the existing system in favor of Western-style democracy.

It was this reluctance to accept all that came with political freedom that had sustained the status quo for so long. Without it, even the most elaborate internal security mechanism, no matter how skillful and brutal, could not have protected the old system. This would become more apparent a few years later when the dictatorships of Eastern Europe began to collapse and the Soviet Union started to undergo more systematic, thorough, and irreversible disintegration than anybody could have imagined possible. As these countries started to embrace the democratic principles preached by the West, there was no sign of similar tendencies in the Gulf.

The main difference was that while the Eastern European countries were casting away authoritarianisms of a single dictator or even of a single ideology, the Gulf countries were clinging to the dictatorship of an old way of life which, although in some ways as uncompromising as the dictatorships of East Europe, was so deeply rooted in the popular psyche of the region that its mere familiarity inspired a sense of security and confidence. The Arabs were too uncomfortable with change to easily accept it, let alone fight for it.

As long as Arab men did not want to change, and their women were veiled and locked up, their "traditional values" as they liked to call them could be protected. Never mind that not all of the women were veiled and isolated. Never mind that not all of those who were veiled and locked up lived in ignorant bliss. The seemingly strict and unbending system could be flexible and tolerant, as long as violations were made with great discretion.

So vital was saving face and keeping up appearances that much dogma and ideology could be compromised in order to keep violations secret. Very often, penalizing a serious, yet unpublicized offense according to the tribal code carried the risk of exposing the offense in public and humiliating the family of the offender. It wasn't worth taking this risk. More often than not, defending the status quo was tantamount to defending this big lie.

"There are no values any longer!" Hassa al-Saud had told James Blackburn two decades earlier. She was one of the Saudi princesses who, under the watchful eyes of an entire contingent of female servants and spies, was allowed to study at the American University of Beirut (AUB). Blackburn, at the time an American student at AUB, was allowed in her presence only as her tutor, and only in the company of her Egyptian maid, a chubby, giggly young woman called Fatima. "There are no values!" Hassa insisted. "Traditional, moral, ethical, religious, or otherwise. There are only the dirty habits of our men. The 'traditional values' argument is a godsend, perhaps literally, for our men."

"What kind of dirty habits?" Blackburn asked, knowing her outburst was a gross exaggeration, but sensing that Hassa was in the mood to talk. In those days Hassa was often high on hashish, which was abundant in Lebanon, smoking it almost at the same rate as Blackburn smoked regular cigarettes. That too was one of those transgressions that were best left unpunished. Occupying a suite at the Sands Hotel in a rich Beirut suburb, with every conceivable material need satisfied, Hassa had only one fear in life, which was having to go back to Saudi Arabia and be forced to marry one of her cousins chosen for her by her father.

"Simple dirty habits," she answered. "Getting drunk, I mean senseless drunk, cheating on their wives, stealing from their brothers, buying women and mistreating them, gambling, and above all, the ultimate luxury for our men who supposedly have been brought up by this strict moral and ethical code, to *get away* with the excesses. Not to be accountable ..."

Princess Hassa took a long drag from her "loaded" cigarette—a regular Marlboro soaked in hashish oil—and gazed at Blackburn through faint, watery eyes.

"Not to be accountable," she repeated, waving her hand around, as if the room were part of what they were not to be accountable for. Then, as if suddenly falling upon a whole new idea, she continued with newfound energy.

"You in the West talk about human relationships. That concept does not exist with us, because all human relationships are already perfected beyond any further discussion! For example, a man is *entitled* to a wife and children. So he is given a wife who gives him children. He *is* the husband and the father. What more is there to do? He already is what Western men try to become, right? He *is* so-and-so's son. He *is*. Therefore, he does not have *to do*, nor earn, nor think much, for that matter. Our equivalent of the famous 'I think therefore I am' is: 'I am, therefore I don't have to think.'"

True values or not, The Symposium's aim was not to destroy the status quo. Its immediate goal—the only goal declared to all the members—was to reform society, to reintroduce whatever good was lost from the past, and adapt it to the specific needs and circumstances created by modern lifestyle, and, perhaps most importantly, to reform the corrupt and unjust governance structure.

The original seven founding members had considered over 2,000 names, but only 400 individuals were approached. The founders initially approached each candidate carefully, speaking in vague and general terms. If the reaction of the potential recruit was found acceptable, more details were provided about the organization. Otherwise, the process was ended.

Two years after its formation, the coalition had 343 members. About 200 were Saudi Arabian citizens, 100 were Kuwaiti citizens, and the rest were divided among Bahrain, Qatar and the United Arab Emirates. Most were prominent members of their communities, including successful business-men, judges, teachers, and representatives of the large merchant families and the ruling families.

The full membership list was a well-kept secret, even from the mem-bers themselves. Members of the executive committee, who had done all of the recruiting, were the common links among all members. The rea-sons for such secrecy were obvious and never questioned by the members of The Symposium. If the existence and objectives of the organization were ever discovered by the intelligence services, the life of every member of the coalition would be in jeopardy.

The organizational mastermind of the coalition was Karim Suliman. A former officer in the Saudi Secret Service, Suliman had one of the sad-dest stories regarding the excesses of the royal family. In fact, it had been the pitiful fate of Suliman's only daughter, fourteen-year-old Fahda, that had pushed the intelligence officer out of the establishment and into an underground organization.

Suliman's work took him to the Eastern Province often. As a senior officer of the Saudi Arabian Intelligence Organization in charge of internal security, he had much to attend to there, home of the vast majority of Saudi Arabia's Shia population, on which the government kept a close eye. This brought Suliman in close contact with the fami-lies of Saudi princes in the Eastern Province. It was through this chan-nel that young Fahda met and befriended a young princess, the daugh-ter of one of the influential princes in the province. Accompanied by a few of her maids, Fahda often went to visit the princess and spend a few days at the family's palace in Dammam, which was about one hour's flight from Riyadh.

It was during one of these visits that the prince, drunk and out of control, stormed into his daughter's quarters, ordered his daughter out, and viciously and repeatedly raped Fahda.

When Suliman found out about the rape, partly from Fahda and the rest from some of the maids who, hidden behind the doors, had managed to witness most of the gruesome act, he went mad. He even contemplated the unthinkable—killing the prince, then his own beloved daughter, and then himself. That would be the only way to wash the shame from the family. His anger had soared to unmanageable proportions when the prince, through an intermediary, offered him $2 million for the "damage" and to keep his mouth shut.

Fortunately for all, Amin took Suliman into his care in that most vulnerable period of his life and convinced him that there were better ways to get even. After a weeklong retreat in Amin's desert refuge in Kuwait, Suliman emerged with a new conviction to fight the system from within. Fahda was flown to a rehabilitation clinic in Switzerland where she stayed for about a month. Later, he enrolled her in an exclusive all-girls school in Montreux. She never returned to Saudi Arabia. Suliman resigned from the government and started his private business, importing residential security devices into Saudi Arabia and advising large commercial concerns on security procedures. He was one of the most dedicated members of The Symposium.

Ashkar, though not one of the founding members, was one of the early recruits. Ramzi Amin had recommended him and approached him. Amin knew and understood Ashkar better than some of his Saudi colleagues and close friends. He knew, for example, that Ashkar's outer image of drinking and womanizing was his escape, his defense from the frustrations and embarrassments of daily life.

"Do you really believe that you *own* anything?" Ashkar asked Amin during one of their early conversations, in an outburst facilitated by alcohol. "Do you really believe that your house, your bank account, your investments are yours? *Really* yours, inviolate, beyond the reach of your ruler? You're a fool if you do, my friend. Because you have no rights, you own nothing, and your life is worth nothing if your ruler so decides."

They were at Amin's desert retreat. That was the site where Amin interviewed and tested many potential recruits during countless long weekends. He masterfully directed the conversation to what he knew would get Ashkar going.

"But why should your ruler so decide?" he asked. "The rulers don't go around confiscating people's property. On the contrary, they're the ones who give people their property, their income; they're the ones who create the investment opportunities so that people like you and me can make investments in the first place."

Amin knew the fallacy of his own argument well. But he wanted to see how genuine Ashkar's sentiments were.

"But that's the whole point!" Ashkar screamed. "Don't you see? They're the ones who give everything. Income, wealth, privilege. *They give, and therefore they have the right to take back!* It does not matter that they don't go around confiscating people's properties. What matters is that if they did confiscate everything you own tomorrow, you'd have no recourse. There's no higher authority where you can appeal. How can you accept living under these conditions?"

"Kamal, you know you're not being fair," said Amin, even though he was impressed with the depth of Ashkar's emotion. "You can't get angry at today's rulers just because they could, if they wanted to, confiscate everything you have. You cannot blame them for hypothetical situations. Besides, today's rulers didn't invent this system. Their forefathers and *our* forefathers did."

"The old system, the one invented by our forefathers, had merits that are now lost. There was accountability then. The old system imposed accountability on the chief."

Ashkar surpassed Amin's expectations. There weren't many people in the Gulf who could transcend the material perks provided by the system and look at the more basic, albeit somewhat philosophical, issues of individual rights and freedom.

That was the legacy of the tribal system; it was also the legacy of life in the desert. Human rights and individual freedom were luxuries in the harsh conditions of desert life, where physical survival was the only relevant human preoccupation and where survival required adherence to a strict tribal code. But the oil boom had alleviated the harshness of desert life. Physical survival was no longer a concern, after having been the paramount human objective and, as such, having determined most of the social norms and tribal relationships.

But how could one maintain a system after destroying a critical determining factor that had given birth to it? That was the inevitable question the defenders of the status quo in the Gulf had to face sooner or later. Perhaps the conservatism of the Gulf Arab, nurtured by his keen sense of self-preservation, combined with his dirty habits and traditional values, could carry things along a bit longer. But for how long?

Ashkar was, of course, right. But Amin felt the need to play devil's advocate a little while longer.

"I still don't see what's so bad about the system," Amin said. "Everybody in the Gulf is better off today than they were ten or fifteen years ago. Everybody has a decent income, a decent home, a free education, free medical care. What's so bad about all that?"

"What's so bad is that we are a nation of wealthy slaves," said Ashkar. He had stopped yelling. In typical Ashkar style, he suddenly shifted from an animated discourse to a soft, barely audible voice and calm manners. That was what Ashkar always did when he wanted to emphasize something—he lowered his voice, stopped moving his hands, erased all expression from his face, and uttered each word clearly.

"A nation of wealthy slaves," he repeated. "What's so bad is that we have no soul. We allow ourselves to be bought and sold every day. We accept privileges handed down to us by individuals for whom we have no respect, and then we meekly and gratefully express our gratitude, just like a cheap whore would pretend she enjoyed every minute of it. We allow ourselves to accept, and we allow the rulers to give us, what should have been ours, and never theirs to give in the first place! We are a nation of wealthy slaves. The reason we value our material possessions so much, the reason we pretend we are the masters of our immediate environment, whether in our homes or in our offices, is that we know, deep inside we know very well, that somebody else owns *us*. That, my friend, is what's so bad about the system."

Amin wondered whether Ashkar understood the true significance of what he was saying, and whether he realized that this was a fundamental and radical departure from the tribal creed that had guided life on the Arabian Peninsula for many generations. What would have been considered a great honor in the old days was taken as an insult today.

Times had changed. The very notion of income distribution, which was the glue holding the old system together, was now being questioned. Ashkar's views could be considered borderline, almost too radical to fit comfortably in the general philosophy of The Symposium. But Amin knew that Ashkar could, when faced with a clear goal, be pragmatic. He was recruited.

Ramzi Amin's notion of the historical progression of the Gulf was not overly complicated. He believed the Gulf States would have been further ahead in instituting quasi-democratic reforms and in achieving certain individual freedoms had the oil boom of the 1970s not introduced certain social norms. The enormous wealth that suddenly became available to the rulers of the region had enabled them to buy off both political and religious dissent and assume certain rights, powers, and privileges, which, under the old system, without all the billions to throw around, would not have been possible or tolerated.

Amin saw the past twenty years as a derailment from the normal course of social and political development in the Gulf, even though it had brought about an enormous leap in the average standard of living of the region. The corrupt elite's appeasement of the religious establishment was by far the most disturbing phenomenon, because it affected education, and therefore had the most lasting long-term impact on society.

"We have to go back a couple of decades in order to be able to go forward again," he had told Majed Al-Shammary more than two years earlier, when the nucleus of The Symposium was being formed. Al-Shammary, a soldier in the Saudi Arabian National Guard, was another early recruit. "We first have to erase the negative aspects of the oil boom and put the slow process of our political maturing back on track. Then, and only then, can we hope to make progress toward achieving a measure of political freedom. The economic boom, instead of helping us liberalize our society, as it would have done practically anywhere else in the world, resulted in more centralization and more religious fanaticism."

"But that's not surprising," Al-Shammary said in one of his rare interruptions of Amin's monologue. "Our tribal system has always used money and favors to buy loyalty and to pay for sins. So when the rulers fell upon enormous wealth, they felt they could afford to sin and abuse loyalty, because they had enough money to pay for the first and buy back the second."

"Of course, my friend," Amin said. "But the result was that our people sold their souls. They sold their dignity. The modern comforts we enjoy cost us far too much. And they didn't have to. And we had no right, even for the unimaginable material benefits, to sell our children's freedom and dignity. How will they judge us?"

This was at the heart of Amin's beliefs and of his political drive. This was the issue that he mourned in his heart. This was what he believed was worth risking his own safety and possibly even his life for.

"How will they judge us?" he asked the rugged desert soldier. "Think about this, my brother Majed. Think about this, keeping in mind that our children have not suffered the hardships our fathers suffered and those of us who are old enough to remember suffered during our childhoods. They have no basis for comparison, no reason to be enamored by the purely material improvement in their lives."

Amin rubbed his tired eyes and took a sip of water. He studied Al Shammary's anxious face for a few seconds before continuing.

"My dear brother Majed, this is our battle to define an identity, or perhaps to rediscover an old one. This is the search for our lost souls. Who are we? Are we the heirs of some great past glory, or simply people stained by the unforgiving shame of our present lives? Are we the almost invincible, desert-hardened people who fought against the Ottoman Turks and the British, who won some battles and lost a few, but who never gave up their inner strength nor their convictions? The only outlet that is allowed to us now is religion. Has the embrace of an illusive consolation in religion become our only hope? How can we allow that?

"Every day, I ask myself that question with the hope that by some divine inspiration the answer will come to me, reconciling the pride I think I should feel but don't, and the constant humiliation I think I should not have to feel, but do. What would your old King Abdulaziz do if he saw how his sons and grandsons live today? Old King Abdulaziz would probably disown most of them!"

Majed Al-Shammary loved to listen to Ramzi Amin. Amin had a way of articulating what Al-Shammary felt but could rarely express. As one of Amin's early recruits, he was also a member of the executive committee.

The current meeting site was inside the Iraqi border, in the Al Muthanna Province of Iraq. The cover of the meeting was a hunting camp. Nine small tents were erected around a central large tent, which served as the kitchen, dining room, and common area for the campers. The eighteen members of the executive committee slept in the small tents, two per unit, but gathered mostly in the large one. Around two dozen shotguns, rifles, and falcons were housed in the common area, while hounds and retrievers stayed outside. A small generator supplied electricity to the campsite, operating the large refrigerator and the air conditioning unit in the communal tent. There were also several tents outside of this cluster for the servants and cooks.

To keep the necessary appearances, a hunting expedition left the campsite at dawn every day and returned by midmorning. Some days, a second expedition went out in the late afternoon and returned after dark. The rest of the time, the eighteen hunters gathered in the large tent. After the necessary meal preparation and cleanup, they dismissed the servants and held their meetings.

When Kamal Ashkar arrived at the campsite, Majed Al-Shammary had already been there for over an hour and had just finished unpacking and getting situated in the tent he was to share with Ashkar. The two embraced with great passion and ceremony. They had not seen each other since their last executive committee meeting, held in Kuwait a year earlier. They were two of the eight Saudi Arabian members of the executive committee and were the furthest apart in family background, personality, and occupation, but somehow they had grown fond of each other.

By sunset, all the campers had arrived.

The first gathering that evening was informal, devoted to socializing, catching up, and re-bonding. After dinner, the eighteen men lounged around the common area, had a few drinks, and talked late into the night. The informal session gradually turned into a pre-meeting session that set the tone and the stage for the formal meetings that would start the following evening.

The next morning, the first hunting expedition, composed of twelve people in four jeeps, left the campsite.

The fourth executive committee meeting of The Symposium lasted four days. During that time, fourteen gazelles, five rabbits, and a dozen bustards were killed. Some were eaten by the hunters and the rest of the game was distributed to the nearby villagers.

The most significant decision made by the executive committee of The Symposium was that King Fahd of Saudi Arabia was a liability and a threat to the stability of the Gulf region and should be replaced as soon as possible. The Symposium would support all efforts to expedite the succession of his rule by Crown Prince Abdulla. Majed Al-Shammary was trusted with the task of serving as the main liaison between The Symposium and the crown prince. Amin would be the main liaison with the Kuwaiti government. The plan was to depose King Fahd and bring Abdulla to the throne in less than two years—before the middle of 1989.

PART TWO

1988

Everything that one needed to predict the next twenty-five years was right there, happening in broad daylight. The problem was, that reality did not have to be plausible to be true. And the seeming implausibility of events was the ultimate camouflage, blinding even some of the more seasoned observers.

III

"What's Going On?"

I t was a few minutes past 5:30 on Tuesday morning when the telephone in James Blackburn's Washington, DC apartment started to ring. He had gone to bed only a few hours earlier, his senses numbed by the countless flasks of sake he had consumed at the sushi bar on 20th Street. The first several rings were lost somewhere in his subconscious as faint, blurry noises always present in the city night. Or perhaps they were the incessant chatter of the Japanese businessmen still echoing in his ears. His mind jumped from bedroom to office to sushi bar, unable to focus on the reality of the moment. By the fifth ring the telephone seemed to be blasting like thunder. As he opened his eyes, a sharp pain exploded somewhere inside his brain, burst outward to his temples and forehead, and crept down to his eyes. The thunder was getting louder and, it seemed to him, more impatient with each new ring. He managed to move. His mouth tasted like seaweed and the smell of stale sake rose from his breath in a sudden jolt and enveloped him. He reached over to the handset on the nightstand and collapsed back in bed.

"H'llo," he mumbled in a barely audible voice.

"Jim!" somebody answered. "What's going on? We *have* to know what's going on!"

"What? ... Uhh ... Who's this?" Blackburn struggled to awaken his mind. He thought about the question still pounding in his brain. *What's going on?* Yes, that was what the person had said. What were the Japanese up to now? Was this Mr. Takao? Blackburn was vaguely aware of his mind making a heroic effort to formulate a response. Who *is* this, he thought at last, exhausted from his futile attempt to answer the question.

"Jim, this is Stan!" declared the agitated voice. "How can you still be asleep? We've been at the office since four this morning. They broke up the meeting a few minutes ago. They're going back in fifteen minutes, 11:45 Vienna time. We *have* to know what's going on."

Oh, shit, thought Blackburn, finally realizing what this was about. The meeting ... don't these bastards ever listen to what I tell them?

"Okay, Stan," he said into the cold handset. "I'll ... I'll make a few phone calls and get back to you." He heard himself make that promise automatically, almost instinctively. How many times had he been through this? "Let me make a few phone calls and get back to you." What a great line. The perfect way to avoid giving an immediate answer to any untimely query.

"Make sure you call us right back, Jim," Stanley Simmons said, still agitated but now in a calmer tone. "We have too much at stake here as you know."

"Yeah, Stan, okay, but don't worry." Blackburn was more awake now. "I've told you before. Nothing will come out of this meeting."

"Then what are they holding so many damned sessions for? First, the non-OPEC guys met alone. Then they met with the OPEC guys. Then they came out for a break, but they're going back in a few minutes. After this, OPEC will meet alone. What are they talking about? If nothing is going to come out of it, why don't they just end it and go home?"

"Stan, relax. You're in good shape. This is how they always do it. They have to go through the motions."

"But you'll check it anyway, right? We really don't have much time."

"Yes, don't worry. I'll call my friends in Vienna. But I'll be surprised if ..." Blackburn felt exhausted. He was almost out of breath. "I'll get right back to you."

Pushy bastards. Why were commodity traders such nervous wrecks all the time?

Actually, he knew the answer to that question all too well. He had briefly traded in energy futures to see what his clients went through, and had seen how rough things could get on the floor. Prices could swing so rapidly that a trader could lose a fortune before being able to place a call to his broker. Trading in oil was driven by greed and fear, often reinforced by rumors. Even if the rumors were wrong, traders usually acted on them, driving prices up or down.

Stanley Simmons, largely relying on Blackburn's advice, had built a huge short position in crude oil futures when prices had started to rise a few days ago. He had sold short over 10,000 contracts during the past week, which represented ten million barrels. *Ten million barrels!* This was twice as large as the 5000-contract limit imposed by the New York Mercantile Exchange on open positions held by speculative accounts. A. Nitzen could go over this limit because it owned Jade Petroleum, which owned and operated a refinery in Philadelphia. The refinery could process 300,000 barrels of crude oil per day, and kept a crude oil inventory of over ten million barrels. This made it possible for A. Nitzen to describe its futures trading as hedging, rather than speculating. For all legal and regulatory purposes, A. Nitzen & Company did not speculate in oil markets.

If the Vienna meetings resulted in a new agreement to restrain oil production, prices could easily rise by a further $3 per barrel on the New York Mercantile Exchange, affectionately known as the Merc, and Stanley Simmons, or rather, A. Nitzen & Company where Simmons worked, would lose $30 million. If, as Blackburn had reassured him, the meeting broke without any concrete agreement to cut back output, prices could collapse by as much as $4 per barrel. Then Simmons would show a profit of $40 million. *Forty million dollars in about ten days!* Yes, Simmons had thought, it can happen so easily. Oil prices could crash to $13, maybe even lower. He had sold his contracts at above $17 per barrel, some blocks at as high as $17.65.

The clock radio next to the telephone on Blackburn's nightstand displayed 5:43 a.m. If Simmons was right, the five oil ministers of OPEC's Pricing Committee and the seven oil ministers from the non-OPEC countries would reconvene in the conference room in the OPEC headquarters building in Vienna in about two minutes. In reality, though, these meetings never started on time. There was always at least one minister who arrived late. The young, alcoholic oil minister of Qatar was a standard late arrival. They probably won't start until 12:30, thought Blackburn, which was odd, since it was so close to lunchtime. In fact, he found it odd that they would break for only fifteen minutes. Why not break till after lunch? Well, who knows, he thought as he yawned.

About a week earlier, when the joint meeting of OPEC and non-OPEC producers had first been announced, oil prices had shot up from $14.50 per barrel to over $17.50 per barrel. The meeting was an unprecedented event. Informal talks between OPEC and non-OPEC countries had been taking place for years, but never before had an official and public gathering like this one been held between the two groups for the explicit purpose of controlling oil production. Seven oil producing countries, none belonging to OPEC, had surprised the world by getting together and collectively pledging support for OPEC. They were: Mexico, Egypt, Oman, Malaysia, Angola, Colombia, and China.

Speculators were not about to take chances with such an event. Most were still buying futures contracts of crude oil, heating oil, and unleaded gasoline. They will agree, said most traders. OPEC alone could not fix things in the market now, but with the support of these other countries, they could pull something big out of their collective hat. There was too much at stake. The difference between $14 and $19 per barrel translated into billions of dollars in revenues for these countries. Besides, as experienced OPEC watchers pointed out, had they not been close to an agreement, they wouldn't have gone through the trouble of holding a formal meeting. Had it not been for the frantic buying of these traders, Simmons wouldn't have had the market liquidity to sell all that volume.

Blackburn lit a cigarette and walked to the bathroom. He stood in front of the toilet, with eyes closed, a cigarette hanging from the corner of his mouth, his head and face throbbing with his colorful sake hangover, and tried to urinate. After a few seconds he gave up. He threw the cigarette in the toilet, splashed his face with cold water, and looked into the mirror. His thick black hair was a mess, with about two dozen gray strands sticking out around his temples. There were several gray hairs in his mustache also, but he had stopped counting them a long time ago. Without their normal sparkle, his dark eyes looked asleep, and the heavy bags under his lids made him appear as fatigued and exhausted as he felt. "You're getting too old for this," he said to the face staring back at him. "You're thirty-five and still acting as if you're twenty." To wash away the fatigue, he splashed his face again and, without drying himself, went back to the bedroom, sat at the edge of his bed, and picked up the telephone.

His telephone had twelve speed-dial buttons, one of which reached the Marriott Hotel in Vienna. That was where most of his contacts stayed whenever OPEC ministers or the organization's various committees met. He hoped Amin would be in his room. He could try paging him if he was in the hotel lobby, but it would be impossible to reach him if he was at the OPEC Secretariat. He pushed the fifth button from the top marked "Marriott" and closed his eyes. His head felt heavy. He rested his cheek on the knuckles of his hand, with the handset squeezed between his palm and his ear, his elbow digging into the top of his knee.

"Vienna Marriott Hotel, *Gutentag*," the cheerful voice of the receptionist said.

"Yes ..." Had the telephone actually rung? "I'd like to speak with Mr. Ramzi Amin, please," said Blackburn, slowly pronouncing every syllable of the name as clearly as he could. He hated to spell names over the telephone.

"Yes, certainly, I connect you. Just a minute please," continued the whiny singsong of the hotel receptionist. "It is ringing, sir."

"Aaallooo." It was Amin all right.

"Ramzi, Jim here. How are things in Vienna?" Blackburn asked in classical Arabic.

"Boring. Big waste of time." Amin never used long sentences unless he was talking about the philosophy of The Symposium.

"Will you be in Kuwait next week?"

"I'll be there. As soon as this meeting ends."

"Something's come up. I'd like to come see you. I'll probably get in late Tuesday night."

"I'll be there. Something interesting, I hope. This meeting has bored me to death!"

"I'm not sure what to make of it yet. It has to do with a bunch of nosy Japanese traders. I'll tell you more in Kuwait. By the way, any positive surprises from the meeting?"

"None. It may even be worse than we thought."

"The market's nervous here."

"Why?"

"Traders are worried about all the different meetings."

"No surprises," Amin said in a reassuring voice.

"The Saudis are still mad at the Mexicans?"

"Yes. As of this morning they hadn't forgiven the Algerians yet either. It will be tough. But no surprises."

"When do you think it'll end?"

"Not much longer. Nothing left to do here. Maybe today. Latest tomorrow."

"Thanks, Ramzi. I'll see you in Kuwait next week."

"*Insha-Allah*." God willing.

That was enough for Blackburn. Would it be enough to put Stanley Simmons' mind at ease? Blackburn dreaded the thought of calling him back and being bombarded with questions about *exactly* what was going on. What were they talking about? What was the Saudi position? The Kuwaiti position? What were the Nigerians saying? They had already changed their minds three times in the past two weeks on whether OPEC should cut output. Was Blackburn sure, *really* sure, that the Gulf States were united this time? "Any chance of an agreement?" Simmons would ask. "*Any chance at all?*"

Blackburn wiped his face with the hem of his T-shirt and yawned again. His mouth was dry and the stale taste of seaweed clung to his tongue and the inside of his mouth. The previous night's conversation and alcohol still buzzed in his head, sending random flashbacks to his brain. He thought of Mr. Takao's questions, his uncharacteristic chatty enthusiasm, and still could not figure out what the man really wanted. Why was he so interested in Kuwait and the plans of the Kuwait Investment Office?

Takao had questioned Blackburn about the business ethics of KPC. Was the corporation reliable? Did it uphold contract sanctity? Did Blackburn-san know of any cases where it had not honored a contractual commitment? Blackburn-san didn't. Had it ever been sued or taken to court for any reason? Or had it resorted to an international arbitration panel, perhaps? So sorry, but Blackburn-san didn't know of any such cases either. Had KPC ever sued any of its clients or business associates? No.

Wait a minute, sure it had. Blackburn-san reminded Takao-san how KPC had taken the U.S. government to court and won its case. Ah, so? The U.S. government? Yes, Takao-san, the U.S. government. Remember when it bought Santa Fe? Santa Fe was producing oil and gas over lands leased from the U.S. government, and the secretary of the interior said that Santa Fe could be barred from those leases because Kuwait didn't allow U.S. companies to explore on its territory. Ah, so! Really? It was some obscure U.S. law the secretary dug out. But you're sure they sued the U.S. government and won? Yes, very sure.

Then Takao had shifted his line of questioning to another area. Do you think KPC will start investing in Asia? More specifically, does it plan to buy refineries in Asia? I see. You're not sure. If it is, which countries do you think it'll consider? Ah, so sorry, you're not sure about this either. No one has mentioned anything to you about investing in the Far East? No, Takao-san, we usually talk about the oil market, not KPC's investments. Ah so, I see. But you can find out if it has such plans, right? Oh, of course we'll pay your expenses if you go to Kuwait on our behalf. Of course, no one should know we're asking the questions.

Of course, Blackburn had reassured Takao, trying to read through his expressionless eyes. Blackburn also threw in some questions of his own. Why was Takao-san so interested in KPC's reliability? Was C. Itoh considering a joint venture with Kuwait? Oh no, no, Takao had answered. Tokyo office is curious, that's all. We buy a lot of oil from Kuwait, as you know, that's all. Yes, Tokyo office is curious. And what about Kuwait's investment plans in the Far East? Was there a potential conflict with C. Itoh? No conflict, Blackburn-san. Just curious.

But there's no such thing as idle curiosity, Blackburn reminded himself. Not in general, and especially not in *this* business. "Tokyo office is curious," he said to the four walls of his room and started to laugh, remembering Takao's facial expression and the humor in the phrase. "Tokyo office is curious!"

None of it made much sense. Takao had asked him to dinner several times the previous week, even though they talked on the telephone almost every day. Takao had never brought up the question of Kuwait's investments on the phone. Last night, that had been the only subject he talked about. He did not seem to care about the OPEC meeting, even though that was the hottest issue on every oil trader's mind. Takao had not once mentioned Saudi Arabia during the evening. Blackburn remembered thinking it must have been his first conversation with Takao in which Saudi Arabia did not come up.

"When can you leave?" Takao had asked as soon as Blackburn indicated he would be willing to go. There was a sense of urgency in his voice.

"The earliest would be this weekend," Blackburn answered, even though he was not sure a trip would be required to answer Takao's questions. Why not just make a few telephone calls? But Takao was already finalizing the deal.

"Very good, Blackburn-san," Takao said, showing his satisfaction with a wide smile. "That would certainly be early enough. I'll brief our Middle East office about your trip. You know Mr. Kato in Bahrain, right? If you need to clarify anything while you're there and you can't find me, you can contact Kato. He'll know about the purpose of your trip."

Now Blackburn looked at the telephone for a long moment, unable to gather enough strength to put in the call. He *had* to call Simmons. The first four buttons on the telephone's speed-dial panel were devoted to Simmons. The first one, marked "Nitzen," was the general number of the company, which he rarely used. The second one, marked "Simmons," was Simmons' private line at the office. The third and fourth buttons were marked "Stan1" and "Stan2." One was the number of Simmons' home telephone, and the second was for his car phone. It would be another six months before Nokia would come up with the first truly portable telephone.

I better brush my teeth first, Blackburn thought, glad to have found an excuse to postpone the telephone call.

He was halfway to the bathroom when the telephone rang again.

"Well?" Stanley Simmons said in his hurried, impatient voice. "What did you find out?"

"There's absolutely no chance of an agreement, Stan," said Blackburn, trying to think how to end the conversation as quickly as possible. "They're miles apart and angry as hell at each other. Some of the ministers are already making plans to return home."

"But what about the Indonesian minis ..."

"Stan, listen to me," interrupted Blackburn more abruptly than he had intended. "Indonesia has nothing to do with this. The Gulf countries have ganged up on the rest. Now, I really have to go. I'll talk to you after the opening or when they end the meeting. Okay?"

Blackburn's confident tone helped. Simmons knew Blackburn would dismiss any other question as irrelevant. He had received all the reassurance he was going to get, but would still remain a nervous wreck until the final outcome of the meeting was officially announced.

"Okay, Jim," he said finally, "but stay in touch, will you?"

"Sure thing, Stan. I'll talk to you in a few hours."

It was already 6:00 a.m. Three hours and forty-five minutes before the crude oil market opened on the Merc. Three hours and fifty minutes before the heating oil and gasoline markets opened. Blackburn sat at the edge of his bed and lit another cigarette. That did not help his headache, or his dry mouth, or the pungent taste of seaweed. I need some coffee, he thought. I should send a fax to the other clients, he was thinking the next second. They're all dying to know *what is going on,* but only Simmons would have the nerve to call me at home at ungodly hours. True, they're my largest clients, but they're also a big pain at times like this.

A. Nitzen & Co. paid Blackburn's firm $250,000 per year as retainer, plus three to five cents per barrel commission on all physical oil deals that Blackburn arranged, depending on how profitable the deal was. This made Stanley Simmons Blackburn's largest client and, in Simmons' mind, gave him the right to call anytime and anywhere. What bothered Blackburn the most was not the calls, but the repetition. The constant demands for reassurance that nothing had changed since the last conversation.

But that's what I'm really selling, he often thought in defense of Simmons. Not just information, but confidence. Reassurance.

Although every cell in his body was ordering him to crawl back into bed, Blackburn knew he wouldn't be able to go back to sleep. What a way to start the week!

It had been 2:30 a.m. and he had been drunk when he got rid of Takao and managed to drive to his apartment. But he had not felt as terrible as he did now. The few hours of sleep seemed to have made matters worse. He had even listened to his telephone messages and then unplugged the answering machine before going to bed—a habit he had started because he could not afford to sleep through calls. Without the answering machine, the telephone would keep ringing until he woke up.

There had been a message from Simmons. "Jim, call me as soon as you can." And one from Sophie. "Thinking about you; hope you enjoyed your sushi dinner. Call when you get a chance. Bye." Simmons' message was standard. Blackburn would have been surprised if there hadn't been one from him. But Sophie's voice had an unusual quality. It was pleasant, as usual, but had an added softness, almost a melancholy, which he had vaguely noticed but was too drunk to dwell on for long. They'll both have to wait till morning, he had thought as he undressed and collapsed into bed.

Now, with a conscious effort, Blackburn got up and walked to his study and plugged in the coffee machine. He threw away the old filter, full of the muddy residue from yesterday morning's coffee, placed a new filter in the container, filled it with fresh coffee, and shoved it in place. After filling the machine with water, he pressed the button, collapsed on a chair, and waited. In a few minutes the familiar crackling sounds emerged from somewhere within the machine. Coffee, his early morning savior, was on its way. He dozed.

When the flow from the top of the machine had slowed to a trickle Blackburn got up, removed the pot, and pushed his mug under the dripping nozzle. A few drops fell on the hot plate, boiled with a violent hiss, and disappeared in a second. He filled the mug from the pot, sat back down, and lit a cigarette.

There was a sudden tranquility in the room. The first rays of sunlight fell from the slats of the blinds onto his messy desk, and the branches of the lone, tall pine tree outside his window shone and shivered in the morning breeze. It was a cool, crisp morning, the type that comes to Washington for only a few days in the spring and again in the fall. Days like these were the saving grace of an otherwise unbearable climate, with impossibly hot and humid summers and cold winters.

After the commotion of the past half-hour, Blackburn felt calm and detached from the hectic pace of nervous traders. He sank deeper into his leather armchair, raised his feet onto the desk, and stared out the window, all the time feeling his mind settle down and an inner peace take hold of him. He was no longer a participant in the drama.

That's the secret, he told himself on the countless occasions when he felt the panic that plagued his clients rise in him also. You're an observer. You're watching a play. You understand the actors and their roles, but you don't care about any one in particular. You know them well, but they're not your friends. The act goes on whether you watch or not, whether you understand or not. That's why you're calm and confident when the players are in a panic. That's why you inspire confidence and get paid for it. That's one of the reasons you quit trading after around a week. Trading and consulting simply do not mix.

IV

Leaky Faucets and the Meaning of Life

Blackburn held his coffee mug in his lap with both hands and stared at his desk. The tip of the antique Yemeni curved dagger, a gift to his father from Gene Theiss, peeked from under a pile of papers. His mind drifted back. He momentarily forgot the meeting in Vienna and the traders in New York.

The son of a U.S. Foreign Service officer stationed in Beirut for eight years, Blackburn had studied at International College and later at the American University of Beirut, where he had spent the best years of his youth. His father, Henry Blackburn, was an iconic figure in the intelligence community. The younger Blackburn knew very little about his father's accomplishments, but could not miss the body language of his associates and colleagues when they dealt with him—it was nothing less than reverence. Blackburn knew that one day he would spend long hours talking to his father in an attempt to better understand the man and his career.

But Henry Blackburn had died in a car accident in Virginia soon after the family left Beirut in the mid-1970s. Blackburn was not prepared to lose his father. The phrase "sudden and untimely death," which he had read in various obituaries, acquired a whole new meaning. Henry Blackburn was healthy, in his mid-fifties, at the prime of his career, and was getting ready to leave for his next post in the Far East when he died. The void James Blackburn felt was immense.

His mother, Martha, did not take the loss any better. She had just turned fifty, and was attached to Henry in every way—emotionally, socially, and in most practical daily matters. Henry had always been so central in her life that she lost perspective. A month after the car accident, she was convinced that his death was not accidental. "They killed him," she'd tell Blackburn. "Mark my words, Jim, they killed him. He knew too much. He knew too much not only about the enemy, but also about them. He had weighed and measured everyone at the CIA. He knew their secrets, their weaknesses. They killed him for it."

Blackburn had no idea how to handle his mother. He was not over the loss of his father either, and it pained him to see his mother disappear into a world of her own, drawn into what he considered a fantastic paranoiac realm of her imagination.

Then his mother got more specific, citing names and incidents she believed provided motives for his father's killing. Blackburn thought she could not have made them all up.

That was when he went to Gene Theiss for advice. Theiss and Henry Blackburn had been long-time colleagues in the CIA. They had been stationed at various posts in succession, taking over from each other and keeping each other regularly briefed. Although the two families did not get together often, they were close. Blackburn used to call Theiss "Uncle Gene" when he was growing up. It was after Henry Blackburn's death that Theiss started taking the younger Blackburn more seriously.

On the day of the visit they sat in the library of Theiss' house in Old Town Alexandria, where Blackburn had been several times with his parents. Theiss looked like his father to him that day. Gray hair combed back, long, strong chin, blue-green eyes, solemn, undecipherable expression, and slim physique, suggesting a disciplined and frugal lifestyle, which was in fact far from the truth. Theiss listened patiently to Blackburn, showing no reaction to the various suspicions of foul play.

"Do you know if Henry was indebted?" he asked when Blackburn was finished.

"Indebted?"

"Yes, was he in debt? Did he owe people or banks a lot of money?"

"I have no idea," responded Blackburn, puzzled by the question. "Why?"

"Jim, listen to me carefully. The CIA will not hit one of its own, especially someone like your father. I would even have said 'never,' except that I would not want to give you the wrong idea. It has happened. But only in extremely special cases when the person in question has been considered to be a major liability. And the most common cases of potential liability are agents who are heavily indebted, the idea being that they can be bought."

"He was not indebted. No creditors have been knocking on the door since he passed away."

"I didn't mean to upset you, Jim. I'm just letting you know about the rare situations when such dark possibilities may be contemplated. That's all."

"What do you make of the stories my mother has been telling?"

"There is no way that the agency could have anything to do with Henry's death. He was not a liability. He was the type of man the agency would have gone out of its way to protect. I don't believe there was any foul play in this case, Jim. And I give you my solemn word that I would tell you if I suspected anything like that."

Less than a year after his father's accident, Blackburn's mother passed away. Heart failure was the medical explanation. The more likely reason was her loss of a lifetime partner and her subsequent grief. Given all the noise his mother had made about foul play, Blackburn had some eerie feelings about her untimely passing as well. But none of it made sense to him.

Over time, with a lot of help and reassurance from Gene Theiss, he learned to let the doubts and suspicions lie.

Blackburn's eyes drifted back and scanned his desk. The ashtray was full of cigarette stubs. It had been more than fourteen years since he had taken it from the Horse Shoe Café on Hamra Street. The red and white lettering on the black ceramic ashtray had faded, with the "s" and the "e" of "Horse" barely legible. Just as the place itself has faded away, he thought with nostalgia. He cherished the old ashtray as a valuable memento from his days in Beirut. The Horse Shoe had had its time. It had been part of Beirut's intellectual history. It had been the favorite hangout not only of the Lebanese political and literary elite, but also of the international intelligence community that thrived in the city in those days.

But that was not just fourteen years ago. That was in a different era. Now the city was associated with terrorists and hostages. To most Americans, Beirut *meant* terrorism. To most Lebanese, it meant terror. Neither the Horse Shoe ashtray nor the poster of the Cedars of Lebanon hanging on the wall of the study could make Blackburn lose sight of that. But they helped him relax. Staring at them, he withdrew into a world where everything ran at a slower pace; a world where he could think more clearly, at least about matters related to the Middle East. James Blackburn was one of the few Americans who had managed to adopt part of another culture. He had learned Arabic and spoke the classical version of the language fluently.

The sunrays had moved from the scattered papers on his desk to the keyboard of the old personal computer, and were creeping up its screen. He rarely used this PC now. He had a much faster model in the office, with four times the memory. This was an old IBM clone with ten megabytes of memory on its hard disk, which had served him well until the new models started appearing on the market, one almost every week. Only two years old, the machine now gathered dust on his desk and was of less use to him than the fourteen-year-old ashtray.

He noticed the stack of bills at the corner of the desk, from the telephone company, electric company, gas company, and a few magazines whose subscriptions he had let run out. He wouldn't be able to get around to paying them until the weekend. Or maybe Thursday, he thought absently.

He knew he was going to have an extremely busy day. At least a dozen telephone messages would be waiting for him when he arrived at his office, and the telephone would not stop ringing until evening. He would have to explain to his clients what went on and what it all meant for oil prices. The same conversation, repeated over and over again. Some clients would be far more inquisitive than others, demanding an explanation of the details, bombarding him with questions about specific figures, positions, and conversations. Some would press him for specific recommendations on how to trade, how much to buy or sell, at what price, when to cover.

He didn't like to get that specific. The irrefutable conventional wisdom in commodity trading was "buy low, sell high." Simple enough. But it was impossible to recognize the lows and the highs. How low is low? How high is high? You sell at what you think is the high, but the market can go higher. You cover with a profit, but the market can keep moving in your favor and you kick yourself for having left money on the table. Specific recommendations were a headache. He would dwell only on the overall direction of the market. He should telefax a memo to all the clients to cut the telephone calls short. It helped to have the major points and figures down on paper. It reassured the clients and saved him time.

Blackburn suddenly realized he had been thinking about Bianca ever since Simmons' call had woken him up and reminded him of the meeting in progress in Vienna.

Bianca was what turned Vienna into a magical city for Blackburn. And she was what colored OPEC meetings with passion. Originally Italian, she was married to a Viennese banker named Stefan Kraus. As the executive assistant to the secretary general of OPEC, she did more than assist the secretary; in effect, she was the chief of staff in the organization.

Important as her job was for Blackburn, that was not what Bianca meant to him. He loved her zest for life; her insatiable and unending passion; her reluctance to miss an exciting moment, a charged experience, an elevated level of being; her devotion to friendships she considered worthwhile; her unusual ability to share her innate joy of life with those around her. In short, even though he did not know it as such, he loved her.

It was not an easy relationship. Blackburn also knew and liked Stefan. In fact, he had known Stefan longer than he had known Bianca. Stefan's bank, LGT bank headquartered in Vaduz, Liechtenstein, had financed two energy projects that Blackburn advised. Professionally, they had grown to respect each other. In many ways, Stefan was a rare phenomenon—solid as rock, settled, at peace with himself and with his surroundings—exactly the type of man Bianca gravitated toward, a man who served as a reliable anchor for her. And, prone as she was to emotional excursions, she needed a reliable safe harbor to always return to. Stefan was perfect. And he liked Blackburn, and enjoyed his company, but did not know about his relationship with his wife.

Bianca had a habit of telling Stefan everything. But Blackburn had made her promise to keep their relationship a secret.

"I could never face him again," he said. Bianca laughed, but agreed to grant him his wish.

Another complication was Blackburn's budding relationship with Sophie Myles, a public relations professional based in Washington, DC. But he told himself that as they had no firm commitment, no one would get hurt, as long as Sophie did not find out about Bianca.

He had met Bianca three years earlier during one of his frequent visits to the OPEC Secretariat. Bianca was twenty-eight then, full of energy and radiating a contagious type of joy so unique that it defined her. The first time their eyes met, his gaze lingered, and so did hers. Something clicked, but he thought it would be inappropriate to make a move, given the official contacts he had in the organization.

The next day, she sent him a message at his hotel on behalf of her boss proposing a meeting the following morning at 8:30. Blackburn hated early morning meetings. He considered any appointment before 10 a.m. uncivilized, and had told her that. So he left a message on her voice mail.

"Bianca, are you trying to kill me?"

Later that afternoon, she left a message at his hotel. "Yes, I'd love to kill you, but only by little deaths. B."

She managed to reschedule the meeting to 10 a.m. It was with the OPEC economic research unit, and resulted in an invitation to dinner the same evening. To Blackburn's surprise, Bianca was also there, with his old acquaintance, Stefan Kraus. That was when he found out they were married.

Throughout dinner, Bianca showered him with short, intense glances, often lifting her glass and silently offering him a private toast across the table. As the dinner came to a close, she walked over to Blackburn and bent down to his ear.

"Did you understand my message?" she whispered, sending shivers down his spine.

He looked up, their faces an inch apart, and shook his head.

"Dying a small death means having an orgasm," she purred. "*La petite mort* ... It's a French thing. I'd like to kill you over and over with small deaths."

Every word resonated in his groin. And a stormy affair soon started, which survived against all odds.

On their first date after that dinner, neither Bianca's charm nor her passion had limits. Her boundless sensuous energy filled the space and overwhelmed him.

"I love your hands," she told him early in the evening. "The first things I look at in a man are his hands. Long, slender fingers are key," she said, holding his hand with both of hers and running her fingers up and down his palm and fingers. "Fat, meaty fingers won't do. There can be no romance behind chubby hands."

She initiated the seduction, led the dance, filled the air, overwhelmed the emotional space.

But the charm that made Bianca so addictive was precisely what made it impossible to keep her exclusively. She had other lovers, aside from Blackburn. Stefan somehow tolerated that a lot better than Blackburn. That intrigued and troubled Blackburn. If her husband can accept her love affairs, who am I to complain, he told himself. But he couldn't get over his jealousy.

One man she had just started seeing who had managed to keep her affections was someone she called Roberto. Stefan knew about him, and Bianca had told Blackburn about him as well. Roberto was becoming a presence in her life, no question about it.

Blackburn had learned early on that if he wanted Bianca, he had to take her as she was. He somehow had managed to get over his initial jealousy of Stefan, although he still hated imagining them together. But Roberto was an entirely different matter. There was no logical explanation for his presence. Roberto was her choice. Just like Blackburn was. Another choice. Another role player, filling another gap in Bianca's world. That was difficult—in fact impossible—to get used to.

Now, in spite of his state of mind and what the day promised to throw at him, Blackburn could not resist the urge to call her. The phone had barely rung when he heard her voice. Caller identification had just been introduced in the OPEC Secretariat.

"*Amore mio!*" His heart missed a beat.

"Hello Bianca."

"Why aren't you in Vienna? Eh? Tell me, why? If you no longer care about me, don't you care about the meeting?"

She chuckled so sweetly that Blackburn couldn't help smiling ear to ear.

"I'll do better than visit you during the OPEC meeting. How about this weekend? Maybe until Monday?"

"You made my day! The last ten days have been too stressful here. I need to decompress."

Blackburn could not keep a silly, childish smile from spreading all over his face. He loved to be with Bianca when she decompressed; that was when she was at her best.

"I'll stop by Europe for a couple of days on my way to Kuwait. You want to meet in Vienna or somewhere else?"

"Let's get me out of Vienna!" She declared. "What's most convenient for your connection? London?"

"You are a sweetheart. So considerate. Yes, London. I'll send you my itinerary as soon as I finalize it. Count on two nights, Saturday and Sunday."

"I miss you sooooo much, Jimmy. Don't expect to have much rest in London."

"I can't wait. By the way, how is Anthony doing?"

Anthony was her four-year-old son, an adorable little boy whom she loved more than anything in the world.

"Thank you so much for asking, Jimmy. You are so sweet. He is doing great. He's very smart and very good natured—so much more like his father than like me, wouldn't you say?"

Blackburn laughed. "See you soon," he said, getting ready to hang up.

"Wait, you're not going to ask me about the meeting?"

"What's there to ask? It will be over soon, right? Probably this evening. And not much will come of it, right?"

"You already know more in Washington than a lot of people here. Soon you will not need me anymore."

"You know I'll always need you … *ciao*, Bianca."

His head was feeling better. The throbbing had subsided and the coffee had managed to wash away some of the stale taste from his mouth. The prospect of seeing Bianca in a few days made everything he had to face today so much easier.

He filled another cup, lit a cigarette, and tried to compose the memo in his head. His right index finger gently stroked his mustache, gliding over it in slow, steady movements. That was trademark Blackburn in thought, especially when trying to compose a note. The broad outline of the memo was already taking shape in his mind. It wouldn't be difficult to write it once he sat in front of his computer at the office. The keyboard and the screen would somehow inspire him to write the two or three paragraphs it would take to sum up what had happened and what it would mean for oil prices.

He would then telefax the same memo to the dozen reporters on his mailing list. But not before all the clients received it first and had a chance to call him. And when they later read the same analysis in *The Wall Street Journal*, *The New York Times*, and several specialized oil-market trade journals—*Petroleum Intelligence Weekly*, *Platt's Oilgram News*—they would have the deeply satisfying feeling that they were not learning anything new. When they saw Mr. James Blackburn of the PCG quoted by the energy reporters and the wire services as a "leading oil expert," they would recognize not only the quotes, but also the background to the analysis, which the average reader would miss. They would feel they had access to the "inside story." And, when Blackburn sent them their renewal notices with an invoice, they would not hesitate to renew their retainer agreements and pay their fees.

Blackburn had started the Petroleum Consulting Group around ten years ago, with one associate, an analyst named Patrick Hagan, and a secretary, Linda Hays. Both were still with him, but the group now included over a dozen other analysts. They researched global product markets, focusing on gasoline and heating oil and production, consumption, inventory levels, prices, and refinery margins in Asia, Europe, the Middle East, and the United States. They produced regular reports, short briefings, and memos for distribution to PCG's clients. Blackburn followed these reports and occasionally delved deeper in them to assure quality and professionalism, but his heart was in the politics of crude oil markets. The geopolitics of the energy sector captured his imagination in a way that the commercial details of refineries and retail markets could never do. Early on, he delegated those tasks and responsibilities to Hagan, and focused mainly on the political economy of crude oil.

The preference for the latter had come into focus soon after he had returned to the United States with his parents from Beirut, and in the most unlikely way.

Blackburn had watched a lot of commercials on television in those days. While most people would mute the TV during commercials or go to the restroom, he'd skip the show and focus on the commercials. "These people have paid good money to research what sells to the average American," he'd tell his father, who voiced his puzzlement about his infatuation with commercials. "If you want to know what the average American is like, watch TV commercials."

One of the commercials that made an impression depicted a simple, lower middle class American, dressed in a yellow and brown plaid pair of pants and a blue flannel shirt, climbing up a mountain. He climbs through the thick vegetation and mist, out of breath, but with an unwavering determination to reach the top. Finally at the peak, he comes face to face with an impressive figure, a guru of sorts, seated on the ground with his legs folded under him, his long, white beard swaying in the light breeze. The American, startled, falls to his knees, over towered by the larger-than-life presence of the meditating guru.

"Oh wise one," mutters the man. "I need your counsel. How can I fix the leaky faucets in my house?"

The guru momentarily opens his eyes, and the intensity of his gaze pins the man to the ground. Then, without even opening his mouth, a voice fills the wilderness. "Come back to me when you want to learn about the meaning of life," it echoes through the entire mountaintop. "As for your leaky faucets, go to the plumber." And the name and phone number of the sponsoring plumbing company echoes through the mountains, as the guru shuts his eyes and goes back to his meditative state.

The commercial so amused Blackburn that he later created two departments at PCG. He dubbed one "Leaky Faucets" and the other "Meaning of Life." Leaky Faucets dealt with refinery margins in Singapore, bunker fuel prices in Europe, lube oil production and demand globally, and all the other detailed nuts and bolts of the oil business that needed to be quantified and monitored in excruciating detail on an almost daily basis. Meaning of Life, on the other hand, dealt with the policy aspects, the geopolitical shifts, the competitive environment of the large commercial interests, and the strategic challenges faced by both governmental and commercial actors—none of which could be quantified or entered into a spreadsheet.

"I don't do Leaky Faucets," Blackburn told Patrick Hagan soon after they started the company. "Will you take it?"

And Hagan took it.

It was past 7 a.m. when Blackburn finally rose from the leather armchair in his study, turned on his answering machine, and walked to the bathroom. He showered, shaved, trimmed his mustache, and left for his office on Pennsylvania Avenue and 20th Street.

V

The Oil Traders' Backstage

There was an air of excitement in the Marriott lobby. Perhaps it was the novelty of the OPEC/non-OPEC collusion; or maybe everyone realized that this time the stakes were higher than usual. Whatever it was, it did not make life easier for the reporters. Although the ministers were still at the OPEC headquarters, rumors of a new deal had already spread through the lobby. Jim Purdy, the correspondent from *The Financial Times*, had heard from "authoritative sources" that a deal had already been made and was waiting only for the formality of the signing of a new agreement. He was seated at a table at the front of the Garten Café, near the elevators, along with the correspondents from Reuters, *The New York Times*, and the *Middle East Economic Survey*. There were several others standing around the table, listening to the conversation being conducted in a deliberately low, but audible voice.

"They have a deal," Purdy said. "Non-OPEC has promised to cut their exports by 5 percent if OPEC agrees to cut its production by 5 percent. The way I understand it, OPEC can't turn them down." Purdy was clearly excited. His cheeks were redder than usual, and the curly white hair on his temples was a mess.

"I don't believe it," said Joe Edwards of *The New York Times*. "I can't see how Saudi Arabia and Kuwait could agree to any cut in their quotas, not to mention the UAE, which has not even ..."

"*Why?* Don't you think they want higher prices too?" interrupted Purdy, ready to defend the validity of his information. "Do you *really* believe this garbage about Saudi Arabia and Kuwait wanting low prices to punish Iran? Or to help George Bush win the U.S. election?" That sent Purdy into a fit of laughter, which soon became an uncontrolled coughing frenzy.

"I don't know about the U.S. elections, but they've said they're going to defend their market share," answered Edwards, trying to control his temper, and not waiting for Purdy to fully recover from his cough.

"But they're *boxed in!*" Purdy had caught his breath and was already lighting another cigarette to calm his cough. "Non-OPEC is unanimous on this. Maybe what you're not aware of is that many key OPEC countries are for it also. Algeria is for it, Iran is for it, Venezuela is for it, Nigeria has changed its mind again and is for it. They're all for it except the Gulf States. Saudi Arabia and Kuwait cannot turn them down."

Joe Edwards was furious. How could Purdy get all this before he did? Had these countries actually confirmed their official support for the production cuts? Edwards had to admit that Purdy wouldn't make it all up, but he could be misled; he could overreact; he could be used by one minister to test an idea on the others.

In fact, OPEC ministers had become quite good at using the press in that fashion. Under constant threat of being cut off from an official news source, the press would usually go quite a distance to appease the egos or wishes of various ministers. The most notorious in this regard were the Nigerian and Saudi Arabian officials. Rulwanu Lukman, the oil minister of Nigeria and the president of the OPEC conference, believed he had to cultivate the press in order to improve the image of Nigeria within OPEC and the international oil community.

In this environment, it was no wonder that some trade journals were dubbed as the "voice of Saudi Arabia" or the "voice of Kuwait." When an OPEC minister or his press secretary appeared to be close to a certain reporter, it could discredit both the reporter and the publication. Unfortunately, this was not always fair nor an accurate representation of the reporter's integrity.

Edwards and Purdy had always been in bitter competition over sources and the reputation of being the best energy reporter. Purdy was at least ten years older than Edwards, but had been covering energy for only the past eight years, the same as Edwards. Edwards' contacts with the Arabs were better than Purdy's, but Purdy had managed to cultivate the Nigerians. That must be his source, Edwards thought. It cannot be a done deal, no matter what this fool says. The Nigerians must have taken their fight to the press again.

"It won't be easy to box in the giants," said Steve Kudairi of the *Middle East Economic Survey*, whose contacts in the Saudi and Kuwaiti delegations were best of all. He had been listening silently, unable to decide whether Purdy's story had merit.

A few tables away, Ramzi Amin had finished his lunch almost two hours earlier, but had decided to stay for lack of anything better to do. He had come down soon after his telephone conversation with James Blackburn. What a waste of time, he kept telling himself. It was April and, elsewhere, it was spring. But Vienna was still cold, windy, gray, and depressing. Amin skipped as many trips to the OPEC headquarters as he could, preferring to stay in the Marriott lobby. Although the OPEC building was no more than five minutes away by car, he still had to put on his coat and walk out in the wind.

Several people had joined his table, tried to chat with him for a while, then excused themselves quietly and left. It wasn't easy to stay in the company of Ramzi Amin unless one accepted silence as a perfectly normal way of keeping company with another human being. Reporters rarely got anything out of him. Only those who had learned how to interpret his short and curt phrases could sometimes deduce relevant facts from a conversation. But this required patience and years of experience in dealing with Amin personally, something most reporters did not possess.

All that did not bother Kamal Ashkar, Amin's colleague who was with the Saudi Arabian delegation. As long as somebody was listening, Ashkar could talk for hours without any feedback. He joined Amin, went through the usual pleasantries, and then turned his attention to the waitresses. They were charming. Wearing white, low-cut blouses and long, black skirts with slits on the side that came up to mid-thigh, they scurried around, taking orders, bending over tables to gather dishes and cups, and exposing their breasts to gaping Kamal Ashkars all over the Garten Café.

In both physical appearance and personality, Kamal Ashkar was the antithesis of Ramzi Amin. The permanent smile on his round, chubby face was far more natural than his goatee, which looked as if it had been glued on as an afterthought. His big black eyes were warm, outgoing, and friendly. Amin's boney face and small, dark eyes gave him a stern look that fit his personality perfectly. Ashkar did not just love to talk. He *needed* to talk, constantly, about any subject, with anyone. For Amin, talking was like undergoing surgery; it was one of those human activities that one did only when absolutely necessary, with as few words as possible. The Symposium recruiting sessions at his desert villa in Kuwait were the only exception.

Steve Kudairi excused himself from the journalists' table and walked over to Ramzi Amin. His chair was immediately taken by the person standing nearest to him, and the debate, in an almost conspiratorial whisper, continued. Kudairi greeted Amin and Ashkar in Arabic and sat down. It would have been inappropriate to ask the burning question right away, even though that was precisely what Purdy or Edwards would have done. As the waitress came to take Kudairi's order, Ashkar's face lit up.

"Aila, honey," he said, grabbing her hand. "I want you to meet my good friend Steve. Steve, this is Aila. She's from Denmark, but she loves Vienna more."

The waitress, barely twenty-two years old, blushed. "What would you like?" she asked Kudairi, ignoring Ashkar.

"I'll have a cup of coffee, thank you," said Kudairi. The waitress was gone in an instant.

"Can you imagine her in bed?" Ashkar said, his eyes pinned to the behind of the departing waitress. "Can you imagine *those* legs thrown across *your* shoulders?"

"Leave her alone," Amin said coldly.

"Ramzi here doesn't care about women," Ashkar said to Kudairi. "He doesn't drink alcohol, he doesn't joke, and he doesn't flirt. Now you know why the Kuwait Petroleum Company is so successful. That's the real secret of its success. And you reporters go around looking for far-fetched reasons."

Amin didn't seem to have heard any of Ashkar's remarks. He knew Ashkar well. He took a sip of coffee and absently watched the lobby.

"Have any of you been outside today?" Kudairi asked in an attempt to change the subject and the mood. "It's terribly windy outside. I don't know how people live in this city."

"With women like this, who cares about the wind?" said Ashkar. Neither the waitress's cold shoulder nor Amin's curt reprimand had fazed him one bit.

"It's amazing how rumors start and spread in this place from thin air," Kudairi said softly, turning to Amin. It was finally time to hint at what was going on at the front table.

"So what is it this time?" asked Amin, gesturing with his head toward Purdy's table.

"They say the deal is done," Kudairi replied in a disinterested tone. "Somebody mentioned something about a 5 percent cut. They say everybody has agreed and they're working on the wording of the final communiqué."

"Interesting. Especially since I know nothing about it," Amin said with a smirk, which Kudairi took as an emphatic refutation. But the gathering around Purdy's table had grown larger, and he was dominating the discussion. By now, almost everybody in the lobby knew about the plan and most believed the deal had already been made. Representatives from oil companies had already called their offices to alert their traders.

Amin had ordered his third cup of coffee and a beer for Kamal Ashkar when a commotion started in the lobby. Within a few minutes, the café stood empty as some thirty reporters rushed toward the elevator lobby. Kudairi was gone and Purdy's table was deserted, leaving a dozen coffee cups and glasses of water and a few plates of half-eaten deserts abandoned. The waitresses of the Garten Café dreaded these scenes. These were the times when unpaid bills accumulated in the pockets of their pretty aprons; they would have to remember which faces were sitting at which table and hunt them down later, when things settled down.

But as far as the reporters were concerned, the Nigerian oil minister, Mr. Rulwanu Lukman, was more important than paying their bills. He had entered the hotel and was headed toward the elevators with a small entourage of four assistants. Amin had barely caught a glimpse of him when the reporters surrounded him. All Amin could see now were the stretched, almost distorted, bodies of the unfortunate reporters at the periphery of the crowd, their arms extended toward the center, hoping their small, hand-held tape recorders would capture the statements made by the minister. Sudden outbursts of questions were followed by total silence, indicating the minister had started responding to one of the questions shouted at him.

On the marble counter opposite the elevator doors sat four house phones. The Reuters crew had somehow managed to hook one of them to their temporary editorial headquarters at the Intercontinental Hotel. That was smart, for they now had the best spot, right next to Lukman, and one of their reporters was on the house phone repeating everything Lukman said into the handset and straight into the Reuters station at the Intercontinental. Even as he spoke, the reporter's words were being entered into the Reuters system and transmitted to subscribers all over the world. At that instant, somebody sitting in New York in front of his screen could find out what Lukman was saying faster than Amin, who was sitting no more than twenty yards away.

"Your Excellency, is it true that the meeting is breaking apart?" shouted one of the reporters.

"We just broke for a recess, but I am not aware of anything breaking *apart*," Lukman answered in his calm manner.

One of his aides stood with his back to Lukman's, facing the crowd. Two others were at each side, nervously scanning the reporters and their equipment, and the fourth stood in front of the minister, with his back turned to him, also focused on every move made by the reporters.

"Your Excellency, is it true that non-OPEC has made a proposal to cut output?"

"Yes. We have a concrete proposal from our non-OPEC colleagues."

"Your Excellency, can you tell us what exactly is the non-OPEC proposal?"

"The group of non-OPEC oil producing countries that met with us is as concerned about the stability of the oil market as we are. They would like to support our efforts to stabilize oil prices at an acceptable level. To this end, they have proposed to cut their exports by 5 percent, in return for a 5 percent cut by OPEC."

"How much is 5 percent of their exports? From what level will these cuts be applied?" shouted the reporter from *Petroleum Argus*. She was a small woman with short, black hair, who was squeezed in the middle of the crowd, barely able to move her hand to write on her notepad.

But Lukman chose not to answer her question. At any given moment, there were at least five questions thrown at him simultaneously, and he answered the one he felt most comfortable with.

"Would you say that OPEC is prepared to accept the non-OPEC proposal?" This was clearly Jim Purdy's voice, rising triumphantly above the others.

"Obviously that is what we are discussing. I think it's a good proposal and deserves our serious consideration. All I can say at the moment is that we have had a constructive dialogue with our non-OPEC colleagues."

"Your Excellency, are you saying you're optimistic that a positive response will be given to the non-OPEC countries?" persisted Purdy, giving a side look to Edwards who was standing next to him.

"Well, as you know, we are always optimistic. There is no room for pessimism in our business. We have had differences in the past, but we've found ways to work them out."

"Will Iraq join the OPEC production agreement?" Iraq had not been party to OPEC quota-sharing decisions since 1986, insisting it should have quota parity with Iran, which Iran categorically refused.

"This meeting is not about Iraq. This meeting is about our non-OPEC colleagues and their proposal."

"Your Excellency, how long do you think your next meeting will last?"

"There is no set time limit. We will be here as long as it takes to discuss all the issues."

Lukman moved toward the elevator doors. His aides, arms stretched out to keep the crowd away, followed in such unison that their formation around Lukman was not disturbed. The impromptu press conference had come to an end. Lukman, satisfied that he had said everything he wanted to say, ignored the last several questions thrown at him. At that same instant, the story was taking shape on the Reuters screen:

"NIGERIAN OIL MINISTER LUKMAN SAID THAT OPEC MINISTERS ARE SERIOUSLY CONSIDERING A NON-OPEC PROPOSAL TO CUT EXPORTS BY 5 PERCENT, IN RETURN FOR A SIMILAR MOVE BY OPEC. HE EXPRESSED OPTIMISM THAT OPEC MEMBERS WILL ACCEPT THE

PLAN AND WORK OUT THEIR DIFFERENCES. ASKED
HOW LONG HE EXPECTED THE MEETING TO LAST,
HE ANSWERED 'AS LONG AS IT TAKES' TO COME UP
WITH A SOLUTION. HE DESCRIBED THE JOINT OPEC/
NON-OPEC MEETING, WHICH JUST CONCLUDED, AS
'CONSTRUCTIVE.'"

It was almost 3:30 p.m., about 9:30 a.m. in New York. In fifteen
minutes, trading on the New York Mercantile Exchange would begin.

"I wonder what kind of garbage he's feeding them now," asked Kamal
Ashkar, watching the crowd around Lukman, his attention temporarily
distracted away from the waitresses.

"Lukman has his garbage, we have ours," Amin said quietly as he got
up from his chair.

The Kuwaiti delegation was expected to arrive from the OPEC headquarters soon, and there was bound to be another meeting upstairs. He
did not want to be caught in the crowd when the other ministers arrived.
If this is bad, wait till the Saudis and Kuwaitis arrive, he thought.

Up in his suite, the Kuwaiti oil minister, Shaikh Ali Khalifa Al-Sabbah,
had already changed from his Western business suit into an Arabic *thawb*,
the long, flowing white robe he always wore in Kuwait. He had let out
a sigh of relief while taking off his tie and unbuttoning his shirt, and a
longer sigh while taking off his trousers. This must be the most unnatural
way to dress, he thought for the thousandth time as he tossed the Western
clothes on his bed. His shoes and socks were gone also, replaced by light
leather sandals. Then he received his colleagues, the oil ministers of Saudi
Arabia, the United Arab Emirates, and of Qatar.

Tea was served, which the ministers sipped with long, loud slurps.
"They seem more sure of themselves after each session," Hisham Nazer,
the Saudi oil minister, said. He rested his left foot on the couch and his
arm on his elevated knee. His string of amber worry beads was partially
wrapped around his index finger.

"Oh, yes," said Shaikh Ali. "They're really getting overconfident. It
will be interesting to see how long it will last once this is all over."

Shaikh Ali desperately missed the old days. He and Ahmad Zaki Yamani, the former oil minister of Saudi Arabia, understood each other. Ali respected Yamani's intellect, tact, and understanding of international affairs. Even when they had disagreements, Yamani was a real colleague. Ali could talk and plan with Yamani. He could bargain and plot with him. There was a rapport between the two men that had been built over two decades of camaraderie. At countless OPEC meetings, they had confronted the Nigerians, Algerians, Iranians, and Venezuelans together. They had survived the diplomatic nightmares created by the downfall of the shah in Iran and, soon afterward, the eruption of the Iran/Iraq war.

About two years earlier, King Fahd had fired Yamani. After representing Saudi Arabia as the Kingdom's oil minister for twenty-four years, Shaikh Ahmad Zaki Yamani was unceremoniously pulled away. Hisham Nazer, a long-time minister of planning and friend and confidant of King Fahd, was brought in. Shaikh Ali looked at Hisham Nazer as a bureaucrat, or perhaps a glorified messenger of His Majesty King Fahd. He couldn't plot with Hisham Nazer. There was no history in their relationship, which sometimes made it difficult even to communicate.

"Hey, Ramzi," yelled Shaikh Ali. "What was Lukman telling those reporters earlier?"

Amin told him about the Reuters story one of his aides had read to him over the telephone from Kuwait. That was at 9:30 a.m. New York time. Now it was almost 10:15 in New York. The market had been open for half an hour. Amin dialed his office in Kuwait again. After listening for a few minutes, he hung up to report that WTI prices had opened limit up—that meant one dollar per barrel higher than the previous day's settlement for all the future months except the first trading month, which had no limit. The first month—in early April, the first trading month was May—was up $1.62 per barrel, to $19.15 per barrel.

Then Ramzi Amin left the room, went to one of the two bedrooms of the suite, and closed the door behind him. He immediately picked up the telephone and dialed James Blackburn's office number in Washington.

*   *   *

When Blackburn received the telephone call from Amin, the May WTI contract was trading at $19.22 per barrel. Stanley Simmons had been in a panic all morning. His paper losses since the opening of the market were approaching $1 million. Although Blackburn had received Amin's reassuring "no surprises" verdict about five hours earlier, Lukman's statements and the market's reaction had him concerned. What if there were last minute changes? What if King Fahd had changed his mind, as he had done so many times before? If Chadli, the president of Algeria, had put more pressure on him at the last minute, the king could have caved in. Amin might not have found an opportunity to warn him.

Blackburn had been relieved when his secretary, Linda, interrupted one of his impossible conversations with Simmons to announce that Mr. Amin was on the other line from Vienna. He cut Simmons short and immediately picked up the second line.

"Ramzi, I'm so glad you called," he almost shouted before taking control of himself. "Tell me, what's going on out there, what's all this talk from Lukman?"

"Jim, listen, forget Lukman. I can't talk long. When it hits 19.50, I want you to sell 600 contracts for my account. Don't spread this around yet. Let Tony do it gradually, as usual. A hundred at a time."

"You want them all sold at 19.50?" asked Blackburn, barely able to conceal his relief. This was the biggest proof of all that there would be no agreement.

"No, no. Just start selling when it hits 19.50, and keep selling till you have 600 done. That's all. I have to go."

"Okay, Ramzi, consider it done. I'll see you in Kuwait next week. And Ramzi, thanks."

Amin had already hung up. Next week I'll find out the details, thought Blackburn, as a wide smile spread across his face. The relief was enormous. He had spent the past three hours reassuring his clients that there would be no agreement, even as strong doubts were beginning to creep into his own mind. When Lukman's statements appeared on the Reuters screen fifteen minutes before the market opened, he could not put his phone down as Linda transferred call after call. Some of the callers were relatively restrained, asking only what Lukman was talking about, and checking whether Blackburn had changed his mind about the outcome. Others were downright abusive, yelling at him, cursing, and threatening to never listen to him again.

"You analysts know nothing about the real world!" Don Underwood of Tafco Securities screamed at him. "They will *not* agree, you said, they will *not* agree. If thirteen OPEC countries can't agree, you said, then how on earth can *twenty* countries agree. Well, *they just did!*"

Blackburn's efforts to convince Underwood that there was no agreement yet, that even Lukman had not said there was one, were fruitless. He closed his short positions at a huge loss by buying back 400 contracts at over $19 per barrel, and started reversing his position by buying more.

Now Blackburn called his broker. He told Tony to sell 600 contracts for Yousef's account when May hit 19.50. It was already trading at 19.42 when he called. "Tony, do it gradually. A hundred at a time."

As they spoke, a small rally hit the market. Prices rose to 19.46, then 19.48, hesitated a second, and the screen registered 19.52, 19.53, 19.55, 19.60 in quick succession. "Tony go!" Blackburn ordered and then hung up.

There were three calls waiting, one of which was from Simmons. Blackburn asked Linda to put Simmons through first and keep the others holding. This would take only a second.

"Stan, I only have a sec. The Arabs started to sell. There's no deal. Hang in there. Gotta go." The next call was from Don Underwood. Blackburn took it, his eyes pinned to the screen. May crude had gone as high as 19.74, but was retrenching rapidly: 19.62, 19.60, 19.55, up to 19.58, 19.53, 19.50, 19.47, 19.48 …

"Don, I only have a sec. There is no agreement. Don't be fooled by all this. Now is no time to be long, I assure you. Got to go."

"Wait a minute, *wait just one fucking minute!*" screamed Underwood. "What are you telling me here? The market's up *two fucking* bucks for nothing? What do you know, Jim?"

"Don, I've told you before, I'm telling you now. There is no agreement. I can't go into the details of why the market's up now. If you don't want to sell short again, at least cover your longs. I *really* have to go."

"Tony's holding," Linda shouted as soon as she heard Blackburn hang up. "And Sophie has called twice already."

"I'm afraid she'll have to wait. Put Tony through."

"We're all done, Jim. It's crazy out there, you know. *Holly shit.* We're down to 19.20 already. *Look* at this!"

Blackburn was still staring at the screen. The prices were now jumping five and sometimes ten cents at a time: 19.20, 19.25, 19.15, 19.19, 19.18, 19.32, 19.20 ... The forward months were still stuck limit up, one dollar above the previous day's settlement price. June was at 18.05, July at 17.78, August at 17.65.

"What did we do?" Blackburn asked after a few seconds.

"Yousef sold his 600 in blocks of 100, 75, and 50, all above 19.50. Want the details?"

"Yeah. Give them to me, but fast."

"One hundred at 19.62, 100 at 19.65, 100 at 19.70, 100 at 19.55, 75 at 19.56, 75 at 19.54, and 50 at 19.52," Tony recited almost in one breath. "It averages at about 19.60 per barrel for the whole thing."

"Thanks, Tony. Great fill," Blackburn said as he jotted down the information on a piece of paper. "Got to go."

VI

Of Brothers and Cousins

S hortly after 6 p.m. in Vienna, the thirteen OPEC ministers assembled at OPEC headquarters. Lukman brought the meeting to order with an elaborate, ten-minute speech outlining the main points of the non-OPEC proposal. He was clearly setting the stage to have OPEC officially endorse the plan. "I know we've made all the sacrifices in the past," he said in an uncharacteristically upbeat voice, "but this is a golden opportunity for OPEC to finally benefit from the restraint of others. The least we should do is consider the non-OPEC proposal seriously."

But Hisham Nazer would not allow any drawn-out debates. He announced that the Gulf States were not prepared to cut their output by 5 percent, but would match non-OPEC cuts barrel for barrel. He allowed Kuwait, the UAE, and Qatar to formally endorse his counter-proposal, and asked the conference to respond, without delay, since he had been instructed by his king to return to Riyadh immediately. The others were stunned. None of them had expected the four Gulf States to show such unity. The bit about his instructions to return immediately to Riyadh was a nice added touch. There was no room for maneuver. The "barrel-for-barrel" strategy had won the day.

The meeting did not last long. A few minutes before 7 p.m., the ministers emerged from their third-floor conference room and headed out. Lukman alone went down to the first floor press room to announce to the reporters assembled there that OPEC was not ready to accept the non-OPEC offer at this time, that a counter-proposal had been made by the four countries of the Gulf, and that OPEC needed more time to study various ways of cooperating with the non-OPEC countries in the future.

*   *   *

In Washington, Blackburn's telephone lines remained busy the entire afternoon. But it was at 1:12 p.m. that speculation ended and hard reality set in. The Reuters story, with similar accounts on A.P. Dow Jones and Telerate, was what everybody had been waiting for:

"OPEC MINISTERS EMERGED FROM THEIR FINAL MEET-ING WITHOUT AN AGREEMENT TO ACCEPT THE NON-OPEC PROPOSAL TO CUT OUTPUT BY 5 PERCENT. THE FOUR ARAB STATES OF THE GULF REFUSED THE PRO-POSAL. ACCORDING TO NIGERIAN OIL MINISTER LUK-MAN, WHO IS ALSO THE PRESIDENT OF OPEC, THEY PROPOSED INSTEAD TO CUT TOTAL OPEC PRODUC-TION BY 185,000 BARRELS PER DAY, THE SAME VOL-UME OFFERED BY NON-OPEC. THIS PROPOSAL WAS CONDITIONAL BASED ON THE CUT BEING DIVIDED EQUALLY AMONG THE THIRTEEN MEMBERS OF OPEC. THIS WAS REJECTED BY THE OTHER OPEC COUNTRIES
..."

In the next half-hour May prices plunged to $16.53 per barrel, and the forward months shifted to limit down, one dollar below the previous day's settlement price. By the time the market closed at 3:10 p.m., May was down to $15.66. June settled limit down at $16.05, July at

$15.78, and August at 15.65. At settlement that day, Ramzi Amin's account showed an unrealized profit of $2,358,000, made in four-and-a-half hours.

A year-and-a-half earlier, Amin had approached Blackburn about his account. He had full discretion over a bank account in Vienna, he told Blackburn, which was under the name of his nephew, two-year-old Yousef Anis. He wanted to open a trading account with a New York broker under the same name, and give Blackburn discretion to trade for the account. But only when he called Blackburn and told him how to trade, he had insisted. Could Blackburn arrange this with a trustworthy broker? Yousef Anis had transferred $800,000 to the broker and opened a trading account under James Blackburn's discretion. Since then, Amin had called Blackburn with specific trading instructions only six times, including today. Six trades in eighteen months, and the account stood at a little over $11 million. Only Blackburn, Tony the broker, and the Viennese banker, who Blackburn later found out was Stefan Kraus, knew the account really belonged to Ramzi Amin.

Soon after the market closed, when Blackburn was finally getting long sought relief from the barrage of traders, he received a call from Bianca.

"I'm so excited about the weekend," she said. "And I'm so happy this drama is over. It has been ten days of hell."

"I'm excited about the weekend too. Can hardly wait."

"Did everything work out for you with the meeting? You kept quiet almost the whole time."

"Everything worked out fine, my sweet Bianca. Thanks for your concern. I have proven to you again that it is you I love, not your job," Blackburn said and chuckled, making light of the word "love."

*   *   *

Later that night the Marriott Garten Café was once again full. Most reporters had already sent in their stories, made flight reservations for the next day, and had nothing to do but kill time in the lobby. The discussions about what had actually taken place inside the closed doors of the OPEC conference room were as heated as the speculation had been earlier that afternoon.

Jim Purdy was stunned. He had been so sure there would be an agreement that he had spent some time writing his story for the next day's paper, describing the "new agreement" and the circumstances under which it had been achieved. There were only a few last minute details to add to his text, which had to wait until he received the final communiqué.

After 7 p.m. he had to go back to his room and rewrite the story, which to his surprise, did not prove to be difficult. Once he changed several instances of "did" to "did not" and added "failed to" in front of "achieved a new agreement," the new story was born.

But that did not help Jim Purdy understand what had occurred.

"I don't get it," he said desperately to the tired but relieved faces of Kamal Ashkar and Ramzi Amin. "I just don't get it. Wasn't their offer any good? Wouldn't it have raised oil prices? Wouldn't it have kept your market share constant? What was the problem?"

It was past midnight. Ramzi Amin had been trying, to no avail, to get Kamal Ashkar out of the reporter's grasp and up to his room.

"Darling, please darrrleeeng," Ashkar said to a waitress as she passed by. "One more beer for me please, but a cold one, yes darling?" He was probably too drunk to notice how loud he had yelled. Then, turning his attention to Purdy, he raised his forefinger and shook it in the air as if he were reprimanding a child.

"They were too aggressive, Jim," he said.

"Too aggressive? What do you mean 'too aggressive'?"

"They tried to force our hand. How could we accept? Nobody can try to force our hand and get away with it."

"Force your hand?" Purdy sounded more confused. "What do you mean 'forced your hand'?"

Kamal Ashkar was busy lighting a cigarette. He flicked his lighter several times, but it would not ignite. He put it down hard on the table, and reached for a Garten Café matchbook. He struck a match several times before it finally ignited. Then he lit his cigarette, blew out the match, and put it carefully in the ashtray, all in slow motion, or so it seemed to Purdy.

"How did they try to force your hand?" Purdy asked again. Although he was getting impatient and annoyed, he knew Ashkar was his best bet for getting an explanation of what had happened. Purdy only hoped that Ashkar would tell him something before Edwards, the one person Purdy did not want to face, appeared in the lobby.

"Do you know what those bastards did?" Kamal Ashkar asked without noticing the stern look on Ramzi Amin's face. "Do you know what those Mexicans did to Hisham? When he was in Houston a week ago, they begged him to visit Mexico. 'It would mean so much for us,' they said. They pleaded with him to honor their country and to honor Pemex by agreeing to a visit. 'A short stopover,' they said, 'on your way to Vienna. It won't cost you more than one night.' So finally Hisham agreed to go. Just for one day. He was too embarrassed to refuse them. That's how badly they were pleading. You understand what I'm telling you here, Jim?"

"Yes, yes. Of course. He was too embarrassed to refuse them because …"

"Do you know what happened as soon as he landed in Mexico?" interrupted Ashkar, as if he had never intended for Purdy to answer the question. Then the waitress came with his beer, and his face lit up again.

"Oh, darling, darrrleeeng! Thank you. It is cold this time, no? What's your name, darling?" But the waitress, who would normally have poured the beer, had already left. Now Ashkar had forgotten both the waitress and Purdy; he was busy filling his glass, very slowly, with great concentration, to avoid making too much foam.

"What happened when he landed in Mexico?" Purdy asked impatiently. He was beginning to lose hope that Ashkar would ever get to the end of the story.

"They all *dumped* on him!" said Ashkar, snapping back into the conversation as if the past few minutes' interruption had never taken place. "They *lectured* him about Saudi Arabia's responsibility to stabilize the oil market. They lectured him! About *our responsibility*. Can you imagine that, Jim? It was a plot, and Oman, Malaysia, Egypt, all of them, had planned it. Do you believe their nerve? Poor Hisham was livid. He was *furious*."

Jim Purdy had to digest all this for a few minutes. A plot? Shaikh Ahmad Zaki Yamani had always talked about Saudi Arabia's responsibility to stabilize the oil market. He had bragged about how responsibly the Kingdom used its vast oil wealth. *What is the big fucking deal here?* He wanted to scream this at Ashkar, at Amin, at anybody who could explain to him what had gone wrong, why the deal he thought had already been signed was never signed.

But Purdy had not paid attention to how things had changed since Yamani was sacked. How Saudi Arabia had decided to abdicate the leadership role. How Hisham Nazer had not talked about Saudi Arabia's responsibilities since he took office. Not once had he mentioned the phrase. Purdy did not understand that it had become almost blasphemous to remind the Saudis of their *responsibility*. That approach had cost them dearly in market share. "We don't want to be leaders anymore," young Prince Abdul Aziz had told James Blackburn more than six months earlier. "In this business, leadership means you make all the sacrifices. That's what the great Yamani brought on us. And the whole world thinks we call the shots. Well, we don't want to call the shots anymore."

Purdy had somehow missed all this. But he decided to let go of the "plot" and pursue another question that had been bothering him since the outcome of the meeting was announced.

"But how did the UAE and Qatar join you on this?" he asked, getting more irritated with Ashkar's cigarette smoke. "Weren't they against Saudi Arabia at the last meeting? I remember it well. Then you were livid *at them*! How come you're all together again?"

Ramzi Amin stood up. This conversation had gone too far. He had to pull Ashkar away from the grip of this reporter before he gave him more ammunition to spread around the lobby. He tried to talk to Ashkar in Arabic, telling him it was too late, they should go. But Ashkar couldn't resist making one last statement.

"My dear Jim," he said, staring at Purdy through a cloud of cigarette smoke. Purdy noticed he had stopped shouting, but it was not the sudden calmness in his voice that was startling. It was the intensity in Ashkar's gaze. "My dear Jim, it is really simple. There is an old Arabic saying. It is one of the few sayings that we Arabs actually practice. It says: My cousin and I against you, my brother and I against my cousin, and I against my brother. Do you see? It is really very, very simple."

It was close to 1 a.m. when Blackburn called the Marriott Hotel again and asked for Ramzi Amin. Amin had just returned to his room. "Thank God it's over," he said several times. In one of those rare moments when he volunteered information, Amin even admitted that controlling Ashkar had been more difficult than usual at this meeting. Blackburn told him about his trade and asked when he should close the positions. "Wait till it gets to $13.50 and then close them all," Amin said, confident that prices would fall that low.

When Amin closed his short position several days later, his realized net profits from the trade were $3.7 million.

VII

Mr. Russell in Tokyo

Sophie Myles was upset. She had not heard from Blackburn for a full week. She had called him several times, leaving messages on his answering machine at home and with Linda in the office. It was an absolutely crazy week, Linda explained, feeling sorry for Sophie.

She settled on her living room sofa with a tall vodka and tonic, determined not to think about Blackburn. Then her telephone rang. On the third ring she picked up the handset from the wall unit, leaned against the refrigerator, and somehow managed to come up with a casual "Hello."

"Hi Sophie."

"Well hello there, stranger! I was beginning to give up on you." Her voice was normal, thank God.

"Sorry I couldn't call earlier. It's been hectic."

"That bad, eh?" She moved the phone to her left hand and wiped the sweat from her right palm onto her jeans.

"So when are you going to tell me about this great week of yours?" Her voice had fully recovered its quasi-cheerful, seductive quality.

"Have you had dinner yet?"

"No," she lied, even though, strictly speaking, it was not a lie. In the past hour she had finished two small bags of potato chips and was halfway through a bag of pretzels, but she had not *dined* yet.

"Well, then, I suggest you get here in less than forty-five minutes. It would be a shame if your dinner got cold."

"You mean you found time to prepare dinner, with your impossible schedule and all?"

"Just come over, Sophie. You can give me all the hard time you want after you get here."

The round dining table was, by Blackburn's standards, immaculate. It could comfortably seat eight, but it was set for two, leaving the damask tablecloth, a piece of art in its own right, largely exposed. There was no elaborate layout of china, crystal, and silver. Two plates, two forks, two knives, two wine glasses, and two candles sat neatly on the table. There was no flower arrangement, just a single, long-stemmed red rose lying across one of the folded napkins.

Blackburn opened one of the three bottles of Chateau Pavie that had been in his cabinet for the past three months. He smelled the cork, then the wine, and shrugged indifferently. James Blackburn was not a wine connoisseur. The French sommelier in the wine department of Sutton Place Gourmet had given him a five-minute lecture on the qualities of the 1982 Chateau Pavie, and he had felt obliged to buy a few bottles. "The 1982 is the best Pavie ever," the Frenchman had insisted in his heavy accent. "It is uncommonly rich and full for Pavie, with a ripe bouquet, almost fruity but not fruity, with a faint hint of toasted almonds. It has a dark color, wonderfully structured, deep and profound." All that about a wine, Blackburn thought. Every trade has its jargon, and this guy sure knows his. Now he smelled the wine again looking for the faint hint of toasted almonds, but did not detect any. How do toasted almonds smell, anyway ... or maybe it's supposed to *taste* like toasted almonds. "We'll see," he said.

The knock on the door was unmistakably Sophie's. In fact, it was not a knock, but the rapid rolling of fingernails on the wood that let out a soft rrrumppppp—something between the sound of a distant tap dancer and a cat scratch. He gave the table a last, critical look before going to open the door.

"Sophie, you look stunning!" She was wearing a jade-green silk dress, the top crossed demurely at the bust.

"Hello, Jim," she said, almost in a whisper, as she entered, radiating sensuality. She walked past him a little too hastily, which gave away her anxious excitement, placed her purse on the small table in the entryway, and turned back just as he shut the door, holding open her arms for the big hug she'd been waiting for all week.

If she did not know James Blackburn better, she'd have thought this dinner had an agenda. None of the men she'd dated before would have gone through all this trouble, unless they were trying to apologize for an indiscretion, or set the right mood so they could ask an important favor. There had been one man in particular who specialized in creating romantic moods as a prelude for asking favors. Could Sophie introduce him to Senator Paul Sarbanes, he would ask in the middle of a candlelight dinner, or could she arrange for the chairman of the board of his company to be seated next to George Shultz at the state dinner next Tuesday?

Not Blackburn. He offered her evenings like this without guilt and without seeking favors from her lobbying firm. In fact, it was through Blackburn that she had secured the largest foreign client for Wilks, Russell & Co., leading to her promotion from an administrative assistant to vice president. Yet all he seemed to want was to be with her. He either truly loves me, or he's just an old fashioned gentleman who doesn't belong in this town, she thought.

James Blackburn was full of contradictions, however. I'm just a modest consultant, he told her often; don't expect sophistication or long conversations about classical music, museums, and paintings. I'm a simple man who likes luxury, comfort and most of all, to live well.

But this was no simple man filling her wine glass and toasting her, with a gracious charm that was so effortless, so natural, that she had to make an effort to hide her hopeless admiration of him.

"Tell me if it has a faint hint of toasted almonds," Blackburn said as she took a sip.

"It has no such thing," she said, laughing at his imitation of the Frenchman's accent. "It's quite good. Toasted almonds?"

"Yes. It's supposed to have a faint hint of toasted almonds."

Blackburn disappeared into the kitchen and came back in a few minutes with two plates. He placed one in front of Sophie, put the other on his side, and returned to the kitchen to get the breadbasket. Lying in the center of each plate was an artichoke heart, with two quail eggs placed on top as if in a nest, and an ample serving of a creamy sauce surrounding the dish. There were two thin carrot sticks, crossed like swords on one side, and three baby corns on the other. He passed her the bread, took a piece himself, and raised his glass again.

"*Bon appetit*! I hope you like this."

"It looks wonderful. You've imposed on your friend at The Peacock again, haven't you? I really don't know why he puts up with you."

"Because I'm a great guy, that's why. The same reason *you* put up with me."

"Well, I hope it's not for *exactly* the same reason," she said with one of her most seductive smiles.

He smiled and refilled their glasses and they started to eat. Her blue-green eyes, fully complimented by the color of her dress, sparkled in the candlelight, their glow sharper than the subtle luster of her pearl necklace and matching earrings. Her light brown, shoulder-length hair, normally pulled tight and tied into a ponytail, flowed loosely over her shoulders. Even though they had been dating for two years, Blackburn could still be taken by her charm.

They had met at a State Department reception given in honor of the Angolan foreign minister. Blackburn's contacts at the Department of Energy had arranged an invitation for him. Representatives from Wilks, Russell & Co. were there, along with those from a dozen other public relations and law firms. The event was a total bore. Diplomats, lawyers, senior staff members of the Departments of State and Energy, and more diplomats, all trying to appear as though they were enjoying every minute, but trying way too hard. Some twenty people were clustered around the Angolan foreign minister and George Shultz. The rest of the 200 or so people stood around, pretending to be deeply absorbed in conversation with each other, while constantly searching the room for somebody more important to talk to.

That was when he noticed Sophie, one of the younger and more beautiful women in the hall. She was talking to a small group of men. He watched her for a few minutes, and though he was unsure whether she had come with someone, went straight to her and introduced himself. As soon as they shook hands and exchanged names, he commented on how stiff and boring everybody looked. That was the last thing she expected anybody to say at a State Department reception. "And," he added with total conviction, "I don't believe you're having any fun here either."

If it hadn't been for his plain, honest charm, she would have been offended. Instead, she was simply astonished. "What did you say your name was?" she asked through a burst of laughter, which he found endearing.

"James Blackburn," he replied. "And may I suggest that we leave this haughty and venerable reception, before we start believing we're doing something important, or even worse, start believing this is what fun is supposed to be like?"

She left her colleagues and went with him. The combination of their personal chemistry and the synergies of their respective professions was dynamite. The connection that followed was anchored in so many different facets and dimensions that it needed no deliberate nurturing. It just flowered.

"So, tell me," said Sophie, taking another sip of her wine. "How bad was your week?"

"Oh, it wasn't bad at all. Just hectic and quite productive. You remember I had to go out with the guy from C. Itoh on Monday night? That was some night! I got home after 2:30 in the morning, was woken up by the Nitzen boys at 5:30, and haven't had a break since."

"What did he want?" asked Sophie, picking up one of the quail eggs on her fork and studying it carefully.

"You don't have to eat that if you don't want to," said Blackburn, noticing her hesitation. "Of course, Marcello assured me that it's fresh. Have you had quail eggs before?"

"No, but I'll try ... It's not bad, actually. It doesn't taste much different from regular eggs."

"I'm not sure what he wanted," said Blackburn. "They think KPC is eyeing a refinery in Asia, and would like to know more. By the way, I'm leaving for Kuwait on Friday night, on their behalf. I'll be back by Thursday night."

"Oh. I don't see you during the week, and now you'll be traveling on the weekend?"

"Sophie, their weekend is Thursday and Friday. I need to be there on their first workday, which is Saturday."

Blackburn filled their glasses again. He did not like to lie to Sophie, but could not tell her he planned to spend the weekend with Bianca in London. Sophie did not know about her.

"What makes them think the Kuwaitis are eyeing a refinery in Asia?"

"Good question. I didn't ask him that directly. It could be coming from a banker or financial advisor who helps structure such deals. What puzzles me is why they should care."

Blackburn did not like to talk about his clients, even when they were in the news and he was asked about something that was already public information. He had never disclosed any privileged information or broken confidentiality when it came to his clients. But he knew Sophie would be interested in anything to do with Japan. Wilks, Russell & Co. had many Japanese clients, and so did Blackburn, and some were from the same organizations. Otherwise, he would not have even brought up the little, insignificant account regarding C. Itoh.

"Time for the next course."

"You need any help?" she offered, knowing very well that he would refuse.

"Everything's under control. Tonight, I spoil you. At least until we finish dinner." He was already in the kitchen so she did not see him smile.

He walked back with two dishes, each topped with four slices of pork tenderloin, covered with a thin layer of herb-butter sauce, and two new potatoes and some green beans. "Be careful, the plate is hot," he said, just like a waiter in a restaurant, and sat down.

"According to Marcello, this sauce works as an aphrodisiac," he said.

"According to Marcello, half the edible plants in Italy are aphrodisiacs. And I bet he assured you it works on ladies, right?"

"Of course he did. According to Marcello, men don't need aphrodisiacs. We're always horny."

"Except maybe when they're too busy having a hectic week."

Blackburn smiled and proceeded to tell her the basics of the saga with the traders—the speculation, price swings, amounts of money made and lost by various traders—without giving names. "That's incredible," she said, genuinely impressed. "Were you in the market too?"

"Sophie, you know I don't trade. I cannot give anyone objective advice if I have a position in the market."

"Too bad. You could make a lot more money trading than consulting."

"Traders live a tense, nervous, and dull life. Besides, in order to trade effectively, you have to get into Leaky Faucets, and I don't do that either. I travel all over the world, and clients seek my advice, which, I have to admit, is an ego boost. My life is less tense, less nervous, and more ambitious."

"Ambitious, you are. Ego, you have … here's to you, Jimmy."

He leaned over and kissed her lips.

"Enough of my week. What have you been up to?"

"Well, you'll be interested to know that the Angolans finally started letting us earn the money they pay us."

"You don't say!" He filled their glasses with the last of the wine. "I was wondering how long your free ride was going to last."

"It hasn't been exactly free, you know. We've been sending them a fat report every week, covering every single energy related issue that's being discussed on the Hill."

"They don't read reports."

"I know. But now they want us to start campaigning against an oil import fee. To be honest with you, I'm not sure it's worth the effort. Even if Congress passed something like that, Reagan would veto it anyway."

Blackburn held a bottle of brandy and two snifters in one hand, took Sophie's arm with the other, and led her to the sofa in the living room. He rested his feet on the coffee table, put his arm around her, pulling her toward him, and kissed her long and deep. He held her tightly at the waist, enjoying the feel of her body pressed against his; he felt her warmth spread through his side, arousing him.

"I may be able to help you figure out Takao and his bellyache," she murmured, catching her breath between kisses. "Mr. Russell was in Tokyo last week. At the invitation of MITI."

"*The* Mr. Russell? As in Wilks & Russell?" he asked, gently moving his hand from her waist to her buttocks.

"*The* Mr. Russell," she replied. She sat up straight and raised his arm above her head, freeing herself from his grip. She filled the snifters.

"I know he met with a few Japanese oil companies, all appointments arranged by MITI. At the staff meeting yesterday he briefly mentioned a program of restructuring of Japan's oil sector, and its potential impact on us."

"But what would they need from Russell?"

"They're getting ready for a buying spree here in the States. Mostly acreage. Oil exploration or something like that."

Her fingernails stroked the inside of his thigh with slow, leisurely movements.

"Mr. Russell said billions are involved."

"Every American company is moving its exploration out, and the Japanese want to come here? I don't buy it."

"Maybe they don't want to explore. Maybe they want to buy discovered reserves. Would you buy that?"

"I might buy that," he whispered without stopping their kissing.

"Mr. Russell said there is a new push in Japan to buy crude oil reserves around the world."

Blackburn took a big gulp of brandy, put the snifter on the coffee table, pulled Sophie over to him, and held her body tightly over his.

"That's all very interesting, Ms. Myles, but right now I'm too tired to think about what your Mr. Russell had to say. What do you say we talk about this over breakfast?"

With that, he rolled her gently to the floor, undid the snap that held the two flaps of her dress together at the waist and, without fully undressing her, made love to her.

VIII

A Different Fight

"The showerhead is a girl's best friend," she sighed. She danced with it on the shower floor, dragging him into a rhythm he had not experienced before.

The mystery for Blackburn was that Bianca was one of the most professional women he had known. He had been in meetings with her with the Economic Research Unit of OPEC, as well as with the secretary general, and had witnessed the unusual respect she enjoyed. She was unobtrusive, unpresumptuous, low key, but at the same time an effective contributor to discussions so technical they seemed to be above her head.

She also displayed a quality of sophistication unfettered by any pretense and unencumbered by a conscious attempt to look that way. Yet it was obvious she knew it. She knew who she was and the impression she was making on the outside world. Blackburn often thought of her as a skilled sculptor who consciously cultivated her image and then fit in it effortlessly.

That was the public Bianca.

The private Bianca had all that, plus an intense sensuality that intoxicated whoever was lucky enough to be with her.

She moved the showerhead between his thighs.

"See what I mean?"

Blackburn grabbed her arms, pinned her against the wall, and made love to her with a passion he had known only with her.

In late afternoon they went to Hyde Park. When it wasn't raining, April was a good month to walk in London. Bianca took Blackburn's arm and leaned against his shoulder as they strolled down the pathways through the park. The freshness of spring was everywhere. They were mostly silent, taking it all in, taking each other in.

She remembered an evening a few years earlier when, as they were leaving a jazz concert in Montreux, Switzerland, Blackburn had told her in one of his less guarded moments: "I think I can love you." She had held on to him and, uncharacteristically, kept quiet.

The next morning, over breakfast at the Montreux Palace Hotel, she casually asked, "What does 'I think I can love you' mean?"

"It means I could lose myself in you," he said without a moment's hesitation, looking her straight in the eye. "It means you could take me away, bury me in you. It means I could forget everything else when I'm with you. And most of all, it means I can once again feel that innate, childish joy which, unfortunately, fades as we get older. It means I can love you."

This was not a typical breakfast conversation, which made it so much more powerful. She was so moved that she was lost for words, and Blackburn noticed her eyes getting wet. She got up from her chair, walked over to him and gave him a warm kiss. Once back at her seat, she recovered her composure, and started bubbling again like newly poured champagne.

The memory warmed her. She pulled his arm tighter to her side, rose on her toes, and gave him a kiss.

After an hour, they left the park and ended up in a small café on Curzon Street. If they had tried to retrace their steps, they would have failed.

"There was something unusual this week in Vienna," she said casually, taking a sip of her white wine.

"Isn't there always?"

"I mean unusual even by OPEC standards."

She had her serious, professional look. The flirty Bianca had gone back stage.

"It could be nothing, but it could also turn out to be important for you. So listen. I got the impression they were pretending. Just going through the motions."

"Who? What are you talking about?"

"The four Gulf countries. Ten days of supposedly intense bargaining, and they were not stressed. The other delegations were working their butts off. The 'Gulfies' were relaxed, almost oblivious to the whole saga."

He nodded, gesturing her to continue.

"My sense is that they had agreed among themselves even before they got to Vienna. They let the others jump through all the hoops for ten days, knowing they'd say no in the end."

Blackburn looked at her for a long moment. She was right—this could be nothing, or it could be significant. They knew their decision would hit the price of oil very hard, yet they stuck to it. This smelled very much like local Middle East politics.

"Who else noticed this?"

Bianca seemed to grow tired of the conversation and turned away. But Blackburn was anxious to get her to talk shop for a few minutes longer.

"Do you think this was common knowledge in Vienna?"

"Of course not. What? You think everyone is as perceptive as I am?" She laughed, refusing to turn serious again. Then, seeing Blackburn's frustration, added: "Some in the Secretariat noticed. But none of the press, and none of the other observers. At least I didn't hear any gossip about it, during or after the meeting."

That was all the shoptalk either of them was prepared for that day. It was time to think about dinner. Blackburn had arrived that morning on the overnight flight from Washington and slept a few hours. After a light lunch in the lobby of the Dorchester, he had arranged for a car to pick Bianca up at Heathrow Airport. It had been midafternoon when she arrived at his suite.

"How about we order room service and stay in tonight?" he asked. "I promise you a more exciting evening around town tomorrow."

"What makes you think staying in won't be as exciting, *amore mio* Jimmy?"

He ordered a basic meat and potatoes meal—steaks, fries, and grilled vegetables. And a bottle of 1980 Chateau La Tour Figeac.

"So when are you going to marry that nice girl you're dating in Washington?" she asked, with an almost reprimanding tone.

"You want me to marry her?" He seemed surprised.

"Look, Mr. Blackburn. You can have a wife, and you can have me. Nothing else. Right now, she doesn't fit with us. But if you marry her, I'll accept her as your wife."

That was a mouthful but, coming from her, it kind of made sense.

"And if I tell you that you can have Stefan, and you can have me. No one else. Will you accept?"

"No. That's different."

"How is it different?"

"I'm egocentric and greedy. But I make everyone happy and no one gets hurt. But if you do it, I'll get hurt."

Blackburn did not know whether to laugh or get mad. Bianca had always been jealous and possessive, in spite of her own lifestyle and philosophy. When you do it, I get hurt too, he thought, but did not say anything.

"Is Sophie egocentric and greedy like me?"

Bianca, you're made of fire, he thought. Sophie is made of earth. I need you both.

"You're not egocentric," he said at last, ignoring the question about Sophie. "You're an egoist. You are selfish and greedy."

She raised an eyebrow and was about to protest, when Blackburn added: "Your energy goes to nurture your own soul first. That's why you cannot belong to anyone. But once your soul is nurtured, you can become the most caring person I've known."

"Thank you. And yes, I am caring. And giving."

"But let's be careful here. You are not caring like Mother Teresa. Even your caring side comes from your selfishness."

"You better say something nice to me now, and quickly." She looked hurt.

"Look, Bianca, you want to have Stefan, Roberto, and me, right? And you don't want any of us to seek someone else, right?"

"Right. But you can have a wife."

"Fine, except for a wife, you want each of us to be satisfied by only you. That's why you become an incredibly generous, giving, caring person, so we'll never need anyone else. Doesn't that basically cater to your possessiveness?"

"There are many layers of me, where different people can fit. Stefan also has everything with me."

"Okay, let's take Stefan. To him, you're a classy wife he can be proud of in any social setting. I bet you also cater to his every sensual fantasy, even if it requires that you act less classy once in a while. You give him a whole range of women—from a most honorable wife to a common courtesan and every shade in between. You also give him a great companion, business confidant, sounding board on any issue, and basic friendship. Why? So he won't find anything outside that he doesn't already have. Ultimately, is that only for his happiness, or also for your possessiveness?"

"How did we end up talking about me? We were talking about Sophie."

"Actually, we were talking about me marrying Sophie so I would have only a wife and you and no one else, remember?"

Bianca was adorable even when scattered. Blackburn could tell she was beginning to lose focus. He had seen her in states of such intense concentration that an earthquake under her feet would not distract her, which made her scattered moments even more formidable.

But she also looked vulnerable and lost. She did not like to be analyzed like this, her character and motives peeled open like an onion. It made her feel helplessly naked.

He poured her another glass of wine, and got up, walked over to her, and kissed her—exactly the type of thing she would have done.

"You know who you remind me of right now?" he asked, staring in her dark eyes. She gave him a focused but unsure look, hoping his comparison would not be one that could hurt her.

"Nefertiti," he said. "Right now, you have her gaze, her refined facial features, her poise."

"Nefertiti?"

"We should go to the British Museum tomorrow. They have a great Egyptian section. Nefertiti's bust is in Germany, but I'm sure we'll see images of her."

"I know what she looks like," Bianca said, smiling. She had resolved that he was giving her a compliment, even though she did not consider Nefertiti beautiful.

"Don't you want to go anyway? I'll show you exactly what features remind me of you. I want to take a picture of you two side by side, you posing like her."

That brought to life Bianca's addictive and seductive laughter. She was back.

"Stefan says I look like the early photos of Audrey Hepburn."

They lay in bed for a long time in silence. She cuddled him, stroking his chest. His mind drifted, from DC to Vienna to Kuwait to Tokyo. Then the drifting narrowed down to all the European cities where he had been with Bianca for two to three day get-togethers—Florence, Paris, Bern, Monte Carlo. They had such escapes once every two to three months. She decompressed, and so did he.

As he thought about her, he realized again what an extraordinary life she had. Ambitious, rich, multi-layered, as even she would say, surrounded by men who adored her, and happy, professionally respected. But there was also a sadness to Bianca, an occasional melancholy that broke over her like a wave and swept her away. After more than five years, Blackburn had not been able to decipher it.

"I wonder what it was like to be a queen in Egypt 3300 years ago," she whispered.

"She had hundreds of slaves and servants, and her every wish was carried out, and she probably was super elegant, classy, with an aura that moved thousands of men to tears."

"Imagine that, Jimmy."

"But remember, she was the great royal wife of the pharaoh. He probably had hundreds of concubines, secondary wives, and slave girls. But the royal wife could not have any other men. You have it better than Nefertiti."

"Don't make fun of me, Jimmy, it's not nice."

"But I'm not making fun of you. Here are the facts: You have three adult men in your life. Nefertiti had only one. Your husband has only you. Her husband had a thousand other women. Who's better off?"

She got up from under his arm, straddled him, and bent over to kiss him.

"What's bothering you, Jimmy? Tell me."

"We are exactly alike, you know. You are the female version of me."

She laughed. "I love that, Jimmy! Tell me, why am I a female version of you?"

He did not lighten up, as she wanted him to.

"Exactly alike," he repeated.

"Jimmy, talk to me. What do you mean?"

"I can accept Stefan," he confessed at last. "But Roberto? Why do I have to share you with him? Why do you need him?"

"You are jealous."

"I am more than jealous. I am furious. I am livid. Every time I think of you with Roberto, my heart sinks to my stomach and starts pounding."

He could tell his words made her happy. She would have been devastated if he had been indifferent.

Then she put on her devious, naughty smile.

"I will now give you something that no man has ever had," she whispered. "I will let you play with yourself, through your female edition. Close your eyes, there is no Bianca here, there is only your female alter ego ... you're all alone with yourself." And she started to slide down his torso, slowly kissing and licking every inch. "Oh, how exciting," she purred between kisses. "Have you ever done this to yourself?"

To his surprise, Blackburn did experience a new level of arousal; he closed his eyes and allowed himself to enjoy every sensation ignited in him.

It was immensely enjoyable, but it did not help dull the pain.

The next day they spent several hours at the British Museum, mostly in the Egyptian collection. Bianca kept imagining herself as a queen, ruling with grace, compassion, and firm discipline. Blackburn humored her, adding details to her fantasies.

"If I were there," she said as they were leaving, "I'd be the pharaoh, not the pharaoh's wife. I'd be like Cleopatra."

Blackburn smiled at her.

"I would have been a great pharaoh," she said. "And I would have had the most handsome lovers in the realm!"

"You'd have a male harem, eh? You'd make soooo many men soooo jealous."

"I'd *want* them to be jealous," she said. "I love it when men are jealous over me. I even love it when *you* are jealous, even though I really don't want to see you hurt. And know this: as a queen, I'd execute anyone in my harem who slept with another woman."

"You're not only my exact replica in female shape, but you've mastered the art of thinking like a man while acting like a woman."

"What do you think I do all day in Vienna, Jimmy? My job is to think like a man, act like a lady, look like a teenage model, and treat them all with great reverence and respect even as I herd them around like sheep."

*　*　*

Their flights were twenty minutes apart, so they went to Heathrow together. It was early morning, and they had not had much sleep the night before, so they were mostly quiet. She held his hand and rested her head over his shoulder for the duration of the hour drive.

As much as he had enjoyed the weekend, Blackburn still had a knot in his stomach every time he thought of Roberto. He imagined her having similar days with him, and that somehow took the luster away from what he had with her.

She sensed his angst; she could see it in his eyes as they said their goodbyes at the airport.

"You know what we have is very special, don't you, Jimmy?"

He smiled. "Thank you Bianca."

As they were about to go to their separate check-in counters, she stopped him.

"You know how I was telling you that the 'Gulfies' were just going through the motions in Vienna?"

"Yes?"

"I remembered something else. The Saudi minister didn't attend two ministerial sessions. He sent a representative."

"Was any reason given?"

"Yes, the first time it was something lame, like he was not feeling well. The second time, they said he was on an important call with the king. But it shows they weren't really serious about the agenda."

"Thanks, my sweet Bianca. I'll see what I can find out in the Gulf tomorrow."

"One more thing," she said, moving closer to him. "I heard his press secretary tell one of the analysts: 'If you want to understand this meeting, forget your standard dollars and cents analysis. This is about a different fight.' Does that mean anything to you?"

"He said that? A different fight?"

"His exact words, my darling Jimmy. *Ti amo ... ciao.*"

IX

The Desert and the Sea

ritish Airways flight 147 took off from London Heathrow Airport for Kuwait at 10:10 a.m. As Blackburn boarded the plane, the flight attendant took his garment bag and coat and hung them in the closet. Tired and sleepless, he was irritated to find his aisle seat, 3B, occupied. "I think you're in my seat," he told the dark young man in Arabic, flashing his boarding pass. The man moved over to the window seat, 3A, barely glancing at the boarding pass, and continued to read his Arabic newspaper, *Al Sharq Al Awsat*, a semi-official paper published in Saudi Arabia.

An hour after takeoff, the man in 3A was nursing his third scotch. He had folded his pale-green newspaper, stuffed it in the pocket at the back of the seat in front of him, and was staring aimlessly out the window. He made no attempt to start a conversation with Blackburn.

Although Blackburn was tired and did not particularly care to talk, he found the young man's reserved solitude curious, a feeling perhaps reinforced by a subconscious desire to make up for his initial irritation with him. He glanced toward the window a few times hoping to catch his eye, but he kept staring out. Finally, the young man turned around and took a cigarette from his pack. Blackburn flicked his lighter and offered him a light. The man accepted, a bit taken by surprise. Then he looked at Blackburn carefully for the first time.

"Are you from Lebanon?" he asked.

"No," answered Blackburn, glad the conversation had begun, but hoping to keep it short. Then, in order to break the awkward silence that followed, he added, "But I lived there for eight years. I learned Arabic there."

"You speak Arabic with a Lebanese accent," the man said. Then turning to Blackburn, he lowered his voice, as if wanting to share a secret, and mumbled: "Too bad, Lebanon."

"Yes, too bad."

Another awkward moment of silence followed. "You used to go there a lot?" asked Blackburn.

"Where?"

"Lebanon."

"In the summers. Before the troubles."

"You're from the Kingdom?" In Gulf parlance, that meant Saudi Arabia. Blackburn wasn't sure how much longer the young man could stay awake and carry on a conversation. He nodded and fell quiet again. Then he picked up his glass, took a sip of scotch, looked out the window, turned back toward Blackburn, and started tapping his fingers on the armrest.

"Before the troubles," he said after a moment's hesitation, "in the sixties, we used to think we were so backward and Lebanon was so civilized. Now we know better."

"I know what you mean, and you're right," Blackburn said matter-of-factly.

He'd had this conversation before. The eternal struggle between the desert and the sea, he called it. In the sixties, when life in much of the Gulf had still been in primitive conditions, the cultural supremacy of the sea had been unquestioned. In the eighties, when Lebanon, the crown jewel of the sea, lay devastated by a decade of civil war, the desert, awash with oil money, looked far more civilized.

The young man was surprised that Blackburn took no offense at his remarks. He would probably have liked to start a debate. But Blackburn, the would-be half-representative of the sea, was not about to put up a fight. He had spent two incredible days in London with Bianca, who had kept her promise of not allowing him much rest. And his mind was still occupied with what Sophie had to say about Mr. Russell's trip to Tokyo.

The flight attendants were serving bite-sized appetizers. The men both took one of each kind. Blackburn ordered another vodka on the rocks, the young Arab another scotch. Blackburn noticed that his eyes were getting redder. He's getting drunk, like they usually do, he thought without malice.

"Where in America do you live?" asked the Arab.

"In Washington."

"You've lived there a long time?"

"For the past ten years."

"So you know your way around Washington?"

"Parts of it, yes," answered Blackburn, unsure if his companion was still making small talk or had become more inquisitive.

"We go there sometimes. To meet with the defense people."

"What kind of business are you in?" asked Blackburn, sensing the man wanted to talk about himself.

"I'm a soldier," he replied with a curious finality. "I've been a soldier all my life."

"That's incredible," said Blackburn, genuinely surprised. "I've never met a Saudi soldier on these flights before. They've always been businessmen. Are you with the Army or the National Guard?"

"The National Guard."

"I'm Jim Blackburn. It's a pleasure to meet you." Blackburn extended his hand for the belated introduction and handshake. "I have a small consulting company in Washington. We advise mostly oil traders."

"Majed Al-Shammary." The soldier shook Blackburn's hand, but showed no interest in his occupation.

"You must have traveled in all parts of the Kingdom. How is it in the desert?"

"Just like that," said the soldier, pointing out the window at the endless blanket of white clouds. "That's how it looks in the Empty Quarter, except for the sand is red, not white."

"From the air?"

"No, no. That's how it looks from the ground. Traveling through it is like traveling through air above the clouds. No landmarks, no signs of any kind. The same boundless sand for as far as you can see. Nothing moves, nothing changes, for hours on end. You can get lost there without equipment, just like you can get lost up here."

"Does it make you wonder how they traveled in the old days? On camelback, with no equipment?"

"Oh yes. Except they didn't really *travel* in the old days. They moved around; they lived there and moved around."

"Do you spend much time in the desert?"

"We change our base every month or so. But we stay mainly in the desert. Mostly in the Eastern Province and sometimes in the Empty Quarter. Every year we spend one month in America. First in Washington, then in different parts of the Midwest. Training, mostly."

This was perhaps the most unusual traveling companion Blackburn had ever come across. Majed Al-Shammary, clearly a Bedouin tribesman from one of the extended families that never fully joined the urban boom in Saudi Arabia, was barely forty years old. His dark skin, rough hands, curly black hair, and short, stocky body were creations of the desert; not the kind of person one expected to meet in the first class cabin.

"Are you married?" Al-Shammary asked abruptly, as if he had just remembered an important question.

"Not yet," answered Blackburn, and momentarily thought of Sophie. "And you?"

"Yes. My eldest son will be eighteen next year. He'll join the National Guard then."

"A family tradition, eh?"

"Oh yes. My grandfather fought with the first king, Abdul Aziz. Since then, there have always been at least a dozen Al-Shammarys in the National Guard."

Al-Shammary withdrew into himself again. He looked as if he had suddenly been absorbed in a new thought process, in the white blanket outside. Blackburn couldn't help feeling that he was in the presence of someone who had traveled through time. He doesn't belong in the present, he thought. At least not the present that's visible to me. He comes from a different period, landed here next to me by accident, and I'm not sure which one of us is having a more difficult time coping with the other.

Blackburn lit a cigarette. The flick of the lighter seemed to bring Al-Shammary out of his reverie. He turned away from the window and reached for a cigarette himself. Blackburn offered him a light again.

"Will you be in Kuwait long?" asked Blackburn, even though what he really wanted to know was what business a member of the Saudi National Guard would have in Kuwait, or London, for that matter.

"About a week, to see some people."

"I'll be there for only a few days," said Blackburn, shifting the conversation to him in order not to give the impression he was being too curious. "To be honest with you, I don't like going to Kuwait that much. I prefer to go to Bahrain, Qatar, and Saudi Arabia. I have many good friends in those places. But in Kuwait, I have only business contacts."

"They're different from us," agreed Al-Shammary, shrugging his shoulders as if to minimize the importance of the statement. "In some ways they're better, in others worse. They're not friendly people, but they're smart."

"Yes, they're smart. But so are the Saudis. I think the Kuwaitis' reputation as better traders has nothing to do with smarts. I think it is simply a matter of priorities."

"I didn't mean smart only in business," responded Al-Shammary. "It's more than that. They stand up to the West more than we do. They pay more attention to Arab causes."

"But you pay attention to Arab causes too. And you're too big to stand up to the West without causing problems. They're small, that's why they can afford to stand up to the West."

"Maybe. But they're not afraid to experiment."

"To experiment?"

"For example, Kuwait is the only country in the Gulf that experimented with creating a parliament. They would never have the courage to try that in the Kingdom."

Blackburn's mind had automatically gone searching for a Kuwaiti "experiment" in the commercial field. The realization that Al-Shammary was not interested in oil or commerce was beginning to sink in. Unlike most Saudi Arabians Blackburn knew, Al-Shammary did not seem to be even a bit curious about business, let alone preoccupied by it. Blackburn saw an opportunity to pierce the superficial layer of generalities that most of his contacts would dwell upon whenever he tried to delve into the subtleties of Gulf politics.

"But that was not a real experiment," he said, trying to hide his rising interest in the conversation. "Doesn't the ruler have the right to dissolve the National Assembly whenever he wants? In fact, if I'm not mistaken, he dissolved the Assembly in 1986. It hasn't been re-constituted since."

"Yes. He has dissolved the Assembly. But it was King Fahd who pressured him to do it. King Fahd did not want the Kuwaitis to set an example of democracy in the Gulf. It was not because of the problems between the Assembly and Shaikh Jaber. Whatever those problems were, the Kuwaitis could have resolved them among themselves. But King Fahd did not want them to resolve anything. He wanted their experiment to fail."

The information was not new to Blackburn. What was new was that a Saudi Arabian soldier, albeit under the influence of alcohol, was telling him all this.

"Do you think Saudi Arabia should have a National Assembly?"

"Why not? The king can stay king and run the country. Why shouldn't he want to have a representative body of the people, to hear their concerns?"

"No reason at all. Unless he thinks he already knows their concerns."

"Well, he doesn't. Not *this* king. You see, even in a household, where the man rules, you cannot have peace and harmony if the woman and the children are ignored. A man cannot run his house properly if the woman is unhappy all the time. He has to listen, understand, and only then can he rule. It's the same in a country."

This really has nothing to do with democracy or a National Assembly, Blackburn thought. This desert tribesman couldn't really give a damn about democracy. In fact, he probably wouldn't be able to tolerate democracy, because it would interfere too much in the tribal way of life. This has to be tied to the rift between King Fahd and Crown Prince Abdulla, the king's half-brother. Prince Abdulla is the commander of the National Guard. Al-Shammary's loyalty is clearly to the crown prince.

The Middle East had only known vertical political allegiances, and those allegiances got weaker as people moved from immediate family to extended family to tribe. By the time they started thinking about king and country their sense of loyalty was diluted.

That King Fahd and the crown prince did not see eye to eye was no secret. Abdulla had long considered Fahd too pro-West. Too pro-American, to be more accurate. Not that Abdulla was, or wanted Saudi Arabia to be, anti-West and anti-America. He wanted a more balanced foreign policy that took into account the needs of both the West and the Arab Middle East. He believed Fahd's one-sided loyalty to the Americans had compromised Saudi interests in the Middle East, not to mention the huge burden on the Saudi budget created by large purchases of U.S. arms. Abdulla had therefore focused on cultivating his ties within the Arab world, allowing his elder half-brother to flirt with the West. He had no visibility in the West, but was almost single-handedly responsible for maintaining Saudi Arabia's relations with Syria.

But there was more to the rift than differences of opinion about foreign policy. The two men were different. Fahd had a dark past of corruption, gambling, drunkenness, and other vices associated with the industrialized West. By comparison, Abdulla had remained a genuine man of the desert.

"Some of my Saudi friends complain that King Fahd has centralized all power in his hands," said Blackburn, convinced he would not offend the soldier.

"In his hands and in the hands of his sons and full brothers," Al-Shammary added. "You know, in Saudi Arabia, consensus is important. People assume that just because we are a monarchy, our system functions without consensus. That's not true. In fact, we need a broader consensus than a real democracy. In America, for example, if you win 51 percent of the vote, you win an election and you can govern. In Saudi Arabia, nobody could govern if only 51 percent of the people supported him. Our leaders have to have wider support."

"You know what we think?" Al-Shammary said softly, never making it clear who "we" meant. "We think King Fahd is like King Saud, the one who was ousted for incompetence and corruption."

The Saudi soldier would not have disclosed as much to a total stranger had the circumstances not been exactly what they were—a long flight, boredom, being drunk, and for some reason feeling the need to talk about himself. He would never have talked about King Fahd to somebody like Blackburn if they had met on Saudi territory or, for that matter, anywhere else where he could easily leave. On the plane, he couldn't get up and walk away, and he was constantly being served alcohol; his only two choices for companionship were the window and Blackburn. He tried the window for a while, and then turned back to Blackburn.

The flight attendants started serving lunch. The process, which involved a leisurely presentation of several courses, took almost an hour. Al-Shammary ate quietly, often staring out the window between courses. Blackburn borrowed his newspaper and decided to leave him alone.

After lunch, the soldier reclined his seat, pulled a blanket over his head, and went to sleep. The flight attendants had to wake him up when the plane began its final descent into Kuwait International Airport. He brought his seat to an upright position, fastened his seat belt as instructed, and fell asleep again. Blackburn woke him up when it was time to disembark.

X

Living in a Bad Neighborhood

In mid-April, Kuwait was as hot and humid as Washington is in mid-August. As soon as Blackburn stepped out of the air-conditioned airport onto the street, the heat and the pollution attacked his exhausted body, nauseating him. He got into a taxi, but that did not provide the hoped for relief. In spite of the heat and the dust, the seats in the taxi were covered with thick sheepskin and the driver refused to turn on the air conditioning. The windows were open instead, allowing more of the polluted air to blow in, making the twenty-minute ride almost unbearable.

Bianca makes me forget so much, Blackburn thought, and could not resist smiling. This time, he had forgotten to order a private car in advance from the hotel to pick him up, as he usually did.

When he finally checked in at the Sheraton Hotel, he called Ramzi Amin, arranged a meeting for the following morning, showered, and collapsed into bed. He slept fourteen hours.

"This is the story: First, the Japanese think you're getting ready to buy a refinery in the Far East, and they'd like to know which one. Second, they have developed an interest in oil exploration. They're preparing the ground to launch a campaign in the United States, sanctioned by MITI and supported by JNOC. Third, new alliances are being forged between different Japanese oil companies, but these are not the usual alliances; Japanese trading firms are involved, and the focus is outside Japan. Fourth, I think the collusion of trading firms and oil companies in Japan will have an impact on how oil trade is conducted here in the Gulf."

Ramzi Amin put four teaspoons of sugar in his cup of coffee, and stirred for a full minute, while listening quietly to Blackburn's succinct presentation. They had spent the first half-hour recapping some of the events in Vienna the preceding week, and Blackburn had explained that he had a standing order with Tony to close all of Amin's open positions in the futures market at $13.50 per barrel, as he had requested. "We should get there today or tomorrow," he told Amin.

"How do you think it will affect oil trade here in the Gulf?" asked Amin, taking a sip of the syrupy coffee, finally satisfied that the mound of sugar at the bottom of the cup had dissolved.

"Well, for one thing, they'll gang up on you guys again. Five or six companies start lifting more than 50 percent of the oil from Qatar, Dubai, maybe even Kuwait; then they come together asking for a discount. Otherwise, they say, they regret that they won't be able to lift next month. Or now that the prices of Gulf crudes destined for the Far East are tied to either Dubai or Oman, they can manipulate those markets. If spot prices of Dubai and Oman come down fifty cents, the price of your crude sold to the Japanese will come down by fifty cents. It's not difficult to manipulate the Dubai and Oman markets if they collude."

As he spoke, Blackburn could feel that Amin was losing interest in his arguments. This sort of story had never failed to grab his attention in the past.

"So crude oil prices will come down," Amin said after watching Blackburn for a few seconds. "Is that what you mean by them affecting oil trade here in the Gulf?"

"Well, yes," Blackburn said defensively. "Oil prices will come down. Isn't that enough of an impact?"

"It is an impact. But who's complaining? Let the prices come down. If they succeed, I may even thank your Japanese."

"You mean you prefer lower prices? Lower than what they already are? Ramzi, the market has already crashed by more than four bucks in two weeks!"

Up to a certain point, Blackburn could understand the Kuwaiti policy of keeping oil prices relatively low. They needed low prices in order to buy some of their international oil assets cheaply. They needed low prices in order to maintain growing demand for oil in the West. They needed low oil prices in order to keep the bigger powers in the region, such as Iraq and Iran, constantly on the defensive economically and financially; otherwise, those powers would get even bigger and become a threat to little Kuwait.

But none of these explanations could justify a price level lower than the levels reached in the past few weeks. This could destabilize governments all over the Middle East. It could backfire on Kuwait.

"Look, Jim," said Ramzi, checking his watch and standing up. "I have to be somewhere in twenty minutes. Why don't we have dinner at my house tonight? There will be other people from KPC I'd like you to meet. We'll talk about this then."

Blackburn signed the check and went back to his room. It was only 10:30 a.m., too early to call his office; it was 2:30 in the morning in Washington.

He called Rashid Al-Awadi at the Ministry of Finance. Al-Awadi had been his classmate at AUB some eighteen years ago, and now was the head of the economic research department at the ministry. They agreed to meet for lunch.

Blackburn had nothing to do for the next three hours. He lay on the bed smoking and thought how little he knew about his own area of expertise. The thought was sobering. Some of the largest players in this game relied on him and on his advice. And not only oil companies; governments, including the U.S. intelligence agencies, were his clients. He was expected to anticipate major changes and forewarn his clients, yet here he was unable to fully understand what was going on right under his nose. Amin's attitude toward the Japanese and the price of oil didn't make sense. Takao's paranoia didn't make sense. These were hard-nosed businessmen focused on commercial ventures. Things were supposed to fit more neatly than this.

It has to be real simple, he kept telling himself, just as he realized his right index finger was in overdrive stroking his mustache, and brought his hand down. Reality always is. Too simple to attract attention. You must be missing an important piece in this puzzle, he thought. Takao hasn't told you everything. Despite its size and importance, the oil game is still a simple game, played by simple people. The largest traded commodity in the world, the most politicized commodity in the world, is in the hands of a handful of simple people.

But everything is relative. "Life used to be so simple," Lou Elmer at Exxon had told him years ago. "The majors controlled everything. We knew everything there was to know about our business; what's more important, nobody else did. There were no oil consultants in those days, you know. No offense. We knew where the oil was, how much was being produced, who was producing it, where it was going, at what price. Now there are too many players, too many interests to keep track of."

But there aren't too many players today, thought Blackburn. And the game is still simple. True, the number of players has increased, but the only real "experts" are still the players themselves.

Are we consultants really experts? We're observers, he thought. We watch. Like fanatic football fans, we watch every game. But we've never played a game ourselves. We've never really been in the field! Have I ever dug a well? Produced a drop of oil? Filled a tanker? Refined a barrel of crude? Sold or bought anything other than paper contracts on the Merc? Paper barrels. How different that game is from the real oil game. The wet barrel game. We're fans of the oil market. Not experts. Not even former players or coaches. Fans advising the players.

The telephone woke him up. It was the hotel receptionist announcing that Mr. Al-Awadi was waiting downstairs. He jumped out of bed, quickly washed his face, and went down to the lobby to meet his old classmate.

Whenever alumni of the AUB met, especially outside of Beirut, there was the obligatory hour of reminiscing about the good old days. Nostalgia ran high as professors and classmates were named individually and information about their whereabouts was exchanged. By the end of the hour there was a renewed sense of camaraderie and closeness, regardless of how long it had been since the alumni had seen each other. Al-Awadi, one of the few Kuwaiti students at AUB in the late sixties, had started as a freshman when Blackburn was a senior. Blackburn had tutored him and a small group of other students from the Gulf in statistics, a subject they found difficult.

"So tell me," asked Blackburn, finally satisfied that the necessary AUB-related talk was complete. "How do you like it at the ministry?"

"If you're going to work in the government, this definitely is the place to be," answered Al-Awadi. "All other ministries, including your famous oil ministry, serve finance, you know. We set the targets for everyone, on both how much they can spend and how much they should earn."

"Oh, I have no doubt that you're in the right place within the government," answered Blackburn. "But frankly, I did not expect you to stay in government for so long. I thought you'd leave and chase a fortune in the private sector."

"I probably would have, had it not been for family pressure to stay on. My father wouldn't hear of it. My brothers were against it also. They made me a full partner in the family business on condition that I stayed at the ministry. They need me here, and not just for the prestige of having a family member serve his country."

That didn't come as a surprise to Blackburn. The Al-Awadis owned the third largest bank in Kuwait and were major shareholders in several other regional banks, insurance companies, and trading houses. And although their influence within the Ministry of Finance ran much higher than Rashid's position as director of economic research would suggest, it wouldn't hurt to have a member of the family permanently planted inside.

"Besides," added Al-Awadi with a sense of exaggerated self-importance, "these days I don't spend much time at the ministry. A few hours a day, at most. I usually get in around 10 in the morning and leave by noon. I never go back in the afternoons. The afternoons are for the family business."

"I won't ask if you feel guilty accepting a full salary for two hours of work each day," Blackburn said with a grin.

"Good. You shouldn't," Al-Awadi said forcefully.

He was clearly disturbed by Blackburn's implied accusation of less-than-exemplary behavior. Then, feeling the need to make a more dramatic impression, he pulled out his Kuwaiti passport from the chest pocket of his *thawb* and flashed it in front Blackburn.

"Do you know what this represents?" he asked, full of passion and drama. "This says I am a shareholder in the company called Kuwait. Citizenship here means you own equity. My full salary, as you put it, is nothing more than the dividends that are due to me. The two hours that I put in every day are time donated to the system. The salary has nothing to do with time or output."

"That's a long way away from the economics they taught us at AUB, eh?"

"You can say that again. In fact, almost everything I've done at the ministry is a long way away from the economics they taught us at AUB."

"Okay, Rashid, I get the point. Sorry if I upset you," said Blackburn, finding it difficult to sound genuinely apologetic. "Tell me, then, what kind of non-economics are you spending your time on these days?"

"Oh, not much to speak of, really. We don't have any financial problems, you know. No matter how low oil prices go, somehow we still manage to generate a trade surplus. Our needs are limited. We're a small country, we don't have big projects like the Saudis, and we invest prudently. Last year, our income from foreign investments was larger than our oil revenues. So what's there to worry about?"

"I've been reading reports of large budget deficits in Kuwait," answered Blackburn.

"Oh c'mon, Jim! Don't tell me even you fell for that. The Kuwaiti budget deficit is probably one of the most successful pieces of non-economics my department has turned out. I wonder what good old professor Khalaf would say if he discovered how we measure budget deficits in Kuwait."

"It's that bad, eh? Are you telling me that Kuwait does not really have a budget deficit?"

"Let me ask you this. This year, we're going to have some $6 billion in investment income from our overseas investments. Should that be part of the government revenue projections?"

"Of course. If it's government revenue."

"It is government revenue. But it is never included in budget estimates as revenue. Let me ask you another question. Each year, we allocate a certain amount of money for the Reserve Fund for Future Generations.

In other words, we save that amount for the future. Should that be part of government expenditures?"

"Of course not, if it's a saving."

"Well, it is a saving, but it gets entered as an expenditure item in the budget. So you see now why we have a 'budget deficit.' With savings categorized as expenditures and investment income absent from the revenue line, is it any wonder?"

"But why should you want to create this artificial deficit?"

"Well, I'll let you figure that one out for yourself. It's OPEC politics, they tell me. It has to do with oil production or market share. We have to look poor to justify higher production. That's for OPEC's benefit. But if you want to figure out the real oil policy, take a careful look at our foreign investments. Everything else is irrelevant."

"You mean investments in foreign petroleum acquisitions, not foreign investments in general."

"Yes, yes. International investments in both downstream and upstream. Non-petroleum investments are purely capital management tools. And we keep adding to the pool of capital to be managed and invested. At the end of this year, Kuwait's foreign assets will exceed $80 billion. That's more than double what the Saudi treasury will have left by the end of this year. Only six years ago, they had over $145 billion in liquid foreign assets! Can you imagine the drain on their financial reserves?"

"Yes, I can imagine," said Blackburn. He knew the Saudi financial situation well. He followed Saudi Arabia much more closely than Kuwait, mainly because the Kingdom's oil policies had a far more profound impact on international markets than Kuwait's. But times were changing. Kuwait could no longer be ignored as a player.

"I hear Kuwait is gearing up for a series of investments in the Far East," Blackburn said in a disinterested way. "Maybe even eyeing a refinery in Japan."

"I don't think we're ready for Japan yet," said Al-Awadi. After a few minutes of reflection, he added, "Let me rephrase that. I don't think the Japanese are ready for us yet. But the Far East, yes. Definitely. And I don't think it's a refinery we're after this time. It's upstream. Crude oil exploration. The downstream will come later."

"Upstream? In the Far East? Why on earth would you go looking for oil in the Far East when you have the cheapest reserves right here in

Kuwait? You're not producing half your full potential here and you want to look for more outside?"

"You're getting warmer, Jim. Maybe if we *could* produce our full potential here in Kuwait we wouldn't be interested in looking for oil outside. It's not as illogical as it may appear at first glance. But that's something else for you to figure out by yourself. Production outside the home country does not count in the OPEC quota. So, again, it's all tied to OPEC politics, or so they tell me."

About thirty-five minutes northeast of Kuwait City, on a ten-acre private beach, lay Ramzi Amin's mansion. The "villa," as he liked to refer to it, was a mini-palace built in the style of old Arabic architecture, and it was the retreat where he had done most of his recruiting for The Symposium. The estate was surrounded by a tall fence to keep in the wild animals Amin had collected over the years.

A small herd of desert gazelles and about twenty Saluki hounds were his prized possessions.

Inside, there were nine men seated around a huge, circular brass tray on the floor of the living room. Furnished in the style of an old Arabic *majlis*, or sitting room, with Persian rugs and hundreds of colorful cushions of different sizes thrown around, the living room could easily accommodate more than fifty guests.

Most were people from KPC that Blackburn had heard about before. Some were from the ministry of oil, and there were a few personal business contacts of Amin's. The men seemed relaxed. Most had taken off their Arabic headdresses and unbuttoned the tops of their *thawbs*. Some were reclining on the thick carpets, with cushions tucked under their arms; others were sitting with their legs folded in front of them and their plates resting on their feet. Two male Filipino servants were serving drinks and bringing dishes of Middle Eastern delicacies to the round tray.

They were unusually friendly to Blackburn when Ramzi introduced him. Compared with other Gulf nationals, Kuwaitis were not generally known to be either hospitable or friendly. If Blackburn had met any of the people in Amin's living room in a different setting, such as in their offices, they would probably have been as cold and formal as their reputation called for. But this was a different gathering. Blackburn couldn't help feeling that he was being *accepted*. An outsider, allowed in an inner circle. He was the only one in Western clothes, but that did not make him feel out of place. It would have, had the Kuwaitis acknowledged the difference.

One of the senior men from KPC sat next to Blackburn. "Ramzi has told me so much about you," he said, passing one of the newly arrived dishes to Blackburn. "I'm glad we could finally meet." His soft-spoken, gentle manners did not fit with Blackburn's perception of the KPC staff. There was an intellectual aura about the man that was rare in oil company executives. His gray hair, deep dark eyes, and impeccable classical Arabic reminded Blackburn of a philosophy professor he'd had at AUB. Then it occurred to him that the Kuwaitis, even among themselves, were speaking classical Arabic, rather than the peculiar Kuwaiti colloquial dialect. This he took as an added measure of courtesy to him.

"It's my pleasure," he said. "I'm glad I'm finally getting to meet some of Ramzi's colleagues."

"I understand you live in Washington. What are the Americans worrying about these days? Now that the so-called second oil crisis is dead and buried?"

"That depends on which Americans you talk to. For some, the oil crisis has just begun! It's called the collapse of oil prices."

"So now prices are too low, eh?" the man said, laughing. "You can't keep all the people happy all the time, right?"

"Right."

Blackburn was tempted to ask what would keep KPC happy, at least most of the time, but judged that it was premature for him to take the lead in the conversation.

"My friend Jim here has aroused a lot of interest in us all over the world," declared Amin, joining them.

"I'm afraid I can't take credit for that!" Blackburn said. "The interest is already there and it's quite strong. I just hear about it and pass it on."

"It's coming from the East this time, I understand. Have the Europeans stopped talking about us, then?"

"I don't think the Europeans will ever stop talking about you. Your buying of BP shares is still more controversial than if you had bought half of metropolitan London, and your Q8 gas stations are all over the place.

The Europeans may be less paranoid about you than the Japanese, but they won't stop talking about you for a long time."

"So the Japanese are paranoid. Very well put, my friend! And I would say mysterious, too," said Amin. "But haven't they always been so? About everything?"

"Perhaps. But now they think you're up to something in their own backyard."

The roar of the fighter jets was deafening. It came suddenly, without warning. Blackburn imagined the sky being ripped apart, with wide cracks left behind the jets, like a strong earthquake would rip the ground apart. Despite the thick padding of the carpets and the cushions, they could feel the violent vibrations of the floor and hear the dishes rattle on the brass tray.

A few seconds later the silence became equally deafening, broken only by the barking dogs and the stampede of the gazelles outside. The echo of the fighter jets was replaced by the faint rumble of artillery shells, no more than ten miles away from Amin's villa.

Blackburn had not realized how close to the Iran/Iraq war Kuwait really was. When his initial shock had subsided, he looked at the quiet, somber faces of his Kuwaiti hosts and, for the first time, saw their fear firsthand.

"Those were Iraqi jets returning from a mission in the Gulf. They probably raided some Iranian oil tankers," Amin explained, breaking the silence. "And that artillery sound you hear in the distance is from Fao." He was calm, his voice soft but firm. There was a chilling intensity in his eyes.

"Now, you were saying?"

He was interrupted again by the thundering return of the fighter jets, as sudden and violent as before. He waited a few minutes, then continued. "You were saying? We're up to something in Japan's backyard?" He pointed out the window toward the battlefronts in the north and softly added, "Would they rather we stayed in our own backyard? *Of course* we're trying to get in their backyard! We're probably even negotiating with the very same people who sent you on this fact-finding mission."

The shelling lasted for about half an hour, often interrupted by the noise of the fighter jets. But even after it ended, things didn't return to normal in Amin's living room.

Something was lost. The few words exchanged among the Kuwaitis were in their dialect.

It was close to midnight when Amin's driver dropped Blackburn off at his hotel. He went up to his room thinking what an eye-opener this trip had been. How he had ignored the simplest and most obvious realities that affected life in the region.

The Kuwaitis, so close to the Iran/Iraq battlefronts, were hedging their bets and buying oil reserves as far away from the troubled waters of the Gulf as they could find them. Their own oil was a source of income, but not a source of security. They must feel like a midget sitting right under the feet of wrestling giants, thought Blackburn.

What would the young Saudi soldier say if he were present at Amin's villa? How civilized *is* the desert? If one could pierce the veil, what would be waiting underneath? Majed Al-Shammary, I hope I run into you again someday, thought Blackburn. It didn't seem likely, however, that he would meet the young soldier again.

Amin's outburst had impressed Blackburn. It was not like him to show that much emotion.

Blackburn called his office, checked his messages with Linda, and asked her to change his return ticket from Kuwait-London-Washington to Kuwait-Bahrain-London-Washington. He had to stop by Bahrain and confront Mr. Kato of C. Itoh.

Then he called Gene Theiss in Old Town Alexandria, Virginia. He felt the need for his perspective now more than ever.

XI

A Stone Thrown from Afar

The following morning Blackburn made two calls to Bahrain. Then he called British Airways to confirm his new flights.

His entry visa was arranged as promised by BMA, the Bahrain Monetary Agency, the country's central bank. The young officer inside the glass cubicle at passport control had no trouble finding Blackburn's name in his fat book, and stamped the visa in the American passport.

He took a taxi straight to the BMA building on the Corniche. He was going to fly out of Bahrain that same afternoon, so didn't plan to check into a hotel. As he entered the building, the armed guard rose from his chair and approached him.

"I have an appointment with Shaikh Saqr Al-Khalifa," said Blackburn, handing him a business card.

The guard picked up the telephone to announce Blackburn. After a few moments he pointed Blackburn up the staircase to the second floor. Blackburn was barely halfway up the circular staircase when Shaikh Saqr appeared at the top to greet him.

"Jim! What a great surprise. Welcome, welcome!"

"Greetings, Shaikh Saqr. I'm sorry I had to impose on you with such short notice. Until this morning I was not planning to be in Bahrain."

"I would have been angry at you if I heard later that you went all the way to Kuwait and didn't bother to stop by to say hello!"

The two men embraced and Shaikh Saqr took Blackburn by the arm and led him to his office.

"What's your schedule like? How much time do we have? Would you like some tea or coffee?" Shaikh Saqr threw out the questions as he picked up the phone, as if he was not going to wait for any answers.

"Well, I have to be at the C. Itoh office in half an hour," said Blackburn, glad to see that Shaikh Saqr had not slowed down over the years. "That should not last more than an hour. I can meet you for lunch afterward, if you're free. My flight is not until this evening, but I'll need to spend some time at the lounge at the airport. I have to catch up on a lot of reading."

"Tea or coffee?" asked Shaikh Saqr, cupping his palm on the handset.

"Tea would be fine, thank you."

Shaikh Saqr gave the order for tea service for two, hung up the telephone, then lifted the handset again. "You'll be needing a car, right?"

Before Blackburn could answer, Shaikh Saqr was speaking rapidly into the phone, arranging for a car to pick Blackburn up in twenty minutes in front of the BMA, wait for him while he finished his business, and then take him to the Taverna. That arranged, he came to sit near Blackburn.

"Welcome, welcome!" he said again. "We'll have lunch at the Taverna. Is that okay? I hope everything is fine with you. Are you married yet or still fighting it? I haven't seen you for almost a year!"

Shaikh Saqr was a phenomenon in the Gulf. He was by far the most hyper individual in the entire, laid-back and leisurely Middle East. He moved, thought, and spoke several times faster than anybody around him. For that reason, many of his local peers avoided him, although he had the confidence and respect of the few that really mattered.

"Everything is fine, Shaikh Saqr. And no, I'm not married yet. Do you really think I would dare get married without letting you know?"

"Good, good. But don't fight it too much longer. Can I help you in any other way? Do you need to see anybody else in Bahrain?"

"No, no, Shaikh Saqr. Thank you very much. But I have to admit things have changed here quite a bit. I saw traffic signs pointing toward Saudi Arabia. I understand the occupancy rates in hotels are way up. Is it all good?"

"Oh, the causeway. Well, yes. Our little island is finally linked to the mainland. It's a real piece of work, you know. You should drive on it sometime. It was built with military considerations in mind. I'll tell you more some other time."

"Has it been good for Bahrain so far?"

"In its non-military uses, you mean?" Shaikh Saqr laughed. "Well, I guess it has. It's difficult to find hotel rooms on weekends. Saudis pour in here every Thursday and start drinking until Friday evening. They somehow manage to get back Saturday morning to start the week. They spend the week getting over their hangovers, in time to make the trip again the following weekend. But I guess it's been good for business."

"This should be strengthening GCC ties, don't you think?"

"GCC ties? What are you up to now? I can never be sure what you're up to when you ask questions like that."

"I'm not up to anything, Shaikh Saqr," Blackburn laughed. "I'm talking about basic relations between brotherly countries, you know, the type of relations you guys talk about all the time. Is the causeway going to improve the already good relations between your little island of Bahrain and the big Kingdom?"

The two men had met over eight years earlier. Shaikh Saqr was at the Ministry of Industry at the time, attending a conference in Doha, Qatar, on Gulf industrialization. The conference, organized by the Gulf Organization for Industrial Consulting, was held at the magnificent facilities of the newly built Doha Sheraton. Blackburn, who was attending the conference as an invited guest of the Qatar General Petroleum Company, met Shaikh Saqr there and the two instantly hit it off.

"Jim, your car will be here soon. We'll discuss GCC ties over lunch. Give me a call when you leave C. Itoh so that I can leave here in time for us to arrive at the Taverna together. I'll see you there. You're sure I cannot do anything else for you? The car will take you to the airport after lunch, so you can leave your bags with the driver."

"Thank you very much, Shaikh Saqr. You shouldn't have gone to all that trouble. I'll see you in an hour or so."

"*Insha Allah.*"

*   *   *

"Yes, Mr. Takao has told me about your mission to Kuwait. I'm glad you made the stop in Bahrain," Suzuki Kato, head of C. Itoh's Middle East operations, told Blackburn.

"My mission, Kato-san, is about to be aborted unless you tell me *exactly* what is going on. I'm sorry, I do not mean to be rude, but I am sure I've been misled by Mr. Takao. I do *not* appreciate being sent on a wild goose chase."

Even as he spoke, Blackburn was surprised to feel his anger rise. The strategy had worked in the past, and he had decided to try it again. Confront them directly, he had told himself the night before. Pretend you know what they're up to, sound angry and hurt. Threaten to call off the whole deal.

"Is that so?" said Kato, his smile and initial friendliness lost. "Is that so? Oh, so sorry, Blackburn-san."

"Yes, that is so, Kato-san. How long have we known each other? Five, six years? Have I ever given you reason to suspect my integrity during this period? Have I ever broken a confidence?"

"No, Blackburn-san, no. Never. So sorry we upset you." Kato was clearly taken by surprise.

"Much is going on here that you are aware of, and perhaps even *part* of," Blackburn said in the same angry tone. "And I was sent here by your company to find out what the Kuwaitis were up to in the Far East. They're up to a lot, but I think you already know that. Now, I want two things from you; otherwise I will consider my mission, as you call it, void."

Blackburn stared at Kato and took a sip of his green tea. Kato nodded, anxious to hear what Blackburn's two demands were.

"First," continued Blackburn, satisfied that he had Kato's full attention, "I want you to tell me *exactly* what kind of new arrangement you and KPC have for cooperation in the Far East, and particularly in Japan." He waited to make sure Kato had understood his demand. Kato nodded again.

"Second, if you want me to continue this mission, I want you to ask me the questions you *really* have about Kuwait. Don't waste my time on meaningless indirect questions, hoping I will reveal what you really want to know without realizing what I've discovered. Of course, you are free not to do this. But I should bring to your attention that I probably will find out the answers on my own anyway, and when I do, I will not be bound by any confidentiality with you since I will not be retained by you. That is all."

"Oh, I see, I see, Blackburn-san," Kato said so softly that Blackburn could barely hear him. "I think we better call Takao-san right away."

"Now?" asked Blackburn, checking his watch. "It's three in the morning in Washington!"

"Oh, so sorry, but never mind. Takao-san doesn't mind, I'm sure. We'll call him immediately."

* * *

The Taverna, one of the popular restaurants on the island, was on the second floor of the Grundy Hotel. Blackburn referred to it as the hangout of the Bahraini yuppies, since it was always full of the young professionals employed in Bahrain's banking sector. Expensive, but with a decent mix of Italian and intercontinental menus adapted to Gulf tastes, the Taverna, with its adjoining disco, Infinity, had become an institution.

Shaikh Saqr was already there, chatting with a dozen people at once when Blackburn arrived. When he saw Blackburn walk in, he grabbed his arm and led him to their table, at the far left corner of the room. "Did everything go well?" he asked, waving at the waiter to follow them to their table. "Are the Japanese giving you any trouble? By the way, I'd like to introduce you to Shaikh Khalifa, the emir's younger brother; he's the prime minister and owns half the island. Have you met him?"

"No, I haven't had the honor," said Blackburn, wondering how he could focus Shaikh Saqr's attention on one issue for more than a few moments while casting a watchful eye toward the waiter, who was passing them the menus.

"One day I'll introduce you to him. He's very smart," said Shaikh Saqr, waiving the menus away. "You don't want to waste time reading these, do you?" he said, pointing to the menus. "Will you trust me?"

"I'll trust you," Blackburn said laughing, and handed his menu back to the waiter.

"Tell your chef to prepare two Shaikh Saqr Specials," the shaikh told the waiter. "He'll know what to do. And get us some beer. You want beer?" He turned to Blackburn, who nodded. "Okay, two beers."

"Shaikh Saqr, can we talk about the GCC for a minute? Is there any problem between Saudi Arabia and Kuwait? I mean something more serious than the ordinary."

Shaikh Saqr slowed down for a minute. His gaze stopped on Blackburn's face for a fraction of a second and his hands stopped moving around.

"If you're asking me that, you must know something," he said, leaning over the table to get closer to Blackburn. "But I won't play games with you. I'll tell you what I know, but you keep it to yourself. Will you?"

"I will."

"Do you know about Prince Mohammad, the king's son?"

"The governor of the Eastern Province?"

"Him. Well, he's crazy, you know. A bit like our own Shaikh Mohammad, the emir's youngest brother."

"I didn't know the emir had a third brother," interrupted Blackburn, and regretted it immediately. This was bound to get the conversation off course again.

"Oh, yes, Shaikh Mohammad. He probably would have had a high position in the government, but he's a bit crazy. So the emir handed the government over to Shaikh Khalifa. The British didn't want Shaikh Mohammed involved. They couldn't possibly communicate with the man, let alone control him. He does not understand diplomacy. Now Shaikh Mohammad has a small personal army and roams around in the desert. He's a big man, with a thick black beard. He looks as crazy as he is!"

"Are you saying the British control Bahrain?" asked Blackburn, even though he was impatient to get the conversation back to Prince Mohammad.

"It's true, isn't it? Why shouldn't I admit it? They control everything."

"I thought you didn't like the British."

"I don't. You know, it's totally incomprehensible to me how these people conquered the whole world at one time. They're all faggots! Even the most macho Brit talks like a faggot, walks like a faggot, thinks like a faggot." Then, to demonstrate his point, Shaikh Saqr lifted his arm, allowing his hand to dangle loosely at the wrist and, in the most effeminate voice and manners he could muster, tried to imitate the British. "Jolly good!" he said, batting his eyelashes frantically. "Jolly good, cheerio ..."

The sight of Shaikh Saqr, with his thick, black mustache and huge nose, imitating what he perceived to be the manners of a "British faggot," was too much for Blackburn. His uncontrolled laughter rolled across the restaurant, turning heads and inviting unwanted attention.

"And their women are even worse!" continued Shaikh Saqr, encouraged by Blackburn's laughter. "The most lady-like British woman is a whore. I'm telling you. The *most* lady-like has a price!"

"Okay, okay, Shaikh Saqr. I wouldn't know much about that. I can see you still dislike the British. But you started telling me about Prince Mohammad of Saudi Arabia, remember?"

"Well, the prince is more crazy than our Shaikh Mohammad, and worse. Much worse. He's also greedy, vindictive, and corrupt. As governor of the Eastern Province, he spends his time chasing Shia dissidents. Most of the Saudi Shias live in the Eastern Province, you know, and they've been resentful that there has not been enough development spending in their region."

"Yes, I know. But what does this have to do with Kuwait?"

"Well, Prince Mohammad does not discriminate between threats in the Eastern Province and the rest of the Gulf. After the Iranian Revolution, Shias in the Gulf were viewed with suspicion. Aside from that, many of the supporters of Juhayman al-Oteibi, the guy who led the siege in Mecca, escaped to Kuwait. So he persecutes, arrests, and sometimes executes them inside Kuwait. He crosses borders himself with his troops, without letting the Kuwaitis know. He has arrested Kuwaiti nationals *inside* of Kuwaiti borders without letting the Kuwaitis know about it! In a few cases he has executed these people on the spot. How do you think they feel about all this?"

"I had no idea it was *that* crazy."

"You won't read about such things in the press. There are armed skirmishes almost every week. By the way, the Kuwaitis have no love for their Shia dissidents, nor for the Sunni zealots. But they don't appreciate this infringement on their sovereignty. They've asked King Fahd to have a talk with his son, but nothing has changed. That's the real problem, if you ask me. King Fahd thinks the entire peninsula belongs to him. He thinks he's king of the GCC, not just Saudi Arabia."

"Where does all this leave little Bahrain?" asked Blackburn.

"Where do you think? We don't like what Prince Mohammed is doing at all. Seventy percent of our own population is Shia. They get upset when they hear these stories. But what can we do? If King Fahd won't listen to Kuwait and Abu Dhabi, why should he listen to us?"

"What about others in Saudi Arabia? The crown prince, for example? Or Prince Nayef, the interior minister?"

"Oh, they're angry as hell, too. Especially Prince Abdulla. He thinks Fahd is overreacting to the Shias and overextending his influence. I'll tell you something else, but this is top, top secret." Shaikh Saqr leaned farther over the table and lowered his voice almost to a whisper. "Prince Abdulla has secretly apologized to Kuwait and Abu Dhabi. Do you understand the *implications* of an apology from him? It means he's telling them 'I don't agree with my brother's policies, and I won't mind at all if you show your own disapproval.' That's what his apology really means."

The Shaikh Saqr Specials arrived. Hammour—a prized fish in Gulf waters—stuffed with a variety of Bedouin spices provided to the chef by Shaikh Saqr, baked in a parchment paper bag. Not baked in an oven, though, but by burying the bag under a thin layer of sand and building a fire over it. The Italian chef probably resented this alien intrusion into his kitchen, but felt obliged to humor the young shaikh. The waiter ripped the paper bags open, revealing the steaming hammour and all the condiments inside. Shaikh Saqr ordered two more beers and concentrated on his meal.

Blackburn was silent for a long time, trying to put all he had learned on this trip into a logical context. He watched Shaikh Saqr eat his lunch in the same rapid and disorganized pace as he spoke. He attacked the fish from all sides and angles, picking steaming slices from it with his fork and practically swallowing them without chewing. Blackburn had barely made a dent in his own food when Shaikh Saqr, having finished his lunch, gulped down the last of his second glass of beer.

"What's the matter?" he asked, showing some irritation at Blackburn's much slower pace. "Don't you like our hammour?"

"No, no, that's not it, Shaikh Saqr. It's quite good, in fact. I've just been thinking about what you said. That's all."

"Well, you can think about it all you want as long as you don't forget your promise to keep it to yourself."

"I won't," Blackburn said again, with every intention of keeping his word.

"Okay, good. Now, if you're not going to eat, at least tell me what you were thinking when you asked the question."

"Oh, I was way off base. I suspected something because of things I heard on the flight to Kuwait and later in Kuwait. I thought all along that the Japanese were trying to meddle in these waters again. You see, I tend to focus only on the commercial stuff. I forget the politics too often."

"The *Japanese*? What can the poor Japanese do here? You know, I feel sorry for them. They have no idea how this place operates."

"I wouldn't be too sure about that. When they collude, which is often, they represent a credible commercial force here in the Gulf."

"But what does that *mean*? Nothing! We can deal with them anytime we want. Yes, they collude. They get a good deal here, a good deal there. Sometimes we leave money on the table when we're dealing with them. Go beyond all that, Jim. We can cut them off anytime we want. Put everything in a historical perspective. You used to like history, didn't you? When have the Japanese ever been a problem for us? Our problems are much nearer to us; they've always been."

"Do the Kuwaitis have that passive attitude about their commercial dealings with the Japanese?"

"Listen. The Kuwaitis have their own calculations and their own plans. They're not passive, and they rarely leave any money on the table unless they can make it back tenfold in other ways. If you think the

Japanese are manipulating the Kuwaitis, then you're *really* off base. If anything, it's the other way around."

Blackburn fell silent again, halfheartedly turning his attention to his meal. But Shaikh Saqr was running out of patience. He couldn't sit there and watch Blackburn pick at his lunch.

"What's the matter?" he insisted. "You don't believe what I'm telling you? Haven't you heard the old Bedouin saying, 'A stone thrown from afar can't hurt you'? It's a wise saying, Jim. If a stone reaches you, if it *hurts* you, it must have been thrown from very near. Very, very near. Only those close to you can hurt you. The Japanese are too far. Forget them."

* * *

Could it be true?

Could so many tribal rules be broken in such a short period of time? Rules that have governed the Arabian Peninsula for centuries?

I'll never find out for sure, thought Blackburn as he reclined in his seat on the flight out of Bahrain. But if Crown Prince Abdulla *really* believes that King Fahd's reign is hanging from a thin thread, and if he *really* believes that intensifying the financial pressures on him will help cut that thread, and if Kuwait and Abu Dhabi are *really* so tired of the king's excesses that they're willing to break some unwritten rules themselves, and if the crown prince's apology has truly been made—that apology would mean more than Shaikh Saqr was willing to admit. It would be a promise from Prince Abdulla that he would not repeat the mistakes of his brother and his king. *It would represent a deal* ... Could it be true?

I can neither confirm it nor ignore it, thought Blackburn. If it's true, Kuwait and the UAE will turn into mavericks within OPEC; they'll stall agreements, produce as much as they can, push prices down. They'll fight against each other, they'll fight against Saudi Arabia, they'll fight against any other OPEC country. They'll embarrass the king politically. They'll force him to continue to deplete his financial reserves. Fahd won't reduce his spending just because revenues are low, he won't be able to control Prince Sultan's insatiable appetite to buy more arms, he won't be able to reduce the flow of money to his branch of the family, he won't be able to stop paying off every potential political opposition, including the religious elite. Maybe they'll even force him to start borrowing money, something that has not been done in Saudi Arabia since the time of King Saud.

How does the unity of the Gulf States in Vienna last week fit in all this? They cooperated, didn't they? Could the Saudis be so oblivious to the designs of their neighbors? Or was that a one-time show of force to ward off the others?

And the Japanese? Do they know what they're involved in? Of course not. If all this is true, they'll get their cheap oil and their good commercial deals, and, without having a clue about what's really going on, they'll even contribute to the plan in a small way by helping keep oil prices down.

KPC will make the deal with C. Itoh and its small partner in Tokyo. A small deal with a small partner. Poor Takao. He had been deeply embarrassed. "So sorry, Blackburn-san. We did not mean to mislead you, so sorry." Shaikh Saqr could be right. They have no idea how this place operates. And they're dispensable.

If the plot to overthrow Fahd is true and fails, what will happen to Prince Abdulla, to the GCC, to OPEC? How will Fahd take his revenge?

I wonder what the boys in Washington would do if they suspected there was a plot against Fahd, thought Blackburn. Losing Fahd prematurely, having to deal with Abdulla, going back to the drawing board—like the rest of the world often does when America elects a new president. I wonder if they know. I wonder if they *suspect*, Blackburn corrected himself. Far-fetched though it is, a change of the guard in Riyadh would be too important for the United States. At least it'd be too important for Washington.

A visit to Gene Theiss was a must now, given what he was beginning to understand.

XII

The Slippery Samurai

Kiyochi Kurai was lying face down on the foam mattress on the floor of his bachelor apartment in the Shinjiku district of Tokyo. His concubine, twenty-two-year-old Kyoko, had finished bathing him and left him to soak in the bathtub for a while, then helped him out and onto the mattress.

She was kneeling between his legs, running her hands up and down his thighs, from the back of his knees to his buttocks. She had no feelings for the sixty-year-old Kurai, the chief executive officer of a small, hardly known, Japanese oil company called Fuji Kosan. She did not care for him, nor hate him, nor did she resent the hours she spent with him. But she knew what he liked and performed her duty for the generous wages she received.

What Kurai liked was to have his ass licked by the young Kyoko. It was not just for the physical pleasure; to have his anus licked with great tenderness and passion gave the sixty-year-old man a sense of *power*.

Kyoko gradually increased the force on the back of his thighs and let her palms linger longer and longer on Kurai's buttocks. She watched the old man's back, his balding head, his skinny arms folded under his face, and came to the same familiar conclusion. Men were ridiculous creatures. Vain, childish, in constant need of pampering. Oversensitive where their egos were concerned, crude and insensitive when dealing with women. But none of this bothered Kyoko. This was life, real and simple.

Kurai's breathing had fallen into a calm, regular pattern. He was totally relaxed, oblivious to everything around him, responding to Kyoko's touch by absolute inaction. She then took a deep breath, spread his buttocks and gently placed her face in between. She shut her mind off, and her senses, and let her tongue earn her wages for her.

In that state of mind, Kyoko did not hear the soft ring of the telephone. Neither did Kurai at first, but after the third ring he started to come out of his daze. She sensed his irritation, came up for breath, and heard the telephone. She jumped up like an agile kitten and brought the telephone to him.

He answered with an agitated grunt, listened for a few minutes, then uttered a final grunt into the handset and handed it back to her. "Proceed," he ordered. And Kyoko proceeded, but she could feel that something was lost. The tension in his muscles did not disappear, nor did his total submission to her fingers and tongue return. That afternoon was not destined to be as magical as usual; he dismissed her early.

But it was a magical afternoon for Kurai in a way that poor Kyoko would never know. The deal he had been trying to put together for over nine months was beginning to materialize. One more wrinkle had just been ironed out, bringing him closer to pulling off the most unexpected turnabout in Japan's rigid corporate hierarchy.

As he left the building half an hour later, he actually smiled at the doorman. The apartment building was designed and built for high-level business executives, who needed a place other than their homes to unwind and relax. But neither Fuji Kosan nor Kurai had the status or the financial strength of the other occupants of the building. This entire facility was out of Kurai's league. And he knew it, and the doorman knew it, and Kurai knew that the doorman knew it, so he made a point of always treating him as a doorman. This was the first time Kurai had acknowledged the doorman, let alone smiled at him.

A fine rain was falling over Tokyo. The narrow and crowded streets of Shinjiku were wet, but the air smelled fresh and almost clean. Kurai felt elated as he walked to his car, parked on the street a block down from the entrance of the apartment building. He opened the back door and got in, waking up the sleeping driver by slamming the door. "To the office," he said curtly, pulling out his handkerchief from his back pocket to wipe the rain off his eyeglasses.

In midafternoon traffic, it would take them about forty minutes to drive back to the Fuji Kosan offices on Nagata-cho. But this afternoon Kurai's mind was too occupied to be bothered by the traffic. KPC had accepted the principle of swapping equity crude for his small refinery. And he had a great Japanese partner. He still couldn't understand why a large and prestigious trading firm like C. Itoh had agreed to go into partnership with a dubious outfit like Fuji Kosan, or with an equally dubious character like him. His operation was the black sheep of the Japanese Motouri. A small, unprofitable refinery that handled mostly fuel oil, some naphtha and kerosene, but no gasoline, which was the prize profit-making product that kept most refiners financially afloat those days. He and Fuji Kosan had been a financial burden on MITI for years. In keeping with established tradition, MITI, the mother hen of Japanese industry, could not allow Fuji Kosan to go under. It had to be subsidized and kept in business.

MITI's efforts to merge Fuji Kosan with a larger, more profitable Japanese oil company had failed. It wouldn't be that easy to get rid of Kurai. He was a hustler. He had set so many conditions that none of the larger companies would come near him. Most considered it beneath themselves to even negotiate with Kurai. Why merge with a losing company and put up with this most obnoxious executive? MITI couldn't deal with Fuji Kosan as an isolated case. In the broader scheme of things, it was too small a problem. Kurai was a symptom of a mismanaged sector of Japanese industry.

What MITI didn't know yet was that Kurai was about to present a far more difficult problem for its bureaucracy than financial drainage. He would launch a campaign to repeal the law that prevented foreigners from owning more than 50 percent of a Japanese refining company. This would raise an uproar in the Motouri brotherhood and threaten the Protocol. Kurai understood that well.

But he was not without supporters. Times were changing. The world was turning anti-Japan. Japan's huge trade surpluses were a thorn in the sides of industrialized countries. How many U.S. senators had gained

political visibility and prominence by Japan bashing? Kurai had followed religiously the development of these sentiments in the United
States. Non-tariff barriers had become a household phrase. Economists
talked about it, senators talked about it, congressmen talked about it.
Presidential candidates were building their campaigns around the issue of
trade reform. In America, trade reform meant "let's get even with Japan!"

And the issue had gone beyond trade. Japan's enormous trade surplus had to be invested somewhere, mostly outside of the country,
where cheap labor and abundant natural resources made such investments far more viable than in Japan. Foreign investments were also
a must to camouflage Japan's growing trade surplus. What Japanese
companies produced abroad and sold in foreign markets all over the
world wouldn't count as Japanese exports. "Reciprocity" was the catch
phrase now. Kurai believed that it too would soon become a household
phrase in the States, if it hadn't already.

If Japanese companies could go and buy anything they fancied abroad,
then foreign companies would sooner or later have to be allowed to buy
into Japan. Japan had to learn how to become a more responsible member
of the international community.

And what better place to start than the oil sector, the Achilles heel
of Japanese industry? Let the foreigners in! Let them buy into the ail-
ing and outdated Motouri brotherhood. Maybe that would shake some
sense into the antiquated system. Deregulation. I challenge you, oh
great MITI, thought Kurai, to put your money where your mouth
is. What a great saying. For all their immature and unwise practices,
Americans can still come up with sayings that our thousand-year-old
culture has failed to produce.

But this is not about America, Kurai thought. This is about Kuwait.
This is about the Arabs. The same elitist society that looks at Fuji Kosan
as an outcast is going to fight the intrusion of inferior people into Japan.
We who buy out Americans and train them in our ways are going to
accept working under the direction of Kuwaitis! Oh, yes. They will fight
it. Japan has regained its old pride. The humiliation of defeat in World
War II has gradually been replaced by a new superiority complex.

In every field ... except in oil. That's the difference.

This may be about Kuwait, but it's also about oil. That will be my
argument. That's the simple fact, which even the pompous Mitsubishi

can't refute. Here is where we have no right to introduce pride into the picture. With one small deal I'll achieve what they have failed to achieve. I'll set a precedent. And I'll upset the hierarchy.

They passed in front of a dilapidated building as two young lovers emerged from the gate. They were holding hands, the girl leaning on the young man, her head on his shoulder, swaying as she walked. A third rate "Love Hotel," that's what the dilapidated building was. The type of institution that had turned the Shinjiku district into a haven for young and broke lovers. Cheap rents. Rooms by the hour. Shameless public displays of affection and passion. Yes, times had changed, Kurai thought. Ask the young people of Japan. Do they feel humiliated about their country's defeat in the war? Do they feel proud of their country's achievements since then? Do they feel superior? Don't fool yourself, MITI. Don't fight the inevitable. You've already lost what you're so desperately trying to defend. Just look at your young people in Shinjiku, not the pompous young executives of Mitsubishi. Japan's future is already no different than the rest of the world's. What the Americans failed to destroy by force, they have already destroyed by peace. The Japanese won't be different from anybody else when these kids reach my age.

Kurai jumped out of the car in front of his office building. He decided to take the stairs. The old brick building had a tiny and terribly slow elevator. Fuji Kosan's offices were on the third floor, and Kurai normally would not go up the two flights of stairs by foot, because it was not becoming of a chief executive. But that afternoon he was too impatient to wait for the elevator. Not because he had kept Noburo Sato, their contact at C. Itoh, waiting for almost an hour and a half, but because he was anxious to hear the details of the progress made in Kuwait. In fact, it was good that Sato had to wait for him so long. Let them get used to it.

He went straight to the small conference room adjacent to his office, where he knew his assistant, Shinji Kawasaki, and Sato would be waiting. He opened the door without knocking and burst in. Kawasaki and Sato jumped to their feet.

"I came as fast as I could," Kurai said as he returned Sato's bow. He ignored Kawasaki altogether. "What's the latest from the Middle East?"

"We have good news and bad news," Sato said coldly, resenting Kurai's treatment of him as a messenger. He was a senior executive at

C. Itoh. The annual budget of his division alone was several times larger than the entire turnover of Fuji Kosan.

"Bad news? What bad news?" Kurai raised his voice. His gaze moved to Kawasaki. "I was not told of any bad news over the telephone an hour-and-a-half ago!"

"Kurai-san. Perhaps it's best if we first hear what Sato-san has to say," answered Kawasaki sheepishly. It wasn't the first time Kawasaki had felt embarrassed for his boss's manners.

"KPC absolutely refuses to grant us any production rights inside Kuwait," stated Sato.

"*What!* Kawasaki-san, I thought you told me that the oil equity issue was satisfactorily resolved. I rushed to get back to hear *this?*"

"That's the bad news," Sato continued, ignoring Kurai's outburst. He watched Kurai for a few seconds, enjoying his annoyance.

"The good news is that KPC agrees to give us production rights *outside* Kuwait. They're prepared to make a more generous offer if we accept this condition."

"Outside Kuwait?" asked Kurai, trying to compose himself. "What rights outside Kuwait? What do *they* have outside Kuwait?"

"They have some now, they will have more by next year, and much more in the future."

"Next year! In the future! Next year is next year. What do they have *now?*"

"We can give you the details in writing, Kurai-san. They have production in Australia, Egypt, and Tunisia, and they have significant exploration rights in China, Indonesia, and South Yemen. In addition, they'll be getting new concessions in Australia, Thailand, and China. But these are confidential at this stage. Now, are you interested in what they've proposed?" Sato's voice was cold and stern.

"Of course I'm interested in what they've proposed," snapped Kurai. "I just want to make sure they can deliver."

"Well, that's a legitimate concern, Kurai-san. But you certainly can't judge whether or not they can deliver if you don't know what it is that they've offered, can you?"

"Okay, Sato-san. Tell me what they've proposed." Kurai was furious. Things weren't as neat and straightforward as the telephone call that had disturbed his afternoon had led him to believe. He had let his imagination get the better of him. And to top it all, this messenger from C. Itoh had the nerve to patronize him. The only reason that KPC was even talking to them was *his* refinery. That's what they wanted. *He* had what they wanted. No other refiner in Japan would have the courage to stand up to MITI and propose what he had proposed.

"The KPC proposal is this," Sato said calmly, handing Kurai a twelve-page document from his briefcase. "I'm sure you'll want to study it carefully. I can outline the main points now, if you wish."

Kurai leafed through the document with mounting anxiety. After a few minutes he put the document on the small coffee table. "Proceed," he told Sato.

"The main points are the following: They'll guarantee us 45,000 barrels per day of equity crude oil for a period of twenty-five years. That's almost double what we had originally thought we could secure."

"Why are they willing to be so generous?" interrupted Kurai, almost jumping from his seat. "You know I don't believe in pleasant surprises!"

"Kurai-san, please let me finish," said Sato. "When I'm done, you might not think of this as either pleasant or surprising." Then, as if the interruption had never occurred, he continued.

"Ten-thousand barrels per day takes effect immediately after signing the final contract. The balance comes in different phases, to be completed within three years of signing. This volume can come from several different production facilities in several different countries. The exact composition is at their discretion, and we have no say in it."

Sato stopped for a second, expecting another interruption from Kurai, but it did not come. Kurai leaned back on the sofa, listening intently.

"They agree to pay $100 million up front, upon signing," continued Sato. "The balance of the $250 million total price—which they agree with, even though they pointed out to us that it was a highly exaggerated valuation of the Fuji Kosan refinery—will be paid through a 50 percent discount of the price of equity oil that we lift. Exact details of the proposed pricing formula will be worked out when the grade and source of oil is determined. Some examples are worked out in the document."

Sato stopped again and looked at Kawasaki, then at Kurai. They looked back at him expectantly. He's beginning to get the picture, thought Sato. "When the discounts fully cover the remaining $150 million, including finance charges, we will pay 85 percent of the market price for our equity crude. At today's prices, they would cover their debt in about a year-and-a-half—twice as fast as we had originally anticipated."

"And you don't think all this is too good to be true? Assuming, of course, that they could deliver all that you've mentioned so far." This time Kurai's voice was as calm as Sato's. He had not even moved. He was leaning back and gazing at Sato.

"There's more," stated Sato, ignoring the remark. "They will also allow us to participate in their future upstream investments in the Far East. They will allow us to buy up to 10 percent of any upstream venture they start in the Far East after we sign the contract. At cost."

"They sure know how to bait us, don't they," Kurai said so softly that Kawasaki couldn't hear him. "I wonder if they know about the Motouri Protocol."

"In return for all this," said Sato, again pretending that Kurai had not spoken, "they want three things. First ..."

"First, my refinery," interrupted Kurai.

"No, Kurai-san. Three things *in addition* to 100 percent ownership of the Fuji Kosan refinery. First, it will be up to us to convince MITI to change the rules of foreign ownership. KPC will not participate in this campaign in any way. They do not even want their name to be involved with the campaign. We will have to achieve this without reference to them or their merits."

"That's what's really in it for them, isn't it?"

"I think that's a fair statement. They think we'll need ..."

"They want us to change the rules for them!" Kurai interrupted again. "Once we change the rules, they can do anything they want. They can buy anything. Once we change the rules, they don't have to offer such attractive deals ever again."

Kurai was on a roll. He had seen an important piece of the puzzle from the Kuwaiti perspective.

"They think we'll need at least two years to accomplish this," said Sato. "Maybe three. By that time they expect to have over 150,000 barrels per day of crude oil production outside Kuwait. They'll be able to deliver."

"Okay, Sato-san. Maybe they will. What's their next condition?"

"Second, they want us to guarantee marketing contracts with Fuji Kosan's current dealers for at least five years from the date of signing the contract. Obviously, we cannot help you here. It's up to you to secure a five-year purchase agreement with your current dealers. For the full capacity of the Fuji Kosan refinery. Is that feasible?"

"It can be arranged," said Kurai. "Given the right incentives."

"We leave that up to you," repeated Sato.

"And third?" asked Kurai, sensing Sato's hesitation to continue.

"And third, they want to change the timing of your 'no repeat' condition."

"*Impossible!*" shouted Kurai. "The 'no repeat' condition is *absolute*. And you know very well why."

"They do not want to repeal it, Kurai-san. Just change the timing."

"To what?"

"To one year."

"*Impossible!*"

"They feel strongly that five years would be too long. But they can commit themselves not to enter into similar agreements with any other Japanese Motouri for one year after the contract is signed. They will not offer equity oil or production rights to any other Japanese company for one year."

"That doesn't give us enough time, and you know it. The others can secure bigger deals than we can. Once we change the rules and make it possible for them. We'll lose in the end."

"That's why they've offered us the option of buying into their future upstream investments. With that option, we still have a good chance. We don't *have* to lose."

"So they *do know* about the Motouri Protocol!" snapped Kurai, sounding as if he had managed to trick Sato into admitting something he didn't want to admit.

"I don't know how much they know," said Sato. He was beginning to show his impatience. "We haven't told them anything. Frankly, it doesn't matter. We have to judge the proposal on its own merits."

"They *have* to know. They couldn't have structured an offer like this without knowing. What does your management think?"

The reference did not escape Sato. Kurai still did not consider him an equal. But he had decided not to allow that to interfere with the business at hand. He wanted to finish the meeting and get out as fast as possible.

"About what?" he asked coldly, returning Kurai's gaze.

"About the offer, of course."

"Well, *I* think it's a good offer. By the way, it is not negotiable. Take it or leave it. That's what we've been told. And we have only one week to respond. After one week, the offer is void."

Kurai wanted to be left alone. He had to digest all of this in peace. Those Arabs were certainly not as stupid as he'd thought; in fact, this was the smartest offer they could have made. And they couldn't have made it if they didn't know exactly what he was fighting for. He had to go back to Shinjiku and surrender his body to the able hands of Kyoko. And think. Think calmly. Sato was right. It didn't matter what or how much KPC knew, as long as the plan allowed him to win.

"Thank you, Sato-san," Kurai said with unexpected courtesy. "We will study the offer carefully and get back to you soon. Please give my regards to your management."

"There's one more thing," stated Sato as Kurai stood up. It was an awkward moment. Kurai couldn't decide whether he should sit down again or continue the conversation while standing. Sato had remained seated in the same position. Kawasaki was feeling uncomfortable too, unable to decide whether to stand up after his boss or to remain seated.

"What is it?" asked Kurai finally, still on his feet, looking down at Sato across the coffee table.

"Upon your insistence, we tried to find out if KPC was trying to secretly negotiate with other companies in Japan." Sato stopped, waiting for Kurai to take a seat.

"Yes?" Kurai's patience was running thin.

"We thought you should know how that went." Sato stopped again and glanced at the sofa where Kurai had been sitting.

"Well? How *did* it go?" Kurai asked as he gave in and sat back down.

"It backfired," said Sato.

"*Backfired*? What do you mean it backfired?"

"We sent a person to Kuwait to find out if KPC was planning any new acquisitions in the Far East. One of our regular consultants. After one day in Kuwait, he figured out that we had misled him. He demanded an explanation. We had to tell him."

"You *had* to tell him?" shouted Kurai, his calm and good manners lost. "And what exactly did you have to tell him?"

"We had to tell him that we were negotiating with KPC, and that we had a partner in Japan."

"I see. And did you have to tell him what you were negotiating about?"

"Yes, we did."

"I see. And did you also *have* to tell him the name of your partner in Japan?"

"Yes, we did."

"I see. And what is *his* name, this boy scout of yours?"

"His name is James Blackburn. And he's not a boy scout. He's the best in his field. He knows the people we're dealing with, the people who might change our future, better than *we'll* ever know them."

"I see. And I guess you'll insist that this disclosure could not have been avoided."

"Yes, Kurai-san. I will insist on that. May I remind you that this whole idea was yours? May I also remind you that we warned you about precisely this type of outcome? I believe my exact words were, 'You can't ask questions without giving people ideas.'"

"Yes. You might have said something like that."

"I did."

"Do you trust this—what's his name? Blackburn?"

"Yes. We trust Blackburn-san. We've known him for many years and he has never broken a confidence."

"Well, then, I guess there's no damage."

"There may not be any damage, but the story doesn't end there. KPC also figured out that it was us who sent Blackburn on this fact-finding mission. They were not amused."

"Ah, so? And what did *they* say?"

"They said if we did not trust them we shouldn't have talked to them in the first place."

"That's all?"

"That's all. That's enough for us. We had to apologize to Blackburn-san, and we had to apologize to KPC."

"Who at KPC told you that?" asked Kurai. He did not seem to be interested in C. Itoh's apologies.

"The main mastermind behind Kuwait's Far East strategy told us that. His name is Ramzi Amin."

Kurai had heard Amin's name, but was not sure how to process the information. He thought for a moment.

"Well, since they made their generous proposal anyway, I guess no harm has been done. I still say it was important that we investigated, just in case ..."

"No, Kurai-san." It was Sato's turn to interrupt. "It was *not* important that we investigate. We knew that all along, and we tried to explain it to you. In the end, we agreed to do it to pacify you. And, as I said, it backfired. Now we have promised KPC that we will not behave in that manner again. We have every intention of keeping our promise. And since we are conducting the negotiations in Kuwait, you will have to accept our judgment on such matters from now on."

Sato waited a few minutes for a reaction from Kurai. But there was none. He wasn't sure whether Kurai had actually understood what he had said, or would remember it in the future. Sato didn't care.

He stood up. "I believe I've covered everything now," he declared. "I expect to hear from you in due course. Goodbye."

Kurai and Kawasaki stood up together. The three men were quiet as they walked out of the small conference room and into the lobby of the Fuji Kosan offices. At the door, Sato turned around and bowed. They returned his bow. As he stepped out of the door, Kurai walked after him.

"By the way," he said, "did your boy scout find out anything about what was worrying us?"

"Kurai-san," answered Sato, showing his utter dismay at Kurai's insensitivity. "We are no longer interested in pursuing that issue. The KPC proposal speaks for itself. Please get back to us as soon as possible."

*   *   *

It was a private joke between Akio Miyazaki, the director general of MITI's Agency of Natural Resources and Energy, and Makoto Itai, the director of the Petroleum Department of the same agency. It had started almost a year ago. When Itai's third attempt to merge Fuji Kosan with a larger oil company failed, he had walked into Miyazaki's room.

"Kurai slipped again," he said. And he was pleasantly surprised when Miyazaki just smiled.

"That reminds me of an interesting quote," Miyazaki said. "'All oil relationships are slippery.' It is attributed to Calouste Gulbenkian, also known as 'Mr. Five Percent.' Have you heard about him?"

"Yes, I have," Itai answered.

"He was arguably the founder of Iraq Petroleum Company and quite a master in handling slippery relationships. I wonder how he would have handled Kurai. In any case, it is an appropriate quote, don't you think?"

"Yes," answered Itai, relieved that his boss found humor in their failed attempt to close the books on Fuji Kosan. "It fits Kurai perfectly."

"The slippery samurai." Miyazaki laughed.

Now, a week after Sato's visit to Fuji Kosan, Itai called Miyazaki.

"Miyazaki-san, sorry to disturb you," he said almost in a panic. "We have to talk, urgently, if possible."

"What's the matter?"

"The slippery samurai has struck again. This time greasier and more slippery than ever."

XIII

Kicking Ass

I ssam Al-Tikriti arrived at the offices of Petroleum Consulting Group Inc. a few minutes early for his 11 a.m. appointment with James Blackburn. He was a small man, barely five feet tall, weighing about 120 pounds. In his early fifties, he felt full of energy. His thick, bushy eyebrows were the most pronounced feature on his otherwise bald head and clean-shaven face, but they did not conceal his small, dark eyes, which had a permanent luster and moved constantly, as if unable to focus on any one object for more than a few moments. The vest of his gray suit was buttoned tight, emphasizing his smallness.

This was only the second time that Blackburn and Al-Tikriti had met. Gene Theiss had introduced them two months earlier. Al-Tikriti had just arrived from Baghdad, where he had presented the Iraqi government with an offer from GE to build a hydroelectric plant near that city. Blackburn had immediately recognized that Al-Tikriti's contacts in Iraq were substantial. Theiss was the most credible person Blackburn knew in Washington. So he skipped the routine background check he usually carried out on people with connections. He later found out that Al-Tikriti also had connections in the Reagan Administration and that on several occasions he had served as the unofficial liaison between the Iraqi and U.S. governments.

Al-Tikriti's energy and enthusiasm were contagious. He greeted Blackburn warmly, accepted his offer of coffee with a hearty "that would be absolutely great!" and sat down, his eyes scanning Blackburn's office with a rapid but methodical sweep.

"We're all set. We'll catch the 12:30 Pan Am shuttle and should be at A. Nitzen by 2:30 easily. But first tell me, you got in okay? Everything was in order?" asked Blackburn, as soon as he had asked his secretary to bring in some coffee.

"Oh, yes. Yesterday afternoon. Everything was great. Just great." Eyes shining, smile beaming, Al-Tikriti was radiant. This is odd, thought Blackburn, who had not known anybody from Iraq to be so outgoing with somebody they had just met; those who had dealings with the Iraqi government were particularly cold and reserved. Most officials at the embassy did not even know how to smile, at least not in public.

Although Al-Tikriti was not a government official, he dealt with the Iraqi government and maintained a private office in the Iraqi Embassy building in Washington, DC. Al-Tikriti's official description of his occupation was "retired public servant." Blackburn had considered it impolite to ask any further questions.

"You've been to Baghdad again since we last met, right? How are things there these days?" asked Blackburn, closing the door of his office.

"Just great, Jim. As I'm sure you know they have been taking back a lot of lost territory from Iran. Morale is high, the Iranians are tired, and the president is determined to recapture every inch of Iraqi soil lost to Iran."

"Iraq's oil production has increased a lot, too," added Blackburn in the same upbeat tone as Al-Tikriti's. "I understand they're pumping 2.8 million barrels per day now."

When the Iran-Iraq war had started eight years earlier, Iraq's oil production had plunged from 3.5 million barrels per day to about 1 million barrels, and had stayed at that low level for over three years. Blackburn had been amazed at how the Iraqi government managed to conduct the war during the early years, with both oil production and oil prices cut by two-thirds and oil revenues at rock bottom. True, the other Arab states of the Gulf, particularly Saudi Arabia and Kuwait, were pouring in financial help, but that was no substitute for the huge drain on government finances. During the first two years of the war, Iraq had exhausted its foreign reserves, some $25 billion, and started to borrow heavily. But more remarkable than all this for Blackburn was the speed with which Iraq had managed to build new export channels and expand the old ones. By late 1987, Iraq was pumping about 2.8 million barrels per day, almost three times as much as it had produced from 1982 through 1985.

"Oh, yes," Al-Tikriti said. "Now they can easily do 2.8. If they had the export channels, they could do four, maybe even five million barrels per day. Iraq now is producing more that Iran, you know. And they're busy at SOMO, Jim, *very* busy. They had to move from selling only 700,000 barrels per day to more than 2.4 million. Can you imagine? Domestic needs are still around 300,000 barrels a day, so they export the rest."

SOMO was the State Oil Marketing Organization that handled all of Iraq's oil sales.

"Well, here is where A. Nitzen could be of some help," said Blackburn, happy that they were finally on the issue at hand. "In a few years they have become the largest oil traders in the world. They surpassed Pool Oil on trade volume this year. Do you know much about them?"

"Just what you told me on the phone the other day. Tell me more."

There was a knock on the door and Blackburn's secretary entered with the coffee. She was a short, heavyset woman, in her early forties, with traces of gray in her short dark hair. She greeted Al-Tikriti with a polite 'excuse me' as she set the mugs on the small coffee table. Blackburn introduced her to Al-Tikriti. "This is Linda. She's the only one in the whole world who knows all my secrets and the only one who can control my life," he said, joking. "And this is Mr. Al-Tikriti. You better practice that name, Linda. I have a feeling we'll be hearing from him often from now on."

"Well I'm delighted!" Al-Tikriti had already stood up to shake Linda's hand. "But you might as well forget the Mr. Al-Tikriti business. If you're going to practice pronouncing any names, practice Issam. That's my first name."

"Thank you, Issam," said Linda, genuinely charmed by the man. "It's a pleasure meeting you."

"Thank *you*," said Al-Tikriti, pointing to the coffee, "and the pleasure is all mine."

Blackburn noticed how quickly Al-Tikriti had won over Linda. He hadn't been in his office for more than a few minutes and he already had an ally.

"Well, as I was saying," he said after she had left the room and closed the door behind her. "They are now the largest oil traders in the world. On a good day, these guys trade more than forty million barrels! That's between physical crude and products and the futures market. Forty million barrels in one day. That's almost as much as the total free world production."

Even as he spoke, Blackburn was aware that he was adopting Al-Tikriti's flamboyant style. This was another one on Blackburn's fabled list of consultants' trade secrets. Adopt your client's frame of mind. Get on his wavelength. Try to think like he does. That's the only way you'll understand what his questions really mean.

"Also," he said in the same animated tone, "they are a fully owned subsidiary of Kramer Brothers, one of the most respected securities firms on Wall Street, as I'm sure you know. Roughly speaking, we're talking about $5 billion of capital backing them, give or take a few hundred million."

"That's just great, Jim. You know how people from my part of the world are. Credibility means everything. But do you think they can handle 100,000 barrels per day? It's so easy to get burned in this game, you know. If for any reason A. Nitzen cannot lift the crude later on, we all lose, you know. I lose credibility, you lose credibility, and of course they lose credibility."

"That's one thing you won't have to worry about. Did I tell you they own a refinery? A large, state of the art, 300,000 barrel-per-day refinery? I'm sure you've heard of Jade Petroleum. They understand the business. They buy and sell crude oil cargoes every day. They refine 300,000 barrels every day. They manage a ten-million-barrel storage facility every day."

"That's fascinating, Jim."

"In any case, you'll meet them soon. I'm sure you'll form your own sense of how much they can do."

"Yes. Very good, Jim. You understand me well. Because once I go to Iraq with a proposal, we cannot back down. I will lose face."

"We'll make sure that does not happen. Now, how do you think SOMO will react to the price-hedge idea? Nitzen is interested in that."

"Explain that to me again, if you don't mind. I want to be 100 percent sure I understand it first, before I can present it to SOMO."

Blackburn lit another cigarette. This was the most important part of the bargain. Simmons had insisted on it. "No direct market-related pricing," he had said. "We'll take all the downside risk, and share the upside risk."

"It is both simple and ingenious," started Blackburn. "Let me explain it by an example. Suppose the market price for Kirkuk blend now is $13 per barrel. They will guarantee $12.50 per barrel, no matter how low prices fall in the future. You can look at the 50 cent difference as your insurance premium. If prices drop to 10, Iraq still gets 12.50; if they drop to 8, Iraq still gets 12.50. And if prices rise above 13, they split the difference 50-50. For example, if the price of Kirkuk blend goes to 14, Iraq gets 13.50, Nitzen gets the 50 cents. Of course the exact numbers have to be negotiated, but this is the idea."

"Fine. You say if prices fall to 10, for example, they will still pay SOMO 12.50. They will lose $2.50 per barrel. On 100,000 barrels per day, that's a loss of $250,000 per day, every day. How can they live with that? How can they afford that?"

"No Issam, no. They don't lose a cent. They hedge the whole thing in the futures and options markets. If you're interested, one day we'll talk about how they do that. But believe me, it is possible to hedge the risk. What they're offering Iraq is essentially an insurance policy that protects SOMO against any future price collapse, at least for a small part of their total sales. This can come in handy the way things have been going the past few days."

"I see, I see," said Al-Tikriti, obviously thinking about the implications of all this. In the past few days alone oil prices had crashed by over $3 per barrel, and SOMO was facing more and more competition from rapidly increasing oil supplies from other producers. Something like this should appeal to them a lot, he thought. Not only do they get a secure outlet for 100,000 barrels per day, but they're also guaranteed a price floor. Maybe next year or even in a few months we can increase the volume. And if prices do crash, the Iraqis will be grateful to me. Very grateful indeed.

"I think it's definitely worth trying," Blackburn said, as if he had read Al-Tikriti's mind. "Who knows, if this works out maybe we can raise the volume."

"Jim, I agree that it's worth trying. But I have to have *absolute* guarantees that the Nitzen people will act exactly as I tell them. Iraq is not like the other Gulf countries. There are no agents, bribes, or princes. Commissions and middlemen, which are the only ways to do business in the rest of the Gulf, are forbidden by law in Iraq. We have to deal directly with the government, and everything has to be above board and professional. This whole thing must also remain confidential. If word gets out that Iraq is even talking to Kramer Brothers, the deal will be off before it starts."

Blackburn lit another cigarette and took a sip of coffee. Al-Tikriti would not have said all this if he had not seen the possibilities of forging a relationship between SOMO and A. Nitzen. "We are dealing with professionals who understand all that," he said. "We won't face breach of confidentiality."

He checked the Reuters screen on his desk. The futures price of West Texas Intermediate for the May contract was trading at $14.53 per barrel. It was 11:50 a.m.

"We have to head for the airport," Blackburn said, rising from his chair. "I think we'll have a productive afternoon in New York. And we'll explain all your concerns to Simmons."

Blackburn called the car service company after they landed at La Guardia. They stopped at the Vista International Hotel to check Al-Tikriti in while the car waited, and then drove to Wall Street, to A. Nitzen & Company. During the forty-five-minute flight and later in the car, they talked about the financial arrangement that Al-Tikriti should propose to Simmons. They agreed that three cents a barrel was the minimum Al-Tikriti should have if he could arrange the contract. On 100,000 barrels a day, that meant Al-Tikriti's commissions would amount to over a million dollars per year. Not bad for a retired public servant, whatever the hell that means, thought Blackburn as they drove into Manhattan. In addition, Simmons had to pay five cents a barrel to PCG, Blackburn's Petroleum Consulting Group. So Al-Tikriti had to make sure the deal was profitable enough for A. Nitzen after all these costs were deducted.

They arrived at the offices of A. Nitzen & Company at about 2:40 p.m. Simmons was all smiles when he came out to the reception area to greet his guests.

"Jim, my man!" he yelled. "My *main* man."

He had reason to be cheerful and happy. Going against his instincts and the advice of his aides, he had refused to cover any of his short positions when the market had soared the previous week. Now A. Nitzen's oil trading account was $31 million richer. All in a week and a half.

Simmons turned his attention to Al-Tikriti. "And this must be Issam," he beamed again, shaking his hand with great energy. "A pleasure meeting you! Jim here has told us a lot about you. Come in, come in. I'd like to show you around our little operation before we get down to business."

Stanley Simmons was a short, husky man in his early thirties. Slightly balding, with small eyes and thin, very thin, lips. His hips and thighs were too bulky compared with his upper body, giving him a pear-shaped look, which belied his otherwise muscular build. Despite his rimless glasses and striped shirt, Simmons did not fit Al-Tikriti's mental image of a typical, aggressive Wall Street type.

They entered a side door from the reception area, passed through a short hallway, and came into a large open hall cluttered with desks, screens, and telephones. There were no individual offices except for a few located around the corners. Clusters of desks stretched through the entire open floor space, with hundreds of people shouting into telephones.

"This is the oil trading group," explained Simmons as they approached the first cluster of desks. Blackburn knew all the traders here. Simmons introduced them to Al-Tikriti: Mike Goldberg, Steve Summers, George Ackley, Tom Bricks, Andy Zeller, and Jon Solomon. The ones who could not get off the phone gave a thumbs-up to Blackburn, smiling apologetically for not being able to interrupt their business, and quickly turned back to their screens. The twelve metal desks that formed the oil cluster had a center aisle of eight desks, arranged in two rows of four desks each. There were two desks at each end of this formation. A dozen Reuters and Telerate screens cluttered the desktops, with telephone handsets hooked to wires that popped out of holes drilled on the desks adding to the muddle. The oil-trading group consisted of fourteen people huddled around this twelve-desk formation.

"Jim, what can I tell you man, you called it. You really called this one," Andy Zeller told Blackburn. He was the most risk averse in the bunch and had argued with Simmons to cover some of their positions at a loss.

"Once in a while I get lucky," Blackburn answered with such exaggerated and obviously fake modesty that everybody within hearing started to laugh. Then he approached the screen to check the latest prices. May was down to 14.03.

"It's come off fifty cents since we left Washington," he told Zeller without looking up from the screen. "How far do you think it will go?"

"If it closes below 14, it can drop another buck next week," said Zeller; "14 is major support. If it closes above 14, you might see a short-covering rally on Monday."

This was one aspect of the market that Blackburn had not been able to fully understand. They called it technical analysis—a whole different level of Leaky Faucets to Blackburn. The technical analysts identified support and resistance levels, based simply on the charts of past price movements. Support was a price level that would trigger significant buying interest, making it difficult for prices to fall further. Resistance was a price level that would trigger significant selling interest, making it difficult for prices to rise further. But if prices did break below the support level, they could fall sharply and rapidly to the next support line. The same was true if prices broke above a resistance line. In addition, technicians distinguished between major and minor support and resistance levels. Between two major support levels there could be several minor support levels.

According to Andy Zeller, who was the chief technician of A. Nitzen's oil trading group and who believed in his technical indicators more than anything else, $14 per barrel was a major support level for May WTI. If prices did not fall below 14, traders would assume the support was holding and would start to buy, bidding the prices back up again. (Initially those with short positions would buy to cover their positions and book their profits, and later new buyers would enter the market to establish long positions.) But if May prices fell below 14, then traders would know that the major support could not hold, and everybody would expect prices to fall rapidly to the next major support line, which, according to Zeller, was $13.20 per barrel. With this expectation, everybody would try to sell, causing prices to fall. As in most commodity markets, widespread expectations, when acted upon, turned into self-fulfilling prophecies.

May prices were still hovering around the $14 per barrel level: 14.02, 14.01, 14.00, 14.03, 14.02.

"It may need a small push after all," Zeller said to no one in particular, and Blackburn noticed how everybody around the cluster started to pay attention to his every move. It was 3:02 p.m., and the crude oil market would close in exactly eight minutes. Zeller picked up the phone and pushed the direct-line button to the Merc floor. "It's beginning to slow down," the Nitzen floor broker told him amid the hysterical noise and commotion coming from the crude pit. "It's thinner. It's mostly the locals who're buying—they're holding support."

"Get ready ..." Zeller mumbled after he put down the receiver, again to no one in particular. But suddenly the oil traders were quiet, and the tension around the twelve desks seemed to rise by the second. Everybody had their telephones to their ears, eyes jumping from the screen to Zeller.

"Get this guy out of here," Zeller whispered to Blackburn, gesturing with his head toward Al-Tikriti. "I don't want him to see this."

"What are you going to do?" asked Blackburn, his senses on full alert and his curiosity at its peak.

"Just get him out of here. Tell Stan to take him around!" Zeller whispered again impatiently. But Simmons had already taken Al-Tikriti by the arm and was casually directing him toward the next cluster. "This is the metals trading group; they do mainly gold, silver, and platinum. Over there is the currency desk. Behind them are the coffee and cotton traders."

It was 3:06 p.m. Four minutes to go. Prices had still not dipped below $14: 14.01, 14.02, 14.00, 14.03, 14.05, 14.04 ...

Zeller lifted his right hand and pointed at Mike Goldberg. "Go!" Goldberg said quietly into the telephone. A few seconds later the numbers on the screen started to change faster, briefly dipping below 14, but coming back up again: 14.03, 14.02, 14.03, 14.00, 13.99, 13.98, 13.97, 13.96, 13.98, 13.99, 14.00, 14.01. Zeller lifted his hand again and pointed at George Ackley. "Go!" Ackley said into the telephone: 14.02, 14.00, 13.98, 13.95, 13.96, 13.94, 13.93, 13.90 ...

It was 3:09 p.m. "We may be home free," whispered Zeller, but the tension did not subside. The others were waiting, on full alert, in case they got the signal from Zeller at the last second. But Zeller did not move. The prices were well below $14: 13.90, 13.89, 13.88, 13.85, in quick succession. It was 3:10 p.m. and a bell rang on Zeller's desk. The market was closed. Relief spread around the twelve desks. Everyone started talking again.

"What the hell happened here?" asked Blackburn, without even attempting to hide his astonishment. He knew he had witnessed an operation of almost military precision, but was unable to guess what exactly had transpired. But the traders around the oil cluster were too busy unwinding to take notice of him. Ackley and Goldberg had sunk in their chairs, watching the dead screen with satisfaction.

"Andy, what the hell happened?" repeated Blackburn as he walked over to where Zeller was standing.

"It's called kicking ass, Jim," explained Zeller, pleased with himself, and mimicking with a kick to his desk. "It needed a push to close below 14. So we gave it a push. That's all."

Andy Zeller was clearly in his element that afternoon. A week earlier, during the OPEC/non-OPEC meetings, his technical indicators had been useless. Support and resistance lines were broken by the slightest rumor from the Marriott lobby in Vienna. But now that the OPEC storm had passed and the dust had settled, Zeller was king of the market. The outcome of the meeting had long ago become public knowledge. But who was to say how low prices would fall? Well, Zeller would. He would *make* the market from here on. This was his turf, where even Blackburn, the great hero this week, was no match for his skill.

Blackburn later found out that four traders around the twelve desks had standing orders to sell pre-specified volumes with the floor brokers, who were waiting for the go-ahead for execution. Goldberg had only 100 contracts. Ackley had 200. Bricks 300. Solomon 400. On the floor, the brokers had the phones to their ears. Goldberg's "Go!" had released the first 100 sell orders. Ackley's, the next 200. Had it been necessary, Zeller would have unleashed Bricks and Solomon too, with 700 more contracts. But it was not necessary.

After the market closed, Simmons, Blackburn, and Al-Tikriti went to one of the private offices in the corner and closed the door. It did not take long to strike a deal along the lines that Blackburn had worked out with Al-Tikriti on the flight up to New York.

XIV

To Isolate an Ayatollah

ssam Al-Tikriti lifted the antique brass knocker and let it fall against the door of the historic mansion in Old Town Alexandria. He waited for a few minutes, then knocked again, with greater force. When he heard footsteps inside, he moved a step away from the door and felt his excitement rise. He had much to tell Gene Theiss, the sixty-seven-year-old retired U.S. Foreign Service officer.

It was only fitting that Theiss would be his contact man in the administration. He had started his career forty-three years ago, as the political officer in the American consulate in Basra, Iraq. Although he had then moved to numerous posts in the Middle East and Asia, Iraq had remained the cradle of his Foreign Service career. And Theiss knew Iraq, even if it was a totally different country in those days. He could tell war stories about the American-British power struggle of the 1940s in Iraq and how the Iraqi faction supported by the British won. But he would not talk about all this as a historian. He would not talk about it as an eyewitness, either. The only way Theiss would talk about this—or any other subject—would be as a *participant* in events. If he had not been a participant, Theiss would not have opinions. "I don't know," he'd say. "I was not there."

The heavy door swung open and Gene Theiss greeted Al-Tikriti with his understated formality.

"Hullo, Issam. Come in, please."

Neither man talked again until they were seated in the library. The short walk from the entrance hall was enough to give visitors the impression that they were in a museum. It was filled with antiques collected from all over the world during Theiss' lifetime of Foreign Service appointments in Iraq, Egypt, Lebanon, Jordan, India, and Sri Lanka. In fact, with the exception of the kitchen utensils, there was little in the fully furnished twenty-room mansion from the twentieth century. Al-Tikriti often wondered whether Theiss' obsession with antiques was acquired during his travels, or whether it was the innate fascination of the old man with antiques that made his travels more tolerable and enjoyable. But it was never easy to analyze a man like Theiss.

The library had not changed much since construction in the 1800s. It had the original wooden shelves, the original crown molding, the original windowsills and, what was perhaps most remarkable, the original hardwood floors. Only the books, framed photographs depicting Theiss with various secretaries of state, the rugs, the leopard skins bought in India, and the sofa and chairs had not belonged to the original owner.

When they were settled on the sofa, Theiss poured Al-Tikriti a cup of tea from the pot on the coffee table.

"The message from the White House is that we can't keep them quiet much longer," he stated calmly, passing the cup to Al-Tikriti. "You may have a few more months, at most. Then they'll break loose like a bunch of angry and hungry dogs. When that happens, even the president cannot stop them."

"If we can be *guaranteed* a few months, it may be enough, Gene."

"Oh?"

"That's the message *I* bring from Baghdad." Al-Tikriti tried to subdue his excitement. There was nothing to be gained, and possibly much to lose, by appearing over-excited in front of Gene Theiss. But this was the most important breakthrough in Baghdad's thinking about the war. The assessment had been made carefully. There was no wishful thinking. The Iranians were showing signs of fatigue. It could all be over soon.

"We know for sure the Old Man in Tehran is preparing for his death," he explained as calmly as he could. "This time it's for real. His doctors have finally managed to convince him and his advisors that he's not immortal. Ending the war is the most important step in preparing for his death, because only *he* can stop the war. If he dies without accepting the cease-fire, *nobody* in Iran will be able to make that decision, sell it to the country, and survive the consequences. At the rate things have been going in the past few months, continuing the war after his death could mean the end of his Islamic Republic, and he knows it."

"And what makes you think that'll happen in the next few months?"

"Oh, he might not die in the next few months. But we believe he'll complete his *preparations* in the next few months, especially if we keep up the heat."

Theiss stared at Al-Tikriti for a long moment, as if trying to assess the credibility of what he had heard by studying his shiny bald head. The two men had been dealing with each other for over four years, but they did not meet face to face often. Theiss, who had spent a lifetime analyzing the credibility of local informers in the Middle East, knew how easily some Arabs could take to exaggeration, especially when dealing with good news. He didn't trust those who couldn't think and express themselves calmly. For Theiss, any enthusiastic recounting of events or description of situations was automatically suspect.

"How important is it that we keep quiet about Iraq's chemical weapons?" he asked, slowly moving his eyes from Al-Tikriti's forehead to his bushy eyebrows and then to his small, animated eyes. He knew what Al-Tikriti's answer would be, but also needed time to think. So he posed the question hoping that Al-Tikriti would embark on a long-winded explanation of the familiar thesis. As usual, Al-Tikriti obliged.

"Well, Gene, you *know* that's important," he said, trying to introduce a measure of patience and wisdom in the quality of his voice. "Any anti-Iraq outburst now, especially from the States, will alleviate the Iranians' fears about getting more and more isolated. They *have* to feel isolated. Besides, you know very well that Iraq doesn't have much choice about using poison gas. It's a fight for *survival*, Gene. Iraq is outnumbered. We can't stop them any other way. We can't demoralize them any other way."

Al-Tikriti suddenly realized he had been talking about Iraq in the first person and abruptly stopped. That was bad form. That was something he always tried to avoid. He was an American citizen and, when talking to Americans, he was supposed to address Iraq in the third person. Theiss noticed the break in his voice, but did not realize what had caused it. For Theiss, Al-Tikriti would always be an Iraqi, U.S. citizen or not.

"Let's not go over that again, Issam," he said so softly that Al-Tikriti wondered if his lips had actually moved. "The relevant facts are these: Some senators are out to discredit Iraq. It's pointless to question their motives or to tell them Iraq is fighting for survival."

Al-Tikriti felt like a schoolboy being lectured about the facts of life. But Theiss was so matter-of-fact and so unpresumptuous that he did not take offense.

"Fortunately," continued Theiss, "it so happens that these same senators don't have much love for Iran either. That's another relevant fact. And that's the only reason we've succeeded in convincing them to keep this issue of chemical warfare on the back burner. But they don't like what they see, and they've been seeing a lot of it lately. Chemical weapons used on civilian targets, poison gas bombs dropped on small towns and villages, pictures of corpses lying in the streets ... It's the kind of thing they thrive on. They'll bring it up, sooner or later."

Al-Tikriti watched the old man's face and wondered whether Theiss was capable of expressing any emotion. What hid behind those ice-cold blue eyes would remain hidden forever. Even when Theiss talked about the corpses of the poison gas victims, he maintained his clinical dispassionate disposition. Those were things that would have the senators all worked up. Otherwise, they wouldn't be relevant to the conversation they were having.

"Then the relevant question that goes with those relevant facts is whether the uproar will come before or after Iran accepts a cease-fire," answered Al-Tikriti, trying to sound as objective and impersonal as Theiss, and clearly failing; he simply could not display the same cold, dispassionate demeanor. "If it comes before, it could be a serious blow to our efforts to stop this damned war. It would delay the cease-fire considerably. If it comes after, I'm sure Iraq can survive the heat."

"We can't guarantee the timing. There's no way *we* can defend or justify what Iraq is doing. All we can count on is that, for the time being, these people hate Iran more than Iraq."

"And possibly the fact that Iraq wants to end the war and Iran doesn't? Or possibly that Iraq has accepted the United Nations Resolution 598 and Iran hasn't?"

"Yes, possibly those points count too. But had it not been for the fact that Iran-bashing is in fashion in this town right now, those would not have helped much. Don't fool yourself, Issam. It won't be easy to turn Iraq into a friendly country in the minds of Americans overnight. The extreme anti-American rhetoric of the Iranians is one of the best things that could have happened for Iraq. The Iran-Contra scandal is another God-sent development for the boys in Baghdad. The hostages in Lebanon are another nice touch. But don't believe any of this means sympathy for Iraq."

Scattered on the big brass tray that served as the coffee table were a dozen antique daggers. There was one from Yemen, the solid silver sheath decorated with semi-precious stones. Another from India, the sheath made of wood with inlaid mother of pearl designs. Unlike the short, curved dagger from Yemen, this was long and narrow, with a pointed tip. Al-Tikriti picked up the Yemeni dagger and studied the sheath and the handle. At the middle of the handle was a large, ruby-like red stone, with smaller stones lined up above and below it. He pulled on the handle, exposing half of the blade. It was dirty, almost black, but when he casually ran his thumb across the edge, he realized it was sharp.

"A few more months," he said slowly, looking up from the dagger to Theiss. There was a new quality to his voice. It was steady, but a trace of the typical Al-Tikriti theatrics lingered on. "That's all we need. Once the Old Man accepts the cease-fire, we will deal with any problem. And he will accept, to save his Islamic Republic. In the next few months, Iraq will hit hard. Air raids will continue at great intensity. Chemical weapons will have to be used. And none of this should cause an outrage anywhere. Only then the Old Man will know it's all over."

Theiss was watching Al-Tikriti's face again. This time, he was mentally formulating his report to the White House. He would have a very short time with the president, no more than ten or fifteen minutes. In that period, he would have to communicate to him both the literal message and the state of mind of Al-Tikriti. Then he'd be asked to give his opinion. This was a particularly difficult case for personal opinions. He had no way to validate Iraq's assessment of Iran's war fatigue. "We have to check the diagnostics from Baghdad carefully," he'd have to say. "If they're right about Iran and the Old Man, then by all means let's go all out and help them! Let's end this war."

"I'll pass that on, as usual," Theiss said to Al-Tikriti with a sigh. "You realize of course that we'll have to confirm your assessment of the Iranian situation through our own sources. If it can be confirmed, it will be welcome news at the White House."

"Great, Gene. That's just great. I'm sure your sources will confirm my report. I'm betting this war will be over before the end of the year."

"Have you talked to our mutual friend lately?" Theiss asked, changing the subject.

"You mean Blackburn?"

"Him."

"Yes. Last week. He had just come back from the Gulf. Has he talked to you yet?"

"Yes he has. What do you think of his theory?"

"I think the whole thing is staged. I told him so."

"Staged?"

"Staged. There's no real problem in the Gulf. Neither within the Saudi ruling family, nor between Saudi Arabia and Kuwait, nor anywhere else."

"Did he tell you the *details*? The basis for his suspicions?"

"He did."

"Well?"

"It's all circumstantial."

"Everything?"

"Everything."

Al-Tikriti noticed Theiss' quizzical look and knew he wouldn't be able to dismiss the matter that easily. He didn't want to talk about any other subject at this meeting, for fear of diluting the importance of his main message from Baghdad. But Blackburn's story had clearly captured Theiss' imagination and he wasn't likely to let it go. In fact, it wouldn't be surprising if Theiss had already gone to the White House with the story. This was perfect Theiss material—tribal intrigue, treason, changing of the guard, with strong implications for U.S. interests.

"I have to admit that Jim did a remarkable job of putting the pieces together," he said at last, wishing Blackburn had taken his advice and not talked to Theiss about his theory. "But every piece is circumstantial. He told me that it was too far-fetched. Didn't he mention that to you?"

"Yes, he did. But when he spoke to me he seemed quite sure of a plot. A *real* plot to force Fahd out."

"I still think it's staged."

"Is that the view from Baghdad?"

"It is. It's also my personal view."

"But why would the Gulf States stage something like this?"

"They're afraid of Iraq, Gene. I don't think you truly appreciate that. They've always been afraid. And now that we have the upper hand in the war, they're *very* afraid. If they appear as united as they really are, Baghdad can deal with them as one front. Or so they figure. But if they're divided and antagonistic against each other, they feel they can mislead and confuse Baghdad. Then, they figure, Baghdad will not have one easy target to deal with, but several different and opposing targets. It will make life more difficult. It will divide attention. It will complicate strategy."

"I'm afraid I don't understand," said Theiss, even though he was beginning to understand perfectly. It was ingenious. As ingenious as the "plot" that Blackburn had described to him so carefully. This was tribal politics, Gulf style, at its best, with the highest possible stakes.

"Let me give you an example," said Al-Tikriti, glad to have an opportunity to do some lecturing of his own. "The biggest game of all in that part of the world is oil, right? These countries have been at each other's throats for years, trying to grab and defend market share from each other. Now suppose that the Gulf States believe the war might end soon. Suppose they think Iraq might emerge relatively intact from the war. What will be their first fear?"

Al-Tikriti paused, even though he did not expect an answer from Theiss. He wanted Theiss to fully envision the scenario he was describing.

"They'll think Iraq will start to bully everybody," he continued. "In everything! But especially in oil. Iraq will demand a higher market share than what it has had during the war. Who'll have to give up this share? The Gulf States. They know they won't be able to confront Iraq directly. They can't tell Baghdad to go to hell. They're too scared. So they stage a fight among themselves and fight each other. They'll pretend that they're stealing each other's market share. Except that they won't really be stealing from each other, because they'll *all* be increasing their exports. They'll be stealing from everybody else. Which one does Iraq go after? Kuwait will blame the UAE, the UAE will blame Saudi Arabia, Saudi Arabia will blame Kuwait. They'll each show solidarity with Iraq, but fight each other. That's a disguised fight against Iraq. Gene, this is one case where the old adage 'strength in unity' does not apply. They're stronger by appearing divided than they would be united. Or so they figure."

After all these years, the Middle East can still be intriguing, Theiss thought. Two versions of the story, equally credible and equally incredible at the same time. I could convince anybody at the White House or at the State Department of the first version, then turn around and, in the next breath, convince him of the second version.

"But what you're suggesting implies tremendous coordination," he said, turning to Al-Tikriti. "These countries have never been able to cooperate, *really* cooperate, on foreign policy. What makes you so sure they'll manage something of this magnitude, of this delicacy, now?"

"Fear, Gene. Again, you underestimate fear. If you accept that they're really afraid of Iraq's political and military force, that they look at Saddam Hussein as an ambitious leader with designs over the entire Gulf, that they see him *dictating* everything to everybody in the Gulf, if you accept that they're *afraid* of a world like that, would it then be *that* far-fetched to assume that they could collude and coordinate something like this?"

Probably not, Theiss thought. But that would represent a major breakthrough in intra-Arab relations. If they pulled this off, it would give them a taste of real cooperation, something that would be without precedent in the Middle East. They might just discover the importance of strategic political cooperation. For them, that'd be like discovering a new weapon. If they succeeded in using a weapon like that on Iraq, wouldn't they try using it on others? Would the United States be exempt?

"If your theory is right," Theiss said, looking Al-Tikriti in the eye, "how long will it be before they start to ease Iran's isolation? Perhaps you shouldn't worry about the United States as much as the Gulf."

"The difference, Gene, is that the Arabs won't jump the gun. They'll keep Iran well isolated until *after* a cease-fire is reached. Fortunately, Iran has been its own worst enemy in these past months—attacking Kuwaiti ships and Abu Dhabi's oil installations, and alienating every country in the region. The Arabs won't start flirting with Tehran while the war's still going on."

"And will they after the war ends?"

"It won't matter what they do then. But Iran will probably continue to be its own worst enemy. It'll try to mobilize the Shiite communities in the Arab world, burning any bridges with Arab governments."

"How will Baghdad deal with this staged fallout in the Gulf?"

"They haven't had much time to think about it. That can't occupy their minds right now. But Jim asked me the same question, and then provided an interesting answer. He said whether it's staged or not, there's one good strategy to deal with the situation. Interestingly enough, the name of the game is still 'isolation.' He said Iraq should isolate Saudi Arabia by making a pact with King Fahd. If the plot is real, such a pact would spoil it. If it's staged, it would neutralize its impact. Isn't that interesting, Gene?"

"Yes. Interesting," murmured Theiss. "Jim suggested that to you?"

"Yes. His exact phrase was 'tie the big donkey in the stable.' That way, he said, if the plot is real, you protect him; if it's staged, you stop him from causing damage outside. If the big donkey is kept tied in the stable, he said, the small donkeys can't damage your field too much, no matter how wildly they trample around. Isn't that great? James sure has a way with words."

"Yes, he does," Theiss murmured again, deep in thought. That would sure eliminate the cooperation weapon, he was thinking. That's the real long-term advantage of the plan. I wonder if Issam knows that. I wonder if Baghdad knows it. I wonder if Jim knows the real significance of what he has suggested.

I should bring him into the government, thought Theiss. He is being wasted in this private consulting business. Jim would make his father proud.

"Do you want me to check this suggestion out at the White House?" he asked Al-Tikriti, as if it were another routine piece of business in which he had no interest whatsoever.

"I leave that up to you, Gene," Al-Tikriti said in a disinterested tone. He knew it was up to Theiss anyway; the only reason Theiss had asked the question was to see if Al-Tikriti expected a response. "It may be premature. I'm afraid that kind of donkey tying won't take place until after the war's over, if at all."

"Did he suggest exactly how you might want to keep the big donkey tied in the stable?"

"We didn't go into details, Gene. He just mentioned something about a Saudi-Iraqi treaty of some sort. What he had in mind was a security treaty."

"What makes him think that King Fahd will go along?"

"I asked him that. He thinks it would be too tempting for the king, even if the so-called plot were staged. Jim thinks Fahd would not be able to turn down an opportunity to be the first to befriend the great bully of the Gulf. Especially after the war ends when the great bully's hands are freed. Of course, if the plot is not staged, then his motive to go along will be obvious."

*   *   *

During the next several months, Iraq intensified its aerial attacks on Iranian economic targets. Iranian oil tankers leaving the Gulf were hit at an increasingly successful rate. Iranian oil exports dropped sharply, while increasing exports from the Gulf States kept prices depressed, a double blow to Iran's finances. Civilian targets were bombarded with alarming frequency. Iraq did not spare anything within its military capability.

At the same time, the U.S. Navy in the Gulf adopted an intolerant stance relative to Iran. At the slightest provocation, Americans hit and sank Iranian speedboats and vessels and destroyed oil platforms. The State Department tried to defend the Navy's actions by declaring them necessary to secure freedom of international navigation in the Gulf. But it didn't need to try very hard. Nobody in America or abroad seemed to care much about a few Iranian boats and platforms.

The incident that drove that point home in Tehran did not occur until early July, when missiles fired from the *USS Vincennes* shot down an IranAir Airbus with 290 passengers on board. The Airbus happened to be on a regular civilian flight from Bandar Abbas to Dubai. Although the U.S. Navy initially tried to explain the shooting as a perfectly justifiable action provoked by hostile intent on the part of the plane, it later had to admit that an error in interpreting radar data had caused the shooting. But that too was wrong. There had been no error in interpreting radar data. The shooting was deliberate. "A necessary killing of mercy," as an insider in the Washington intelligence community explained to Blackburn.

The most frightening aspect of the incident for Tehran was not that the U.S. Navy had become more daring. Nor was it the loss of innocent lives. It was that the incident did not cause any genuine remorse in America, or any outrage internationally against America. *Nobody cared.* The U.S. president expressed his regrets to the families of those who died and offered financial compensation. Some U.S. congressmen opposed the idea of compensation, however. Some Ayatollahs in Tehran called upon the Muslim world to declare an all-out war on the United States and its interests. But there was no reaction, let alone outrage. Others in Tehran tried to take the moral high road, but they were not taken seriously either. *Nobody cared.* Iran was truly isolated. Even the most radical ayatollahs could see that.

The Old Man in Tehran saw that.

Only two weeks after the shooting of the IranAir airliner, Iran's president announced that his country was ready to accept the United Nations Security Council Resolution 598, which called for an immediate ceasefire in the Gulf.

XV

When the Guns Fall Silent

Two months had passed since Iran had shocked the world—the Middle-East-watching part of it, at any rate—by announcing it was ready to accept a cease-fire. One month had passed since the cease-fire had taken effect.

At first, the news had been good for business. The announcement had wreaked havoc in oil markets. Every trader *had* to have a view on what it meant. It did not have to be a complicated view, nor did it have to be based on an in-depth understanding of the situation in the Gulf. But it had to be clear as to the direction of oil prices: Is the cease-fire bullish or is it bearish? That was all that mattered. Everything else was irrelevant, the sort of stuff historians and academics tried to figure out and explain. But a trader *had* to take a position in the market. As Blackburn had often been told by an irate client who simply would not accept "no opinion" for an answer, no position *was* a position. One took it only when one thought prices would not change, which was almost never.

But this time Blackburn did have an opinion. A clear opinion. And, as was often the case, a minority opinion. Amid the confusion that overwhelmed the market in the few days immediately following the announcement of the cease-fire, oil prices soared. The bulls had outnumbered the bears. Cease-fire meant peace, peace meant a more coherent OPEC, a more coherent OPEC meant better coordination of oil policy, which meant less oil production, which meant higher prices ... that was how the short-term conventional wisdom of the traders on the Merc was formulated and expressed.

Blackburn had a lot of fun with that, not to mention a lot of profits for those clients who listened to him. The cease-fire did not mean peace, he insisted. And peace, if and when it came to this godforsaken part of the world, would not mean a more coherent OPEC. If anything, the cease-fire meant that both Iran and Iraq would now be free to produce and export without having to worry about each other's bombs, which would mean more oil on the market, which would mean lower prices. If you *had* to have a quick and superficial view of the situation, that was the one to go by. Once again, while most traders were buying oil, he advised his clients to sell short. Some of his clients did. Ramzi Amin sold short. Selling short in a bullish market took a lot of guts and deep pockets; Ramzi Amin had both. Simmons had deep pockets and possibly guts too, but he managed to hide the latter in his eternally nervous state.

Even before the cease-fire went into effect, Iran raised its exports by almost one million barrels per day, and Iraq started boasting about its huge production capacity and great oil reserves. The bulls quickly sobered up and oil prices crashed. Nobody involved in trading oil talked about peace in the Gulf or a coherent OPEC after that.

But these types of nerve-wracking trading sessions were not the problem. They did not consume much time, they did not require travel and, best of all for Blackburn, they did not require him to rely on other people. He formulated his views and then it was a matter of responding to the torrent of questions.

What took most of his time, and caused the most frustration, were two other projects he was involved in. First, there was his new arrangement with Takao, and second the SOMO-A. Nitzen deal.

Takao had arranged for a consortium of Japanese oil and trading companies to retain Blackburn to help them identify strategic partners for Japan's international upstream efforts.

For this new assignment alone, he had made a couple of one-day trips to London in the past two weeks. Once, he did not even stay in London overnight. He flew over on the evening flight from Washington, arrived at eight in the morning, took a cab from Heathrow straight to Shell Center, then went back to Heathrow to catch the early afternoon London-Washington flight.

The second trip was not only physically tiring, but also frustrating. He arrived in front of Britannic House on Moore Lane, headquarters of British Petroleum, straight from the airport.

Templeton's secretary met him as soon as he stepped out of the elevator on the thirteenth floor and escorted him to a large corner office. Paul Templeton came to greet him from behind his large desk and they sat on the sofa.

"Thank you for agreeing to see me at such short notice," said Blackburn, studying Templeton's face closely.

"No problem at all," said Templeton. "Now then, how may I be of service to you?"

He personifies everything that Shaikh Saqr is allergic to, thought Blackburn. Milky white skin, pink cheeks, freckles, dirty looking light brown hair, blue-gray eyes with bags under them, and that uniquely British affectation that no British aristocrat would be caught without and that, viewed from the desert culture of the Gulf, was seen as repulsive and degenerate.

"I have a Japanese client who is interested in establishing long-term strategic alliances with various multinational oil and gas companies," started Blackburn. "Given the specific needs and strengths of my client, I thought perhaps it would make sense to look for a possible match with BP."

In spite of Templeton's initial friendliness, Blackburn had an uneasy feeling about the meeting. His instincts told him that Templeton was not going to be open to the idea of entering into any sort of meaningful partnership with the Japanese, especially with a trading firm like C. Itoh.

"Possible match with BP, you say? And what might the specific needs and strengths of the client in question be?"

Behind the smiling and friendly face, Blackburn could feel the impregnable steel wall. It was the old imperial attitude, the "I-already-own-planet-earth-and-all-that's-in-it-so-what-could-you-possibly-offer-that-would-be-of-value-to-me" posture, something Shaikh Saqr must have run into on countless occasions.

Blackburn decided that since he was already there, he might as well ignore the attitude and proceed with his presentation. There could be substantial amounts of capital, he explained; the Japanese were willing to put billions into projects that would give them access to crude oil and that would enhance their sense of security. There would also be huge benefits in the form of access to Eastern markets where the Japanese traders had a clear dominance. This would be a truly strategic, long-term partnership where the benefits to both sides could go far beyond the provisions made by any single contract or joint project.

Templeton was listening more intently than he wanted Blackburn to notice. This was not the first time he had heard the arguments, nor was it going to be the last. What interested him in the conversation this time was the messenger, not the message. What business did this American consultant, with known close ties to Kuwait and Saudi Arabia, have promoting Japanese/British strategic alliances? Why would a Japanese company resort to such an intermediary?

"But what can the Japanese offer BP that we don't already have?" asked Templeton, interested to see how far Blackburn would push the classic arguments in this area. "You mention capital," he continued before Blackburn could have a chance to answer. "I'm sure it's true that they're willing and able to bring in substantial capital, but that isn't exactly one of our problems now, is it? Access to markets, well, perhaps there is something there, if we can hook up with some of their large trading conglomerates, but then again, I wouldn't know how one can quantify the financial benefits associated with that."

Blackburn was beginning to develop some of Shaikh Saqr's allergies. Templeton was being disingenuous. BP did need capital. That was the main reason for the BP-Statoil alliance, where BP brought international experience, and Statoil capital. So there was a clear precedent for what he was proposing. He could sense his aggravation rising and suddenly felt a strong urge to stand up and leave. But this had been his idea; it was he who had convinced Takao to try the British, as a fallback position, in case the negotiations with the Arabs came to a dead end. The least he could do was put in the necessary good faith and try to push his point across.

"Look, Paul," he said, sitting up straight at the edge of the sofa. "I think it would be better if we stopped beating around the bush. The Japanese will make their deals and they'll get their oil, with or without BP's participation. I don't think I'll have to prove that to you. If they do it without you, it will be either with producing countries or possibly with other majors. In short, *without* you could very well mean *against* you. That's what's at stake here for BP. I'm sure you have highly qualified accountants who would be happy to quantify the financial benefits you're asking about. But that is not the key question. In my view, the key question is how much BP's global competitive position will be weakened if the Japanese cultivate their strategic alliances with your competitors, instead of cultivating them with you."

Templeton was clearly taken aback, perhaps even offended by this unusually direct approach. He probably had become unaccustomed to being talked to in this tone a long time ago. Blackburn sensed this, but did not care. He had delivered his message.

"What you're saying is true only if the Japanese finally do succeed in joining the game." That was all Templeton could say.

"Keeping them out of the game is simply not an option any longer, Paul," said Blackburn, feeling satisfied that he had made his point. "Please keep that in mind when you think this over."

Exhausting as these trips were, he would have enjoyed them had they been productive. But they were not. Sophie's right, he thought. I need a break. A real break, not just a vacation. Vacations are for normal people working normal hours and living normal lives. What I need is a clean break.

But not quite yet.

*　*　*

Blackburn rushed out of the A. Nitzen offices and headed straight to the black car from Bell Radio Taxi that was waiting at the corner. The white cardboard sign at the side window read "Bell 809." That was his number. "La Guardia," he said, handing the driver the voucher. "Marine Terminal, Pan Am shuttle." He had barely enough time to make the 5:30 shuttle back to Washington. It would be aggravating if he missed the flight by just a few minutes. That would mean either wasting an entire hour at the airport to catch the next flight, or trying to catch the 6 p.m. Eastern shuttle. He didn't like either option.

That afternoon Blackburn was feeling old, tired, and frustrated. He had not had much sleep during the past few weeks. Too many one-day trips to New York, too many fruitless conversations with the Nitzen boys and Al-Tikriti, too many inflexible positions on all sides, too many disappointments in big time deal making.

All that on the SOMO-Nitzen deal alone, which had occupied most of his time during the past few months, and was supposed to be the deal that was going to secure Al-Tikriti and Blackburn a flow of income on which they could retire. Nitzen had agreed to pay both Al-Tikriti and Blackburn's Petroleum Consulting Group their respective fees. Once the oil started to flow, neither Al-Tikriti nor Blackburn would need to lift a finger to earn their fees; the fees would flow, too.

He made it to the airport on time and boarded the Pan Am shuttle to Washington. There was a community of regular New York - Washington, DC commuters, and he recognized several faces on the plane. But he was not in the mood to talk to anyone that afternoon. He gave a quick nod to a couple of acquaintances, took his seat, and closed his eyes. His mind drifted back to the SOMO-Nitzen deal.

In order to make the deal attractive for Nitzen, the crude would have had to be acquired from Iraq at substantially below market value, so they could still make a profit after giving away all the commissions. One of Al-Tikriti's important functions was to make sure that Iraq accepted a "good deal."

Al-Tikriti had secured the necessary clearances for A. Nitzen from the Iraqi government and from SOMO. These clearances had to be obtained from one of the most capricious bureaucracies in the world, with arbitrary delays and even more arbitrary new requirements at each step. The Nitzen boys had resented being put through all the checks. The Iraqis had resented the resentment of what they viewed as a bunch of New York traders who were expected to show more respect toward the requirements of a sovereign state. And Blackburn had resented being stuck in the middle, receiving the complaints, grievances, and threats of both sides.

But it seemed the worst was over. A. Nitzen & Co. was finally a "registered" buyer of Iraqi crude. SOMO had made an allocation for Nitzen. The two sides had even agreed on a specific price formula for the sale of 100,000 barrels per day for one year, automatically renewable for another year unless explicitly terminated by either party. In effect, that meant a perpetual contract that would end only in extreme circumstances. All that was left to do was sign the contract.

Then came the announcement of the cease-fire, which raised everybody's hopes even higher. Now that Iraq was no longer at war, the deal would be far more meaningful and easy to implement. Iraq would have more crude oil to sell, and a secure contract of 100,000 barrels per day. The chances of raising the volume were better than ever. In a year's time they could probably raise it to 200,000 barrels per day. The commissions that Al-Tikriti and Blackburn would make would also double.

Then, almost overnight, everything fell apart. It was barely three weeks into the cease-fire. Simmons had just sent Blackburn a copy of the final contract, which they would present to SOMO for signature. On the same morning that Blackburn called Simmons to say it looked great and ready to go, the U.S. Department of State announced it had definite proof that Iraq had been using chemical weapons against its own minority citizens, the Kurds. The secretary of state issued a public statement warning Baghdad that if this practice continued, it would affect U.S.-Iraqi relations.

The following day, the Senate introduced a resolution calling for a wide range of economic sanctions against Iraq, including a ban on imports of oil. Although the resolution was never adopted, it was enough to scare conservative Wall Street firms away. Kramer Brothers, the owner of A. Nitzen & Co., gave instructions to the A. Nitzen traders to stop all dealings with Iraq.

Now Blackburn felt the plane going through some turbulence, which momentarily brought him out of his musings. Soon thereafter the captain announced that the final descent into Washington National Airport had started. Blackburn buckled his seatbelt and closed his eyes again.

The Nitzen order to stop all dealings with Iraq had started as a true nightmare for Blackburn. Al-Tikriti had raised hell. He called

Blackburn at home at three in the morning the day after the decision was made. "I can't believe they're actually going to back down!" he yelled to an exhausted Blackburn, who nonetheless felt he owed Al-Tikriti the courtesy of listening. "Do you remember our conversation a few months ago? You remember what I told you about credibility? You remember? I said once we start, we can't back down. Once I go to Baghdad with an offer and they accept it, we can't say 'oh, sorry, we changed our mind.' You remember? This is precisely what I was talking about. You said, 'No Issam, don't worry, they won't embarrass us, they're professionals.' That's what you said, Jim. On that basis, we proceeded. Now look where we are. How can I face them again?"

Those sessions were most distasteful for Blackburn. Al-Tikriti was right, of course, but only partially so. It was true that they'd had that conversation, but that was before Iraq was portrayed to the world as a terrorist state with the mass murder of a civilian population on its record. That was before Iraq, in an angry response to the U.S. accusations, had announced it would not accept New York as the site of the UN-sponsored Iraq/Iran peace talks, and the negotiations were moved to Geneva. That was before the U.S. Senate started playing with legislation to ban trade with Iraq. Blackburn patiently explained all that to Al-Tikriti. "Issam," he said, "surely you can understand the significance of these developments. None of them were foreseen a few months ago."

But no, Issam couldn't understand what the whole commotion was about. Was there an actual law banning American companies from importing Iraqi crude? No. So where was the problem? Did A. Nitzen want to start obeying a law that was not yet passed? A bunch of petty lawmakers, who couldn't give a damn about the Kurds, who probably hadn't even heard of Kurds until now, were all worked up about nothing, trying to discredit Iraq and undermine the new Iraq-U.S. friendship. And the Nitzen boys were falling right into their trap and retracting all the goodwill they had so painfully built during the past several months.

"Jim, how can you honestly claim to understand their position, let alone defend it?" Al-Tikriti retorted. "If they were willing to enter a long-term contract with Iraq when the country was *at war, for God's sake,* how can they find it unacceptable now, during peace? The whole world is rushing to benefit from the business boom that's about to start in Iraq, and they decide to back down? Where is the logic in all this?"

And Al-Tikriti's rant continued like a flooded rapid: Did Jim know there were no vacancies in any hotel in Baghdad right now? Did he know that every hotel room was booked solid for weeks? Did he know that half the hotel rooms in Kuwait were occupied by businessmen seeking to get to Baghdad? Did he know who these businessmen were? Well, they were Japanese, Korean, German, and French businessmen. Entire teams of businessmen, from the largest and most prestigious companies in these countries. They were pouring in to make sure they did not miss out on the new opportunities that were going to spring up all over Iraq. And now, all of a sudden, a bunch of Americans decided to worry about the Kurds?

For some reason, Al-Tikriti considered this charade necessary. He was not surprised by the Senate action, although George Shultz's statements did take him, and many others, by surprise. Why would the secretary of state come out so strongly against Iraq? "The Jewish Lobby" was the standard explanation to any action against any Arab country, and George Shultz was not spared. The administration was going to change soon and Shultz was going to need a lot of friends; he couldn't offend the Jews now, during the last few months of his term.

The Senate action was predictable. Gene Theiss couldn't have been clearer on that in their various conversations. Even the reaction of Kramer Brothers was predictable. Al-Tikriti did understand. But he felt he had to go through the motions of showing what a great disappointment everybody had been.

Blackburn promised himself that this was the last trip he'd make to A. Nitzen to discuss the fate of the Nitzen-SOMO deal in person. He had done all he could and the Nitzen boys would not budge. They could not budge. They had their orders from above.

But there had been an interesting twist in the talks in New York that afternoon. As Blackburn disembarked the plane and headed for his car in the parking lot, he could not help thinking how Simmons, who was the real gambler in the group, had seemed almost relieved that the deal had fallen through. That surprised Blackburn. But the thing he found even more surprising was that Andy Zeller, who had preached caution while the deal was being negotiated and appeared to have been against it all along, had been furious. He was furious at the U.S. Senate, furious at the top management of Kramer Brothers. "Those assholes have no right to interfere in our business!" he said. "What the fuck would a shitty senator know about trading oil?"

"Hey, let's cool it a bit," Simmons said, feeling embarrassed for Zeller.

"If they could do anything useful with their miserable lives, do you think they'd run for office?" Zeller asked. "Noooooo ... They enjoy poking their snotty noses where they have no business and making our lives miserable!"

This side of Zeller was new to Blackburn. It wasn't the anger, or the hostility or the foul language that was shocking. All that was standard on the trading floor. The novelty was that those emotions were aroused by something other than the market or a specific trade or a specific trader. To the chief technician of the oil-trading group at Nitzen—who didn't even fully understand the nature of the physical trade involved in the SOMO deal—the issue was freedom and autonomy. The Senate had no right to interfere with Wall Street. Period. More aggravating than that, senators were not *qualified* to interfere with Wall Street. Regardless of what he thought of the Nitzen-SOMO deal, this was not the way to end it. There was an issue of principle involved. Principles! On Wall Street. By a technical specialist in commodity trading. Remarkable.

Principles or not, Blackburn was fed up and ready to drop the issue. He could no longer take the stubborn, hot-headed rhetoric from the Iraqi side or the almost paranoid "we can't afford to appear to be in contempt of the Senate" rhetoric from the Nitzen boys, who were simply repeating the party line dictated to them by some fat vice president at Kramer Brothers. His break, the clean break, had to come from somewhere else.

＊　＊　＊

Blackburn was at his apartment in Washington by 7 p.m. He had barely finished washing his hands when the phone rang.

"Amore mio ..."

Bianca's voice rang through his entire tired body like a magic potion. He was so ready for a couple of days of unwinding with her that he ached all over. But he had not been able to take the time. He had even gone on two business trips to Europe without contacting her.

"Bianca, it's past one in the morning in Vienna. Is everything okay?"

"Everything is okay, Jimmy. But I wanted to talk to you. I've promised to tell you every time I see Roberto. He'll be in Florence tomorrow on a two-day business trip from Rome, and asked me to join him. It's been such a difficult month, Jimmy. I want to go. Would you be upset? Please be direct with me. I'll call you from there, I promise, if you agree to talk to me."

Blackburn felt as if he had been thrown into the vortex of a tornado. Something collapsed all around him, and he could not put his finger on what it was. He just stared at his living room wall.

"Jimmy, please say something."

"Will I be upset?" he mumbled finally. "Yes, Bianca, I'll be upset. I will be more than upset. I have no words to describe how upset I will be."

"Jimmy, please. I need to decompress. Can't you understand?"

That made him so mad that he could not talk for another minute.

"I'll resent that it is him and not me. You would too. I'll resent that I have to share you. I will imagine you with him, in excruciating detail. I already feel a big part of me is beginning to die inside of me. Is that direct and clear enough?"

Blackburn was surprised to feel such charged emotions. This was not his style. Normally, his pride would have stopped him from bearing his soul to this extent. But the timing of Bianca's news couldn't have been worse. Besides, they had made a pact to be direct and brutally honest with each other.

"Now I feel lost." Bianca was sobbing.

"Don't be lost," he said, softening his tone. "I'll take this if I have to. But know that it's killing a part of me."

"I'm lost, because I don't know where we stand. I don't want this to change anything between us. I'm not upset by your honesty. But you never once said you still love me. Not even a hint."

Blackburn was far too bitter to tell her what she wanted to hear.

"This is really exhausting me," he said. "I have to find a way out. I will go for a walk. Sorry. I need to go clear my head. We'll talk later, when you can."

"Jimmy wait. Please don't hang up yet. You knew about Roberto. I told you it's different from us. Has nothing to do with us. He is in a different space ..."

"Bianca, please stop. Yes, I knew about him, and you knew I was jealous. Knowing in advance does not make it easier to cope when it actually happens."

"Nothing, no one, can ever take your place in my heart."

"I need to go, Bianca. I'm sorry."

And he gently put the receiver down.

He still could not figure out why he was taking this so hard. He was old enough to have been hurt before, but never like this. Maybe because I am so drained, physically and mentally, he thought. This could not have come at a worse time.

He thought for a minute about calling her back in order to finish the conversation on a different note. She was right. He knew about Roberto. He knew her personality. He knew he could never have her just for himself. He knew she was married. He knew her husband somehow tolerated the relationship with Roberto. Stefan and Roberto knew each other. They had even cooperated on a couple of business projects and on work with a charitable foundation helping poor families in Italy. Blackburn knew Roberto had inherited a family fortune and spent a lot of time on the boards of various foundations and NGOs. He could not understand how Stefan could accept Bianca's occasional get-togethers with Roberto. Stefan knew she planned to spend two romantic and sensual days in Florence with Roberto. Yet he would welcome her back with open arms. And they'd carry on, in love as always, as if the two-day absence had not even taken place, let alone changed anything.

That amazed Blackburn. Maybe the three of them are more evolved than I am, he thought. I am still a simple man at heart.

One way he had of coping with difficult emotional situations was to focus on something that only he could do. It was a habit he had started as a teenager, when one of his teachers had given his class an unusual assignment: write a composition about things that only you can do. Then his teacher had told him, "Do something every week that *only* you can do." It was a powerful way to get to know oneself. Normal everyday activities—eating, drinking, reading, playing games—were excluded. Everyone else could do those things. It forced the young James Blackburn to focus on what was unique about him. He'd write a letter to his uncle that only *he* could write. He'd try to help his father at home in a manner that only he could. And, mostly, he'd just think. No one else in the world could think his own thoughts.

The practice stayed with him when he grew up. It was useful in stressful situations. This was the way he kept his consulting business different from the competitors. What he was selling was *his* judgment, *his* views, *his* unique way of handling contacts, *his* unique interpretation. No other consultant could duplicate that. That was why he rarely accepted consulting assignments that involved only the gathering and dissemination of raw data. He insisted that the trademark of the PCG was the unique intellectual context it brought to raw data.

So he closed his eyes and focused on something unique to him. Love was age-old, hurt was age-old, betrayal was age-old. What was uniquely James Blackburn? His inner strength, his independence, his awareness, his consciousness of his surroundings.

His other way of fighting situations like this was *knowing* the details. That was uniquely Blackburn too. Others in his situation would prefer *not* to know, *not* to think about what Bianca would be doing with Roberto in Florence. With Blackburn, ignorance was not bliss; it had never been. Not knowing was the most scary state possible. Not knowing the details left him helpless in front of an invisible enemy. He could fight and overcome anything if he could see it, if he could know everything about it.

He knew he would have to talk to Bianca again. He would want to know every detail, her itinerary, their plans in Florence, where they were going to stay, what they were going to do. And later, he'd even want to know how they made love, how often. Yes, those details would torture him at first, but without them he'd be lost, his vivid imagination would take over and create even bigger monsters. Only by knowing could he hope to eventually cope.

But this was not the time to call Bianca back. He knew he was too bitter to say anything nice to her.

He called Sophie.

"Hey, Jim, you're back!"

"Sophie, I don't want to be alone tonight."

That was not the type of opening he'd normally use. She sensed the angst in his voice.

"I'll come right over."

"Do you mind if I come over there instead? I need to get out of here."

That was rare too. He had always preferred to have her over to his place than to go to hers.

"Sure, Jim. Come over."

XVI

Reputation Management

Sophie had not known Blackburn in this state of mind. He was distant, yet focused. Restless, yet calm. Kind, yet abrupt. Intense, yet vulnerable. In bed, he was eager, yet reluctant at the same time. Passionate to a fault, but she felt something was off.

Only once did she ask what was bothering him.

"Oh, nothing serious, really," he said. "The Iraq-Nitzen deal fell through. Months of hard work, and my first real chance for a clean break, all down the drain." That was serious, but somehow she was not sure that was everything.

His intensity told her to hold off on further questions.

The next day, he called her more often than he normally did. They went to dinner at The Palm on 19th Street. Then he asked her to spend the night at his place. She felt he was fighting an urge to tell her something. She decided to give him the space he needed.

Later that evening, as they finally settled on the sofa, Al-Tikriti called to find out how things had gone in New York. Blackburn was in no mood to listen to the standard lecture again. He wanted to cut the conversation short.

"I think it's about time we faced up to the facts, Issam," he said. "They *cannot* do the deal. It has nothing to do with commercial viability or goodwill or anything like that. Believe it or not, it also has nothing to do with how professional they are. They simply cannot do the deal. They have orders. I think we better drop the whole thing for now. When things calm down a bit, hopefully in a few months, maybe we can revive it."

To Blackburn's surprise, Al-Tikriti didn't try to argue.

"I agree," he said with uncharacteristic calm. "Iraq has lost face. There's no question that we're suffering from a damning image problem. Which brings me to the real reason I called. They want me to find a good public relations firm to represent them in Washington. Got any ideas?"

"You mean a lobbying firm?" asked Blackburn, emphasizing the word "lobbying" for Sophie, who was lying on the sofa reading a magazine. He gave her a thumbs up as she looked at him.

"Yes, you know, a professional firm that can present Iraq's point of view to the honorable congressmen and honorable senators of this honorable town." The sarcasm in Al-Tikriti's voice was spewing out of the phone. "Not that I'm convinced it will make any difference. Sometimes I feel there are professional Iraq-haters in this town who won't give up for anything. But in any case, we're going to try."

"Well, I can't think of any specific firm off the top of my head," said Blackburn, winking at Sophie and giving her another thumbs up, "but I'll give it some thought. How serious are they about using this option?"

"Very serious. They've finally realized that's how things are done over here. It wasn't easy to convince them, you know. They still can't believe they have to spend money to explain their position to the political establishment of another country. But after they saw the damage done by the Senate resolution, they were convinced it was necessary."

"I can imagine," Blackburn said, wondering about all the other deals that must have fallen through because of the Senate resolution. Iraq could get particularly hard-hit if there was a similar change of heart in the banking community. Credit, which already was scarce, would get even scarcer. Nobody would want to lend to a country that was about to be put on the black list by the U.S. Senate. Iraqi letters of credit traded on the open market at a 50 percent discount over their face value during the war. That meant Iraq was paying more than double for the imports it financed through short-term borrowing.

When the cease-fire was first announced, the discount dropped to 25 percent. The Senate action could easily have raised it back up to 50 percent and possibly even higher. That alone would have been enough "damage" to sober up Baghdad.

"What type of firm should we go after?" asked Al-Tikriti.

"I think it should be a firm that has a good rapport with both Democrats and Republicans; you don't want to get squeezed by U.S. partisan politics, especially given that this is an election year and we don't know who's going to be in the White House next year. Also, it has to be a firm that has had some experience in representing foreign governments; that always requires a special touch. Those two conditions should narrow it down somewhat. Do you agree with the conditions?"

"I agree. Absolutely."

"Good. Why don't I sleep on it and call you sometime tomorrow? This is going to cost Baghdad a bundle, you know. It's not going to be easy to find a firm worth its salt that'd accept an unpopular assignment like this for peanuts."

"Oh, I know. And they know. At least that's one thing we don't have to worry about right now. This has been cleared at the highest level."

"Good. Can I ask questions around town?"

"You can ask questions, but don't mention Iraq just yet. No point in warning the gladiators in the arena and raising the ante."

Blackburn didn't quite understand that last comment but didn't want to ask. His mind was already preoccupied with the possibilities that this new turn of events represented.

And his heart still dropped to his stomach, pounding, as he thought of Bianca and Roberto.

"You got it," he told Al-Tikriti. "I'll talk to you tomorrow afternoon."

He walked over to the sofa where Sophie was lying.

"I think it's time for you to have a heart-to-heart talk with Mr. Russell," he said, sitting down and taking her feet in his lap.

He was aware that he was fighting a bitter inner battle that was secret from Sophie, and felt a pang of guilt.

"This deal is going to make you a partner in the firm. Promotions aren't enough for you anymore."

"I don't think Wilks, Russell & Company is ready to accept a female partner, Jim," said Sophie, but she could not hide her excitement.

"They're one of the most conservative firms in DC, and they're not going to change their image for one more account."

"One more big, fat, incredible account, Sophie. But it doesn't have to be a formal partnership. You can make them a different type of offer."

"Such as?"

"How much was the retainer from the Angolans?"

"Four-hundred K a year."

"Good. Tell your Mr. Russell that the next big account you bring in, you want 75 percent of anything above 400K as a bonus."

"He'll never go for it!"

"Why not? You're not asking for anything if the account is 400K or less, right? Even a 400K retainer is pure gravy for the firm. Anything above that would be theft anyway. He should be happy to keep only 25 percent of it."

"How much do you think the Iraqi account will be worth?"

"Oh, at least a million the first year."

"*What?*"

"Oh, yes. By our formula, 400 of it would go straight to the firm, and 75 percent of the remaining $600,000 would be yours. That's $450,000."

"That would be almost half of the total retainer, assuming we do get that much. Jim, they'll never let me get away with that kind of dough!"

"They wouldn't have much choice if you had a contract with them, would they? I think they'll sign a contract because they'll never expect you to bring in that kind of account. They might think you'll bring in a 450 or, at best, a half-million dollar retainer, which they figure will get you a bonus of 50,000 to 60,000 bucks, which is okay, so they'll sign. Then you spring on them a million dollar contract."

"I don't know … I can't even think of that kind of money."

"You'll get used to it," said Blackburn, relishing the moment. "But not a word about Iraq to anybody. And definitely not a word about any of this to Mr. Russell until he signs your new contract."

It would be interesting to be able to follow more closely, through Sophie, Iraq's public relations efforts in Washington, Blackburn thought. His own involvement with Iraq and particularly with SOMO had grown considerably after the cease-fire, even though the deal with Nitzen had fallen through. Iraq was faced with formidable problems, almost entirely due to a financial squeeze. Its creditors, who had been willing to lend it vast amounts of money during the war, had started to demand repayment of the old debt before any new lending could resume. Potential foreign investors were also reluctant to step in. The cease-fire had somehow failed to trigger the widely expected economic boom. Even worse, it had raised expectations among the people of Iraq for a period of economic prosperity and abundance, following eight years of deprivation caused by the war, but no significant improvement in economic conditions was visible anywhere. The government was heavily in debt, oil prices were low, and Iraq's civilian economy was suffering from years of neglect.

In order to break the cycle of capital shortages, payments delays, and borrowing problems, Blackburn had been advising Iraq on various types of long-term financing arrangements for big revenue-generating projects. But the credit market seemed to have dried up. Banks were largely preoccupied with investigating the emerging opportunities in Eastern Europe, which, almost overnight, was recognized as the new "growth area" for international lending. Only Iraq's old creditors were still interested in talking to Baghdad, not about new loans, but rather repayment of the old loans.

One of the old creditors was Japan. Unlike France and Germany, Japan's loans to Iraq were not military in nature. They were for large civilian projects, with some started before the war and others during the first few years of the war. Throughout the war years, Iraq had favored those creditors that supplied arms to the country, namely, France and Germany. Japan had thus taken the back seat in the Iraqi leadership's mind. But even now that the war was over Baghdad still would not take Tokyo seriously. The vast commercial potential of the Japanese conglomerates, financial institutions, and trading empires somehow eluded the leadership in Baghdad, which was conditioned to prioritize everything solely on the basis of its military strategic value. Blackburn viewed this as a grave error in judgment.

The Japanese were acting under what appeared to be increasing confusion. They had launched a major investment drive in the United States and had hired Wilks, Russell & Co. to help mitigate the inevitable anti-Japan sentiments Their paranoia, helped by Mr. Russell's shrewd negotiating tactics, had led to two separate retainer agreements: one to pave the way for Japanese investments, and a second for watering down anti-Japan sentiments because of Japanese trade protectionism. As usual, there was one Japanese front company per deal, but Mr. Russell knew that a whole consortium of companies stood behind the agreements.

Blackburn remained baffled by the clumsiness of the Japanese when it came to public relations and oil. Somehow, the ease and ingenuity with which they achieved their success in other industrial and trade areas were absent from these two fields.

Even as his mind spun with all this, Blackburn still thought of Bianca and could not get rid of the knot in his stomach. He tried to focus on things that only he could do, but the knot always reappeared. Roberto was at least ten years older than Blackburn, but had captured Bianca's imagination, if not her heart.

She had never said she loved Roberto, but Blackburn knew she enjoyed being with him. Could it be because he was Italian like her, flamboyant, outgoing and a person who enjoyed life to the fullest? Could it be that she missed an Italian factor in her life, given that she lived in Vienna, worked in a multilateral organization where there were no Europeans, let alone Italians, and was married to an Austrian banker? Wouldn't all this put Roberto in a position to give her something that neither Blackburn nor her husband could?

The only thing that was going to give him a fighting chance was to know everything, all the details: whether Bianca was already in Florence, if Roberto had met her at the airport personally or sent a car for her, where they were staying, where they planned to have dinner the first night, and how passionate Roberto was with her.

*   *   *

Ramzi Amin looked at the faces of the two Japanese businessmen with an almost academic curiosity, as if understanding them was more important than negotiating the deal. Could our tribal culture evolve into their level of sophistication one day? he wondered. Well, it's not really sophistication. They're not really sophisticated. They're structured, disciplined, and possibly more knowledgeable, and they can focus, on *any* level of detail. We can't.

Takao and Kurai stared back at the face of what Blackburn liked to call the philosophy-professor-that-never-was. Neither had a clue as to what Amin was thinking, nor would they have believed him had he at that instant bared his soul to them. This contract was too important. Not just for them, but also for KPC. Academic curiosity had no place in a meeting such as this.

"Mr. Amin," Takao said gently, breaking the silence that had filled the room for the past few minutes. "Mr. Kurai and I are curious to know how KPC will respond to our minor alterations in the original KPC proposal. We're sorry, Mr. Amin, we don't want to rush you in any way, but we presume that since you bothered to fly all the way to Tokyo and honor us with a visit, well, we assume that you have an answer for us."

Amin had arrived in Tokyo a day earlier, and this was his second meeting with them. The Japanese had entertained their guest at one of the most exclusive restaurants in the Akasaka district, and had questioned him about the general conditions in the Middle East. They had also invited him to their headquarters and shown him around.

Now they were at his suite at the Okura Hotel. Amin had been hospitable, offering them tea and fruits and presenting each man with a small gift that KPC's public relations secretary had wrapped and insisted he take with him. "The Japanese love presents," the secretary had insisted.

"Ah, the proposal," said Amin, turning to his briefcase and pulling out a bunch of documents. "Your, eh—how did you put it? Minor alterations? Yes, I believe that's what you said. Well, your minor alterations were indeed minor, Kurai-san, and we have no problems with them, and I am ready to sign the agreement on behalf of KPC, if that would be acceptable to you. But before we do that, I'd like you to explain to me why you chose to make those alterations, since they're so minor that they shouldn't have mattered anyway and since we had insisted that our original proposal was not negotiable."

Takao and Kurai were taken by surprise. This was the most ridiculous question they'd ever heard. What did it matter why, especially since he had accepted the terms and declared his acceptance in advance? When Amin had announced that the alterations were acceptable, Kurai's first instinct had been to go and celebrate the birth of what he believed would turn out to be a historic agreement. But now something was keeping him down. Something about Amin's attitude didn't sit quite right with him.

Could he really trust these people? Amin did not sound serious enough about the deal. He didn't seem *excited* enough about it.

"Mr. Amin, first I'd like to say that I am very pleased with KPC's decision and that I look forward to a long and fruitful association with you." Kurai was engaged in the rather futile effort of trying to extract a firmer commitment from Amin, a reassurance that his complacency about the substance of the agreement did not indicate indifference about honoring its terms. "The nature of this agreement is such that it necessitates a constant renewal of commitment and trust, and we hope that our personal friendship will grow and flourish along with the commercial aspects of the agreement."

Takao was becoming uncomfortable with this monologue; Amin was listening intently, but the expression on his face had an almost amused quality. Kurai talking about commitment and trust! Kurai begging for reassurances, verbal reassurances, beyond those provided by the letter of the contract. This was ridiculous; the whole thing should have been over by now.

"As to your interest in our minor alterations," continued Kurai. "I'm sure you have noticed that none of them are related to the commercial aspects of your original proposal. In fact, what we've done is to make our commitments to you more binding, more airtight, legally, that is. We have even added a few clauses that would make us liable for any future breach of good faith by our current distributors. I assume this was welcome at KPC as a sign of our commitment to the agreement."

"Oh, it was. But you have to admit that it is somewhat unorthodox for one party in an agreement to tighten the legal terms on itself, don't you think? As I said, we can't find any reason to object to the substance of the changes you have proposed. But we'd like to know why, simply because I cannot be at ease when I don't understand an important aspect of an agreement I'm about to sign."

"The legal details have no bearing on you," stated Kurai a bit too curtly. His patience, along with his stock of goodwill, was beginning to run thin. "They were introduced into the agreement to give our lobbying efforts here in Japan some teeth. Just in case we need it. That's all."

"What Mr. Kurai means is that the agreement might one day have an impact on how Fuji Kosan's lawyers deal with MITI," Takao added. "The more binding the agreement, the more ammunition they'll have when they start fighting for a change in the rules of foreign ownership. That's all. It will in no way affect you or KPC."

"I see, I see, yes, I do see." Amin was almost whispering the words. "But are you sure it won't affect us? We've said we don't want KPC involved in your campaign in any way whatsoever. How could you avoid that if one day you end up resorting to this agreement to make your case?"

"We can, Mr. Amin, easily in fact," said Takao before Kurai could answer. He did not want Kurai to snap at Amin again. "You see, the issue is not going to be KPC at all, but rather an airtight, binding contract for Fuji Kosan. It could have been signed with any other organization and it would still serve the same purpose from the point of view of the lawyers. Please understand that this is a strictly internal Japanese matter and we have as much incentive as you do, if not more, to keep the name of KPC out of it."

That seemed to satisfy Amin. The foreigner doesn't really matter. It is an internal battle. Obligations are internal matters. A curious phenomenon and very Middle Eastern, he thought. *We* use foreigners to settle scores among ourselves. Sometimes we leave so much on the table without any apparent reason that they get confused. How should they know that we're making the deal just to stab one of our own in the back? The Americans are the most hopeless in situations like that. They would never understand that sometimes we act irrationally with good reason and that there is no contradiction in that. But I would never have thought the Japanese did the same. To the rest of the world, they appear much too united and harmonious for that kind of thing. In the Gulf, especially, they gang up on us, as Jim explained so aptly. They gang up *on* us, not together with us against one of their own. Perhaps the differences between us are more form than substance after all, Amin thought, without fully believing they were.

They signed the agreement. Amin couldn't understand their eagerness. The agreement would become binding on KPC only after the rule that limited any foreign investment in a Japanese refinery to less than 50 percent share was repealed. Until then, it was just a piece of paper. It will take them years, thought Amin, two, perhaps three years. After all, the only credible external source of pressure on

Japan is America, and why should the Americans care about Japan's oil refining and distribution industry? The majors are already here. The Americans have bigger interests in this region. They don't care about the infamous Motouri; they don't—and they couldn't—understand it enough to want to invest in it.

So who knows when the old rule will be repealed, if it is repealed at all, he thought. But regardless of what each of them might have thought about the prospects of changing Japan's foreign investment rules, they signed the agreement with a great sense of ceremony. Three original documents were ceremoniously signed and passed along. At the end, each man took his original and bowed to the others. Even Amin bowed. Then they all laughed.

Kurai apologized for having to leave soon after the signing. He instructed his driver to go straight to Shinjiku. He needed Kyoko to help him decide whether he should celebrate or worry, to help him understand why he wasn't jumping with joy.

PART THREE

1989-1991

"The meek shall inherit the earth, but not its mineral rights." J. Paul Getty

XVII

Tying Down the Big One

I t was the most elaborate state reception ever given to any visiting dignitary by the government of Iraq. It was in the spring of 1989, and all of Baghdad, including every agency of the government, was mobilized and put to the task of "celebrating" the visit of His Majesty King Fahd bin Abdulaziz Al Saud, king of Saudi Arabia and the custodian of the two Holy Mosques. There were schoolchildren lined up on both sides of the main highway from Baghdad International Airport all the way to the official state guesthouse, waving the Iraqi and Saudi Arabian flags, trying their best not to show their fatigue and boredom. Such flags also decorated every street where the king was going to pass. And there were pictures, thousands of pictures, of Saddam Hussein and King Fahd.

"It pleases me, at this moment, when I, and the accompanying delegation, arrive at my second home, the fraternal Republic of Iraq, to salute with all pride and admiration my brother, His Excellency President Saddam Hussein of the Republic of Iraq," announced King Fahd in his arrival statement. This was his first visit to Baghdad, which diluted the credibility of the claim that Iraq was "a second home" for His Majesty. But the language was standard and expected.

As King Fahd's motorcade drove from the airport to the state guest-house, His Majesty had a hard time keeping up the necessary appearances. The children, in their freshly laundered and pressed school uniforms, were waving their flags and throwing flowers on the street for his car to pass over. But he clearly was becoming tired of continuously waving and smiling to the endless line of chanting schoolchildren.

Watching him on television in his room at the Al Rasheed Hotel in Baghdad, Blackburn thought it was a rather unflattering public appearance the king had been trapped into making. The camera seemed to be pinned on his forced smile and his waving hand, which increasingly resembled a mechanical arm that needed re-winding every few minutes.

During the next few days, Iraqi television showed little else than the king's visit and Saddam Hussein's reception of him. There were speeches, full of brotherly love and Arab nationalist rhetoric. In one of his many public appearances with Saddam Hussein, King Fahd took off a gold medal from his neck and, with great ritual, hung it on Saddam Hussein's neck. It was the highest Medal of Honor that Saudi Arabia could bestow on an individual, and was usually reserved strictly for members of the royal family and ultra loyalists.

Saddam Hussein, in his turn, presented the king with a sniper rifle manufactured in Iraq, and a gold plated automatic gun made of the weapons of the Iraqi dead in the Iran/Iraq war, or as the announcer of the evening news on Baghdad television put it, "made of the weapons of the glorious Saddam's Qadisiyah martyrs, donated by the glorious Iraqi women." In another appearance, Saddam Hussein called the king "our elder brother." King Fahd was elated that day. He had been waiting for that recognition, formally and officially, and it finally came, from Saddam Hussein personally.

The meetings were not all love and brotherhood. It was rumored that when Saddam Hussein and King Fahd met behind closed doors for several hours, there were fierce arguments and debates, even threats and counter-threats. Blackburn tried to find out what was going on, but it was impossible. There was a total blackout on their dialogue. The two men did not need interpreters or aides; they talked alone, one to one. No leaks. Just a lot of guesses and rumors.

The problem was that while Saddam Hussein had all the authority he needed to speak on behalf of Iraq, King Fahd did not have the authority to decide and speak on behalf of Saudi Arabia without first consulting with his brothers. That was the irony that distinguished the "absolute monarchy" of Saudi Arabia from the "republic" of Iraq. Saddam was more of an absolute ruler than King Fahd, who could not rule without appeasing the peculiar sensitivities of the Al-Saud family. But it wasn't until later that this problem became evident. During the few days of the royal visit to Baghdad nobody knew enough to worry about the powers of the Saudi king. It so happened that the king was inclined to break a few rules. Saddam Hussein had managed to convince His Majesty that the heads of the other Arab sheikhdoms had already betrayed him; worse still, certain members of his own family had sold him out.

King and president finally emerged to have their aides announce the existence of a series of secret agreements, which were later referred to as the Saudi-Iraqi "non-aggression pact." Of course, nobody thought of the pact as a bilateral treaty between two countries not to invade each other. It was clear that it was a non-aggression promise from Iraq in return for certain financial favors by Saudi Arabia, which essentially meant that the king had finally agreed to pay protection money to the big bully of the north.

For Blackburn, however, the Saudi-Iraqi non-aggression pact had a unique significance. In many ways, he considered it his own brainchild.

Later that evening, Al-Tikriti called and whispered over the phone, barely able to contain his excitement. "The big donkey is tied in the stable. He is secure. *Very* secure." Blackburn heard Al-Tikriti's restrained chuckle just before he hung up the telephone, and a chill went up his spine. This was *his* advice, his idea, unfolding in front of his eyes, even though he had no clue what the details entailed. But His Majesty was finally cornered and neutralized by Saddam Hussein through a security pact.

During the following weeks and months, the non-aggression pact became a sticking point almost everywhere. With the exception of Saddam Hussein and King Fahd, nobody seemed to like it. The inner circle in Riyadh, composed of King Fahd's brothers, did not like it. The rulers of Kuwait, the United Arab Emirates, Bahrain, Qatar, and Oman were furious. They saw the pact as an unforgivable capitulation by Fahd to Saddam's pressures. They also saw in it a decision by Fahd to betray everybody else in order to save his own neck. Some even argued that the pact was illegal, since Saudi Arabia was tied by similar security agreements to its GCC members, which prevented the Kingdom from signing non-aggression pacts with other countries without prior consultation with the GCC.

*   *   *

Six months after the signing of the Iraq-Saudi Arabia non-aggression pact, the Marriott lobby in Vienna was buzzing again with the usual group of reporters, delegates, and oil company representatives. The Garten Café was full and the charming waitresses were scurrying.

For many veteran observers, it was clear that once again something was different. Ever since the great excitement of the ill-fated OPEC/non-OPEC meetings of the preceding year, OPEC meetings had started to become boring. Even the jumpy oil markets had started to ignore some of the more routine statements that came out of the Marriott lobby.

But this OPEC meeting had the clear potential to turn into a major political showdown. The usual questions and issues—such as how much oil the group should produce, what the price of oil should be—were still on the table, but the delegates did not seem interested in them. The main issue was that Kuwait was absolutely furious at Saudi Arabia and was going to do everything in its power to disrupt the meeting and OPEC's quota structure.

"We are tired of saying 'yessir' to His Majesty King Fahd," Ramzi Amin explained to Blackburn. "Shaikh Ali has instructions from the ruler of Kuwait to be totally uncooperative, with everybody, but especially with the Saudis. If he cooperates in the slightest way, he will be fired."

This was quite a mouthful for the quiet and reserved Amin. But they had a moment alone at their table at the Garten Café and Amin thought he owed Blackburn at least a hint of an explanation of the way the Kuwaitis had been behaving.

"We are an independent sovereign state," continued Amin, sensing the surprise, perhaps even disbelief, in Blackburn. And, as if trying harder to drive a point home before somebody joined them and he couldn't talk any more, he added, "The Saudis have to realize that we are not Qatar! They simply cannot push us around. If they have a plan, they should consult with us, ask our opinion, and if we like it we will cooperate with them. Kuwait's oil policy is made in Kuwait, not in Riyadh."

"Ramzi, what does this have to do with oil policy?" asked Blackburn, who was getting somewhat frustrated with Amin's uncharacteristically emotional diatribe. "We're alone, you volunteered an explanation about the Kuwaiti stand, so why don't you come to the point?"

"The point," Amin snapped, "is a re-declaration of our sovereignty and our independence. For those who have ears to hear, it is very clear and direct." He was getting irritated too, at Blackburn's refusal to talk around the subject.

"Fine. Let me ask you this. How much of this has to do with the Saudi/Iraqi non-aggression pact?"

"Jim, we'll talk about this later," said Amin, pointing at the group of people approaching their table. But Blackburn knew it wouldn't be easy to make Amin say much. For a more honest and complete account of the Kuwaiti agenda, he would have to find someone else in the Kuwaiti delegation to talk to. Amin was a perfect source for all the questions that could be answered with a short phrase, but not for something that needed to be analyzed.

The meeting lasted for five days. Kuwait was the ultimate and masterful troublemaker. Shaikh Ali challenged almost every assertion made by every other minister during the meetings. He insisted that Kuwait's production quota should be raised disproportionately to the other quotas, because Kuwait had a huge spare capacity, which had to be utilized. He tried to win the support of other countries, notably Iran, in order to isolate Saudi Arabia, but did not succeed. In the end, he declared that since his quota demands were not met, Kuwait would simply assume it was free of any quota restriction and would produce out of the OPEC quota system.

The media had a field day with the controversy, partly because the preceding meetings had been relatively boring.

There was no question in Blackburn's mind that the Kuwaitis felt betrayed by both Iraq and Saudi Arabia. The bilateral agreement had hit a raw nerve somewhere in the Kuwaiti psyche. They did not appreciate being left out of a deal that the "big boys" struck.

I have to get the Iraqi perspective on this mess, thought Blackburn. But there was no one in the Iraqi delegation in Vienna he could talk to freely. Rather, there was no one in the Iraqi delegation in Vienna who would freely talk to him. So Blackburn left the Garten Café, went up to his room, and called Issam Al-Tikriti in Washington.

"I'd like you to call some of your Iraqi friends here in Vienna and find out what they think about the Kuwaiti performance," said Blackburn.

"I don't have to call anybody," replied Al-Tikriti. "I can tell you exactly what the Iraqis are thinking right now about the Kuwaiti performance. They are disgusted by it. I assure you that Kuwait will regret this. I can't say exactly how or when, but they will regret this."

"Do you think Kuwait has a bone to pick with Iraq?" asked Blackburn, aware of the highly emotional tone in Al-Tikriti's response, which meant the Iraqis must have been discussing this among themselves and riling each other up in the process. "I thought their fight was largely against Saudi Arabia."

"Look, Jim. They can pick their fights with anybody they want and fight them in any way they want. What they *cannot* do, what they will *not be allowed* to do, under *any* circumstances, is trash the Iraqi economy in the process. And this little fight they've picked with the Saudis happens to do just that. I don't have to explain that to you."

"They're saying they're a sovereign state and they're free to set their oil policy as they like," said Blackburn, hoping to get Al-Tikriti to carry on.

"Well, they're *not* a sovereign state! *They're a bunch of Bedouins*, for God's sake. Since when has Kuwait become a nation? They are a miserable little desert *tribe*. They can't *afford* to act like a sovereign state. They will pay for this, Jim. I guarantee you that."

"But Issam, why the hostility? They're saying they supported Iraq during its war with Iran. They paid Baghdad billions. They gave Iraq more than Saudi Arabia. They're saying they *risked* more by siding with Iraq than any other country in the region. And now they feel betrayed because Baghdad won't sign a non-aggression pact with Kuwait, after having signed one with Saudi Arabia."

"You've answered your own question, Jim," Al-Tikriti said with sudden calm. "Now you should understand why the hostility is there. Because these shitty little Bedouins, who think they're so smart, are trying to *force* Saddam Hussein to sign a non-aggression pact with them. They want to *force* him to recognize and secure their borders. They're trying to force him, Jim, economically. They have the balls to show him that they can do great damage to the Iraqi economy by trashing the oil market. They've taken on the wrong man, Jim. They really don't know what they're dealing with."

"Why won't Iraq sign a non-aggression pact with Kuwait?" asked Blackburn, glad to have finally come to the heart of the matter.

"Oh, they will. But not under duress and definitely not under Kuwait's terms. The pact will cost them. It cost Fahd, as you know. It will cost that dog Jaber even more. They can't have it for free and they definitely can't have it by force. They are so afraid right now, you wouldn't believe it! They have never been more scared of Iraq. They believe the non-aggression pact between Iraq and Saudi Arabia has made them more vulnerable to an Iraqi aggression."

"Has it?"

"Sure it has. We've tied the big donkey in the stable, remember? Now we're free to go after the small donkeys!"

"Issam, wait a minute. The purpose of tying the big donkey was simply to protect it. It was not meant to make the smaller ones more vulnerable!"

"Well, why not? The idea is not to invade Kuwait, you know. The idea is to scare them enough so they pay full price for the non-aggression pact. They'll get their pact eventually. But this behavior is just raising the price."

Later that evening, four people from the Kuwaiti delegation, including the chief officer from the KPC London office, gathered in Amin's suite. Blackburn joined them.

"How can we believe them anymore?" a frustrated Kuwaiti trader said, referring to the Saudis. "They put this $15 price floor idea on the table last November, then backed down. Then the king talked about $26 oil, almost as if he had seen it in a vision in his dreams! Then he wanted the $15 floor again. Then he took it back again. Then he wanted to eliminate the $18 price as target. Now $18 is 'reference.' How can anybody say all this and still have any credibility left?"

By some stroke of fate, Kamal Ashkar from the Saudi Arabian delegation showed up at Amin's door. Blackburn, who was beginning to feel outnumbered by the Kuwaitis, was happy to see him. The Kuwaitis felt so comfortable with Ashkar that this type of Saudi-bashing could take place in his presence without anybody giving it a second thought. Ashkar was Ashkar, the eternally jovial, talkative, more often drunk than sober member of the Saudi Arabian delegation, who rarely listened to what was being said to him, let alone around him. And Ashkar was getting quite drunk that night. After finishing everything in the minibar, he had already taken the liberty of calling room service from Amin's suite and ordering a bottle of scotch.

"What would you have done if OPEC had accepted your quota demands?" Blackburn asked Amin, knowing full well that Kuwait's main objective had been to disrupt the meeting and not to secure a higher production quota.

"If they had accepted our demand, then we would have produced 1.35 million barrels per day and oil prices would have increased. They all would have been better off. Now we are not bound by 1.35 because they did not accept it and that's not our quota. Now we have no quota."

"Ramzi, what would you *really* have done?" insisted Blackburn. "I mean, could you simply have declared your satisfaction with your new quota and behaved normally? Was this really the strategy?"

"Look, Jim. I don't know what anybody has told you, but we do not want to be troublemakers at any cost and for no reason. There really is a good reason behind all this. I asked the Iranians, 'Why are you siding with the Saudis? Don't you want higher prices? Accept our quota demand and you will have higher prices, because we will stick to it. If you reject our demand, you will lose revenue.' But they did not listen to me. Now, do you really believe that if the Iranians had listened to us and supported us against the Saudis, we would have reneged on our promise to stick to the agreement? Why would we have done that? Can't you see that pulling Iran to our side against Saudi Arabia would have been a bigger victory for us than any quota calculation?"

Blackburn could see that. But he also could see that this feud would not end with just one victory at one OPEC meeting. Kuwait could not afford to start behaving better within OPEC if it really intended to add some muscle to its protest against the Saudi-Iraqi non-aggression pact. It had no other means. It had no political or military weight. The only thing Kuwait could do to force its neighbors to take it seriously was to cause them economic and financial hardship.

"What puzzles me is how the Gulf countries can still support Saudi Arabia," the Kuwaiti trader said. "The Saudis are corrupt. Whenever we have approached them to buy gasoline they have turned us down, because we do not pay commissions. They betray anybody without the slightest hesitation. They betray each other. How can you trust people like this? That's the real puzzle."

"I'll give you a better puzzle, my friend," said Kamal Ashkar, butting into the conversation. He was drunk, his face was flushed, his eyes bloodshot and his smile wide. "It's actually a riddle, not a puzzle. Now let's see how smart you really are." And Ashkar proceeded to recite with all the great theatrics and fanfare that the Arabic language affords:

> *He sleeps and he wakes up.*
> *He sheds tears, but does not cry.*
> *In Damascus, they call him "The Pigeon,"*
> *Because he perches on two eggs.*
> *In Iraq, they refer to him as "The Treacherous,"*
> *Because he's been known to stab from the back.*
> *In London they call him "The Gentleman,"*
> *Because he stands up in the presence of ladies.*
> *And in Paris they call him "The Rumor,"*
> *Because he moves from mouth to mouth.*

"Well? Did you figure it out yet?" he demanded amid general laughter. They were all somewhat tipsy.

"Won't your brain ever leave your genitals?" asked the Kuwaiti trader. But the mood in the room had lightened considerably. More Scotch was ordered and Arabic music was put on. Blackburn excused himself and left.

*   *   *

At Blackburn's insistence, over dinner his first night in Vienna, Bianca had told him everything that had happened in Florence. Everything, especially the sexual details. She was reluctant at first, resenting the intrusion into her privacy. But then she went along. If this is what he needs to overcome his inner demons, she thought, I won't spare the details. She was fighting a battle too, doubtless as bitter a battle as his, to save her relationship with Blackburn.

The "full disclosure" sessions were completed that first night. Back in his room, Blackburn absorbed everything again, with as much detachment as he could muster, and, in the absence of the fear of the unknown, resolved to stay with Bianca. He also resolved to live in the present. Her presence with him then and there, rather than with Roberto, helped. The present was his.

She was to spend the next night with him. He booked a suite at the Imperial Hotel, which he considered the best and most romantic hotel in Vienna, if not in Europe. He did not intend to follow the OPEC meeting closely, and did not want anyone to see him with Bianca at the Marriott. This would be their first night together since her rendezvous with Roberto in Florence. He had decided to do everything he could not to show her any lingering angst. He had grown to regret his initial openness. There was, after all, something called pride.

Bianca was especially sweet that night. She wanted to overwhelm him so he'd forget the details he'd asked for and she had shared. She gave herself to him with such abandon that it drove him to distraction. But in the back of his mind, he was thinking, did she give all that to Roberto too? Is this unique? Is this a pure Bianca-Blackburn moment, or is it shared with many? If only he could be sure this was just theirs, not repeated with others. Despite his new resolve, the pain of having to share her never fully left him.

Later that night, as they were lying in bed in each other's arms in silence, he remembered Ashkar's riddle and smiled. She was cuddling him, her head resting in the crook of his shoulder, his face touching the top of her head. She felt his smile.

"What now?" she whispered, without moving.

"I have a riddle for you," he said, trying desperately to sound serious.

"What kind of riddle?"

He recited the riddle.

She listened, with her face buried between his arm and his chest, chuckling at the various descriptions, holding him tighter with each new clue. When he was done, she looked up to him.

"You want me to solve your riddle, Jimmy, *tesoro mio?*"

"I bet you can't, even though it's right under your nose." He couldn't help a spontaneous burst of laughter.

"You want me to go looking for the solution, don't you," she whispered so seductively that he was instantly taken by her spell.

"*Luce dei mie occhi ...*" she purred, as she dove inside the covers and started walking her fingers on his abdomen, whispering sweet nothings under the sheet, looking for the solution to the riddle.

This was the present, and this was Bianca. And at that moment, she was his. Deep inside, Blackburn knew she would hurt him again. But he was not dwelling on his "deep inside" at that moment.

XVIII

Death of a Protocol

The doorman of the bachelor apartment building in Shinjiku had been bribed in advance. He let the young Yakuza gangster in and quietly slipped Kurai's apartment key into his hand.

The man walked straight to Kurai's door. Before opening it, he pulled down his mask. There was no need to harm the woman as long as she did not see his face. He opened the door and stepped in so quietly that neither Kurai nor Kyoko noticed. When the man finally made a noise, he was standing over them, sword raised with both hands far above their heads.

"Move over!" he ordered a horrified Kyoko, who had been kneeling in her customary position between Kurai's thighs, with her face buried in his buttocks. The entire operation did not take more than ten seconds: Her leap away from the arced path of the sword, Kurai's attempt to turn around, the first blow on the back of his neck that severed the bone, the second blow, which hit diagonally from his right shoulder to his left buttock, and the young Yakuza's calm, satisfied walk to the door.

Blood was still gushing out of Kurai's neck and back when the Yakuza quietly closed the apartment door behind him. It took poor Kyoko a good ten minutes to recover her voice and call for help.

The slippery Samurai had finally been dealt with, the old-fashioned way.

Kiyoshi Kurai had gone a step too far. He had taken his battle out of Tokyo and into the highly sensitive game of Japan-bashing in the United States. In order to put the squeeze on MITI, he had started to cooperate with the anti-Japan lobbies in Washington. The information and insights he transferred to Washington could one day have bigger implications for Japan than Fuji Kosan or even the Motouri Brotherhood. He had to be stopped.

∗   ∗   ∗

Kurai's dramatic murder quickly turned into a political sensation in Japan. It wasn't every day that corporate executives got hacked to death in their bachelor apartments by Yakuza gangsters, and it wasn't every day that the excitement-hungry Japanese could find an event so fertile, so full of possibilities for gossip, mystique, scandal, and intrigue. The picture of Kurai's blood-drenched body made the front page of most newspapers for a day. But the pretty and tearful face of his concubine, Kyoko, graced the pages of Japan's newspapers for weeks after the killing, as real and imaginary pieces of the puzzle of Kurai's murder were uncovered or manufactured by the Japanese media and offered to a seemingly insatiable public.

A few reporters actually managed to put together a story that was quite close to the truth. But by then so many different versions of what might have happened were floating around that the truth was easily lost in the shuffle. Most of the theories appeared to be more likely than the truth anyway. To the average Japanese, it was unthinkable that MITI would resort to Japan's criminal underground and hire a gangster assassin to get rid of a corporate executive, regardless of how troublesome the executive might have been for the ministry. In fact, to the average Japanese, it was inconceivable that a corporate executive could have been too troublesome for MITI in the first place. MITI was the undisputed overlord of Japan's vast industrial and trade complex. Even the more skeptical Japanese, who did not have much respect for their government, found it hard to believe that a single individual, the head of a small, insignificant oil company, could put MITI in such a compromising position.

The most popular versions of the episode remained those that revolved around love and jealousy, since the media had invented more than one young, jealous, but poor lover who couldn't continue watching Kyoko waste her life with the dirty old man.

With all the attention, Kyoko's initial shock and sorrow wore out rather quickly. She was actually fanning the speculative fires of love triangles and untamed passions running wild. She did not publicly deny any of the stories. She confirmed only a few factual details that the police had been forced to release to the press. Everything else was fair game for the reporters and the astonished public. And it was not only attention that she received or sought. She was in the process of negotiating with the most promising reporter from one of Tokyo's tabloids an authorized biography, with movie rights and all. Although Kurai had not given Kyoko one joyous moment when he was alive, his death had served her well.

By the time the MITI resignations came, the Japanese public was too absorbed in the love stories to detect any correlation with Kurai's death. Outside Japan, people either hadn't heard of the incident or didn't know enough to make the connection. Despite all the attention the Kurai killing received in Japan, and even though his death was closely related to his overseas wheeling and dealing, the event was not even reported abroad.

Blackburn read about the MITI resignations on Reuters. The story was short and to the point:

"JAPAN'S MITI HAS NAMED NEW CHIEFS FOR ITS AGENCY OF NATURAL RESOURCES AND ENERGY AND FOR THE PETROLEUM DEPARTMENT OF THAT AGENCY, A MINISTRY SPOKESMAN SAID.

"MASAJI YAMATA WILL REPLACE AKIO MIYAZAKI AS THE AGENCY'S DIRECTOR GENERAL. NOAKI GURODA WILL BECOME DIRECTOR GENERAL OF THE PETRO-

LEUM DEPARTMENT, REPLACING MAKOTO ITAI, THE
SPOKESMAN SAID.
"THE APPOINTMENTS ARE EFFECTIVE JUNE 27."

Although Blackburn couldn't grasp the full significance of the news, Miyazaki's departure was not altogether irrelevant to him. Takao of C. Itoh often talked about Miyazaki as a person who would transform the Japanese oil industry and make it competitive with the best in the world. Takao had explained to Blackburn the basic thrust, agreements, and targets of the Motouri Protocol, even though that phrase was not used to describe the deal. It was referred to as Japan's oil industry plan, and Miyazaki was identified as its main architect.

It could not have occurred to Blackburn that Miyazaki's replacement also marked the death of the Motouri Protocol, at least in the form in which it had been conceived and agreed upon that fateful day two years earlier in the small village of Gora. The error in the Motouri Protocol was not its final objective. The error was that it left too much to private oil companies to sort out. That was unwise. One loose cannon like Kurai had come so close not only to destroying an essential plan for Japan's future economic well-being, but also to embarrassing the Japanese government at one of the most sensitive periods in the country's relations with the United States.

In retrospect, the whole idea of letting the oil companies, through competition, decide for themselves which of them would survive to inherit Japan's oil industry was too naive, too half-cooked an idea, and it left too much to chance for MITI to have tolerated. Had it not been for Miyazaki's record and enormous prestige within the industry, it probably would not have been approved.

The question was what the government could do to secure a long-term supply of oil. Oil is a government business, Blackburn had told his Japanese clients time and again. Well over 90 percent of the world's oil reserves were owned by governments, not by private companies, including the majors. In order to secure oil, the government had to not only get involved, but also deal with other governments. The time had definitely come for MITI to start advancing the main objectives of the Motouri Protocol, but without relying on the Motouri. Perhaps even without the cooperation or knowledge of the Motouri.

Thus it was that during the first few months after Kurai's murder, the pressure on the newly appointed team at MITI's Agency of Natural Resources and Energy started to rise. They had to do something to alleviate Japan's dependence on foreign oil companies in a significant way.

*   *   *

It wasn't until a year later, long after Iraq's tanks had rolled into Kuwait and started a major international crisis, that Yamata finally understood what he had been offered. But at the time, as a fine perspiration enhanced the shine on Issam Al-Tikriti's bald head, and as his small beady eyes darted around with excitement, all Yamata could think of was the one-stop shopping analogy advocated earlier by Blackburn. "You can't go after a few thousand barrels here and a few thousand barrels there," Blackburn explained to him patiently. "You'll never reach two million barrels per day of meaningful production that way. Your costs will be too high, your production will be dispersed all over the world, with different types of crudes from different fields. You have to go after something substantial. Focus your efforts in one or two areas where you have some advantage—maybe areas where you can have some leverage over the local government."

"But where?" Yamata asked with enough sarcasm in his voice to irritate Blackburn. He could have read too much into the two words that Yamata uttered, but the tone seemed to tell him "stop preaching concepts and get to specifics; tell me exactly where and how and spare me the lectures."

Blackburn had been spending a lot of time in Tokyo. He had met both the new team and the old team at MITI's Agency of Natural Resources and Energy. After his formal resignation, Miyazaki had been retained by MITI as a senior advisor. He still had the confidence of the minister of international trade and industry. So Blackburn had a chance to meet the architect of the ill-fated Motouri Protocol.

Sensing Blackburn's irritation, Yamata tried to elaborate. "We tried the British, we tried the Americans, we tried the French, we even tried the Kuwaitis," he recited, which irritated Blackburn even more. "In fact," he added, with a deliberate emphasis, "I understand that we tried these people with some direct or indirect help from you. Now where do we try, Blackburn-san?"

"You're right," Blackburn conceded. This was no time to raise tensions between him and a new client who probably was testing him. "The British won't deal with you. It is mostly arrogance, of course, but that's immaterial. The Americans, at least those worth dealing with, are far too big in this business to take you seriously."

"And the French? We seem to have a problem linking up with them too. We tried to deal with Elf and Total, without any success. We offered them a lot, as I recall. Access to markets in the Far East and cheap capital."

"Your problem with the French is a combination of your problem with the British and the Americans," answered Blackburn. He wanted to come to his main point of introducing Iraq's potential, but felt courtesy required that he humor Yamata. "What complicates the French situation even further is that both French oil companies are extensions of the French government and French intelligence. Especially Elf. They won't deal with you because they're too big; they feel they don't need you, and they'd rather you stayed out of the competition."

"So where does that leave us?" Yamata asked.

"Why has MITI been refusing to talk seriously to Iraq?" Blackburn responded, with growing dislike for the man. Yamata was an argumentative little man, with dirty, crooked teeth, who often turned inexplicably hostile in the middle of a conversation.

"Iraq? I am not aware that we have a meaningful chance in Iraq."

"Yamata-san, Iraq just emerged from an eight-year war with Iran. Its economy is shattered. All of its creditors are demanding repayment at once. It has enormous long-term potential, but happens to be in a short-term bind. Most importantly, the government is politically strong but economically vulnerable. That's exactly the combination you need. You can help them, and they can deliver to you in one lump sum what you will not be able to get from ten different deals. Just listen to what they have to say."

So it was that Al-Tikriti was given an audience. He had come prepared. He had maps, geological surveys, and seismic surveys. Some were spread over the large conference table, others remained rolled into a neat pile near his briefcase. He patiently explained the full potential of the Rumaila oil field to six expressionless Japanese faces. Yamata invited Akio Miyazaki to attend the meeting. The others were geologists and production engineers from MITI. Al-Tikriti presented details about the Iraqi government's development plans for the Rumaila field, with cost estimates and future production profiles. Although toward the end of his presentation the Japanese faces started to look human, emitting a sound or two and showing some movement in the tiny muscles around the eyes, Al-Tikriti had no idea what portion of what he said, if any, had registered anywhere, let alone impressed anybody.

At the end of the presentation, Yamata broke the silence. He glanced toward Miyazaki, conscious of his presence and seniority, then turned to Al-Tikriti.

"Mr. Al-Tikriti, may I please see the general map again? The one you showed us at the beginning?"

"Certainly!" Al-Tikriti was glad there would be some dialogue after all. He cleared the table of all other maps and charts and spread open the map that Yamata had requested. It was a large, detailed map of an area of some 900 square kilometers between Southern Iraq and Northern Kuwait. It covered a thirty kilometer wide area of about twenty kilometers into Iraq and ten kilometers into Kuwait. Around the center of the four-by-four-foot map was a long, banana-shaped area, shaded light green and marked "Rumaila."

Yamata pointed at the lower part of the light-green area. "This entire portion of the field falls inside of Kuwait's border," he said. "The plan you presented ignores this fact. It treats Rumaila as if it were entirely inside of Iraq."

"Rumaila is an Iraqi field," answered Al-Tikriti, trying hard to remain calm. "You can see from the map that a large portion of it falls inside Iraq. Regarding the Kuwaiti portion, it will be sorted out soon between the Kuwaiti and Iraqi governments. Please do not underestimate the strategic alliance between Kuwait and Iraq. As you know, Iraq's victory in the Iran-Iraq war saved Kuwait from imminent occupation by Iran. And Kuwait spent a considerable amount of money to make sure that Iraq won that war. So you see, there are precedents in the Iraqi-Kuwaiti relationship where economic and financial assets are swapped for security. The Rumaila field will fall in that same category."

"Are we being offered half of the production of the *entire* Rumaila field then? I mean, including the Kuwaiti portion of it?"

"You certainly are," said Al-Tikriti, aware that his characteristic genre of enthusiasm might not go down any better with the Japanese than it would with Gene Theiss. "I assure you that there will be no problem whatsoever with either the Kuwaiti portion or the Iraqi portion when it comes to developing and exploiting Rumaila. It is one field. The border between Iraq and Kuwait is arbitrary anyway, and any Kuwaiti will tell you the same."

One-stop shopping, Yamata thought. Politically strong, economically vulnerable. It is the combination you need—Blackburn's words kept coming back to him. Suddenly, everything seemed to fall into place for Yamata. Although a shrewd and experienced negotiator with industrialists and large foreign corporations, he had no experience in oil exploration and production. Otherwise, he would have seen the value of the offer more quickly, as Miyazaki did.

But Miyazaki knew more about Iraq's potential as an oil producer than he let be known at that meeting. He knew, for example, that even though the Iraqi offer could be of great value for Japan, the Rumaila field was not the best deal available in Iraq. There were more attractive projects. The real prize was the Majnoon field, with production potential of some two million barrels per day. Now that was a worthwhile project. There was no exploration risk, as the oil had already been discovered. There was no marketing risk—the development partners alone could easily absorb the entire output. There was no commercial risk—the development costs were well within reason and easily recovered even if one assumed a large drop in oil prices. There was no political risk, at least not for a few years, while Iraq and Saddam Hussein recovered from the eight-year war with Iran and regrouped. Finally, there was no potential border controversy, as the entire field lay inside Iraq's borders.

So, thought Miyazaki, why had the Iraqi gentleman, so enthusiastic and so generous, not offered Japan the chance to participate in the development of the Majnoon field? For the same old reason, thought Miyazaki. Because the big boys are already there; because, once again, we have been left out of the really good opportunities; because of their arrogance or business savvy. In this case, the big boys were entirely European. Even the Americans were left out of Majnoon. The big Europeans. The French, the

Italians, and the British/Dutch. Nations that had armed Iraq in the past and could arm it again in the future. Nations that were more reliable than the Americans in that regard, because they knew how to pursue their long-term commercial and strategic interests better than the Americans.

But what bothered Miyazaki the most was not that the Rumaila field had much less potential than the Majnoon field. It wasn't even that Japan was being offered second-best acreage again. What bothered him was his belief that Japan could never achieve its objectives by chasing opportunities in the Middle East. The Middle East had brought only trouble to Japan. The original version of the Motouri Protocol had been killed by the Middle East. While the most credible oil companies in Japan were being given the cold shoulder by the international majors, a total flake like Kurai could actually find and cultivate a partner in the Middle East.

In Miyazaki's mind, this was a symptom of bigger ailments. The whole region had turned suspect and unreliable, and not just because of the Middle Easterners. Japan could not rely on the Arabs, nor could it ever trust the Europeans and Americans, who had already carved up the Middle East among themselves.

Miyazaki believed Japan should focus on the Far East, where it had a natural advantage. Malaysia, parts of Indonesia, Papua-New Guinea, all had potential and were relatively free of the influence of the majors. True, they could never match the reserves and production volumes that were possible in the Middle East. But when entry was as difficult and full of pitfalls as it was in the Middle East that did not matter. Japan's oil industry should first grow and mature in its own backyard, and only then venture into the political and commercial minefields of the Persian Gulf.

Very few at MITI agreed with Miyazaki that the Middle Eastern connection had ruined the Motouri Protocol. They blamed instead bad planning and excessive reliance on the private sector, both direct criticisms aimed at Miyazaki. The Middle East, in spite of its chronic instability and political and military upheavals, remained the most important oil region of the world.

Miyazaki's anti-Middle East argument was not an easy one to champion. But old statesmen and their influence did not die easily in Japan. If it was difficult to argue the point in the context of oil and the Middle East, Miyazaki was intelligent enough to take the entire debate to a different arena. Beyond energy, beyond oil, beyond even the Middle East.

"This has to do with Japan's *total dependence*," he argued during a private meeting with the minister of trade and industry and Yamata, soon after Al-Tikriti had left Tokyo. "Not just Japan's dependence on imported oil. This has to do with our dependence on the United States. Political and military dependence, that is. It does not have to be the case any longer. We can free ourselves from all of our international economic, political, and even military constraints if we plan this right. It is not just the oil world that has changed. The *whole world* has changed and is still changing."

The three men had a mandate from the prime minister of Japan to finalize a strategy. There was no time to waste. Once the strategy was adopted, the resources of the private sector would be drafted to implement it.

Yamata and Miyazaki couldn't have been more different in almost every respect—appearance, personality, priorities, and outlook. Miyazaki was a classy, impressive man. His white hair, intense eyes, and highly refined manners gave him an aura of nobility. Yamata looked more like a thug: untidy clothes, crooked and yellow teeth, badly groomed hair, and an abrupt and impulsive hostility that never failed to appear in his manners. Miyazaki was the grand strategist: the global thinker, manipulator of situations and grand schemes, student of history and long-term planner. Yamata was a pragmatic executive. He liked to deal with clearly defined, tangible objectives, and did not have much appetite for long-winded arguments and analyses.

The minister of international trade and industry saw the virtues of both men, even though they could not appreciate each other's strengths. He was interested in Miyazaki's arguments more than Yamata was. "When you talk about freeing ourselves from the economic constraints, I understand," he said. "I might even begin to understand how we may shed some of our political constraints. But how can we free ourselves from the military constraints? We still need American military protection and, as far as I can see, we'll need it for a long time to come."

"Yes, we need the American military protection. But against what threat? The conventional wisdom has been that it's the Soviet threat, of course. But who in this room truly believes that the much-dreaded Soviet Union is not in great jeopardy itself? The entire system is crumbling. It may be dismantled in five years, or even earlier. If it is, do you believe our dependence on U.S. military power will disappear? It will not. As long as we rely on the Middle East for our oil supplies—and it does not matter how you define that reliance—we remain dependent on the U.S. military to secure the free flow of oil from the Persian Gulf. Whether we are partners, owners, or importers, we *cannot* secure that flow ourselves.

"The only way to radically diminish, if not totally end, our dependence on America is to end our dependence on the Middle East. The Americans and the Europeans will always have more power there than we do. It is their turf. So why fight it? Why press our luck?"

Yamata was not interested in Miyazaki's arguments. He had already made up his mind. He was going to make a place for Japan in the Middle East. Blackburn was right about Iraq and the special opportunities it represented for Japan. Yamata would have to listen to Blackburn a while longer, even though at some point the consultant had to be left out of the loop. Yamata believed Blackburn was developing too much influence in MITI. He knew too much about Japan's strengths and weaknesses; worst of all, he knew too much about their plans and objectives. We'll cut him off in time, Yamata thought. Right now, we still need him to interpret realms we do not fully grasp.

The compromise decision was to do both: to pursue Iraq through Al-Tikriti's proposals, while intensifying efforts in the Far East. In order to maximize the chances of success in these two areas, all other activities were to be stopped or drastically reduced.

In particular, current efforts by the Japanese Motouri to acquire acreage or existing production assets in the United States were to stop immediately. Entry into the United States was a bad strategy on the part of the Japanese private oil companies. It showed a simple-minded herd instinct of following in the footsteps of the other, more successful Japanese industries. And the environmental and tax-related problems alone were enough to make the United States an unattractive host for upstream oil investments. Add to these the increasingly hostile political environment toward Japanese investments, and you had a sure loser.

They wouldn't waste much time with the European majors either. They would ask the Japanese companies to quietly withdraw from the scene. As much as possible, negotiations would be conducted with either the host governments or their national oil companies. No third-party partners would be cultivated, especially among the majors. Obviously, if the host governments brought them in or insisted on their participation, that would be a different matter. But Japan would no longer ask to be allowed into the big oil club. It would just enter.

Miyazaki was appointed the head of a task force to orchestrate MITI's upstream efforts in the Far East. He would head the research effort to identify promising areas for exploration and development, and be in charge of the negotiations with the new host governments.

Yamata, who seemed to be developing a personal fascination with the Middle East, wanted to keep the Iraqi effort under his own control. That meant Miyazaki had to be kept out of the loop. Miyazaki had his own turf now, and could go on pontificating about long-term strategy to anybody he wanted about his own turf. Yamata would focus on delivering the Middle East.

XIX

So Sorry, Russell-san...

Robert Russell did not take the news well. His $2.5 million a year contract with the Japanese, which had not even run through its first full year yet, was re-evaluated by the client and trimmed substantially. The new proposal was to keep a $200,000 retainer, which would be terminated at the end of the contract year. Cost cutting. Different priorities. So sorry, Russell-san.

At the same time, the Japanese negotiations for the acquisition of oil assets in the United States came to a halt. The Japanese simply withdrew their bids. Meetings were canceled or indefinitely postponed. Some even reneged on existing contracts and offered to settle any reasonable damages. There had been a change at headquarters in Tokyo, they explained. They had no choice but to stop all oil acquisition programs.

The Japanese presence in the U.S. oil sector was so small that the sudden change did not attract any attention. Those directly involved were clearly affected. But it did not become an issue of greater significance. In fact, had the Japanese firms continued their push to buy producing assets in the United States they would have attracted more attention and created more controversy than they did by their sudden withdrawal.

It was a good thing for Wilks, Russell & Co. that the Iraqi contract came in around the same time the Japanese one was lost. Although it was not of the same magnitude—it was worth only $1.2 million for the first year—and exactly half of that amount was to go to an employee called Sophie Myles, Robert Russell should still have been grateful that there was a consolation fee of $600,000 left in the deal for his firm. The money was in exchange for lobbying services for the Republic of Iraq in the U.S. Congress. One day after the deal was signed, Myles called a small staff meeting. "Our assignment is to help improve Iraq's image in this town, smooth over its record of human rights abuses, and create a better environment for financial and trade relations between Iraq and the United States," she announced to her two assistants working on the case.

"It is not going to be easy to achieve all that," said one of the assistants, "especially with little or no help at all from the regime in Baghdad. They keep providing daily ammunition to the anti-Iraq factions in Congress by new violations of international law and human rights."

"I realize that," said Myles, "but we do not have to show results to earn our fee. All we have to do is try. This doesn't make our job easier, however. We have to convince the client that our work will give them the absolute best shot at improving their image. *The* best. Not just *our* best."

"How can we convince them of that?"

"I'm not sure yet. Right now, we need to devise a strategy for Iraq and then help implement it. This really shouldn't take a lot of work."

It won't take much at all, thought Myles. With some behind-the-scenes help from James Blackburn, I can put a strategy together without involving any of the expensive legal talent at Wilks, Russell & Co.

"I've given this a lot of thought, and it does not need to be as difficult as it looks at first," she continued, sensing the skepticism of her assistants. "The strategy has to be simple. Its message should be clear: first, stress Iraq's importance as a counterbalancing force for the potential menace of Iran and its fanatic mullahs, who would not hesitate to take American hostages again. Remind as many congressmen and senators as possible that the Middle East and possibly even the rest of the world would have looked uglier, more unsafe, had Iraq not stood up to the great threat of Iran's Islamic Revolution and stopped its spread beyond its borders."

"Sure," said one of the assistants, "and it won't hurt to remind people every chance we get of the American hostages taken by the Iranian revolutionaries."

"No, it won't," said Myles. "Second, emphasize the economic potential for the United States of good relations with Iraq, show the size of the export market for American goods and services that Iraq represents, translate these exports into numbers of jobs, and show what the congressman or senator would be turning down in his own hometown by ignoring good business opportunities in Iraq. Third, focus on all the good the government has done—economic development, growth in light industry, education and the substantial increase in Iraq's literacy rate and health care. When really pressed by gory accounts of atrocities against the Kurds in the north or the Shias in the south, it might be necessary to attempt to discredit the subversive political motives of these groups, although we have to be careful not to appear as if Wilks, Russell & Co. is endorsing the gross violations of human rights in Iraq."

The strategy was not only simple, but it was also the best anybody could do for Iraq in Washington at the time. The effort had to be carried out in a relatively low-key way. No big media events and no page-long advertisements, which would invite responses from opponents and give more publicity to the negative aspects. The strategy was to work on one congressman or senator at a time. This also meant that very little help would be needed from the company's high-priced lawyers, which was important for Myles' long-term plans.

And it meant that a large portion of the $600,000 that Wilks, Russell & Co. was keeping from the $1.2 million account was profit for the firm.

But Russell was too angry to be grateful for the Iraqi contract. Angry with the Japanese for canceling their retainer, angry with Myles for tricking him into signing her compensation agreement and, ironically, even angrier with her for springing the $1.2 million contract on them. It was almost as if he would have been happier if the total value of the Iraqi contract was only $400,000 and he did not have to pay any commissions to Sophie Myles.

But most of all, Russell was outraged because Myles had tried to warn him about the Japanese contract being in jeopardy, but he had refused to listen. At the time, he could not have thought of a single reason why he should listen to her. How could she know anything of any relevance to the Japanese account? He had been to Tokyo and met with the executives who mattered for that contract. He had negotiated the details personally. He had seen how desperate the Japanese were for his services. What would a relatively junior ex-secretary-turned-officer-by-chance know about the Japanese account?

Several months earlier, when Myles had asked for an appointment to see him, his secretary had forgotten to mention it to him. That was how unimportant Sophie Myles was for Robert Russell. But she persisted. When his secretary finally remembered to mention to him that one of the employees had been asking for an appointment, he put it off, until her persistence was too difficult to ignore.

"Japanese priorities are changing in a way that might affect us," she said when she was finally allowed in to see the big boss, a week after her first request for an appointment. "I thought it was important enough for me to bother you. It could affect our Japanese account."

"What exactly are you talking about, Miss Myles?" he asked, viewing her posture and tone of voice as borderline arrogant.

"I know from reliable sources that there has been a fundamental change in Japan's energy investment policy," continued Myles, sensing her nervousness rise as she fought to control her voice. "They won't be pursuing the aggressive investments in the United States they once planned. In their eyes, this might be cause for re-evaluating the multi-million-dollar public relations expenditures in the United States."

"How come we haven't heard anything about this change in investment policy so far?" asked Russell. "You talk as if it has already been done, right?"

"Right."

"If it is already fact, if it is news, then how come we haven't heard about it?"

"Mr. Russell, it is fact. I did not say it was news. Not yet. I thought perhaps you wanted to know before it became public."

Russell thanked and dismissed her, unconvinced by her story, not even bothering to call his Japanese clients to question them. A few weeks later, Myles requested to see him again, this time to negotiate her commission contract. He agreed to her terms, partly because, as Blackburn had predicted, he did not believe she could bring in an account much larger than the $400,000 base, and partly because he was beginning to get curious about her motives and connections.

A week after he signed her contract, she delivered the Iraqi account. Only a few days after that, the Japanese canceled their contract.

How *did* she know, thought Russell after the Japanese account was lost. I never even asked her. I just dismissed her. How did she manage to learn the facts before they became news, as she so aptly put it?

It occurred to Russell that he knew nothing about Sophie Myles. When she had delivered the Angolan contract almost two years earlier, his curiosity had been aroused a bit, but, as usual, he had been too busy with much bigger issues and soon forgot about her and her surprise Angola connection.

This time, decided Russell, he would not let it slip. He was going to learn about her contacts, her means and methods. He surely had the resources to do that; he had done it on more secretive people than Sophie Myles. He had discovered and sometimes exposed the innermost secrets of some of the most powerful and well-guarded men in Washington. Sophie Myles would be a piece of cake.

Meanwhile, Myles was busy. She took the Iraqi account seriously and arranged various meetings and briefings. She solicited sponsors from the private sector to host seminars in Washington about the business opportunities in Iraq, including "How to do business in Iraq" sessions that attracted many American contractors, traders, food exporters, and exporters of industrial intermediary goods. Often, the sponsors of these seminars came from the oil industry. A few times Blackburn was an invited speaker, talking about Iraq's oil potential and future plans.

Myles organized many private briefings for the benefit of various senators and congressmen, where she invited private sector experts as well as officials from the Iraqi Embassy to confirm her official line: that Iraq was a reliable U.S. ally in the Middle East and should be supported. Iraq's import needs over the next five years were analyzed in detail and presented to various congressmen and senators in terms of the number of jobs those imports could mean for their districts. Myles would often engage former U.S. ambassadors to Iraq and other parts of the Middle East in these sessions. Former ambassadors could be useful. They were generally pro the country where they served, and they gave credibility to the campaign.

Myles went the extra mile on the Iraqi assignment because she wanted to keep total control over the account. Blackburn's obsession with "not working for anybody else" had started to rub off on her. She also thought she owed it to Blackburn to make sure the Iraqis got their money's worth.

The significance of the behind-the-scenes twists and turns of the past year, although neither fully understood nor fully appreciated, did not escape Blackburn's attention. The launching of an aggressive asset acquisition campaign by the Japanese oil companies in the United States was followed by their abrupt and unceremonious withdrawal, which happened to coincide roughly with the unexplained demise of C. Itoh's deal with Kuwait Petroleum Company. This was followed closely by the resignation of one of the most respected Japanese statesmen from MITI, the recognized mastermind of Japan's new energy plan. Blackburn couldn't have missed the possibility that these events might be related, but did not dwell on it either. There was too much to do. The Iraqi-Japanese deal alone could be more important for his future financial well-being than his entire consulting practice.

Neither Blackburn nor Myles had the time or the attention to notice that they were being followed. The private investigators Russell hired had immediately established the relationship between them. Russell had also seen the connection between the Petroleum Consulting Group and Myles' link to Iraq, to the Japanese contract, and to the Angolan contract. He had ordered them to monitor Blackburn as closely as Myles. And they did. Both Blackburn and Myles were under surveillance twenty-four hours a day. The Myles-Blackburn file was getting fatter by the day as photographs and accounts of new get-togethers were reported with meticulous detail.

Russell had no interest in the personal aspect of the Myles-Blackburn relationship—their romance, their occasional mini-vacations to some mountain resort or seaside refuge. His interest was in the business connections and possibly political or even intelligence ties that Blackburn or Myles could be drawing upon. But a large portion of the material filling the Myles-Blackburn files was of a personal nature. There was only an occasional reference to a telephone conversation, a business trip, or an on-site client visit that exposed a client relationship.

One morning, after reviewing the materials given to him by his private investigator, Russell decided to express his frustration.

"This is fine," he said, looking at the photographs of Myles and Blackburn dining in a Washington restaurant, "but we established their relationship a long time ago. I want to know more about his business. His clients—who they are, what he does for them, what he charges them, how long they've been his clients, where he gets his information, who he deals with on a regular basis aside from his clients. Cool it on the personal drama for a while; focus on his business."

"Sure thing, Mr. Russell. But it will cost more. I'll have to buy one of his employees, possibly his CFO, who we gather is going through a difficult divorce and is in serious financial ..."

"Stop right there," interrupted Russell. "Do what you have to. I don't have to know the details. I don't want to know the details."

*   *   *

Robert Russell arrived at his office one morning later than usual. He walked into the fancy marble lobby with a large manila folder under his arm, feeling a little more enthusiastic than usual. The lobby seemed cleaner and shinier to him. Russell had seen too much to feel excited about much of anything. But that morning, he felt more excited than he had for a long time.

He knew the value of what he'd been given at his breakfast meeting as soon as he opened the large envelope and laid his eyes on the computer printout. It was impressive. Probably the most prized and best-guarded asset of any consulting operation was its client list, and that of the Petroleum Consulting Group was now in his hands. His private investigators had surpassed themselves this time. As he went down the list, his curiosity started to mount. It took him enormous effort to fold the printout and slip it back into the large envelope. No point in letting the investigator know that what he had delivered was a big deal. That would raise compensation expectations and betray motives.

Once in his office he told his secretary to hold his calls and cancel his appointments for the day until further notice. He opened the list again and went down the names. Sorted alphabetically by company, it listed the names of individuals, their titles, and company mailing addresses, telephone numbers, and telefax numbers. Most companies had at least five different entries, usually two or three names in the main headquarters and two or three more in regional offices, mostly in the Middle East and Europe. There were 120 companies and 650 individuals in total. And they were not only oil companies.

There were seventy oil companies and oil trading firms from around the world. There were twenty banks and other financial institutions. The remaining thirty "companies" were various government agencies, representing twenty-five different countries. The ministry of petroleum in a dozen oil producing countries, seven different ministries of finance, mostly in Europe and the Middle East, and several other governmental agencies were on the list. There were also ten individual names with just an address and no company affiliation—four in the metropolitan Washington area, two in Japan, two in Europe, and two in the Middle East.

This is a gold mine, thought Russell. He went over the Japanese companies again. C. Itoh, Marubeni, Idemitsu Kosan, Nippon Oil, MITI, Japan National Oil Company. The top five or six executives in each organization were listed, with their direct telephone and telefax numbers. Iraq's State Oil Marketing Organization and the Ministry of Finance were represented on the list by three names each. There was one name with a Baghdad address whose affiliation was simply "The President's Office," and another with an address at the Iraqi Embassy in Washington.

"Absolutely incredible ..." murmured Russell. "Does this Blackburn character know what he's sitting on? Is it really possible to have all these client relationships and run a simple, $6 million a year business?"

It was amazing that just two clients on Blackburn's list, the Japanese government and the person in the Iraqi Embassy in Washington, had been worth $3.7 million to Wilks, Russell & Co. at some point. Two organizations from a list of 120 paid him more than half what the entire

120 paid Blackburn's Petroleum Consulting Group. The potential was mind boggling.

Either James Blackburn didn't care about money or he had no idea how valuable his contacts really were. This guy could make more than the entire revenues of his consulting company working for me on a commission, Russell thought. If I give him the deal I signed with Sophie Myles, he could easily make more than $3 million a year. What would he say if he knew that?

Russell was keenly aware that if he did not plan his next move carefully, he could easily blow this opportunity. Both this Blackburn character and his ex-secretary-turned-officer Sophie Myles had to be treated with care. He had to find out what made Blackburn tick. He had to decide how much of the business potential of a partnership with Blackburn to disclose to him. If Blackburn did not see the potential, he would not be motivated to cooperate with Russell and, in the process, change the entire nature of his practice.

Russell knew there was neither much love nor much respect lost between consultants and lobbying firms—or public relations firms, as the lobbyists liked to refer to themselves. The lobbyists viewed the consultants as a bunch of nerdy technical analysts who did not understand the real power game of Washington and who could never be real players, brokers of real influence, as the lobbyists were. The consultants, on the other hand, viewed the lobbyists as a bunch of immoral, unprincipled operators doing the bidding of whoever paid more, regardless of what their client represented. In order to convince Blackburn to cultivate his existing relationships in a different direction, Russell had to show him how serious the financial rewards of such a shift could be.

But if Blackburn sees the real business potential, he'll get greedy, thought Russell. He undoubtedly gave Myles the idea of the commission arrangement on the Iraqi deal. Blackburn may not recognize the full revenue potential of his client list, but he does not strike me as someone who'd leave money on the table in a business venture.

XX

He Who Knows, He Who Knows Not...

he Symposium was going through a troubled period. There were
divisions among the ranks, as the organization could not agree on
a strategy to cope with the Saudi-Iraqi non-aggression pact. The
end of the Iran-Iraq war and the signing of the historic treaty had been
unexpected setbacks for the organization's plans. They were only a few
months away from their target date of forcing King Fahd out of office
and bringing Crown Prince Abdulla to the throne. Three years had
passed since 1987 when that decision had been made; nobody could have
anticipated these developments back then. New realities on the ground
required revising the plan.

Amin was having trouble choosing a venue for the fifth executive
committee meeting of The Symposium. There were rumors that the Iraqi
intelligence had already infiltrated the organization. Amin had even heard
that Saddam Hussein had managed to extract additional concessions from
King Fahd by disclosing to him The Symposium plan to depose him.
Southern Iraq, where they had held their last meeting under the cover of
a hunting party, was out of the question. Kuwait would be too dangerous,
because Iraqi intelligence would definitely find out and have access to the

meeting. Saudi Arabia would be risky, especially if King Fahd was alerted about the existence of a plot against him. The small island of Bahrain was nothing more than an extension of Saudi Arabia. Some remote corner of the United Arab Emirates would be a possibility, but gathering there would attract too much attention.

Amin initially considered holding the first executive committee meeting out of the Gulf. Europe would be safer. Geneva or Vienna, where they usually met for OPEC meetings. Or perhaps London. What he disliked about the European option was that The Symposium would start to assume the image of an organization "in exile" to its own members. That prospect horrified Amin. To him, and to all other members, The Symposium was a regional organization. Created in the Gulf, from the Gulf, and always *in* the Gulf.

The bigger problem preoccupying Amin's mind involved the divisions within the group after the signing of the Saudi-Iraqi pact. The divisions were formidable. Some were arguing for patience, while others were urging drastic measures, such as assassination.

"Let's just get it over with," Majed Al-Shammary told him. Amin had to take Al-Shammary's views seriously. He was Saudi, related to the royal family, although not a member of it; his tribe was one of the most prominent in the Arabian Peninsula. "Let's just get rid of him," Al Shammary insisted time and again.

"It's not that simple, Majed," Amin said, wondering whether it actually *was* that simple.

"And why not?" Al-Shammary said, getting agitated. After all, this was a Saudi matter, and Ramzi Amin, though a prominent figure within The Symposium, was a Kuwaiti. "King Faisal was assassinated, wasn't he? And he probably was the wisest monarch this country has had since King Abdulaziz. If we could survive losing him, imagine how much better off we'd be losing Fahd!"

But there were those who advised caution. "This is no time for adventure," they said. "The whole world is changing. Look at what's happening in Eastern Europe and the Soviet Union. Entire systems are crumbling. Political ideologies, which until now were regarded as God's truth, are being cast aside."

What concerned those counseling caution most was that reformers were losing control over the process they had started. Change was going *further* than intended by those who instigated it. This was the most dangerous symptom of all—losing control over a process of change and having events force more drastic transformation than was initially planned or intended. This was the danger of moving too fast and risking imponderable unintended consequences.

In the end, the fifth meeting of the executive committee of The Symposium took place in the heart of Riyadh city. And it took place under the cover of an exclusive business forum organized by the Gulf Consulting Group of Washington, DC. Ramzi Amin had simply decided to take James Blackburn into his confidence. That was the most reasonable cover they could think of.

Blackburn's involvement in The Symposium had not come easily or naturally. He had to be briefed, alerted to the risks and dangers associated with being part of The Symposium and, perhaps more importantly, accepted by the members of the executive committee and go through an initiation of sorts. This took several days of discussions at Amin's villa in Kuwait, during which a dozen of the members of the committee "stopped by" and held meetings with him.

What intrigued them about Blackburn were his views about (and his access to) Washington. The politics of Washington and, much more importantly, the institutions engaged in formulating American policy toward the Middle East, were generally little understood in the Gulf. The temptation was to either oversimplify (as in "Americans are naive and allow their policy in the Middle East to be run by Zionist interests") or over-*mystify* (as in "every ill that has ever been inflicted on the Arab world has been the doing of the CIA").

Blackburn's most formidable task in educating his Arab friends was to make them understand that they were not as important to the United States as they thought they were. And although their oil was extremely important, even that was not as important as they thought it was and clearly not for the reasons they believed.

"Don't ever take anything for granted about Washington," he told his Arab hosts. "Not the ideological premises, not the concerns about human rights, not even the commercial interests. And remember, for Washington, the Middle East has always been a side show, never the main game."

"What do you mean, never the main game?" they argued. "Oil *is* the main game, isn't it? Hasn't the West fought wars over it?"

"Oil is not the main game," Blackburn countered. "Oil is an important weapon in playing the main game. The main game, which is about power and influence, is always played among the main players, not you. It is played between the United States and the USSR, between the United States and its own European allies, between the United States and Japan, and among the European allies themselves. But never between them and you. Sometimes *for* oil. Sometimes *with* oil. But it is not oil."

"What's the difference then? For oil, with oil, because of oil, it is an oil game in the end!"

"My friends, it is not an oil game. It is a game to gain dominance over each other. It is a game to become economically more powerful—more powerful than not only our adversaries, but also our allies. It is a game to make our allies depend on us for their strategic resources—such as oil. You and your oil are a side show played for the benefit of the main game."

"But you can't be a player, not even in the side show, without our oil. Oil becomes an end in itself. The fact that it is used as a means to achieve higher objectives is irrelevant! *Our* oil is so powerful that it *becomes* the end in your petty little game!"

There were times when Blackburn lost his patience. Not totally, not enough to tell them all to go to hell, but enough to be less diplomatic than the circumstances called for. How could a culture be so self-centered and so insecure at the same time? How could someone view himself as the center of the universe, yet suffer from an inferiority complex? How could they exaggerate their self-importance, yet feel victimized by the very people to whom they believed they were indispensable?

"It is not your oil," he told the angry faces staring back at him. "If we really believed it was *your* oil, we would have allowed the British and the French to colonize this godforsaken place a long time ago. Why can't you wake up and see the truth, even for one fleeting moment? We are here in Kuwait. Do you really believe Kuwait is a *viable* state if left to fend for itself? It is not your oil. I'm sorry, but it really is *our* oil! We let you keep it because we in the West don't want to fight against each other for it. So instead, we compete over who will control you and, ironically, protect you the best."

Even Amin, who had known Blackburn for a long time, was astonished by this outburst. He knew Blackburn well enough to know it was caused by his frustration at failing to get his point across. But this was not obvious to the others at first. It took many more sessions of heated discussions and outbursts before they finally realized that Blackburn was not interested in winning a debate, but rather, he had a point to make. What nobody realized, however, was the degree to which they had won Blackburn over as an active supporter of their cause.

Blackburn became the first and only non-Gulf national to be included in the inner circle of The Symposium. The question of whether he was a full member of the organization was deliberately left vague; Amin wanted him to have the access of a member, while maintaining some of the freedom and flexibility of an outsider.

The fifth meeting lasted three days. There were several business sessions planned to provide cover, just in case. Presentations on the outlook for the business environment in the Gulf, general economic and trade issues, oil markets, and investment opportunities in various sectors were prepared and ready for distribution. There were slides, handouts, summary tables, and charts.

The three days of discussions went more smoothly than the pre-meeting debates. The committee agreed to postpone any direct attempts at toppling King Fahd. Instead, they would focus on launching a massive campaign against the corruption of the royal family and various abuses of power. They would demand reforms, while exposing the weaknesses of the status quo as much as possible.

But a key question remained unresolved. Had The Symposium, or worse still, the executive committee, been infiltrated by Iraqi or Saudi agents? Ramzi Amin was not sure, and did not want to take chances with all eighteen members. A smaller group met on the last day: Ramzi Amin, Kamal Ashkar, Karim Suliman, Majed Al-Shammary, and James Blackburn.

Their task was to find out whether the executive committee was safe. Amin would check the Kuwaiti-Iraqi rumor traffic. Suliman and Ashkar would check if Riyadh was receiving any information (or disinformation) about them from Baghdad. Al-Shammary would check for rumors in the tribes. And Blackburn would check whether Washington was aware of anything and, if so, whether the information was coming from Iraq or Saudi Arabia.

It was agreed that they'd send simple messages to each other. "He who knows not, is a fool" would mean there were no leaks. "He who knows is a prophet" would mean a leak had been identified. The signals were Amin's idea, taken from a saying attributed to the fourth caliph after Prophet Mohammed, Ali bin Abi Taleb:

He who knows not, and knows not that he knows not
Is a fool. Ignore him.

He who knows not, and knows that he knows not
Can learn. Teach him.

He who knows, and knows not that he knows
Is asleep. Awaken him.

And he who knows, and knows that he knows
Is a prophet. Follow him.

*   *   *

Gene Theiss listened to Blackburn for a long time without interrupting. They were in the library of his old house in Alexandria. The antique daggers were spread as usual on the brass tray. On the library shelf, among a dozen framed photographs, was an old picture of Theiss and Henry Blackburn, James' father, taken in Beirut almost two decades earlier when both men were stationed at the American Embassy there.

Listening to Blackburn, Theiss was reminded of his old friend. He and Henry had been more than colleagues; they had been allies and life-long friends. Allies in the never-ending internal power struggles within the Foreign Service, and friends in times of need. But Theiss was not just remembering his friend that day; he was *recognizing* elements of his old friend in the junior Blackburn, as he spoke, analyzed, reasoned, and argued.

"Let me get this straight," he said after Blackburn had finished recounting the story of the fifth meeting of the executive committee of The Symposium. "You actually promised these people you'd check to see if we knew anything about their movement and, if so, from what source? Are you serious?"

Blackburn was not moved by Theiss' disapproval. He had expected his initial reaction to be exactly that.

"Gene, consider this," he said calmly. "The Symposium is up and running and sooner or later it will probably change the history of the region whether we help them or not. They took me into their confidence, partly because their key people have known me for a long time and partly because they see the value of my connections in this town. Now, can you think of a better way to keep track of them than my cooperation with them? Why shouldn't I have made that promise to them?"

"Because there's no clean way to play both sides, Jim. You can't keep your promise to them and help Washington keep track of them at the same time."

"Why not? They're not against *us*. *We* aren't against them! They are a reform movement, for crying out loud. Why can't I help them without betraying anything?"

"How are you going to control what the State Department tells the Saudis?"

Blackburn stiffened in his seat. "We cannot go to the State Department with this," he said firmly. "They won't understand it. Their first instinct will be to win a few points with the Saudi government, so they'll tell them everything."

"But why shouldn't they do that?" asked Theiss. "An opposition movement is organized, isn't it? They have a plot to depose Fahd, don't they?"

"This is more serious and more legitimate than a few Islamic fundamentalist cells. The Symposium was not formed by a bunch of unemployed and bored youth who have nothing better to do. These men have a lot of vested interest in the system. The reform they're after will actually help save the system, not destroy it. That's what the State Department will not understand."

"So where do you want to keep this?"

"With you. And if need be with the community."

Theiss looked at Blackburn for a few long minutes. Blackburn waited, aware that Theiss was thinking through the possible consequences of his suggestion.

"Fine," he said at last. "Strictly within the community. I'll see what I can find out. But I can tell you this much now: If their organization has been exposed in this town, the source can't be Iraqi intelligence as they think. There is a more likely source. I'm surprised none of you or them thought of it."

Blackburn looked at him and waited.

"Don't miss the Israeli angle in all this, Jim," said Theiss. "They'd prefer Fahd over Abdullah. They have infiltrated the Gulf better than our boys. They probably know about your reformer friends."

Blackburn could almost kick himself. Theiss was right. If Langley knew, they probably learned it from the Israelis.

"I have to remember not to focus strictly on the oil and business side," he conceded. "That's the main reason I did not think of Israel."

"They know the oil side pretty well too. Two weeks ago we received top-secret seismic data of practically every Russian oil field from them. The information is guarded as a state secret in Moscow. I don't think we could have acquired that directly."

"That's impressive. How did they do it?"

"One of the Russian oil tycoons. He had close ties to Israel. He amassed billions by getting his hands on some Russian oil assets, which was forgivable in their chaotic system. But then they found out he had passed the state secrets to Israel. He is now in jail."

"Do you think the Israelis know the oil sector in the Middle East too?"

"I can't be sure, but it wouldn't surprise me."

Then Theiss changed the subject to the Saudi-Iraqi non-aggression pact. "How does it feel," he asked with a faint smile, "to see your own brainchild materialize like that?"

"I'm not sure I have thought this through," said Blackburn. "But I have to admit that watching Fahd's visit to Iraq on TV gave me a huge ego boost."

"What do you mean you have not thought it through?"

"Well, technically, with the Saudis tied down by a non-aggression pact, Iraq is free to go after the others, right?"

"To some extent, right."

"And who is the most troublesome of the 'others'? Kuwait, of course."

Theiss gave him one of his focused, intense looks.

"What are you saying, Jim?"

"In my mind, tying down the Saudis was intended to protect them, not to make the others more vulnerable. But I'm afraid that is what has been achieved."

"How troublesome is Kuwait?"

"From the oil market perspective, very troublesome. They're not alone, of course. But they've become intransigent."

"You know," said Theiss, changing the subject, "you look more and more like your father as you get older. I miss him terribly."

"I miss him too. I'd give anything to be able to talk to him now about everything that's going on."

"Why are you wasting your knowledge and experience in that consulting business? Don't you want to join the community instead?"

"Gene, I don't have the personality, nor the patience, and I especially don't have the discipline. I am happy doing what I do. Besides, I think I can be more helpful to them as an advisor than as an employee."

"Perhaps," said Theiss thoughtfully, "but it's still a pity."

Then he got up and poured them each a glass of sherry.

"What you said about Kuwait being more vulnerable is important. I have heard similar concerns from the field. Let me know if anything concrete shows up in your sights."

"Will do, Gene."

"Of course you know you're being followed, right?" Theiss said casually, as he handed him his glass of sherry.

"Followed? No, by who?"

"You and Sophie have been under twenty-four-hour surveillance for the past few weeks. They are private investigators hired by Robert Russell."

The news hit Blackburn like a bolt of lightning. Theiss saw the shocked surprise on his face.

"Sorry," he said. "I don't know why, but I assumed you must have detected them; otherwise I would have warned you earlier. They haven't been discreet."

"But how did you find out?" asked Blackburn. "Who else knows about this?"

"I have a twenty-four-hour secret security detail. They set it up when my house was broken into over a year ago. The detail saw them follow you last time you came here. Then they ran a check on them. Only a few people in the counterintelligence know."

"Any idea what they're after?"

"Well, you've been photographed everywhere you've been with Sophie. Aside from that, they know about some of your business meetings. They followed you to New York, by the way. So I have a feeling they are after intelligence about your business."

"This is incredible! Robert Russell?" Blackburn was outraged.

"I don't think he intends to harm you or Sophie," said Theiss.

"What do you suggest I do? Should I confront him?"

"You can, of course. But you won't find out what he's after if you do. I'd say leave him alone, but now that you know, be more careful about any sensitive business information you may have. Make sure your client files are secure. How many employees do you have?"

"Fifteen full-time researchers and a couple of consultants."

"Do you trust them? More importantly, do they have access to your files?"

"No, but it wouldn't be difficult for any of them to create an excuse to have access. Of course Linda knows where everything is."

"Who's Linda?"

"My secretary."

"Do you trust her?"

"So far I've had no reason not to. She is loyal. She would have come to me immediately if they had tried to pry information from her or bribe her."

Theiss looked at him somewhat skeptically, but said nothing.

"Tighten security on your files," he said after a while. "I'll try to find out more about what they know so far."

"Thanks, Gene. I really appreciate this. What a shocker! Robert Russell?"

"How's Sophie?" Theiss changed the subject again.

"She's very well, and busy. She's working on Iraq."

"Yes, I heard." That did not surprise Blackburn. Theiss knew everything that went on in Washington that had to do with Iraq. "Give her my regards."

XXI

Sandbox Club

The rains were relentless in the typhoon season. It seemed as if all of Tokyo was enveloped in a boundless sheet of water, pouring, shifting direction, slamming into everything in sight. And although everyone in Tokyo had lived with typhoons all their lives, they still braced themselves when the rains came.

Standing in front of the window of his room at the Palace Hotel, Blackburn watched the gardens of the Imperial Palace across from the hotel disappear into the downpour. The pair of swans, which were a permanent presence in the moat surrounding the outer walls of the palace, had gone. The narrow footbridge was a faint shadow, the green moss around its walls lost in the gray mist.

He didn't care for rainy days. A rainy day in Washington, DC, especially in the summer, would be unbearable—it would raise the humidity to 100 percent in the already muggy city, with temperatures hovering above ninety degrees Fahrenheit, triggering every mold-related allergy in his body and clouding his mind.

But he loved the typhoon rains. This was not an ordinary rain inconveniencing one's day. This was a force of nature that had come with a mission and an unbending determination to achieve it. The blind, relentless drive of the force behind the storm sobered and rubbed off on him. It strengthened his resolve.

The Japanese were kind enough to have agreed to meet at the Palace Lounge in the lobby of the hotel. It was large and, with widely spread tables, would allow them to have some privacy for a small meeting. There were three of them: Mr. Takao of C. Itoh, who had flown from Washington with Blackburn and organized the meeting; a representative of MITI's Agency for Natural Resources and Energy who was one of Yamata's senior staff members; and the senior vice president of Idemitsu Kosan. Blackburn was meeting two of them for the first time.

The greetings and introductions were formal and ceremonial. Name cards, held with both hands between thumb and index finger, were presented solemnly with a bow of the head.

"I am Akiyama, with Idemitsu."

"I am Hayashi, with MITI."

"James Blackburn, PCG Group."

Takao gave a few more details about each person. Then, satisfied that the introductions were adequate, invited them to sit. The Palace Lounge was famous for its wide selection of teas in the afternoon. In the early evening, the service changed to drinks and a diverse menu of small bites and delicacies. The men ordered tea, and Takao asked the waitress to bring a selection of mini sandwiches, scones, and sweets.

After the necessary small talk about the flight to Tokyo and the typhoon season, Takao started the meeting.

"Blackburn-san, both Akiyama-san and Hayashi-san are actively involved in the upstream sector. And they each have experience in both the private sector and the government. We appreciate all the advice you have given us recently, but we have some concerns."

Takao nodded toward Hayashi, a serious-looking man in his mid-fifties, who seemed to Blackburn as though he had been persuaded to come to this meeting against his better judgment.

"The concerns we have are about the Middle East," said Hayashi. "The situation seems to be deteriorating politically, and we are about to sign yet another long-term agreement. We would appreciate your candid assessment of the situation."

The phrase "yet another" did not escape Blackburn. He correctly assumed that the reference was to the ill-fated agreement between KPC and Fuji Kosan and C. Itoh.

"I agree that the political atmosphere is tense, especially in the Gulf," he said, aware that while he had nothing to do with the Japanese agreement with KPC, they would hold him responsible for any deal they ended up signing with Iraq. "But what specifically is of concern to you?"

"As you know, we are negotiating a long-term agreement with Iraq for 50 percent of the production of Rumaila. I believe that offer reached us through your kind intermediation."

"I am not privy to the specifics of your negotiations, but yes, I introduced you to Mr. Al Tikriti, who, I believe, made you that offer."

"The specifics of the negotiations are not important," answered Hayashi, looking toward Akiyama. "The fundamentals of the political situation in the region are."

"If I may, Blackburn-san," intervened Akiyama. "Idemitsu Kosan will be the operating partner of the consortium that will be involved in the Rumaila deal. Our concerns are twofold: First, how stable will Iraq be in the future? And second, how will the Iraq-Kuwaiti relations affect our operations, considering that part of the Rumaila field falls inside the Kuwaiti border? We have tried to analyze the situation based on the recent escalation of tensions, and we do not see hopeful signs."

Blackburn faced an ethical dilemma. He would earn a substantial success fee from Iraq if the deal was concluded, and even larger fees once it was executed. But he also understood that the risks of that deal had increased substantially. And even though in this particular deal the Japanese group of companies was not his client, he had a moral obligation not to misrepresent the situation.

And the situation touched upon more than ethics. There was a question of direct conflict of interest, which, in all his years as a consultant, he had avoided with complete success. Most of his clients were competitors, even though they partnered on many projects. The PCG had never accepted a conflicting assignment from any client. During a wave of mergers and acquisitions in the 1980s, he had often been approached by two opposing companies involved in a hostile takeover, and inevitably had to turn down one, and in at least one case both, due to an irreconcilable conflict of interest. This situation was different, but the conflict of interest was clear and present.

Besides, Blackburn liked Akiyama. He was younger than Hayashi, around Blackburn's age, possibly in his mid-thirties, and there was something warm and friendly about him. Protocol dictated that their business cards be kept in clear sight, so a person could always refer to them, avoiding the embarrassment of forgetting names. Blackburn looked at the cards lined up at the edge of the table in front of him, giving himself another minute to think.

"Akiyama-san," he said, looking him in the eye. "This is the riskiest business in the world. It is infinitely riskier than refining crude oil and marketing it in Japan. I'm sure you know that. Your investments will be in a foreign country, under the mercy of a foreign government."

He waited, but there was no reaction from any of them.

"I'll go a step further," he continued, "and please forgive me for my candor. This business is more risky for you than for the large British, French, and American companies, for the simple reason that the host governments depend on those countries for their security. Rightly or wrongly, they assume the interests of those large corporations will be protected by their governments."

There still was no response from any of them, but he noticed how Hayashi stirred uncomfortably in his chair.

"Now, coming more directly to your point, I have to admit that the risks have increased since the signing of the Saudi-Iraqi non-aggression pact. That pact, instead of having an overall stabilizing effect in the region, has stirred things up in a negative way. So the risks have increased. But by how much, I honestly could not tell you."

Takao finally chimed in. "Would you say the risks have increased enough for us to reconsider the Rumaila deal?"

"It's hard to say, Takao-san. If the situation does not deteriorate beyond just political tension and hostile rhetoric, I would say no, no need to reconsider. However, if the risks escalate further, it would be wise to wait before making any major investments."

They drilled him for another hour. What exactly were the different scenarios they should consider? What was the probability of each? What would be the implications of each for their business?

Blackburn did his best to address their concerns, dividing the various possibilities between high and low probability and high and low impact scenarios. The high probability but low impact scenarios were described but put aside. So were the low probability and low impact scenarios. But the Japanese dwelt a long time on the high impact scenarios, with both high and low probability of occurrence. Among these scenarios was military aggression by Iraq against Kuwait.

Then, as they were about to conclude their meeting, Akiyama raised a new question.

"Blackburn-san, are you aware that Kuwait is already producing from the Rumaila field?"

Blackburn had heard about this, but it was not common knowledge, nor had it been officially confirmed by his Kuwaiti sources. So he was taken by surprise.

"I've heard rumors," he said carefully, "but I'm not sure how accurate they are."

"Oh, it is true," said Akiyama with confidence. "We know, because we were offered a cargo and just purchased it."

As they were leaving, Akiyama invited Blackburn to dinner. "Let me show you a little of Tokyo," he said with a warm smile. Blackburn planned to stay in Tokyo for several more days, and had nothing scheduled for that night. He liked Akiyama, and accepted.

*   *   *

The restaurant was on the ninth floor of a crowded street in the Akasaka district of Tokyo. Blackburn gratefully accepted the slightly perfumed hot towel offered to him. It was a lush steaming marvel, presented over an exquisite ceramic dish. The therapeutic effect of the simple pleasure of wiping his hands and face with the thick cotton was nothing short of magical after a long day. It also foretold culinary pleasures yet to come, unwinding his body and filling it with anticipation of a feast of the senses.

The restaurant was small and simple. The lighting was flawless, with enough brightness to see what one was eating, but so artfully dimmed that it felt like he was sitting inside a masterfully composed photograph. When Akiyama had asked whether he preferred to sit at the bar or a table, Blackburn had chosen the bar. That was where the chef offered a seemingly interminable flow of small and perfectly balanced delicacies, so a patron could consume a lot of alcohol without even realizing it. That fit Blackburn's mood perfectly.

"This place may look new," explained Akiyama, "but it is old. My father used to come here as a young man. It gets renovated and redecorated every ten years or so."

"It is beautiful," said Blackburn. "Thank you so much for this invitation. I was ready for exactly this type of place tonight. The rains create a specific mood, and the lighting and décor here fit that mood."

The bartender put two small dishes in front of each of them, each dish about two inches in diameter. One had a single raw fava bean in it. The second held some kind of pickled seafood. Blackburn picked the fava bean up with his chopsticks with some amusement. He was amazed at the full, rich authentic flavor of fresh fava. That simple flavor took him back a few decades, when he had tasted the first fresh fava beans in season from the vegetable souk in Beirut. But there the beans were served in huge quantities as a salad, or cooked with rice and meat as a special pilaf. Only the Japanese with their aesthetic of minimalism would consider offering a single bean, on its own small plate, to be savored and appreciated as if it were the last fava bean on earth.

Akiyama noticed Blackburn's amusement.

"You like fava beans?"

"We used to buy these by the sack," he said with a laugh. "Our Lebanese cook worked wonders with those beans. But I have to say, I have not tasted anything so good since the sixties."

"They grow most of their prized vegetables themselves," explained Akiyama. "The owner has a small garden in the suburbs. He picks everything himself, just when it's ready, and serves it the same day. Nothing is saved for the next day. What is not consumed in the restaurant, they take home and give to friends. The next day they pick what is ready."

"That's dedication," said Blackburn laughing, and picked up the next morsel. "And this?"

"That's pickled *tako*, octopus. One of the specialties of the house."

The dinner lasted a few hours, as many more delicacies and selected Japanese culinary wonders were served at a leisurely pace. After a few scotches, they shifted to sake and sampled several different types, each with a story and unique feature.

Akiyama was the perfect host. He offered a wealth of information on Japanese culture, history, and cuisine. Whenever he was not sure of something, he'd call the old chef who was more than happy to lecture them about the various dishes and sakes and their history. He asked Blackburn about the United States and the Middle East, and Blackburn talked about Washington politics and Middle East culture, and about his observations of some of the similarities between the Middle East and the Far East.

He then told Akiyama about his trip to the Soviet Union.

"You went there?" Akiyama was puzzled.

"Last year. I had to see with my own eyes."

"See? What?"

"The unraveling of the Soviet Union is the single most important event of global proportions in our lifetime," said Blackburn, aware that he might be in too much of a lecturing mode. "I had to see it."

"What did you see?" Akiyama was clearly taken by this revelation.

"I went to Russia, the Ukraine, Georgia, and Armenia. I was fascinated by the Caucasus. Everywhere, I saw the old structures being dismantled. But there was a void. Nothing was replacing the old system, other than a chaotic opportunism. I think this will be as painful a transition as any in history."

"Did you have any business there?"

"If you mean paid consulting business, no. Nothing like that. Just curiosity. Not even professional curiosity. Personal curiosity."

Akiyama could not hide his fascination. He could never pull off something like that as an employee of Idemitsu Kosan. To get up and go to a region of the world simply because it was undergoing an important change, based on personal curiosity? For the first time, Akiyama looked at Blackburn and did not see the energy consultant; he saw an interesting man he wanted to befriend.

There wasn't much business talk that night. Only once, early in the evening, did Akiyama bring up business.

"You seemed surprised when I mentioned that Kuwait is already producing from Rumaila," he told Blackburn.

"To be honest with you, I was surprised you knew, since I had not confirmed it yet. But when you said you had already bought a cargo, it made sense."

"That presents a complication, you know. How can we sign a deal on the field with Iraq when we are already buying the output from Kuwait?"

Akiyama was right, of course. The deal with Iraq involved 50 percent of the *entire* production from the Rumaila field. Iraq could not deliver on it if Kuwait had already started production and was marketing the crude. It would make Japan look disingenuous, negotiating with Iraq on the one hand, and trading with Kuwait on the other. So Blackburn knew the deal would fall apart, unless Kuwait and Iraq could come to an agreement quickly on Rumaila, which seemed unlikely given the rhetoric of the last several months.

"You have a point," he told Akiyama. "It is a serious complication. As we were saying this afternoon, it would not be wise to rush into any investments until the quarrel between Iraq and Kuwait is resolved one way or another. I'm sorry this opportunity turned out to be so problematic as well."

"No problem, Blackburn-san. Maybe it was not meant to be. There are some at the MITI who think we should not even deal with the Middle East. They want to focus on Asia only."

"It makes a lot of sense for Japan to focus on Asia. But why 'only'?"

"Do you know Mr. Miyazaki? The former director of the Agency for Natural Resources and Energy?"

"I've met him only once, after he was replaced by Mr. Yamata. But unfortunately I did not know him when he was the director of the agency."

"He calls the entire Arabian Peninsula 'The Sacred Sands.' He says there is a 'Sandbox Club' where only the select few are allowed to play. They will never let Japan in."

Blackburn thought of his failed attempts to find partners for the Japanese oil companies among the majors and among some national oil companies. He didn't think his difficulties were the result of a conspiracy to keep the Japanese out, but rather a result of commercial scale and competitiveness. But he also knew that entry into the game was extremely difficult, at least on a scale that could be consequential. Miyazaki's take was interesting.

"This Miyazaki is the ultimate 'Meaning of Life' type," he said, even though he hadn't meant to give voice to that thought.

"Sorry?"

"Oh, never mind, Akiyama-san. I was talking to myself. One day I'll tell you about my Leaky Faucets and the Meaning of Life. But tell me, does Mr. Hayashi share that view?"

"Hayashi works for Yamata, who is committed to the Middle East. I'm not sure what he thinks personally, but his job is to open the Middle East for Japanese oil companies."

Blackburn did not want to dwell on the issue. He wanted to drink and unwind. He sensed that Akiyama was not keen on business talk either.

"Do you feel like going somewhere else?" asked Akiyama. "If you're not too tired, we can go to a club I know in Roppongi. You will see how Japanese businessmen relax after work."

The club was also a small place, with ten low tables scattered in the room, sofas by the walls, comfortable chairs all around, and a small stage on one side full of electronic gear. The room was filled with cigarette smoke and, unlike the restaurant, was loud, and filled almost entirely by men, most of them at various stages of drunkenness. The main hostess and proprietor, a woman in her late forties referred to as Mama-san, wrapped in a beautiful multi-colored kimono, rushed to greet them. She knew Akiyama, and greeted him with the most elaborate outpouring of welcoming pleasantries. Introductions were made, heads bowed, a table offered, drinks ordered.

A man was on stage, his necktie undone, hanging over his shoulders like a scarf; he was swaying with the microphone in his hand, and accompanied by one of the hostesses, singing his lungs out with what seemed to be a love song. Blackburn had been to karaoke clubs in Tokyo before; he had even once been persuaded to take the microphone.

There were four hostesses, in colorful kimonos, entertaining the guests. Most tables were loud and rowdy, with men telling jokes, laughing, toasting. Several people came by to say hello to Akiyama. Some were his colleagues from Idemitsu, others were from other oil companies and banks. Blackburn was introduced to all. As their drinks arrived, the hostess pulled up a stool and sat next to Akiyama. The conversation among everyone was in Japanese, but it seemed like they all knew some English, because they did not hesitate to shift to English when speaking to Blackburn.

Blackburn finished his flask of sake quickly and was feeling pretty upbeat. The empty flask was replaced in minutes. A banker started drilling him about the United States, especially about the anti-Japan sentiments because of Japan's ever-growing trade surplus. Another conversation followed about the low oil prices and tensions in the Middle East. But in spite of the serious subjects, everything was said light-heartedly, with laughter.

Meanwhile, the singing continued, with men taking turns on stage, and one of the hostesses filling in when it remained empty for more than a few minutes. The atmosphere was festive and relaxed, even though the customers were top professionals in their fields—important enough people, thought Blackburn, that one would need to work hard to secure an appointment with them in their offices.

It was well past midnight, and Blackburn had lost count of the number of flasks of sake he had consumed, when the mood in the club changed. Amid many "ooohs" and "aaaahs" and a round of applause, a beautiful young lady in an impeccable silk kimono took the stage. She was in her mid-twenties, graceful, serious, modest yet haughty at the same time. She did not look at anyone, just stared into the wall facing the stage, and started singing an old, whiney Japanese love song. Blackburn could not take his eyes off her.

"That is Mariko-san," explained Akiyama. "She is not a hostess, nor an ordinary entertainer. She is an accomplished actress and singer. She comes here once in a while only because Mama-san is her aunt."

Blackburn was too drunk to be subtle. "She is amazing," he mumbled.

When Mariko-san finished her song, the applause was thunderous. Before the next song could start, one of Akiyama's friends who had joined their table ran to the stage and whispered something to her. She nodded, and the music started. Blackburn was immediately taken by the rhythm of the song. It was a duet. The man sang a line, followed by Mariko-san, then he sang two lines, and they sang a fifth line together. The song carried Blackburn away.

"What's it about?" he asked Akiyama, pointing to the singers.

"It is called '*Wakare no Yoake*.' It means 'Dawn after Separation,' or something like that. It is an old, sad love song."

"Can you write the words for me in the English alphabet, please?"

Akiyama was surprised, but happy that Blackburn was enjoying his evening. There were three verses, five lines each. But the singers were already on the last verse. So Akiyama asked Mama-san if they could please repeat the song so he could write the lyrics from the beginning. They agreed and Mama-san brought him the lyrics in Japanese, which he scribbled phonetically in English. He handed the piece of paper to Blackburn.

An hour later, to Akiyama's astonishment, Blackburn walked over to the stage. He bowed to Mariko-san and uttered: "*Wakare no Yoake.*" She was taken by surprise. She studied Blackburn carefully for a minute, then smiled, her first smile of the evening.

The music started, and Blackburn sang the first male line, with a slight accent, in a shaky voice and a bit off tune, especially when he tried to get the melodic nuances. Mariko followed with the second line, then he sang the third and fourth lines, and then he turned to her as they sang the fifth line together. In the second verse the roles were reversed, and the third verse was like the first, with him taking the lead. When they finished, the applause in the room boomed again. Everyone at Akiyama's table gave them a standing ovation.

The Japanese had seen foreigners (*gaijin*—meaning round eyed) get on karaoke stages before, but only to sing American favorites. This was the first *gaijin* who had actually had the nerve to get up and perform not only a Japanese song, but an old and traditional one at that, after having just heard it for the first time.

Blackburn turned to Mariko-san and bowed low. "*Arigato*, Mariko-san," he whispered, looking her straight in the eye. Then he left the stage.

Ten minutes later Mariko-san was sitting at their table, next to Blackburn. Akiyama and Mama-san were taking turns translating for them. It was mostly small talk, dealing with each other's backgrounds and occupations, but the atmosphere was charged. Neither Akiyama nor Mama-san needed to translate the chemistry.

Around three in the morning, Akiyama told Blackburn it was time to leave. Blackburn thought for a minute, then removed his hotel key from his coat pocket. It was on a large and heavy oval metal key-holder, with "Palace Hotel" engraved on one side in both English and Japanese, and his room number on the other side. He held it low, below the surface of the table, and showed it to Mariko-san, making sure to turn to both sides a couple of times. She looked at it for a minute, raised her eyes to him for a split second, then bowed her head and nodded.

"*Hye ...*" she whispered. Blackburn's heart skipped a beat.

About twenty minutes after he arrived in his room, the concierge called to announce that a certain Ms. Mariko wanted to come up. Blackburn gave his okay, and went to check the water in the bathtub, which he had already started drawing.

She had changed from the kimono into a pair of jeans, a white shirt, and a light jacket. She looked younger and as stunning as she had at the club. When she looked up to him, her pitch black eyes sent shivers down his spine. He held her face between his hands, looked at her for a moment, then kissed her forehead, her cheeks, and finally her lips. He held the kiss for a moment, feeling her warmth engulf his entire body. Then he led her from the entryway into the bathroom and pointed at the bathtub. She nodded. They got undressed and entered the tub to wash away an entire evening's smoke and perspiration from each other's bodies.

They woke up at noon. He clung to her soft, sleepy, naked body with an abandon he had not known for a long time. Gradually, very gradually, the red blinking light on the phone by his nightstand came into focus. It occurred to him that he was in Japan on business. He jumped out of bed, and checked his messages on the hotel phone. All it said was, "Message waiting, please contact the concierge." Then he turned on his mobile phone. There was a voicemail from Linda.

"Jim, call me first chance you get. Regardless of time. It's important. I left a message at the hotel also."

It was approaching 1 p.m. in Tokyo, around 11 p.m. a day earlier in Washington. He called Linda's home number.

"Jim, I'm so glad you called. Theiss is looking for you. He said it's urgent. Call him now. When I told him you were in Tokyo, he said 'let him call me,' regardless of time."

"Thanks, Linda. Anything else?"

"The usual stuff with clients. All that can wait. Call Theiss now."

"Okay Linda, thanks."

"*Daijōbu desu ka?*" Is everything okay? Mariko-san sat up in bed, her long hair scattered over her shoulders and face, only partially covering her breasts. Blackburn went to her and kissed her lips.

"*Chotto mate kudasai,*" he said, pointing to his phone and signaling that he had to make a call. One moment please. It was one of the phrases he had learned right away in Japan.

He called Gene Theiss.

"Your friends have been compromised," said Theiss in his character-istically calm manner. "I was right about the original source. It went to the North. It was used to negotiate the terms of tying the big donkey in the stable."

That meant The Symposium had been exposed by Israeli intelligence, the information had reached Baghdad, and Saddam Hussein had sold it to King Fahd as part of the financial deal associated with the non-aggression pact. Anyone listening in on the conversation would not have a clue as to what they were talking about.

"I understand," Blackburn said. "Many thanks. And I have more information about the issue you asked me to monitor. Those that had become vulnerable and intransigent have just become more vulnerable and intransigent."

"When do you get back?" asked Theiss, which Blackburn took to mean that he understood his message.

"I still have five days here."

"If you can come back earlier, even by a day or two, it may be worth it."

"Understood. Will do. Will send you a message."

Mariko-san looked like she had fallen asleep again, with her back turned to him. Her left shoulder peeked from under the covers, partially covered by her hair.

As soon as he hung up with Theiss, Blackburn called Amin.

"He who knows is a prophet," he said. "And Ramzi, he is a very seri-ous prophet."

"I understand."

"Get totally off the radar. It is serious. Especially serious for the brothers from the Kingdom."

"I understand."

"Maybe they should leave for a while." He meant get out of Saudi Arabia, and was sure Amin understood him.

He also knew he was probably saying too much over the telephone, but felt he had to get the message across. He felt himself panicking, and wished he could have the calm composure of Gene Theiss while com-municating his message. Blackburn was in way over his head; he was not used to communicating in this fashion, let alone playing the role he was trying to play.

"Will you be in Europe anytime soon?" asked Amin. He sounded calmer and more composed than Blackburn, even though he obviously had a lot more at stake in the situation.

"I'm in Japan now. Have to return to DC in a few days. I can't travel for at least ten days after that. It is important that we meet. I also need to check with you on something I learned in Tokyo."

"That's too long. I'll come to Washington. Let me know when you're back."

Then Blackburn called Linda, instructed her to change his return ticket to two days earlier, and crept back into bed.

Love without language, without words. It was a new experience for him, and probably for her too. She knew four English words: hello, good-bye, sorry, and thank you. He knew some twenty-five Japanese words and phrases, half of them related to food. They communicated by gazes and senses, by their presence, and mostly simply by their auras. Blackburn found it exhilarating. It brought out an intensity and sharpness of feeling that language would have dulled. It was similar to when someone, having lost his eyesight, develops a sharper sense of hearing and even smell.

Blackburn spent the next three nights and a good part of the days with Mariko-san. He declined lunch and dinner invitations from his clients, and kept only the most essential business meetings. They went to museums, shows, and dinners; took long walks in various parts of Tokyo; and ate wonderful lunches in the Asakusa district, the low-cost, working-class section of town, as well as in the highest echelons of the Ginza.

She was the guide in most of their outings. On their last night, she took him to a tempura restaurant called *Moto Yama* on Nihonbashi. It was a small tatami-room restaurant, where an old, bald, and skinny Japanese chef sat behind a huge frying pan about three feet in diameter. Surrounding the pan were all sorts of vegetables and fish, which he dipped in his special batter and fried to order. They sat on the mat in front of the mega-frying pan, with their legs crossed, and savored every piece of absolutely perfect tempura presented. Between their orders, the chef sat motionless, his gaze fixed way beyond them.

They had started talking to each other—she in Japanese, he in English—neither of them understanding what the other was saying. But Blackburn had decided that silence was depriving him of her voice, of her facial expressions while she talked, of her tenderness. He loved to hear her talk. And they had taught each other many new words, making basic communication a little easier.

Their last night was peaceful and melancholy. She made love to him, and then lay in his arms, caressing his body. He gestured to her to speak. And she started talking, in her low, soft voice, telling him stories about her childhood, her family, their village some forty kilometers north of Tokyo, her theater, her colleagues ...

After a while, she felt his breathing fall into a slow, steady pattern. Blackburn had fallen asleep. She closed her eyes and lay still, in order not to disturb him.

XXII

Fire and Wind

B lackburn was anxious to get together with Theiss. He tackled the most urgent demands at the office, gave detailed instructions to Linda and to Patrick Hagan for the follow-up communications with Japan, and headed out for Old Town Alexandria.

He needed an Iraqi perspective before seeing Theiss, so he called Issam Al Tikriti from his car.

"Of course we know what Kuwait is doing in Rumaila," hissed Al Tikriti. "All I can tell you, Jim, is that this time they really crossed the line."

"Crossed the line?"

"Jim, you know that Iraq has never recognized the Kuwaiti-Iraq border, right? That border is artificial. The British drew it, without any meaningful participation from either Iraq or Kuwait. So, very conveniently, the southern tip of Rumaila was left dangling inside the so-called Kuwaiti border. What a joke!"

"What do you think Baghdad will do?"

"This is the last straw. You know how they have been trashing the market for the past few years, right? Oil prices could have been at the target level of $21 per barrel by now. Instead we are at $14 per barrel. Every dollar drop costs Iraq over a billion dollars per year in oil revenues, Jim. You can do that math better than I can. Then, as if that weren't enough, they're asking Iraq to pay back the $12 billion they say they loaned it during the war. Can you imagine that? The Saudis wrote off their so-called loans, but this bunch of tribes wants us to repay! Then they start stealing our own oil from Rumaila. Now, what do you think Baghdad should do? You tell me, Jim."

"Is that how they feel in Baghdad?"

"Didn't you hear the president the other day? He said overproduction by Kuwait constitutes economic warfare. This is not some minister talking. The president said that. Economic warfare."

Blackburn could not decide whether to tell Al Tikriti that the Rumaila deal with Japan was, for all practical purposes, dead. He felt he owed it to him to tell him that much, but had an uncomfortable feeling that he'd be adding fuel to the fire.

"It does not look good, Issam," he said instead, having decided to hold off on the Japanese for now.

"They're trying to force our hand again, Jim. Remember what I once told you about their tactics? It will never work. Worse, it will backfire on them. There are some in the Iraqi military who pray every day for a good excuse to march into Kuwait, and the Kuwaitis are answering their prayers."

*   *   *

Gene Theiss looked tired. The flow of news from Iraq had increased in the past few weeks. The bags under his eyes were larger and darker than usual, and his voice was gentler.

"Leave everything here," he told Blackburn, gesturing toward the antique table at the entrance, "including your coat. I don't trust all that new gear. Nothing is safe. We'll talk in the basement today."

Blackburn deposited his mobile phone and coat on the table and followed him down the semicircular staircase.

The basement of the historic mansion, like the rest of the house, was almost in its original form, including the large heavy iron loops protruding from the walls, where owners in a different century had chained their slaves. Theiss had transformed the area into a cozy sitting room, with valuable old carpets and antique divans. It also housed the overflow of some of his prized paintings that he rotated from the living quarters upstairs every once in a while.

They walked to the far corner, where there was a worn coffee table with three chairs around it.

"Would you like a sherry?"

"Sure," said Blackburn, even though it was only three in the afternoon, and he did not like to drink during the day. But he sensed that Theiss needed a drink.

"It would be good if you could clear your schedule this week," said Theiss, handing him a glass. "The boys need to hear from you, and I think you'd be interested to hear from them."

"Sure, just let me know where and who."

"I don't only mean the boys here. You'll have to travel a little."

"Travel?"

"Florida, to meet with CENTCOM, and next week to Maine, to participate in this year's War Games."

He had been to Central Command in Tampa, Florida, and knew about the War Games in Maine, but had not yet participated in them. He had the necessary security clearances to participate through his advisory work for the CIA, but usually the War Games involved scenarios of nuclear engagement with the Soviet Union, something he was neither interested in nor qualified to contribute to. But this year, explained Theiss, the games were about the Gulf. More specifically, about possible U.S. retaliation in case of an Iraqi invasion of Kuwait. This was something he could sink his teeth into.

"About time they put the Gulf on the War Games agenda," he said. "After all those wasted hours on a nuclear engagement with the Soviet Union."

"They weren't wasted."

"Maybe. But this is the real thing, actually happening now."

"Well, your old friend Jim Schlesinger is taking the lead on this one. He asked for you personally."

Blackburn was happy to hear that. He liked Schlesinger, who'd had a unique government career, having served as the head of the CIA, as secretary of defense, and as the first U.S. energy secretary, a position established right after the oil embargo of 1973.

"I'm glad. As I said, this is happening now. The situation in the Gulf has taken a turn for the worse. Iraq is crying economic warfare. And Kuwait is producing oil from the Rumaila field. It will most probably kill an important deal that Iraq was negotiating with Japan. Diplomatic measures by Arab countries to diffuse the tensions have so far failed. We could be looking at a military engagement."

"I know. There are three scenarios our boys are toying with. One, Iraq mobilizes troops to scare Kuwait into better behavior; two, they march in and occupy the Rumaila field; three, they occupy all of Kuwait. As of this morning, they had no favorite scenario. What do you think?"

Blackburn did not hesitate for a second.

"If I have to choose among those scenarios," he said, "I'll say three. Occupation. No question about it. The other two scenarios are shams, as you know."

"What makes you so sure?"

"Because they can. They can take Kuwait in a day. If the diplomatic efforts have failed, why fool around? Besides, Iraq does not really recognize Kuwait or its borders. And after their devastating losses in the Iran war, they need to show some gains."

"So they'll occupy the entire country?"

"Why not? They consider it part of Iraq anyway."

"That is what the War Games are all about, Jim. You'll fit right in."

Theiss fell silent. He refilled their sherry glasses, and looked at Blackburn for a while.

"So when are you going to marry that nice girl you've been dating?" Good old "Uncle Gene" was talking.

Blackburn laughed. "You're the second person to ask me that question."

"You mean Sophie is asking you too?"

"No, not Sophie. It is a long story. It is actually another lady I see occasionally in Europe."

Theiss gave him a quizzical look, but decided not to probe further.

"If Henry were around, he'd put a lot more pressure on you to get married. You know that, don't you?"

"I know, I know. Just need to sort out a few things, that's all."

"How old are you? Thirty-five? Thirty-six?"

"Thirty-eight."

"Thirty-eight. Well, Henry would tell you whatever you have not sorted out by now, can remain unsorted."

"We'll see, Gene. Who knows, maybe she'll propose soon," Blackburn said with another laugh, and this time Theiss laughed too.

Theiss got up to refill their sherry glasses again.

"Russell has pulled off the surveillance on you two," he said, waving his hand dismissively. "It stopped when you left for Japan. I guess he did not see the point of the expense of having you followed all the way there."

"Did you find out what he was after?"

"As I had guessed, it was your business. He has a copy of your client list. He may also have your financials for the past few years. So he knows everything about your business."

Not quite everything, thought Blackburn, but certainly a lot more than he should.

"Any idea why he'd be interested?" asked Theiss.

"Yes, I think I have an idea. I got Sophie two lucrative contracts. With Angola and then with Iraq. I bet he started getting curious then. He probably guessed that Sophie must have had some help in landing those deals."

"Well, whatever it is, he seems to have found what he was looking for." Business details did not interest Theiss. "Now, let me tell you about your friends. What did you say their organization was called?"

"The Symposium."

"The Symposium. If you like these people, tell them to lie low. Very low. Fahd may be hated in Saudi Arabia and the Gulf, but he is liked elsewhere—including here and in Israel. And the reasons for him being hated at home and loved abroad are probably the same. He is corrupt."

"You think Israel or we would go after The Symposium to protect Fahd?"

"No, of course not, but only because they do not present a credible threat yet. If they did, I wouldn't put it past either the Israelis or us. But the Saudis will not wait for these guys to become a credible threat. They will crush them now if they do not lie low."

"Do they know who they are? Do they have names?"

"They think they know several names of the ringleaders. Not everyone. The Saudi members are in the greatest danger."

*   *   *

Two days later, Blackburn picked Amin up at Dulles International Airport and drove him to the Four Seasons Hotel in Georgetown. He briefed him on the extent of the dangers that members of The Symposium faced. He also explained that the Saudi members of the executive committee were in the gravest danger.

"Karim Suliman may be in the most serious danger of all," he emphasized. "As a former member of the Saudi Secret Service, and the mastermind behind The Symposium's security structure, they will not spare him. He should not be in the Kingdom right now, nor should any of his family members."

Amin's mind had already processed those details and moved on. He looked somewhat bewildered.

"So the United States and Israel prefer Fahd to Abdullah," he mumbled, looking lost. "I understand Iraq feeling that way, now that they have signed a deal. But Israel? And the United States? What's it to them?"

"Ramzi, forget all that right now," said Blackburn, not wanting to get into a broad policy discussion with Amin. "We are where we are. Focus on the security of your members. The other crucial issue we need to talk about is the danger to Kuwait."

"We'll come to Kuwait in a second. I could even understand Israel's position—celebrate the corruption of the Arabs, rejoice in their weaknesses. But the United States? Why?"

"Don't go looking for deep reasons. It is simply the devil you know. Have you heard that expression?"

"Yes."

"This town does not know much about Abdullah. And the little they know is superficial and not pleasant—such as Abdullah is Arab-centric, while Fahd is pro-West. Sorry, but even I am amazed when they base foreign policy on crap like that."

"Okay, Jim. We'll leave it there for now. Tell me why Kuwait is in danger."

Blackburn gave him a brief synopsis of Kuwait's production in Rumaila and the Iraqi sentiments about it. He did not hide his own displeasure for being kept in the dark about the extent of production from the Kuwaiti side of Rumaila. He concluded that, given the price wars of the past year and the demands that Iraq repay its war debts to Kuwait, Rumaila had come as the icing on the cake and a confirmation of hostile intent from the perspective of Baghdad.

"I'm afraid the picture does not look good for you right now, my friend," he said, looking at him with genuine sympathy. "Fahd is safe for now, Kuwait is in danger, and The Symposium is in mortal danger."

∗   ∗   ∗

Bianca's call couldn't have come at a worse time. Blackburn was poring over a large file of declassified material sent to him in preparation for the War Games in Maine, which were to be held in a week. The classified material would be provided on site, and collected after the deliberations. He also had a dozen client phone calls to return, which he was putting off. But he did not want to decline Bianca's call.

"How are you, Jimmy? How was Japan? Did you miss me?"

He thought of Mariko for a second, and realized two things in a flash: He had not thought of Bianca while with Mariko, and he had not thought of Mariko a single time since getting back home. That worried him. He always prided himself on seeing the totality of his condition at any given time. The "unified theory," he called it. One may compartmentalize for purely practical reasons of organization, but one should always be aware of the totality of one's circumstances. Compartmentalization may be great as a management technique, he thought, but it is worthless when it comes to existential awareness. Everything forming a person's universe is one whole.

"Of course I missed you," he lied. That was another disappointment. He would not have lied if they had been together when she asked the question. He would have looked her in the eye and said, "Bianca, I'm sorry, but I was with this beautiful Japanese lady who did not know a word of English, and we spent three incredible days together, and during those three days I did not miss you." He could never say that to Sophie, but he could say it to Bianca. She probably wouldn't take it well, but at least if they were together he could explain it better.

"So how was your trip, *amore mio?*"

"Bianca, I'd love to chat and hear your voice, but I am really swamped. Too much is going on right now. Can we talk in a few days?"

"Sure, if you have no time for me now," she said, sulking. "What happened to the fire between us, Jimmy? Please tell me it is still there."

Normally, Blackburn would have dropped everything he was doing to respond and put her mind at ease. But he wanted to return to his reading. There was so much new material there having to do with realities on the ground in the Gulf, maps, statistics of population densities, border conditions, even certain troop positions on the Iraqi-Kuwaiti border.

"Bianca, sweetheart, I am under a lot of pressure. I'd love to talk about us, but not now. But tell me, do you still feel the fire between us? Same as the first time?" He could not resist using the opportunity to see what she was thinking.

"Yes and no, to put it bluntly," she said, to his surprise. He had expected a simpler answer.

"Yes and no?"

"I think the initial spark was spiced up with our physical closeness," she said, taking on a more serious tone. "The ability to touch and get electrified, to exchange glances and feel our bodies respond, to be surrounded with people and yet be alone with each other in a crowd."

Blackburn's mind went back several years to the first group dinner hosted by OPEC, when she flirted with him at the table.

"Yes, I do remember how we were alone in a crowd," he mumbled, "and how you explained to me *la petite mort* ..."

"That was my greatest achievement, Jimmy. What exciting times we had!"

"And now? Is the same fire still there?"

"Let me read a verse from an Italian poem to you," she said. "I'll translate as I go.

Until we meet again, we've lost a part of us
yet gained something more profound
fired into a kiln and emerged more robust
we'll endure this savage, unforgiving distance..."

"Bianca, that's incredible. Do you really feel that way? I mean, can we really endure the 'savage and unforgiving distance'?"

"We already have endured it, Jimmy. I don't think we'd be good for each other if we saw each other every day. We're not meant to be everyday lovers. Distance has actually been good for us."

"I'm not sure how to take that."

"My dear Jimmy, think of love as fire and distance as the wind. If the fire is strong, the wind will make it stronger. If it is weak, it will be easy to put it out. The proof is there—our friendship has gotten stronger with distance, only to be spiced up again when we meet and spend hours chatting about the ways of the world. Isn't that wonderful?"

XXIII

A New Act

Blackburn returned from the two-day session in Maine with mixed impressions. He had not seen such a professional, multi-agency and bipartisan approach to tackling a challenge in all his years in Washington, DC. This is the real strength of America, he thought, not the politicians and lobbyists in Washington. The CIA, the National Security Council and the Departments of State and Defense had been involved. Various civilian and military officers and retired veteran Foreign Service officers led most of the discussions. James Schlesinger led a good part of the policy aspects of a possible U.S. military retaliation in case of an Iraqi invasion of Kuwait. CENTCOM generals discussed details of various military strategies.

There were detailed maps, created by satellite imagery, where one could zoom in on a point of interest with such clarity that the sand pebbles in the desert were visible. They studied the populated areas between Kuwait and Southern Iraq that could be affected by a military incursion. They saw the lineup of Bedouin tents with their camels and goats, and they studied the routes of tribal movements. They dwelt on the areas of the Marsh Arabs in Southern Iraq.

Most of the military strategy discussions were above Blackburn's head. He was fascinated by the information and the analysis, but could not contribute to the discussions. The insights he gained filled a major gap in his understanding of how certain decisions were made. At that level of detailed planning, he saw the importance of Leaky Faucets.

As Gene Theiss had predicted, Blackburn was in his element during the scenario discussions. There was no question that Iraq had the capability to invade and occupy Kuwait. But did it also have the intention and will to do so? Military intelligence knew every weapon that Iraq owned and the size and organization of its army. But when it came to understanding the intentions of the political leadership in Baghdad, and especially its will, Blackburn thought they were clueless.

There were many in the auditorium who doubted that Iraq would invade, and among those who considered it likely, there were many who strongly doubted Iraq would occupy Kuwait. War fatigue from eight years of fighting Iran was cited as a prime reason. Many thought that intra-Arab politics, particularly intervention by the Arab League, Saudi Arabia, and Egypt, would also serve as a deterrent.

How can they know so much about the physical realities on the ground, yet miss so much, wondered Blackburn. Maybe they have not heard Saddam's speeches, or haven't listened carefully. Leaky Faucets and the Meaning of Life had to come together to produce a viable plan.

He studied the analysts as they made short presentations. Crisp, frugal, confident, objective, logical, emboldened by classified information—yet dead wrong. He was amazed at the contradiction. Could it be that having a lot of facts dulled one's judgment? Was the capacity for deductive logic out of necessity sharpened by a paucity of hard facts and details?

Schlesinger called on Blackburn to present his view. He made a strong case that an Iraqi invasion was likely, and if it came, it would be nothing short of total occupation of the country. He tried to explain the anger of the Iraqis, the frustrations with their economic devastation of the last eight years, the high levels of debt the government had to tackle, and the oil price war among the Gulf members of OPEC, which Iraq viewed as nothing but an attempt to cripple the Iraqi economy and budget. He also addressed the intransigence of Kuwait in OPEC, and the production and sales from Rumaila. All this made sense to some, but seemed a waste of time to others.

In the end, there was no clear consensus as to the probability of an Iraqi occupation of Kuwait, but there was almost unanimous consensus that, should such an eventuality come about, it would be consequential and high-impact. So regardless of the probability of occurrence, the occupation scenario was significant enough to call for a whole new set of scenarios of the implications of different possible U.S. military and diplomatic responses.

That became the main issue during the remaining three days of deliberations. The participants divided into separate working groups, each analyzing different U.S. responses and the implications for the region and the world, and then regrouped in the auditorium to present summaries of their conclusions. Here also, Blackburn was surprised. While the military experts could map out exactly how they would push Iraq out of Kuwait, the geopolitical discourse was, according to Blackburn, way off base. Some argued that it would be a mistake for the United States to attack an Arab country, because it would invite pan-Arab opposition and thus jeopardize the U.S. diplomatic position in the Middle East. Retired U.S. ambassadors to various Arab countries were the strongest voices advocating caution in this regard. Others were worried about military setbacks that would embarrass the United States in front of the whole world. Blackburn left this concern for the generals to address.

Blackburn focused on the first concern. He still had the stage, where he would have felt at home while making a presentation to a client, but was somewhat unsettled in the unfamiliar environment of this audience. "First, we will not be invading an Arab country," he argued. "In the scenario we are discussing, an Arab country has already been invaded by another Arab country. We won't be going there to invade, let alone occupy, Iraq. We will be going there to reverse the Iraqi invasion of Kuwait. That is all. Second, if there were plans here in anyone's mind to do more than that, I'd fully agree that it would be unwise and detrimental for both U.S. interests in the region and the interests of the region itself. We should limit our policy objective to a simple target: reversing the occupation of Kuwait, and not an inch more than that. In my opinion, that would be welcomed by the Arab world. In fact, I would predict that you'd hear a huge sigh of relief from the region when we managed that."

Most of the participants did not know Blackburn, so they listened to him with some skepticism. It was Schlesinger's endorsement that gave

Blackburn the credibility he did have. Otherwise, the intelligence community wonks would have dismissed him. But none of that bothered Blackburn. This was an intriguing one-time excursion for him out of his normal audience of commercial and government clients.

By the end of the three-day session, the group had come up with a detailed and elaborate plan for how they would reverse an Iraqi occupation of Kuwait. Aside from the military aspects, which required using Saudi Arabian territory as a launching ground for American troops, the plan outlined the diplomatic efforts required to build a solid coalition for the operation. It was an impressive blueprint for a contingency that had not happened yet; but the plan was ready, nine months before the Iraqi tanks rolled into Kuwait.

*   *   *

It happened rarely, but Sophie Myles recognized the mood. Blackburn seemed restless, yet down, which was unusual, because he usually became restless in upbeat moments. She felt that he needed some closeness, yet he also seemed to want to be alone. The contradictions that made up James Blackburn could sometimes be maddening. The worst was when he did not know what he wanted. Those were the moments when he did not like himself. He had told her once that when that mood hit him, the things dear to him lost their luster, the enthusiasm that normally drove him faded, and he started questioning the meaning of it all. To make matters worse, he said, a fog descended and blanketed his mind.

The Blackburn Sophie knew was an entirely different animal. He was so determined that he would stand his ground against people ten times more powerful. The Blackburn she knew could walk into any room as if he owned the place, and everyone in the room would believe he did, including the actual owners. One of his colleagues had told him that once, and it had left an impression on Blackburn. Later, when he told Sophie about it, it had left an impression on her too.

But that night she had a different Blackburn on her hands, and did not know how to handle him. She pressed his head to her chest, running her fingers through his hair and caressing the back of his neck.

"What's bothering you, Jim?" she whispered. "Please talk to me."

"Shshshsh ..." he mumbled.

"Okay," she whispered. "But I wish you'd just come out with it."

The problem was that "it" was not one thing. Come out with which one? Come out with Bianca? Mariko? His losing touch with his own "unified theory"? The news that every deal he had tried to make had fallen apart? His inner struggle about where to take his relationship with Sophie? The demise of The Symposium, which he endorsed intellectually? The impending war in the Middle East? "It" covered too much.

"Uncle" Gene was right. If Henry Blackburn had been around, he would have told his son that whatever he had not yet sorted out at the age of thirty-eight could remain unsorted. "Marry that nice girl you're dating."

Then Blackburn remembered his comment to Theiss: "Maybe she'll propose soon," and he started laughing. Even Theiss had laughed at that, and he rarely laughed about a subject he considered important. That was clever.

"What?" she asked, relieved that he was laughing.

"Oh, I bet you'd love to hear this one," he answered, "but I'm not going to give it to you just yet. You'll have to earn it."

"Earn what?" She could not help laughing with him.

"The story."

"The story?"

"Yes. The story. But it's too early."

He did decide to come out with one "it"—the plans gone wrong. "The deal with SOMO and Nitzen is dead. The deal with Kuwait and C. Itoh is dead. The Rumaila deal is dead. Every deal I've worked on very hard is dead. So here we are, with no real break in sight."

"Jim, you cannot be serious," she said, so casually that he took notice. "Is that it? Is that what's bothering you? The deals are dead? You really surprise me sometimes."

He did not expect that pushback from Sophie, even though he realized he deserved it. Sophie was usually far more careful and considerate. That was the kind of reaction he would have expected from Bianca. "Oh, Jimmy, *amore mio*, stop whining and move on ..." He could almost hear Bianca uttering those words in her delightful Italian accent. But Sophie?

"I'd like to invite Gene to dinner," he said. "Just the three of us. I think he likes you. We haven't been together since his wife passed away. What do you say?"

"Great idea!" She did not hesitate for a moment. "Let's do it this week. But what a sudden jump, Jim. How did you get there from where we were? Your dead deals and the story I still have to earn?"

"It's not as big a jump as you think," he said. "Let's get together with him. He is the only person I know who was close to my father. He reminds me of my father."

Sophie knew about Henry Blackburn, but had not met him. The stories she knew, mostly from James, presented Henry as a legend in his time. But it was not uncommon to talk like that about someone close who had passed away. She assumed Blackburn's desire to get together with Theiss was simply a nostalgic urge to think of his father. Of course, to some extent, she was right. But Blackburn wanted Theiss to reconfirm his approval of Sophie; his approval would be a proxy for Henry's.

In reality, it had a lot less to do with approval than with confirmation. Blackburn knew he had already made a decision. He was simply struggling with it, allowing it to prove itself, to survive the test of his own resistance.

*   *   *

The disintegration of The Symposium was faster and more complete than any of them had anticipated. The executive committee suspended all its formal activities, which included communication with its members, through any medium. While various members of the committee met privately in Europe and in the Gulf, mostly to catch up on and analyze events in the region, no planning was done and no decisions of any consequence were made.

What accelerated this process of disintegration was the news of the arrest of Karim Suliman in Riyadh, which spread through the members of the committee like wildfire. He had refused to leave Saudi Arabia in spite of Amin's repeated pleas. No reason or report of the formal charge was given for his arrest. He had no visitation rights, even from family members. Every member of the executive committee imagined Suliman uttering his name, under torture, to Saudi security officers. Kamal Ashkar moved to Europe indefinitely. But Majed Al Shammary refused to move. He stayed in Saudi Arabia and remained in the National Guard. He was not bothered by the security forces. Either Suliman had not cracked under torture, or somehow the security apparatus did not consider him important or dangerous enough to arrest.

Ramzi Amin was devastated. Suliman's arrest and the breakdown of The Symposium were bad enough, but things soon became even worse. The Symposium's ranks did not just dissipate and disappear. The religious fundamentalists, whom he had fought hard to keep out, started to make new inroads into the frustrated remnants of his organization. The Islamic fundamentalist members, whose job had been to keep the radicals out, became even more radical and dogmatic. New renegade groups were formed, under a fundamentalist Islamic banner, advocating the imposition of Sharia law throughout the Arab world. The professional cadre that had aspired to graft civil society onto the foundations of the tribal system disappeared.

Amin watched this process of change, which he viewed as the most cataclysmic wasted opportunity in his lifetime, with horror. What he saw was not just a setback in plans. He saw an irreversible backward step in the historical process The Symposium had aspired to. As if events and fate had conspired to bring about the exact opposite, the very antithesis, of his vision of the future of Gulf societies. He and all those who thought like he did were rendered powerless to stop the trend, let alone reverse it. History had just had a good laugh at their plans.

Blackburn was not following these trends as closely as Amin, but could not miss the overall sense of malaise in the Gulf. The political thinkers with whom he associated the most, basically the Amin-style advocates of civil society adapted to local culture, were in a major retreat. Most had disappeared from public life. Some had disappeared altogether, not responding to his inquiries. It had become difficult to even reach Amin, who in the old days would not leave any telephone call from him unreturned.

George Herbert Walker Bush had won the U.S. presidential election, just as the situation in the Gulf was getting tenser by the day, and the Soviet Union, which had defined and conditioned U.S. foreign policy for over four decades in the post-World War II era, was coming to an end.

Although he had lived in Washington, DC most of his life, this was the first time Blackburn felt the excitement of being in the center of activity. Perhaps that was one of the reasons for his heightened nostalgia for his father. In his time, his father, just like Gene Theiss, had been in the center of activity, whether physically in Washington or abroad. Blackburn remembered Theiss' comment about joining the community, but dismissed it yet again. He knew he did not have the temperament for it.

He never knew where Al Tikriti called from; he could be in Baghdad or Washington, DC, or somewhere in Europe or possibly even on his farm in Fresno, California. Now Blackburn was in bed, having spent a long evening with Sophie celebrating her birthday with a lovely dinner, a concert at the Kennedy Center, and then a few more hours at a bar on K Street. They were both tipsy. They had arrived at his apartment close to 3 a.m., made love, and fallen asleep. So he was not amused by the early morning phone call.

"Sorry to call so early, Jim, but it must be already past 6 a.m. there, right? This is important."

"Go ahead, Issam," Blackburn mumbled, trying to sit up in bed, and patting Sophie's back. "Where are you?"

"I'm in Baghdad. They got a telefax from Tokyo." Al Tikriti's voice was unusually calm, but his tone had a coldness that sent a chill down Blackburn's back. "Idemitsu walked away from the Rumaila deal."

"I'm not surprised," Blackburn said, and almost immediately regretted it. That was probably not the reaction Al Tikriti wanted to hear. The words sounded insensitive. To soften the impact, he added: "Did they give a reason?"

"If you're not surprised by their decision, then the reason will not surprise you either. You already know it; you told me about it, remember?"

"Kuwait. Producing from Rumaila."

"Yes sir! They are not just stealing from our field. They've managed to kill a very important deal for Iraq."

Blackburn had expected this.

"I'm sorry the deal fell through. You know how much I wanted that deal to work." That did not sound any better, but he was too tired and sleepy to play the sensitive diplomat.

"There is nothing that you or I can do now." Al Tikriti's voice had acquired the same calm and cold finality. "Now, the big guns will speak. No more diplomacy. The curtains have closed over everything you knew up to now. Get ready for a whole new act when they rise again."

* * *

Akiyama was expecting Blackburn's call. He was friendly and cordial. Blackburn first thanked him again for his hospitality in Tokyo, then brought up the deal with Iraq.

"Yes," confirmed Akiyama. "We had to back out of the deal. Iraq had proposed something it could not deliver, as we discussed in Tokyo. And the escalating tensions in the Middle East make such deals even more questionable."

"I understand."

"Also, Miyazaki-san's anti-Middle East position is getting stronger as the region becomes more unstable."

Blackburn realized that Japan's walking out of the Rumaila deal might have pushed Iraq's patience with Kuwait over the limit, and the irony of the situation intrigued him. He wondered if Akiyama would understand that their decision could actually create more tension in the already tense region. But he decided not to engage him in that kind of analysis over the phone.

"I understand, Akiyama-san," he said. "I do not blame Idemitsu, or Japan for being cautious at a time like this. Please let me know if I can help Idemitsu in any other way. And if you ever visit Washington, please let me know. I would love to show you around this town."

"Of course, Blackburn-san. But you may have reason to visit Tokyo again before I find reason to come to Washington. You left quite an impression here. Everyone at the karaoke club is still talking about you."

Blackburn laughed. "I hope I did not embarrass you too much," he said, feeling genuinely apologetic. "But that was an incredible night."

"Yes it was, and of course you did not embarrass me. You are now a legend in Tokyo!"

"A legend, eh? I'm not sure I can face Mama-san again."

"She thinks the world of you. I was back there last night, and they all ran to me asking about the 'funny *gaijin*.' But you have made the deepest impression on Mariko-san."

"Oh, oh … Is she all right?"

"She wants my help in finding a translator to translate that song for you. Do you remember it?"

"I remember the song. But please, she does not need to go to that much of trouble."

"She asked for your telefax number. When she has the translation completed, she wants to fax it to you. Shall I give it to her?"

Blackburn had not imagined that he would have ongoing contact with Mariko-san. The language barrier, which they somehow overcame in Tokyo, could not possibly allow for long-distance communication, let alone a courtship. For him, the memory of those magical three days and nights was all that would remain, and he had already resolved in his mind that it was enough. He had his hands full with Sophie and Bianca.

He liked Akiyama enough to make a quick decision to open up to him.

"Akiyama-san," he said in as friendly a tone as he could muster. "I'm sorry you have been put in this position. I do not see how any tie between Mariko-san and me can go anywhere, given the distance and especially the language barrier. So I am in a dilemma. I do not want to be rude to her in any way; she does not deserve that. But I do not want to mislead and encourage her either. What would be your advice?"

"No problem at all," Akiyama said. "We take these things more lightly in Japan. I will offer to fax the translation to you myself, and I'll tell her how busy you are. She'll be all right."

"Thank you, Akiyama-san."

Along with a sense of relief, a sense of loss descended upon Blackburn and momentarily engulfed him. He felt as if he had said his final goodbye to Mariko-san, which he realized he might not have been prepared to do just yet.

XXIV

Something Called Pride

Amin did not sound like his normal self. The characteristic calm and collected voice had given way to an anxiety-ridden, almost breathless tone. It was 6 a.m. in Kuwait, and Blackburn knew it would usually be impossible to reach Amin at that hour. He could call him until around midnight wherever he was, or after 10 a.m. Yet it was Amin who had called Blackburn at that hour.

"Can you meet me in Europe?" he asked. "It's important."

"Sure," answered Blackburn, even though he had already arranged dinner with Sophie and Theiss, and promised Theiss to make it to Tampa to brief the generals at CENTCOM on the intricacies of regional relations in the Middle East. "What's going on?"

"When can you get to Europe?"

"Ramzi, tell me where you want me and when, and I'll come." Amin had been a good friend over the years, and had trusted Blackburn enough to take him into his confidence regarding The Symposium. Blackburn was not about to reject this request, especially when he could sense the urgency in Ramzi's voice.

"I have a meeting in Athens tomorrow afternoon, but after that I'll be spending a few days in Switzerland."

"I'll meet you in Switzerland. Where will you be?"

"Do you know a little town called Coppet, near Nyon, between Geneva and Lausanne?"

"Oh yes, there is a great cigar shop in Nyon. I'll take you there. Where will you be staying?"

"I'm staying with some friends. But there is a nice hotel close by. Hotel du Lac. You'd like it. I'll send you the details."

"No need, Ramzi. I'll figure it out. See you there. If I get there in three days, will that work?"

"It will work. I'll make the arrangements for you. I can have you met at the Geneva airport. Give me the details when you arrange your flight."

"Ramzi, you don't have to worry about any arrangements. I'll call your mobile when I check in."

"I insist, Jim. This one's on me. I've already booked several rooms at the hotel. I will make the other arrangements and fax the details to Linda directly."

Before Blackburn could protest, Amin had hung up.

Blackburn could not resist the temptation to contact Bianca. A trip to Europe was always an opportunity to be with her. He thought of asking his travel agent what Hotel du Lac in Coppet was like, to see if he could have Bianca meet him there. The problem was, he did not know what Amin had in mind. If he had booked several rooms, there might be too much Gulf activity planned. Bringing Bianca could prove to be a bad decision.

He decided to arrange to meet with Bianca after meeting Amin. Maybe in Montreux, where they had been before. Or anywhere else in Europe that would work for her. He was curious to find out what Amin had in mind, but it was being with Bianca that promised to make this trip exhilarating.

She was excited to hear from him, as usual, and said she had been about to call him, but he detected a slight reservation in her voice.

"I'll be in Europe in a few days," he said. "Can you meet me?"

"Jimmy, I was about to call you. Please don't be upset again. But I am meeting Roberto next week in Rome. There are some great art exhibitions that he has sponsored."

Blackburn felt like a part of him had cracked and collapsed. Why do I still put myself through this, he thought. When will I learn?

"Jimmy, please say something."

"It's okay. I understand. No problem. I'll talk to you some other time." Blackburn was determined not to show her his torment again. He tried to sound casual and lighthearted, but knew he was failing.

"Jimmy, wait. I have a great idea. Why don't you meet us in Rome? You'd love Roberto. I know he'd love to meet you."

"Bianca, that is not a good idea. By the way, I hope you have not told him about me."

"Of course I have told him about you, Jimmy. I tell everyone about you. I cannot stop talking or thinking about you. But I have not told him about *us*. I promised not to, and have not. So don't get upset. Meet us in Rome. We'll have a great time. We'll go to the art exhibits together and you two can get to know each other."

He should have known all along, but realized then that although he and Bianca were similar in so many ways, they could also act as if they were from different planets.

"What you are describing can never happen." He feigned a laugh.

"Sometimes I get the feeling that this connection of ours is an exciting movie—it's that interesting and enticing. And then I wake up, and realize I'm actually starring in this movie. The difference between you and me is that I am the one who's trying to enjoy every moment of the movie."

Blackburn was touched by her outpouring. He sensed her fighting to save their relationship, which moved him deeply. But he still could not bring himself to accept the idea of joining them in Rome.

"I need to go. Sorry. Enjoy the art exhibits in Rome."

"Wait. Jimmy wait."

"There's no point to this argument. I will not come to Rome."

"Just tell me, why do you want to know everything but you don't want to meet him?"

"Because there is something called pride. Self-respect. There is dignity in being one, not one of three, just one. Period."

He waited a minute. There was no reaction from her. He gently hung up the phone.

He did not know what he would do next. He did not know if he would try to gather the pieces again, or not. There was a messy wreck in his mind, in the space Bianca had occupied.

In the next several days, Blackburn fought with himself, trying to understand and analyze his own jealousy. Why couldn't he just enjoy his time with her without thinking what else she did? What he had with her was any man's dream. Freedom, no commitment, mind-blowing sex, boundless joy exuding from her every movement, inspiration that never faded—why did he have to mess all that up with his utterly misplaced jealousy?

Could it be that there was more than just sexual jealousy involved? Was he jealous because he saw them as having a life together, meeting frequently with a wonderfully exciting agenda, in romantic cities? She had a married life and a child with Stefan, an almost second married life with Roberto, an incredibly active social circle, a successful career, and then him. Where did he fit?

But where in the hell does she fit in my life, he asked himself. She's right, why do you have to make this so difficult? Enjoy her when you have her, leave her alone the rest of the time.

Even as he reasoned, Blackburn knew he would not be able to let his rational self win the battle in the end. He could never leave her alone "the rest of the time." Maybe there was too much of Bianca in him. Maybe it was he who was like her, not the other way round. A male version of the very feminine Bianca.

*   *   *

The meetings in Coppet did not last long. Amin had gathered five members of the defunct executive committee of The Symposium to brainstorm about their next steps. Blackburn knew most of them, including Kamal Ashkar and Majed Al Shammary. Karim Suliman was still in jail in Riyadh.

Their first gathering was during dinner the night Blackburn arrived. Business was not discussed during dinner, which was a largely social affair. Introductions, catching up on personal news, and mundane updates on the regional situation occupied the long, leisurely meal at the Rotisserie in the hotel.

After dinner, they moved to a private room, and Amin introduced the topic. The Middle East region is about to enter a period of confusion and turmoil, he explained. Too many familiar checks and balances that used to protect the old order are crumbling, both regionally and globally. Iran and Iraq, the two military giants in the region, are licking their wounds from their eight-year war. The emir of Kuwait has tried in vain to get Kuwait's borders recognized by Iraq. The Soviet Union is on the verge of collapse, which raises a long list of questions for the region—questions related both to the space it leaves empty, and to the policy shifts in the West when they no longer fight the cold war. Arab nationalist rhetoric is on the rise. Islamic fundamentalist rhetoric is on the rise. And the only rhetoric that is in retreat is that of liberal society.

"Jim," Amin said, turning to Blackburn. "You may be wondering why I asked you to join us here. Let me first set out the bare basics, and then we can talk details. We now realize, given the new chaos and the rising tides in the region, that a group of professionals like us cannot win this fight alone. As you know better than we do, it was foreign intelligence sources that delivered the most deadly blow to The Symposium."

Blackburn was happy that Amin was directing the conversation to him. He had been having trouble concentrating. Bianca had called him earlier in the evening from Vienna. She would go to Rome in two days. She had showered him with so much love and passion over the telephone that he was in a daze when he joined the group for dinner.

"We know the United States has many organizations that support democracy and civil society around the world," Amin said, "both independent organizations and various offices within the government. Our question to you, Jim, is how can we convince some of them to cooperate with us?"

Blackburn had momentarily returned to Bianca. "I will love you so much, *amore mio*," she had cooed. "I will make you feel so loved that you'll forget our silly aggravations."

Then he tore himself free of her voice and turned his attention to Amin. His efforts to banish Bianca to a far corner of his mind forced him to focus more sharply on what Amin was saying. They spent several hours discussing various options and organizations, from the U.S. AID to the U.S. Institute for Peace, to the German Marshall Fund, as well as several less publicized agencies within the U.S. State Department. Blackburn did not know many important details about these organizations—the mission of each, their programs, and their specific policies regarding how they would work with civil society movements abroad. A lot more research had to be done in order to come up with a more tangible plan. And the only way to conduct such research was to either go to a library or visit these organizations and get their literature.

Amin offered to fund such a research effort, as well as the cost of a concrete plan and recommendation for them to pursue. Blackburn argued that while his consulting firm could do some of the research, this was not his specialty, and he offered to recommend a different advisory firm. Amin categorically refused. "It will take us a long time to build confidence with a new firm," he argued. "Please take the job yourself. If you need assistance from anywhere else, engage others, without involving our name, and include that cost in your other costs."

Blackburn was not comfortable taking money from his old friend for a job that didn't fall in his mainstream advisory work. He insisted that his own time and the time of his staff would be pro bono, because he believed in the cause. He would charge only whatever out of pocket expenses he incurred.

Before retiring for the evening, Amin had one more request.

"Karim Suliman is still in jail," he said. "We've tried to intervene through various channels to have him released, but have not succeeded. These days, the Saudis will listen only to the Americans. Can Washington send a message to Riyadh?"

Blackburn thought for a long moment, stroking his mustache with his index finger.

"There has to be a compelling reason for Washington to be involved in something like that. A high-profile human rights case, perhaps involving someone on death row, highly publicized."

"True, this isn't high profile, but it's a strong human rights case. Someone has been arrested with no charge, and no one has heard of him since, including his family members."

"Can you bring it to the attention of organizations such as Human Rights Watch? Maybe if they raise some noise, Washington will have cause to intervene. Right now, their intervention will raise more questions in Riyadh and will eventually cause more problems."

Amin thought about the scenario and understood what Blackburn was saying.

"Can't the intervention be done through covert channels? No need to involve the diplomats. Just between intelligence agencies."

"I'll check," said Blackburn, but he did not hide his skepticism. It was close to 2 a.m., and he was tired and jet lagged. "But realize that type of intervention will also bring new attention to Suliman."

"We have no options, Jim. Any new attention will be good right now. The man has just disappeared."

"I'll try," Blackburn repeated. "But still, find a way to get his story to Human Rights Watch. They'll bring it to light."

The next day, they reviewed and concluded the arrangements with Blackburn, and after lunch he was no longer involved in their continued meetings.

He decided to return to Washington. He saw no point in calling Bianca. He would never meet her and Roberto in Rome, or anywhere else, as she still wanted him to.

XXV

Undeclared Objectives

B lackburn booked a table at Fleming's steakhouse in Tyson's Corner. That was not convenient for him or Sophie, as they both lived in northwest Washington, but Gene Theiss liked the place, and as much as anything else, this was an "Uncle Gene" dinner. He made sure they reserved a relatively private table, at the far corner of the large restaurant.

Sophie thought Theiss looked adorable, with a dark green bow tie, checkered vest, and black coat. His white hair was combed back, and she could tell he had made a special effort to look good. That touched her, because she sensed the meticulous grooming was for her benefit.

They spent the first twenty minutes with pleasant small talk. Blackburn had cut the tedious process of poring over menus by arranging everything in advance. He knew what Sophie and Gene liked. The food was all American meat and potatoes fare: dry-aged prime rib eye steaks, truffle-parsley mashed potatoes, onion rings, roasted mushrooms, and simple green salads. When it came to the wine, Blackburn would not compromise. He went for a 1980 Chateaux Lynch Bagues Pauillac.

As he poured their wine glasses, Blackburn changed the topic of conversation.

"Gene," he said leaning toward Theiss, "so far, our serious business talks have been in private, strictly between the two of us. But tonight, I'd like to cover some shoptalk in front of Sophie. Are you okay with that?"

"I'm okay if you are," said Theiss, turning to wink at Sophie.

"Actually, I'll need advice from both of you on this one. And this way, I won't have to repeat everything to you separately later."

Blackburn had planned this script beforehand. He wanted Theiss to know that he respected Sophie and her opinions.

He proceeded to tell them about the meeting in Coppet. He carefully outlined the trend toward Islamic fundamentalism and nationalism, the retreat of civil society and basic human freedoms, the concern of the cadre of professionals and their plight, and their appeal for cooperation from the United States. He held off on Suliman, pending their reaction.

Theiss listened quietly as always, but waited for Sophie to react first. Blackburn turned to her.

"The timing isn't the best," she said at last.

"What do you mean?" asked Blackburn. "If they don't do something now, they'll lose the battle against the fundamentalists."

"I mean from the perspective of this town. Everyone watching the region is watching the escalating tensions in the Gulf, the chaos in oil markets, and the impact of an unraveling Soviet Union. As an issue, civil society would be a hard sell right now."

"Gene?" Blackburn turned to Theiss.

"I agree. I can't see this being a priority at the State Department. Nor at the CIA. You may have a better chance with some NGOs, but I'm not sure how effective they'd be."

"The issue is not out there, Jim," said Sophie. "Have you seen any news stories about the plight of those promoting civil society in the Middle East? I haven't. These people have worked so quietly that their cause hasn't been recognized."

"Well, maybe it's worth a shot to try to raise awareness on the issue. If I write an op-ed piece will you help me place it somewhere?"

"Sure. That's a good idea. You highlight the issue and then give it a foreign policy tilt. Make it more than about human rights. Tie it to the long-term stability of the Gulf, as a region vital to U.S. interests. It has to be important to U.S. interests for it to find traction."

"That's not at all far fetched," said Blackburn. "In the end, it is about U.S. interests. Instability in the region cannot be good for us from the energy perspective. But it's more than that; it's also about winning the post-cold war fight."

Blackburn was on a roll. In his mind, civil society, human rights, steering away from fundamentalism, economic development, more income equality, were all tied to a vision of a more stable and rational Middle East, which he saw as good for the region, but also vital to U.S. interests.

Theiss was silent but watched his friends and listened with great interest. He was seasoned enough in realpolitik to know that Blackburn's clean, bright vision of the Middle East was not shared by everyone in foreign policy circles. First, not everyone would agree that it was attainable, but more importantly, not every political interest would agree that a developed, more democratic, more rational region was necessarily a good idea. Blackburn tended to be idealistic in assuming that everyone would naturally be inclined to share a positive vision of the future.

Theiss did not want to burst Blackburn's bubble, but did want to alert him to the hurdles ahead.

"One way you can help your friends," he said, carefully weighing his words, "is to make them aware of the true scope of the enemy."

"Oh, I think they understand the enemy," said Blackburn. "They have been fighting it for years."

"I don't mean just those who don't share their values. The enemy also includes the powers that do not necessarily want the Middle East to emerge in accordance with their—and your—vision. Those who'd prefer a weaker, more corrupt and unstable region, rife with internal problems."

Blackburn realized, in a flash, what Theiss was warning him against.

"Like when they learned that many preferred Fahd over Abdullah," he said almost in a whisper.

"Exactly. Forget the declared foreign policy objectives. Those are rhetoric. In the real realm of policy making, you will not find even an ounce of the idealism that you find in political speeches."

For Blackburn, that highlighted the enormity and complexity of the challenge that movements like The Symposium faced.

"What will you find?" he asked, even though he had a good idea of what the answer would be.

"Interests, more narrowly defined than you'd define them. Commercial interests, political interests, power interests."

"And these interests are in conflict with a stable and developed Middle East?"

"They've always been. Do you know how much we hate popular political leaders in that part of the world? Why do you think that is?"

Blackburn looked at him and waited.

"Because popular leaders tend to be more independent. We need unpopular, corrupt leaders because they will depend on us to keep their power. We like that. The large commercial interests like that. Our European partners like that. Israel likes that."

Theiss was satisfied that he had made his point. He did not want to dominate the conversation. He liked the dynamic between Blackburn and Sophie, and had no problem seeing them as partners, in work as well as in life. So he wanted to change the subject.

"Anyway," he said, smiling at Sophie, "I say all this just so you can assess the nature of the task better, and not to discourage you. Good can still come, even when the odds are against it."

Blackburn saw the concern on Sophie's face as she turned to him, and realized his demeanor had changed noticeably, but he did not want to destroy the mood of the evening.

"Excellent input, as usual, Gene," he said, smiling. "Knowing the enemy is critical, and you've opened my eyes."

"Have you told Sophie about what her boss has been up to?" It was time for Theiss to change the topic.

"Yes, I mentioned it," said Blackburn, "but we haven't had time to talk much about it."

"What do you think?" Theiss turned to Sophie.

"Not sure what to think. First I was mad, but then, I thought, this is Russell. I know him. Conceited, opinionated, greedy. Big believer in the power of knowledge. Jim thinks the two contracts he helped me get had him interested. I think there was a third trigger: I warned him that his Japanese contract could be canceled before he had any inkling it could be in danger. That drove him over the edge."

"How did you know about the Japanese contract?" asked Theiss.

She put her hand on Blackburn's arm and gently kissed his cheek.

"I have only one source of intelligence on anything to do with oil," she said, rubbing his arm.

Theiss looked at Blackburn quizzically.

"It's a long story, Gene. Basically, their push into the United States did not make sense to me to begin with, and then their oil strategy began to change. The United States would not factor in any longer. And if I've learned one thing about the Japanese, it is this: they do not waste a cent on any type of advisory work unless they consider it mission critical."

"Well, whatever the triggers were, Russell now knows everything about your business," said Theiss.

*   *   *

When Blackburn got to his office the next morning, Linda handed him a telefax. She had a playful smile on her face, but turned around and left without saying anything.

The fax was from Akiyama.

Dear Blackburn-san: This translation is from Mariko-san. Not necessarily in the best English, but gives the idea. I pass it on to you just as I received it from her. She said to also tell you that she thinks of you often, and that this song, even though very sad, will always remind her of you.

I will contact you soon regarding a business matter.

Regards,

M. Akiyama

Wakare no Yoake: Dawn of Separation

Man: Omae wa shinu hodo tsukushite kureta: You devoted to me so much (so much you could just die).

Woman: Anata wa dare yori aishite kureta: You loved me more than anyone else.

Man: Kako wo yurushite sasayakana Asu wo mitsuketa koi nanoni: This is a kind of love that forgives the past and finds a modest life each day.

Together: Nande nande nande seken wa kiri hanasu : Why, why, why this world (society) tear us apart?

Woman: Anata ni otoko no tsuyosa wo shitta: I learned the strength of a man from you.

Man: Omae ni onna no itoshisa shitta: I learned to adore a woman with you.

Woman: Atsui ryouteni sasaerare. Ikiru tashikana yorokobi wo: Supported by warm palms of yours, I felt the happiness of life.

Together: Hadade hadade hadade kanjite kitamono wo: Felt it on my skin, on my skin, on my skin (but ...).

Man: Omae mo saigo no gurasu wo hoshita: You, too, had the last sip of your cup.

Woman: Anata mo setsunai toiki wo tsuita: You, too, sighed with heartrending sorrow.

Man: Aiwa moete mo sadameni wa Shosen katenai kanashisa yo: What a sadness, even with our burning love, destiny can't be defeated after all.

Together: Namida namida namida wakeau yoake mae: Shedding tears, tears, tears before the dawn.

Blackburn smiled, then started to laugh. The translation struck him as so innocent and basic, that he found it endearing. He could almost hear Mariko-san trying to read the lyrics. He caught himself humming the song, just as Linda walked back in with a bunch of messages.

"Thanks," he said, handing the fax back to her with a smile. "You can file that under 'Japan Miscellaneous.' You never know, I may have to memorize it one day."

*   *   *

"The situation in the Gulf just got more critical," said Theiss. He had been in touch with Blackburn more regularly since their dinner at Tyson's Corner, and that day had volunteered to meet him in his office, which was rare. "All Arab diplomatic efforts to diffuse the tension between Iraq and Kuwait have failed. That includes a last ditch effort in Jeddah to negotiate a settlement between Iraq and Kuwait directly."

Blackburn had heard about the Jeddah meeting, but was not sure of the details.

"What happened in Jeddah?" he asked.

"The Iraqis had four key demands: stop overproducing; cede the Rumaila field; write off the war debts; and, for good measure, compensate Iraq for lost oil revenues because of the decline in oil prices. Kuwait refused."

"Did they offer anything in return?"

"Forgiveness of debts in return for full border recognition."

"How much of this is public knowledge?"

"As of an hour ago, very little. Our sources say that Kuwait thinks Iraq is bluffing. The political leadership does not believe Baghdad will use military force."

"What other type of force do they wield?" asked Blackburn. "Why is this not obvious to everyone?"

"You're pretty sure about this, aren't you?" asked Theiss, studying Blackburn carefully.

"I see no other way, given what you just told me about Jeddah. Has the State Department been in touch with Baghdad about this, or have we left it entirely up to them to sort things out?"

"Oh, we've been in touch, but I'm not sure we've helped. Our ambassador told Baghdad that the United States does not interfere in intra-Arab border disputes. She also received a commitment from them to resolve their differences with Kuwait diplomatically. Which message do you think takes precedence in this case? Theirs or ours?"

"Gene, if I didn't know you better, I'd say you're kidding. I can't believe we told them we do not interfere in intra-Arab border disputes. Do we want them to invade Kuwait?"

"So you're saying their commitment to resolve differences diplomatically means nothing?"

"Well, given what you told me happened in Jeddah, what do you think?"

Theiss stood up and moved toward the window. Blackburn's office window faced the corner of Pennsylvania Avenue and Twentieth Street. Theiss looked down Pennsylvania Avenue for several minutes, his hands in his pant pockets.

"You know, Jim is impressed by you," he said at last, without turning back from the window.

Blackburn didn't realize what he was talking about. "Jim?"

"Schlesinger. He told me you have an uncanny ability to get straight down to the essence of an issue. I agree with him."

"C'mon, Gene. What does that have to do with anything we're talking about?"

"More than you think," said Theiss, walking back to his chair and facing Blackburn. "I also happen to trust your deductive logic. That is a valuable resource at times like this, Jim. Our boys have more detailed information than you, but they do not arrive at the right conclusions about how someone will behave."

"Gene, I'm touched, because I know you do not BS people, but honestly, this is no big deal. Anyone who thinks about the options Iraq faces given its current situation will come to the same conclusion."

"It's not just about Iraq. Jim also mentioned your predictions about OPEC and the oil market, going back several years. But fine, I won't press the point. I see I'm making you uncomfortable. Let me mention one example though. Do you remember Sophie's story about the Japanese canceling their contract with Russell? How you saw it coming?"

"Yes."

"Moving from a shift in Japanese policy priorities to them canceling a contract with Russell comes naturally to you. But it's not as straight a line as it seems to you. Don't get all uncomfortable when I talk like this. This is important. You have a natural skill that can be helpful to our government at a time like this."

"Gene, please, not that again. I cannot be a government employee. I can't take orders. I acknowledge neither rank nor authority. I can't stand bureaucracy. So given all that, what do you want me to do?"

"I actually agree with you on that. I am not suggesting that you become a government employee. But you can advise the government."

"I do that now already."

"I mean exclusively. With high-level clearances and access. But in order for that to work, you cannot be advising the other clients you have. That would complicate things."

For the first time, Blackburn realized that Theiss was dead serious. He didn't understand what exactly he had in mind, but he knew there was more to what Theiss was suggesting than he understood. It was time for him to find out what the man was talking about.

"Okay, Gene," he said, getting up from behind his desk and pulling a chair to sit next to him. "All I understand right now is that you're serious. You have to explain everything else."

"Just think about this scenario," said Theiss in one his most understated tones. "You told me last time how all the big deals you've been working on fell through. You wanted a clean break, you said. Russell is enamored by your business. You have a staff. What if you sell him your company? You get your clean break. I'm sure he'll pay a lot. Then you're free to do whatever you want. Sophie can be the liaison between you and Russell for a while."

"You *are* serious."

"Why not, Jim? The best deal you can cut right now is with the sale of your company. Forget the other ideas of mega deals."

"PCG is my life. It is my life's work. It is what I love to do."

"So I've heard you say, but then why have you been aiming for a clean break?"

Blackburn had no quick answer. Why indeed. He wanted financial independence. But he had not equated that with giving up his consulting business. He had not thought carefully about what he would do once he achieved financial independence. He made good money through PCG. If he loved it so much, why wasn't he content with how things were?

"Russell will not just buy PCG and let me go. The client list without my connections does not mean much for him."

Theiss realized Blackburn was considering the hitherto imponderable scenario.

"That's true," he said. "But that can be sorted out. You can work out a transition plan with him, involving you and your key staff. And of course you'd get Sophie involved from Russell's end. It can be sorted out."

"Gene, if I've been somewhat effective so far, it is because I am constantly in the oil and Middle East traffic. Clients are not just recipients of advice; they can also be an invaluable source of information and insight. Once I lose my contact with my clients, I won't have my finger on the pulse as I do now."

"You don't have to lose contact with anyone. You just won't be working for them. You can still help your friends. PCG can still advise the traders on the market. You can still keep in touch with your OPEC sources. You can still travel and visit your contacts anywhere in the world on a regular basis. It's just that you will have only one real client."

Theiss paused for a moment to let Blackburn absorb all that. Then, looking him straight in the eye, added: "And you will have access to a new source of information, something you haven't had before. That's what the clearances and the access to the top will give you. I assure you, you'll be far more effective than you've ever been."

That was the most compelling argument for Blackburn. He was beginning to visualize what Theiss had described—him keeping his finger on the pulse, armed with more information, and access to the most effective policymakers.

Before he could formulate a response, Linda buzzed him.

"Sorry to interrupt, Jim, but I think you'll want to take this one."

Blackburn picked up the phone, listened for a few minutes, thanked the person on the line, and promised to call him back.

"That was one of the CIA guys I met during the War Games," he told Theiss. "Iraq has begun deploying troops to the Kuwaiti border. They think the scale is large and could lead to a massive buildup. Apparently the emir of Kuwait is already en route, escaping to Saudi Arabia."

✳   ✳   ✳

Bianca had called a few times, but Blackburn couldn't take the calls. She called from Vienna, from the airport, after arriving in Rome, and late that same night. Blackburn did not decline her calls deliberately. Two came in the early morning his time when his phone was turned off. The other two came when he was in meetings he could not interrupt. The situation in the Gulf was escalating by the hour, and his commercial clients as well as his newly established relations in the U.S. government had become extremely demanding.

He told Linda to get him next time Bianca called. So when Linda cracked his office door open while he was on his mobile phone with someone at the Department of Defense, he cut the call short and asked Linda to put her through.

"Do you want me to stop seeing Roberto?"

He was not prepared for her abrupt directness.

"Absolutely not!" he said, surprised by the finality of his own answer. "Why?"

"Because that would solve nothing. Because you'd probably resent me if you stopped seeing him on my account, and rightly so."

Bianca was silent.

"Look," continued Blackburn. "I can see how well you've organized your life. You have everything—an incredible husband, a wonderful child, a good job, and all the freedom you need to enjoy every minute of your life. I will never interfere in that."

"You're part of that wonderful life you say I have. If you will not interfere by allowing me to keep Roberto, why are you interfering in it so rudely by not letting me keep you?"

What a comeback, thought Blackburn. That was exactly how he would have answered had their roles been reversed. How can she be so much like me? At that moment it seemed to him that she was playing the role of an over-indulgent male in their relationship, while he had assumed the role of the hurt woman. He hated his role. He hated her role.

"Let's talk again when you get back home," he said.

"You're being difficult," she muttered.

He hung up the telephone.

He wondered if, deep inside, he wanted Bianca to get tired of him. He was behaving like a spoiled, high-maintenance girlfriend, the type he would dump without a second thought. But as long as Bianca was with Roberto, her beautiful words of endearment sounded hollow.

XXVI

The Proposal

"**H**ow much do you think PCG is worth?" Blackburn asked the accountant at PWC who filed both the firm's and his personal taxes every year.

"That depends on how one valuates a company that is not traded. There's no market valuation of PCG. It also depends on what you need the valuation for."

"The reason for the valuation matters?"

"Sure. If you want a value on the firm because you want to distribute shares to your key staff, like we have talked about in the past, and you want to know the monetary value of what you're giving away, that's one thing. If you're thinking of selling the firm, then other considerations enter the picture."

"Net each case out for me," said Blackburn. "But take the simplest route. No need for fancy financial projections or formulas."

"The first case can be simple, because it is a matter between you and the staff. You might agree on a multiple of net earnings, say, five to six times net earnings, and take that as the value of the firm. Then, when you issue someone, say, 5 percent of the shares, you know how to put a value on it, and measure it against their contribution to value creation in PCG, and in relation to the salary and bonuses they make."

"And in case of a sale?"

"The pure financial calculus could be similar. Except I'd suggest a higher multiple, say ten times, and not of net earnings, but EBITDA—that's earnings before tax, depreciation, and amortization. Alternatively, you could go for two or two-and-a-half times gross sales. But in a sale, there would be other considerations, such as how PCG's operations would enhance the worth of the buying entity. The synergies."

"Last year we had gross turnover of around $6 million and net earnings of about $1.2 million. So we're talking roughly $12 million valuation—whether we do twice sales or ten times earnings, right?"

"Roughly, yes. You'd get more as a multiple of EBITDA. But that's the ballpark financial calculation—say between $14 and $16 million. But don't forget the synergy value. You could double the financial valuation, if the buyer saw the benefits. Also, buyers will probably look at the average of the last three years' earnings."

"Send me some numbers, would you? The last three years' EBITDA, gross sales, and net earnings."

*   *   *

Blackburn worked late that night. There were a lot of memos and briefings, both to read and to write. The military buildup at the Iraqi-Kuwaiti border continued. Reports confirmed the readiness of five Iraqi divisions, with more than 50,000 troops, to cross the border into Kuwait. To Blackburn's amazement, many in Washington and in Kuwait still doubted that Iraq would launch an all-out invasion.

It was past 11 p.m. He was tired and hungry. Most restaurants in DC would be closed. A few bars would still be open, but their kitchens would be closed. He did not feel like going to his apartment yet. He needed a buffer, a gradual transition, between the hectic office stress and his bed.

He was tempted to call Sophie, but assumed she'd be asleep. She had been working hard also. In spite of the mounting tension between Iraq and Kuwait, or perhaps because of it, the Iraqi Embassy in Washington

had intensified its public relations campaign. She had to organize meetings for the embassy to present Baghdad's perspective to all types of special interest groups. He did not want to disturb her.

But then Sophie called. He was touched to hear her voice, and
impressed by the precision of her timing.

"I can't believe you're still in the office," she said. "Your cell phone is
turned off. I didn't want to call your home, in case you were asleep, but
was hoping to hear your voice, so I took a chance."

"What are you doing now?" he asked, loving the moment.

"I'm in bed. Reading some boring PR memos."

"Do you have anything to eat at home? And some wine?"

"Affirmative to both," she said, chuckling. "And if I didn't, you
wouldn't want to come over?"

"I'd still come, but would stop to pick something up, my lovely,
devious, naughty Sophie."

"Three adjectives in one night! Impressive. I'll warm up something
for you."

The conversation made Blackburn realize how comfortable he was
with Sophie. That's what their relationship was—comfortable. There was
still a lot of passion, a lot of excitement even, but none of the emotional
whirlwinds he experienced with Bianca. Sophie was passionate, loving,
caring to the extent of often being motherly, a joy to be with, but not
crazy, not wild, not uncontrollable and fiery like Bianca. He realized that,
given the specific mood that had taken control of his senses, he would not
trade Sophie for anyone, not even Bianca.

The thought surprised him, maybe because it was new. He had always
known how different the two women were and how strongly he loved
both. But the deeply comforting familiarity of Sophie had never moved
him as much as it did that night. Maybe it is age, he thought in passing.
Maybe I am finally getting ready for this marriage thing.

Sophie greeted him in her nightgown, gave him a warm kiss, and
led him to the kitchen. She had a bottle of Bordeaux open, a bowl of beef
barley soup, and some cheese and crackers.

"Go wash up," she said. "I'll toast some bread."

As he finished the soup, she came and sat in his lap. She stroked his
hair, pressed his head to her chest, and dangled her bare feet down his
knees. He held her tight at the waist and kissed her breasts.

"I'm so glad you called," he said.

"I'm glad you're here, Jim. You want more to eat?"

"No, let's go sit. I have something to talk to you about."

He took the bottle of wine and their glasses and sat on the couch in the living room. Her apartment was small—a one-bedroom, with a separate living room, and a kitchen that also served as a dining room.

As she went in to join him, she felt underdressed. She was still in her short nightgown, which reached around mid-thigh and did not do a good job of covering her breasts, while he was fully dressed.

"Let me put something on," she said as he gestured to her to sit next to him, and started heading toward the bedroom.

"Don't you dare! Come here, just like that."

There was something erotic in the air, in her feeling half-naked next to him, in him ordering her to come and sit as she was. Even though they had been dating for several years, moments like these not only excited Sophie, but also turned her bashful in a way that Blackburn found adorable.

"I've been thinking about Russell's surveillance, and what Gene said about him being interested in my business," he said, passing her wine glass to her and resting his hand on her thigh.

"So have I," she said, smiling and feeling even more self-conscious discussing a business matter in her nightgown. "But you go first."

"If it's true that Russell has somehow managed to get his hands on my client list—which, by the way, I am still shocked about, because I can't believe anyone at PCG would leak that info—then he has seen some 120 client organizations, including Iraq and Angola, which became clients of Wilks, Russell & Co., and he's seen that his own Japanese clients are on my list as well. What do you think is passing through his mind right now?"

"If I know Mr. Russell, he's ..."

"Sophie, stop calling him Mr. Russell," interrupted Blackburn. "I've always wanted to tell you that. He's not in the room. Just Russell, or Robert if you want. But not Mr. Okay?"

"Okay, okay! I didn't know it bothered you that much."

"Calling him Mr. even when talking about him to me conditions your brain to think of him as a higher authority than he is. As far as I'm concerned, he is a thief and a snoop. I'll never address him as Mr. Russell even if I meet him one day. I'll call him Robert."

In a flash, Blackburn imagined meeting Russell and calling him Robert. In the same instant, he thought of Roberto, and a dark shadow glided over his eyes. Stupid thing, to associate two entirely unrelated men based only on their names, he told himself. But regardless, Robert Russell had just received a new black dot next to his name in Blackburn's mind.

"I'd love to be there when you do," said Sophie. "That will certainly shock him. I don't think anyone in the world calls him Robert, except maybe his mother, and I'm not even sure about that."

"Good, so tell me, what is Robert thinking right now?"

"His weakness is his haughtiness. His strength is his shrewd and calculating nature. And if I had to bet on what he's calculating right now, I'd say this: he's thinking he got $1.6 million per year from the two clients of PCG. That averages $800K per client. But since the last contract was well over a million, he'll round up the average to $1 million per client. The last deal carries more weight in his mind. It kind of sets a precedent for a rising trend. Mind you, if Angola had come after Iraq, he would have reduced his average expectations.

"Anyway, then he's going through your client list, and checking which organizations could be possible matches for Wilks, Russell & Co. I bet he has penciled check marks all over that list of yours. He has added probabilities and expected annual retainerships for each client. He has made assumptions and drawn out scenarios—say he gets 20 percent of your clients at an average of a million a year, or 25 percent, or just 10. I bet anything he has a detailed table now, showing him the expected value of revenues derived from your clients over the next year, next five years, ten years. That is your Robert Russell."

Blackburn looked at her for a long moment. He had not seen that side of Sophie. "Brilliant," he said. "Just brilliant. I'd hate to be analyzed by you like that."

"Well watch out, James Blackburn. I can read you like an open book too, you know."

There's so much about me you don't know, my sweet Sophie, he thought. What if I took you in my arms now and told you about Bianca, my unending infatuation with her, with her fire, with her crazy, mad zest for life, with the boundless joy that exudes from every pore of her perfect body? What if I told you I have experienced levels of passion and sensuality with her that we've never had? Would you still be cuddling me on your couch, half naked, bashful and so deliciously aroused? And what if I told you about those magical days and nights I spent with Mariko in Tokyo—my great experiment in wordless love? Three days during which neither you nor Bianca crossed my mind. Reading Russell is easy; there is no emotion involved. Just hard observation. Reading emotion is an entirely different matter, lovely, innocent Sophie.

He pulled her to him, put his feet on the coffee table, and closed his eyes. She nestled comfortably in the nook of his arm. She was about to say something, but changed her mind, and closed her eyes too. This was a precious moment to be savored in silence.

"You and I will cook up an offer Russell can't refuse," he whispered after a long while.

She held him tighter, loving his strength, his determination, and most of all, loving his readiness to involve her in the offer he would make to Russell, as if that was the most natural thing to do.

"And you know what else?"

"What else?"

"We're going to get married."

She did not move. She did not hold him tighter. She did not show any reaction whatsoever. After several minutes, he stirred first.

"Well?" he asked.

"Well what?"

"What do you say to that?"

"If that was a marriage proposal I just heard, it had to be the most unusual one ever uttered by any man. It sounded more like a decision you made while brushing your teeth this morning."

"Every proposal is based on a decision to marry someone. It is the decision that counts, right? And I'll even tell you this, Ms. Myles: I think you made that same decision a while ago, even before I did. I just got tired of waiting in vain for you to propose."

Blackburn burst out laughing, and soon they were both in hysterics. She climbed over him, straddling him, and started pounding her fists on his chest, still laughing while tears flowed down her cheeks.

XXVII

The Invasion

At 10:30 p.m. the Iraqi tanks rolled into Kuwait. By 2 a.m. the next day they had occupied a town called Al-Jahra, around ninety kilometers inside Kuwait. The entire Kuwaiti cabinet followed the emir and the crown prince and fled to Saudi Arabia. The Kuwaiti military resistance, abandoned by their political leadership, fought for forty hours, and then surrendered to the Iraqi forces.

A few days later the number of Iraqi troops in Kuwait had risen to 150,000. The occupation of Kuwait was achieved in twenty-four hours, with another twenty-four hours spent to quell the last Kuwaiti resistance.

The time had come for speculation to end and hard reality to sink in. There was a new reality on the ground, and the pontifications about what Iraq might or might not do were rendered irrelevant within a few hours. Now a new wave of speculation and pontification started. What comes next?

The first wave of reactions was diplomatic. Led by the United States and Britain, the United Nations passed Resolution 660, condemning the invasion and demanding that Iraq withdraw immediately from Kuwait. The

Arab countries, primarily Jordan and Egypt, were desperately trying to find a negotiated solution to the crisis. But it was becoming increasingly clear that only a military response could reverse Iraq's occupation of Kuwait.

The more urgent imperative in Washington was to protect Saudi Arabia. While no one could agree what the ultimate intentions of Iraq were, there was an almost unanimous recognition of the potential risk of Iraq continuing its military campaign into Saudi Arabia. That was an imponderable—a direct and unacceptable threat to U.S. and Western interests.

So it was no surprise that the first U.S. troops arrived in Saudi Arabia, under "Operation Desert Shield," only days after the occupation of Kuwait. Desert Shield was a Saudi defense operation, a preemptive measure to prevent Iraq from moving beyond Kuwait. As for what to do with Kuwait, there was still a lot of uncertainty. Would the hectic Arab diplomatic efforts work? Would Iraq simply withdraw, having made its point and subdued Kuwait, and feeling under pressure from both the Arab League and the West?

Blackburn could not fathom the new wave of "informed" opinions on these questions. In his view, Iraq had seized a historic moment and acted. It had serious historical and strategic issues with Kuwait. The war with Iran had demonstrated the strategic importance of having access to certain Kuwaiti territories in the Gulf. But it had no border disputes with Saudi Arabia. Of course, that did not mean Saudi Arabia was exempt from possible aggression. It simply reduced the odds.

One more wave of speculation ended when Iraq proclaimed the annexation of Kuwait. Diplomatic attempts to have Iraq withdraw were given the final blow. A few weeks later, Iraq would declare that Kuwait was its nineteenth province, and would rename Kuwait City.

The alarms were at full volume in the West, especially in London and Washington. If Iraq got away with the occupation and annexation of Kuwait, no small state in the region would be safe. There was no regional force that could stop the expansion of Iraq, with the possible exception of Israel. Theoretically, Iraq could occupy the entire Arabian Peninsula and move into the Levant. Then it would be a formidable threat to Western interests, not to mention to Israeli security.

At the end, and in spite of the misperceptions and rhetoric, one thing was clear: this was not about Kuwait. Kuwait was dispensable. Other interests were not. The Middle East was a sideshow, as Blackburn had stressed to his Kuwaiti hosts so emphatically, long before the occupation of their country.

Aimi's call came two weeks after the invasion, just when Blackburn was getting ready to leave the office. She was the most impressive person Blackburn had met in Maine. Aimi J. Kaysik, an economic analyst at the CIA working on Third World debt and competitiveness issues, had impressed Blackburn with her sharp insights. They had hit it off, and she had since become his main contact at the CIA.

"The secretary of defense would like to talk to you," she said. "There are questions about the latest events."

"Thanks, Aimi. Will you be present at the meeting?"

"I don't think I can be, Jim. He wants to meet with you alone."

"Alone is fine," Blackburn said. "But I want him to know that if there are others there, such as assistants I don't know, I will not say much."

"I think you will be alone with him. Don't be so paranoid, Jim. So what if he had an assistant or two present?"

"Unless I know who they are beforehand, I will say nothing, Aimi. Sorry. I do not trust Washington. I live here, but this city has no soul."

Aimi laughed. "As dramatic as ever. This city does not need a soul. It needs a brain. But that is another matter. Let's have a drink sometime. After you talk with the secretary."

"You're on, Aimi. And thanks."

Blackburn walked into the office of the secretary of defense of the United States with some trepidation. He had met the secretary before, but this was his first one-on-one meeting in his office. It was an imposing office. A gigantic desk sat against the wall, and a smaller round table was placed at the entrance of the room. As Aimi had promised, there were no aides. The secretary sat at the round table, with a yellow legal pad, and began to question Blackburn about the politics in the Arab world. He took notes as Blackburn talked, covering intra-Gulf relations, and then expanding into Jordan, Egypt, Yemen, and Iran.

The meeting was scheduled for thirty minutes. It lasted over two hours, during which the office secretary knocked a couple of times to remind her boss of his next appointments, but he asked her to reschedule.

Then they talked about how the occupation of Kuwait would affect the political relations in the region, specifically between Saudi Arabia, Egypt, Jordan, and Iraq, and the role, if any, the Arab League could play in diffusing the tensions.

The secretary filled over twenty pages in his yellow legal pad with notes. He wrote double spaced, with large letters and little punctuation. After his initial query about intra-Arab relations, he rarely interrupted Blackburn or even looked up from his pad. He seemed to be getting the type of analysis he wanted, thought Blackburn; otherwise he would have tried to redirect his monologue.

Finally, the secretary stopped writing and looked up from his pad at Blackburn.

"I have a drawer full of cables in that desk from our embassies in the Arab countries," he said, pointing to the gigantic desk, "warning us not to engage militarily. No Arab country can support a U.S. military strike against another Arab country, they tell me. What do you make of that?"

Blackburn recalled the same discussion during the War Games in Maine and assumed the secretary would have been briefed. Aside from that, right before coming to this meeting, he had heard President Bush say in a press conference that he was not contemplating military intervention. It was unusual for the president to rule out an option. It must have surprised the reporters too, because they repeated the question and received the same answer again. No intervention was being considered.

"Mr. Secretary," said Blackburn, "this question was raised in Maine recently. Here is what I believe: If a U.S. military engagement aims to reverse the occupation of Kuwait and stops with that specific objective, most Arab countries will thank the United States, regardless of what they say publically now. None of them want a stronger Iraq. But if the United States goes further, and actually occupies Iraq, or causes major civilian losses, then the words of caution will be justified."

"So even if in the process of forcing Iraq out of Kuwait, we cause devastating losses to Iraq's military, we won't invite massive diplomatic opposition from the Arab countries."

"Absolutely not," said Blackburn without a moment's hesitation. "I'd go further and say that, once it's all done and Kuwait is restored, most Arab countries will be thankful and in awe."

"What are the risks? I don't mean the military risks."

"That we hesitate."

The secretary gave him a quizzical look.

"That we don't finish the job quickly and efficiently," added Blackburn. "That once we start, we do not give it all we have."

The secretary's face lit up. Now Blackburn knew, beyond any doubt, that the secretary wanted to use military force to liberate Kuwait.

"A lot of people I trust value your views, Jim," he said with a warm smile. "And I like your advice better than that of some fifteen U.S. ambassadors, so help me God. Thank you for an informative chat."

When he returned to his office, Blackburn called Theiss.

"We're going to war," he said.

"I'm coming to the same conclusion," said Theiss. "But the White House may not be ready for that yet. Let's try to get together in the next couple of days."

"Good idea, Gene. But I've been ignoring my clients too much lately. I need to focus on them for a couple of days. I'll get back in touch."

He spent the rest of the week answering accumulated client calls, and writing two short memos, which were telefaxed to all his clients. In a nutshell, he alerted his clients to a "highly likely" military intervention in Kuwait and Iraq, which had actually become the minority view following the president's press conference.

Meanwhile, his team produced a detailed report covering various crude oil production interruption scenarios. Periods of total cessation of production from Kuwait, the same from Kuwait and Iraq, with detailed price impact projections, based on how much of the shortfalls could (and would) be compensated for by increased flows from Saudi Arabia and the other OPEC countries. The conclusion of the report was that after an initial spike, prices would stabilize relatively quickly because of a surge of production from other producers. That too was a minority view in an industry used to attributing too much market influence to events in the Middle East.

*   *   *

Blackburn studied the numbers carefully. The average gross earnings of PCG (before taxes and depreciation) for the last three years were $1.6 million per year. If he applied a multiple of ten to that number, as the accountant had suggested, he'd get a derived value of $16 million for the firm. He'd have to incentivize at least three key employees to make sure they stayed under the new ownership. He assumed that would require between $2 and $3 million. So, based strictly on the financial approach, his share of the sale would amount to around $13 million. That did not excite him enough to part with PCG.

The more difficult exercise was to come up with a ballpark figure for the "synergy value" as far as Wilks, Russell & Co. was concerned. Would Russell pay $30 million for a company, which on paper was worth $16 million? If he thought he'd make the money back many times over, he might. Blackburn had seen many of his clients pay "strategic premiums" for assets that were substantially higher than their market value. He figured it would be an attractive deal for Russell if he could see himself recovering his investment in three years. So $30 million would be attractive if he believed he could make $10 million per year of additional income from the synergy with PCG. Blackburn thought Russell could be convinced that his incremental revenues would be at least $20 million per year, assuming just twenty new clients paying a retainer of $1 million each. So a three-year payback would imply a price tag of $60 million. Now that was worth considering.

He knew these computations were rough and would not necessarily stand in actual negotiations, but he had already set his mind on a minimum price of $50 million for PCG, and a target price of $65 million. These figures implied multiples of thirty to forty times gross earnings, too high to be seen in any transaction on Wall Street. But he did not care. That was the price that would make it worthwhile for him.

The next step was to figure out the right strategy to broach the subject. He could not be involved directly in the initial negotiations with Russell. A financial intermediary was critical. And finding the right financial advisor for a transaction of this nature was even more critical. He had seen too many deals go sour among his clients because of mismanagement.

Another factor was how to let Russell know that PCG might be for sale. The offer could not come from PCG itself—that would automatically discount the value.

Finally, Blackburn had learned from the way his clients made acquisition decisions that a little competitive tension always helped expedite closure and boost the premium. Russell had to believe he was not the only one interested in PCG.

An overall strategy was forming in Blackburn's head; what had seemed imponderable only a couple weeks ago was beginning to look real and plausible. Assuming, of course, they were right about Russell's motives and about the nature of his interest in PCG. That had not yet been confirmed.

*   *   *

The diplomatic efforts to gather a coalition against the Iraqi invasion of Kuwait were in full swing. It was important to gain Arab support, as well as the support of the Western allies. In the early days, Arab leaders had advocated caution and calm. They wanted a chance to resolve the issue through intra-Arab diplomacy. But the intelligence reports were getting grimmer by the day. Iraq was not going to withdraw from Kuwait through diplomatic means.

It had come to a choice between a costly and risky military conflict and setting a precedent for accepting a new status quo where a small and defenseless country was overtaken by a more powerful neighbor. The latter had far-reaching and irreversible consequences for American and Western interests.

The secretary of defense was convinced that the only meaningful strategy was to get Iraq out of Kuwait by U.S. military force. Nothing else made sense, given what was at stake. Just as important, nothing else would be effective given the intelligence he had received about the intentions and will of the Iraqi leadership. But the president wanted as large a coalition as possible. This could not be just a U.S. operation.

There was still a lot of ambiguity about whether the White House was considering the use of U.S. military force in the Gulf. International economic sanctions were being considered as an alternative, and some leaders were still hopeful that an oil embargo combined with a naval blockade of Iraq and Kuwait would be sufficient to force Baghdad to withdraw from Kuwait.

But Iraq was becoming bolder and more entrenched within Kuwait every day. Each U.S. and European move triggered a more belligerent reaction from Baghdad. In response to the deployment of American troops to Saudi Arabia, Baghdad had declared a union of Iraq and Kuwait, which was followed by a formal annexation. After the declaration of the annexation of Kuwait, a naval blockade began. A few days later, Iraq declared Kuwait its nineteenth province. The United Kingdom and France announced the deployment of troops to Saudi Arabia.

As the allied military buildup in Saudi Arabia intensified, the UN Security Council passed another resolution, setting a deadline for Iraq to withdraw from Kuwait or face military action. The deadline was January 15, 1991.

* * *

"You're finally going to get your wish," Blackburn told Bianca over the telephone.

She laughed. "Which one? I have so many unfulfilled wishes when it comes to you."

"Sophie and I are getting married."

"You are so cruel," she said in semi-mock protest.

"Didn't you tell me to marry her? You said you could accept her as my wife; otherwise she did not fit, you said."

"I am happy for you, Jimmy, really. Will you invite me to the wedding?"

"There won't be a fancy wedding. Just a small ceremony. Why, would you want to come?"

"Sure I want to come. Don't you want me to come?"

"I don't know. I'm not as evolved in this relationship thing as you are. We'll see."

"Jimmy, we're not just lovers. We've been good friends. We've shared a lot of personal things. In fact, you've been a wonderful friend to me. What's so wrong about wanting to go to a friend's wedding?"

Could it be that the key to understanding Bianca was that she attached no importance to physical intimacy? She loved sex, her passion knew no limits, her elation was so genuine, so unencumbered, so contagious. Yet perhaps for her all that was nothing more than a deserving addendum to a moment already made exquisite by her enjoyment of being in the company of the person she was with at that moment.

What if the Bianca phenomenon was all about living a full life, about not missing any opportunity to have an exhilarating experience?

There is only one problem with that theory, he thought, even though he was beginning to love the idea. The problem is that Bianca would be just like me if our roles were reversed.

"Okay, we'll see. No date has been set yet. I have barely had time to see her lately, let alone marry her! Let's leave it open until things settle down with the Middle East. Okay?"

"Okay, Jimmy. Congratulations. Again, I am happy for you."

"Thanks, Bianca. And by the way, you're right. We have been good friends."

If I remove my jealousy from the picture, he thought after they had hung up, what I had with Bianca was probably as perfect a friendship as anyone could have. We always had a lot of trust, a lot of off the record chats about OPEC, a lot of mutual caring and respect and admiration. It was a truly burden-free friendship—of course, not counting Roberto.

Suddenly he realized he was thinking about his relationship with Bianca in the past tense. He had said nothing to her, nor had she said anything to him. And while, by her own admission, his marrying Sophie would make her "fit" in their relationship, he was not counting on continuing that relationship after he got married. Sophie deserved no less.

XXVIII

Hello Robert

P CG's financial advisors started preparing the firm for sale. The word was out in a small circle of the financial community that a boutique, independent energy advisory firm might be on the market. The first line of potential suitors was thought to be a number of competitive energy consulting firms. Blackburn knew that creating competitive tension was critical and could translate into additional tens of millions of dollars to the sale price. He had not allowed a direct approach to Wilks, Russell & Co. The strategy was for Russell to hear about the sale and approach the financial intermediaries on his own. And Blackburn had instructed his advisors to give Russell the cold shoulder at first, politely suggesting that several specialized energy consulting firms were interested in PCG and had already entered into early discussions.

At the same time, the financial advisors arranged for a full audit of PCG. Blackburn had never bothered to have an audit before, opting instead to produce the minimum reviews he needed for tax purposes. With no shareholders and a nominal board, audits had not been necessary. But they would be required for the due diligence process of a potential acquirer. He had an in-house financial officer who handled his books, client billings, and the filing of corporate expenses, who now dealt with the auditors. But the process proved to be time consuming for him as well. There were details of client accounts that only he knew. Some client relationships were not documented by a written contract so could not be included in the revenue base by the auditors, even though payment had been made regularly. This reduced the revenue base in some years, and brought down gross earnings.

Blackburn was annoyed by these complications, and even more irritated that they were demanding so much of his time.

"We're sorry," said Jerry Fishbine, the main financial advisor working on the deal, "but we have to turn PCG from an informally run personal business to a professionally run corporate business in just a few months."

"What makes you say PCG is not professionally run now? We have an impeccable reputation among our clients."

"Mr. Blackburn, I'm not talking about the way you handle your consulting practice and your clients. I am talking about your books. Everything has to comply with GAAP—generally accepted accounting principles. Right now, it does not. The financial statements have to pass the most demanding audit, and every client has to be properly documented."

At the end, Blackburn had to concede. But in spite of the reduction in his revenue base, he did not reduce his minimum price expectations.

To his surprise, once PCG was properly recast to comply with all the accounting rules, the process of negotiating with potential acquirers fascinated him. As anticipated, there were a couple of serious suitors from the energy advisory sector; there was also one publisher, with a large number of specialized magazines in its list of publications. This surprised Blackburn.

"The owners believe they are in the information business," said Fishbine. "So is PCG. Their magazines are highly specialized—about science, psychology, business, real estate. So they think they can launch a couple of energy magazines."

"PCG is not in the information business," Blackburn answered. "We are in the advisory business. We do not sell information. We sell good, solid, reliable, high-value advice. Forget them."

"Regardless of what they may be willing to pay?"

"I'd be curious to know what PCG would be worth to them, but I don't believe the synergies are there. This could turn out to be a very unhappy marriage. They will suffer, and PCG will probably be ruined."

And then Fishbine received the expected call from the attorney of Wilks, Russell & Co. He had detailed instructions on how to handle it.

"Isn't Wilks, Russell & Co. a public relations firm?" asked Fishbine.

"One of the largest in the nation."

"PCG is a specialized energy advisory firm. How do you see that being incorporated with Wilks, Russell?"

"We believe it can be incorporated very well," answered the attorney. "But shouldn't we discuss those details in person?"

"Yes, of course," answered Fishbine, following the script given to him by Blackburn. "But I feel I need to inform you that at the moment we are in discussions with two energy advisory firms with strong synergies with PCG. The future of PCG matters greatly to Mr. Blackburn, the main principal. So he places great value on synergies with a potential acquirer."

"I understand. I believe we can address these concerns to your satisfaction. Perhaps even better than another energy advisory firm."

One of the two advisory firms dropped out of the race early. It could not comprehend how a practice whose gross earnings were $1.6 million per year would ask a price of $65 million. They did not see any major benefit in added value by combining the practices of the two firms, such as expanded specializations, expanded client relationships to which the services of the two firms could be marketed, and expanded reach into different sectors of the energy industry.

The second, and larger firm continued discussions and decided to conduct due diligence. But subjecting PCG to due diligence by a competing firm was risky. It gave the competitor access to the commercial details, which it could later use against PCG if the deal did not go through.

"How serious are they?" Blackburn asked Fishbine. "How do we know they are not just fishing for information?"

"They seem serious. You have lines of practice that they never developed, they tell me. For example, your crude oil market watch. They also do not do much geopolitical analysis. So they think if they can market their services to all of PCG's clients, and PCG's services to all of their clients, they can increase the combined revenues substantially in just a year or two."

The argument made sense to Blackburn. It was always easier to sell a new service to an existing client, than to cultivate a new client relationship from scratch. And building expertise and services in new areas could be costly.

"And they didn't balk at the price?"

"They did, but they think there's some room for negotiation. At any rate, they're interested enough to go through due diligence."

"I don't know, Jerry. They'll discover everything about my business. They have a lot more to gain by this than PCG. I wish I could be sure they're serious, and if the due diligence results confirm what we're already presenting to them, then they cannot back down from the deal."

"That's easy. We can do that."

"How?"

"We give them the basic bottom line financials. And we put forward a price range. If the due diligence confirms the accuracy of our numbers, they have to go ahead with the acquisition within the price range."

"What guarantees would we have?"

"A written contract."

"Can we make it stronger?"

"A written contract is usually enough, but if you want to, we can ask for a deposit. If the due diligence confirms our claims and they back down, they lose the deposit. If due diligence does not confirm our claims, you'll have to return it."

Blackburn was intrigued with the idea. A substantial, non-refundable deposit, as a pre-condition for due diligence, would certainly demonstrate serious intent.

"What's 5 percent of $65 million?"

Fishbine punched on the calculator he carried with him at all times.

"It's $3.25 million."

"Okay, let's ask for a $3 million deposit. Below 5 percent of the asking price. If they pay it, I'll believe they are serious. But before we go that far with them, where do we stand with Wilks, Russell?"

"They're eager, but I've been stalling them."

"Gauge their interest before we go further with this one. I have a feeling we'll have more fun with them."

When Fishbine responded to Wilks, Russell & Co., things began to move fast. In principle, Russell did not object to the asking price, as long as there was 10 percent room for maneuver. The competitive tension factor was working in full force. Russell believed that PCG was more advanced in its negotiations with the energy firm than it actually was. He had also heard about the publishing company, which happened to be one of Wilks, Russell & Co.'s clients. He did not want to lose this opportunity.

When Russell asked to start due diligence, Blackburn was amused. Don't they already know everything, he thought? And even though he was not worried about being put at a disadvantage by a competitor, he still requested the $3 million non-refundable deposit.

Russell agreed. The money was transferred to PCG's account within a week. A team of financial analysts commissioned by Wilks, Russell & Co. arrived at the PCG offices two days later to start due diligence. Blackburn was amazed that Russell was going through all this trouble to learn what he already knew.

Two weeks later Wilks, Russell & Co. requested a meeting with the principles of PCG, before it made a formal offer. Blackburn was amused by that too. Russell knew Blackburn was the only shareholder of PCG, even though he had issued shares to Patrick Hagan and Jan Gabriel, his financial officer, after the theft of information by Russell. Blackburn agreed to the meeting, but requested that Sophie Myles be present. Given all the pictures of him and Sophie that Russell's private investigators had taken, Blackburn knew Russell would not be surprised by this request.

*　*　*

Blackburn met Theiss at iRicchi, an Italian restaurant on 19th Street. This was an important meeting for Blackburn. A few weeks earlier he had briefed Theiss about Karim Suliman's arrest and Amin's request for intermediation from the community. Theiss had initially resisted the idea. This was no time to interfere in the internal affairs of Saudi Arabia, he had argued. The government needed its full cooperation in the pending military operation, and until recently Saudi Arabia had been holding it back. However, at the end, because of Blackburn's persistence, Theiss had agreed to at least present the case.

Blackburn had learned not to rush conversations on subjects that mattered to him, especially with Theiss. Theiss could get dismissive when pressed, holding back details he might otherwise be persuaded to share. So Blackburn initially focused on the basket of warm bread, dipping a slice in olive oil mixed with balsamic vinegar, and asked if Theiss would like a drink. They ordered two glasses of dry sherry.

Blackburn waited for Theiss to bring up the subject of Suliman. He briefed him on the progress of the effort to sell PCG, making it clear that he was basically following his counsel on that move.

"Let me know when you're ready to talk about your next move with the government," said Theiss.

"Do you know Aimi Kaysik?" asked Blackburn.

"I do. Why?"

"I wouldn't mind working with her."

"How well do you know her?"

"Not well. Met her at the War Games. But she strikes me as one of the smarter ones."

"She probably is. I'll check around. But we should talk about the nature of your engagement with them before any formal approach."

"We can do that anytime, Gene."

Blackburn was anxious to hear what Theiss had to say about Suliman, but could sense Theiss' reluctance to bring up the subject. He didn't want them to get distracted by a conversation about his next career as a special advisor to the U.S. government.

"But before we delve into that," he said casually, "any news about Suliman?"

Theiss realized he could not put off the issue any longer.

"I'm afraid I don't have good news. Our boys believe he is already dead."

"They know this for a fact?"

"No. But there is no record of the guy anywhere. The Saudi secret service denies any knowledge of him."

"They arrested him. That is certain."

"I know. That is why this denial almost certainly means that Suliman has already been murdered. Probably died under interrogation."

Blackburn was quiet for a long time. Theiss focused on his mine-strone soup, allowing Blackburn, who had not yet touched his food, to process the information.

"Jim, there is nothing we can do," said Theiss, finally breaking the silence.

"I know. Thanks for trying anyway. They should at least have the decency to contact his family. Everyone needs and deserves closure."

"They eventually will. But pushing from our end is pointless. Do you know if his family is out of Saudi Arabia?"

"I believe they are. Amin will make sure they're taken care of."

"Eat your lunch. I will keep my ears open, in case any new light is shed on the matter."

"The Symposium was a good organization, Gene. I could relate to them intellectually. Their vision should have been supported. It would have been good for the United States."

"You remember our talk about undeclared objectives?"

"Yes."

"We have supported more corruption in the Middle East than free-dom and human rights. We have tried to topple more democratically elected governments than we supported, and we have usually succeeded. In Syria back in the fifties, in Iran, in Iraq. It is the sad truth."

"Small wonder that we're not trusted."

"That and our obsession with commercial interests, with oil, and with blind support for Israel's policies in the region, leave no room for idealism in our actions."

Blackburn fell quiet again, his grilled chicken already cold on his plate.

"You cannot be effective if you allow events to affect you like this." Theiss had already finished his soup and normally would have wanted to leave. But he ordered a cup of coffee to stay with Blackburn a while longer.

"Maybe you can make a small difference in your future role. But remember, not everyone will share your vision, or your long-term objectives. Cast aside all idealism and enter the arena armed only with Machiavellian calculations. Only then might you make a dent."

* * *

Blackburn walked into Russell's office with Hagan and Gabriel in tow. Russell was sitting at the round conference table by his desk, along with one of his attorneys and Sophie Myles. Blackburn walked straight to him, ignoring Sophie and the attorney.

"Hello Robert," he said, smiling broadly. "Finally we meet. It is a pleasure. James Blackburn. These are my partners, Patrick Hagan and Jerry Gabriel."

As Sophie had predicted, Russell was taken aback by hearing his first name. But Blackburn ignored the reaction, turned to the attorney, and shook his hand. Then, turning to Sophie, he winked and said, "Hi Sophie."

Russell was a handsome man. In his early sixties, slim, slightly balding, with an impressive presence, he exuded confidence. Once he got over the initial shock of Blackburn's dramatic entry and regained his composure, he took charge of the meeting.

The focus was on the transition. The first order of business that Russell put on the table was a set of non-compete conditions, which would include Blackburn, Hagan, and Gabriel agreeing not to engage in similar energy advisory work either independently or through another firm. That was relatively easy to agree to, as none of them had any intention to continue the same line of work elsewhere.

Once the non-compete agreement was out of the way, they agreed that the most immediate challenge was to guarantee that change of ownership would not affect PCG's ability to serve its clients. In order to ensure this, Blackburn and Hagan's continued involvement was critical. Of course, there would be no issue with Hagan's continued involvement, but Blackburn made it clear that they had to work out an orderly transition plan for him, since he intended to withdraw from the commercial consulting business within a reasonable period of time. That was a complicated discussion. Russell wanted Blackburn to commit to at least three years of full-time employment at PCG, which Blackburn could not do.

"I am more committed to the continued success of PCG than anyone," said Blackburn. "This is my life's work. I will make sure it continues and thrives after the sale."

"How?" asked Russell. "Don't most PCG clients insist on talking to you? On some issues they will not trust anyone else."

"That's been true in the past, but it's beginning to change already. Here is what I propose we do: During the first two months after the sale, Hagan and I and a person you appoint from Wilks, Russell will visit every client organization of PCG. We probably need to do this to explain the change of ownership anyway. In the process, every client organization will meet the new faces they'll interface with in the future. We will pass the baton efficiently and effectively."

Russell liked the idea, but something was still bothering him.

"It's not just about the continued operations of PCG," he said, locking eyes with Blackburn. "It's about completing the integration process between PCG and Wilks, Russell. That integration will require more than a few months."

Blackburn understood exactly what "integration" meant in this case. Russell wanted to make sure the PCG clients could be turned into Wilks, Russell & Co. clients. Blackburn looked at Sophie, who was sitting dutifully listening to the discussion, and had not said a word. She gave him the slightest smile, which no one else noticed, but the look told Blackburn she understood Russell's concern. There was something sensuous in being able to communicate with her in public, with such discretion.

"I understand the integration challenge," he said, turning back to Russell. "Here's what I'd propose on that one: I will remain on board as a special advisor to Wilks, Russell & Co. for three years, focusing strictly on the challenges of integration of the two firms. This I can commit to. But my commercial advisory function with PCG has to end in six months after acquisition. I believe we can secure everything in this time frame. This way, I will be 100 percent focused on securing the integration process, which I agree is critical."

Russell was impressed. Blackburn had managed to get his way while alleviating Russell's concerns. Sophie was impressed too. They had not discussed this part of the deal beforehand, so she figured Blackburn had thought of the solution on the spot.

The last issue to cover was how they'd make the announcement, first to employees, then to clients, then to the press. A joint communiqué, signed by Russell and Blackburn, would be drafted and distributed for each of these purposes.

As the meeting was about to come to a close, Blackburn turned to Russell again.

"Robert," he said, "may I have a moment alone with you?"

"Sure." Russell was once again surprised at being addressed by his first name.

"Thanks." Blackburn turned to Hagan and Gabriel. "I'll catch up with you later."

Russell nodded to Sophie and his attorney, and they left the room.

"Thanks again," Blackburn said to Russell when everyone else was gone. "I was going to mention this to you after finalizing the acquisition, but changed my mind. I want you to know it now, so it does not sound like I was being disingenuous."

"Know what?" Russell looked puzzled.

"I know everything about your surveillance. I know you knew about Sophie and me, about my financials, about my client list. I know why you started the surveillance and when you ended it."

Russell's jaw dropped; he was speechless. He stared at Blackburn, unsure what to say or how to look.

"No hard feelings, by the way," added Blackburn with a smile. "You had to find out, right? I have to admit that I was angry at first, but then for a minute I put myself in your shoes, and it all made sense. Iraq, Angola, Japan ... You had to know. Again, no hard feelings."

"But how did you find out?" Russell had finally found his voice.

"Ah! Now that is some story. I'd love to share it with you. But I want something in return. Why don't we make this the cornerstone of our mutual trust and confidence? We're about to enter a mutually beneficial long-term relationship, right? Let's establish trust before we even con-summate the transaction. It will be more genuine this way."

"What are you talking about?"

"As I said, we need to start with trust, Robert. I'll tell you how I know about your surveillance, and you tell me who at PCG sold the infor-mation you bought. This way, we start our new relationship with a clean slate, with the air cleared."

Russell was not used to such a direct approach. In his business, ambi-guity and gray areas were the norm. But he understood what Blackburn was saying, and there was something refreshing in his approach. Still, his hesitation was clear.

"Look, you will never be able to trust the source at PCG. If he sold out to you, he'll one day sell out to someone else. If I've learned one thing about building a team in the professional services industry, it is that skills and knowledge can always be acquired, but character cannot."

The issue bothering Russell was not that he disagreed with Blackburn. On the contrary, he fully agreed with him. What bothered him was being lectured about the ways of life by someone more than twenty years his junior. Blackburn sensed this. "His weakness is his haughtiness," Sophie had said. She had read him right.

"Okay," Blackburn said to help him overcome his reluctance. "I'll make it easier to break the ice. I'll tell you my guess. The person who sold out was here with me in this office today, right?"

"It was Gabriel," Russell said at last. "I was going to fire him right after the acquisition. I wasn't interested in who the source was, until I decided to buy PCG. But then I had to know."

"I understand. Thanks for your confidence. Too bad I issued him some shares. But that's fine too, because I will make him sign the strictest separation agreement before he gets a penny. Now, as for my end, you need to know that I have friends in the intelligence community in this town. In fact, as a further confidence building measure between us, let me disclose that I will be working with them after my six months at PCG are up."

And Blackburn proceeded to tell him how his private investigators were exposed, without giving Theiss' name or location. Russell had a whole new level of respect for Blackburn after that disclosure.

XXIX

Flickering in the Wind

Masahiro Akiyama landed in New York on Friday night. He needed the weekend to get over his jet lag before attending the oil and gas conference on Monday morning. He had seen James Blackburn's name on the agenda as the luncheon keynote speaker, and had decided to come. It was a special event organized by the New York Bankers Association, in collaboration with the Council on Foreign Relations. Idemitsu's chairman was a member of the council, and had received the invitation and agenda, and passed it on to Akiyama.

The title of Blackburn's luncheon speech was "Geopolitics of Energy: The Shifting Tectonic Plates." What a haughty, cocky title, he had thought when the organizers first suggested it. But he had no time to argue, let alone propose an alternative. Besides, at these types of meetings, he gave the speech he thought would be most relevant under the prevailing circumstances, irrespective of the proposed title. And these days, pretentious or not, he did see the tectonic plates shifting in the global energy sector.

Blackburn and Sophie arrived in New York on Sunday afternoon. When Blackburn asked, Akiyama had said he'd prefer to have dinner in an authentic New York restaurant. So Blackburn booked a table at P. J. Clark's on 3rd Avenue and E 55th Street, claimed to be a one-time hangout of Frank Sinatra, Jackie Onassis, and Elizabeth Taylor. The Japanese love stuff like that, he explained to Sophie; I want to show this guy a good time.

Sophie liked Akiyama at first sight. She saw the same pleasant aura around him that Blackburn had seen in Tokyo. "He has kind eyes," she told Blackburn later that night. "Hard to describe, but he inspires kindness." Blackburn was pleased to hear her articulate his own impression of Akiyama, one he'd had a difficult time describing until then.

As usual, the dinner conversation spanned the situation in the Middle East, energy markets, Japan's trade surplus, and the political backlash, plus the main added novelty, the lobbying industry in Washington. Sophie explained to Akiyama what Wilks, Russell & Co. did in general, and a little about what they were engaged to do for a group of Japanese energy companies, including Idemitsu Kosan.

"But what exactly do you do? What is 'lobbying'?" Akiyama seemed fascinated by the very concept.

Sophie laughed. "The industry does not like the term 'lobbying.' We feel it demeans our mission." Self-flagellation, done in humor, was a form of modesty that was common in the industry. It was considered to be a kind of disclosure that built confidence with clients. "We manage our clients' public relations, their image, their relationship with the press, with government regulators, and we often get involved in campaigns that promote policies favored by our clients; that last one is your classic lobbying."

"And your clients include foreign governments?"

"Oh, yes. Foreign governments, both American and foreign corporations, NGOs, and many industry associations. We even have acted as several individuals' publicist, promoting either their specific projects or, in a few cases, their books."

"Iraq is her largest client right now," chimed in Blackburn. "That's a delicate act of what is known as 'reputation management.' You can imagine who would pay money to improve their reputation, right?"

"Doesn't Iraq have bigger headaches now than managing its reputation in Washington?"

"I'm sure it does," said Sophie, "but the threat of U.S. sanctions on Iraq has cost them dearly already. Jim can explain that better. A country's image, as portrayed in the press, on Capitol Hill, in the White House can influence sanction policy, often more than the hard facts on the ground."

They talked late into the night. They asked Akiyama questions about his family, and he was glad to oblige, showing them photos of his two daughters, eight and ten, his wife, even his parents, both of whom were still alive. In contrast, Blackburn was an only child with both parents deceased, and no children. Sophie's immediate family lived on the West Coast, and she rarely saw them. As they were talking about such differences in their personal circumstances, Blackburn put his arm over Sophie's shoulder and drew her closer to him.

"Akiyama-san," he said with a smile, "my personal circumstances will change *very* drastically *very* soon. I am marrying this lovely lobbyist, so help me God."

They had finished their third bottle of wine, and were ready to call it a night. But Akiyama would not hear of it.

"We need to celebrate!" he declared, and ordered a bottle of champagne.

"Unlike the two of you, who are practically on vacation here in New York, I have a speech to give tomorrow," said Blackburn, but he was touched by Akiyama's gesture.

"Oh, you can give that speech in your sleep," said Sophie. "Let's celebrate."

"When's the big date?"

"Next weekend," said Sophie. Then, without a moment's hesitation, she added: "Akiyama-san, can you come? We would be honored if you came."

This was so spontaneous that it surprised even Sophie. She normally would not do something like this without checking with Blackburn first. But the chemistry between them and Akiyama had been so right, and the wine had loosened so many inhibitions, that her impromptu invitation felt perfectly normal, even to Blackburn.

"Can you?" asked Blackburn.

"I was planning to return to Tokyo on Thursday, but I will try to delay. Thank you so much for the invitation."

*   *   *

The formal written offer from Wilks, Russell & Co. came midweek. Fifty-five million dollars for 100 percent of the shares of the Petroleum Consulting Group. Forty-eight million dollars to be paid immediately upon signing, with the balance held in escrow for one year, as a contingency for unexpected liabilities not discovered in due diligence. The detailed conditions in fine print were as previously agreed, covering Blackburn's continued involvement, first as an employee and later as a special advisor to Wilks, Russell & Co., as well as the continued involvement of other key staff, an orderly transition, effective integration, the coordinated announcement of the acquisition to clients of PCG and Wilks, Russell &Co., and coordinated news releases and interviews.

Blackburn's lawyer went through the proposed agreement line by line and saw no reason not to proceed. Blackburn signed the papers one day before his wedding to Sophie Myles.

It was a small civil wedding officiated by a judge, one of Blackburn's old acquaintances. Sophie's parents flew in from San Francisco. Some of her colleagues attended, plus Gene Theiss, Patrick Hagan, and Linda Hays from PCG, a few of Blackburn's clients who lived in Washington, DC, Aimi Kaysik, Akiyama, and, to their surprise, Robert Russell. The ceremony was simple, short, and official—just as they both wanted.

Blackburn had called Bianca to tell her the date, but with no intention of inviting her, despite their last conversation. He had prepared his arguments, planning to suggest that they could all meet sometime in Europe, and deliberately including Stefan to give Bianca a clear indication that it would be a family event. But it turned out that the preparation was not necessary, since Bianca could not fly to Washington on such short notice, and besides, she and Stefan were taking little Anthony to Rome that weekend, to familiarize him with his Italian heritage, and to have him meet Uncle Roberto.

Blackburn could not help feeling that something was off in Bianca; the spark was gone. Maybe we're both getting a little old, he thought, without fully believing it. But at that moment, the distance between them seemed to have grown, and although the wind had not extinguished the fire, it had not made it stronger either. Still, the fire did flicker in the wind, enough to give him a touch of a warm feeling inside.

Uniquely Blackburn

n all his years as the resident keeper of the Executive Resort in Gora, Kobayashi had never seen anything like it. The resort had been used exclusively for executive meetings. Idemitsu Kosan executives used it often for their offsite meetings, and larger groups of corporate executives and high-ranking government officials occasionally gathered there. The gathering of the Motouri Protocol was by far the most high-level meeting ever held at the resort.

So Kobayashi watched with astonishment as Blackburn got out of the car, walked around to the other side, and opened the door for Sophie, not allowing the driver to perform his customary duty. Even more astonishing was the scene when Blackburn picked up Sophie, walked with her in his arms to the large wooden gate, and waited for Kobayashi to hold the door open. Blackburn stepped in, and gently placed Sophie at the entrance, where they removed their shoes and stepped up on the tatami mat.

One week at the resort as Idemitsu's honeymooning guests was Akiyama's special wedding gift to them. An expression of his deep appreciation for being invited to their small and intimate wedding, and a confirmation of a personal friendship that went beyond any business dealings they might have had in the past, or would have in the future. This was one of the perks of the consulting business that Blackburn valued the most—when a client became a personal friend.

The resort had not changed since the spring of 1987, when the ten corporate executives and two government officials had gathered there for their two-day meeting. It was astounding in its simplicity, calmness, and sense of harmony. It took Blackburn and Myles a while to realize that they were whispering rather than talking normally. Everything felt like it had a presence to be respected—the walls, the mats, the bonsai tree, the four-century-old kimono, and most of all, the peace and calm that filled the space.

There were no other guests scheduled to be at the resort until the weekend, when Akiyama and his wife planned to join them. They spent those first four days in a pure "zen" existence, living in their kimonos, meditating, having the most incredible meals served by Kobayashi and his wife, reading, making love, and of course soaking in the hot sulfur spring bath.

Kobayashi showed them the bathhouse and the bathing protocol: Where to undress and hang their kimonos, how to thoroughly wash themselves in the section with the row of faucets protruding from the wall across from the pool, the low wooden stools they could use to sit on while shampooing their heads, the buckets they should use to pour water over themselves to rinse. They could tell he felt awkward giving them this demonstration, and to some extent so did they, but the novelty of the whole setup was interesting, and they found Kobayashi's discomfort amusing. They thanked him repeatedly as he left them alone in the large bathhouse and closed the door behind him.

"So, my venerable husband," whispered Sophie, mimicking how they had read that wives addressed their husbands in Japan, "may I assist you while you wash your body?"

As she took his kimono off and hung it on a peg, she noticed he was aroused.

"Ooh, my very, very venerable husband," she cooed, and then giggled so sweetly that for a second Bianca flashed in Blackburn's mind. He held Sophie close, laughing with her and banning all other images from his mind. They washed with soap and water and then rinsed as Kobayashi had instructed, and walked to the pool, which for a moment looked ominous. The water was dark, almost black, and at the point where it poured into the pool from the volcanic spring up in the hills, it arrived almost at boiling temperature. Steam rose in thick, curly tendrils, and the air was heavy with the smell of sulfur.

The water was so hot that at first neither of them could put more than a foot into the pool. Gradually, four ankles made their way into the water, then legs up to the knees, with many sighs and huffing and puffing. Finally Blackburn ran out of patience and sat on the first step going down into the pool, emitting a long cry mixed with hysterical laughter. Sophie couldn't resist; she shut her eyes, took a deep breath, and sat down next to him, determined not to scream. Gradually, the heat of the water became acceptable, then familiar, then even borderline pleasant. They slid to the second step, then the third, until they were buried up to their chins in the steaming hot water.

The first day, they could not last more than fifteen minutes submerged in the pool. The heat was so overwhelming that they felt faint. Their skin was a bright red when they dragged themselves out of the water, wobbling back toward the faucets to pour cold water over themselves and wash away the smell of sulfur from their bodies.

The great reward after a bath like that was the Japanese massage that followed. The masseuses were so masterful that neither Blackburn nor Sophie could stay awake during the forty-five minute sessions.

But when it was all over, they inevitably emerged from the bath-massage process totally famished. They were amazed at their appetites. Kobayashi and his wife always had the feast ready and spread over three tables in the dining room.

Nothing could have made them feel more decadent and spoiled.

By the fourth day, they were walking into the hot pool with no hesitation, and staying for almost an entire hour. But the effect of the bath and massage on their appetites remained the same.

On Friday evening, Blackburn and Sophie were in their kimonos when they greeted Akiyama and his wife Akiko. Akiyama was still in his business suit and Akiko was wearing a pantsuit when they arrived.

"You two are overdressed," said Blackburn, smiling at them.

Akiko's English was not as good as Akiyama's, but she could carry on a conversation. She took Sophie by the arm and walked ahead of the men, asking her how their stay had been so far and if she needed anything. According to what Sophie had read about Japanese culture and manners, this was unusual. She wondered if Akiko had in turn read about American culture and manners, and decided to adopt the direct and up-close style of breaking the ice with her new acquaintance. She noticed that Akiko had the same quality of kindness in her eyes as Akiyama, and wondered if she and her husband had always been alike in that way, or had rubbed off on each other over time. She wondered if she and Blackburn would grow alike over the years.

The next day they all got acquainted more closely than either Blackburn or Sophie had anticipated. After a few afternoon cocktails in the Japanese gardens overlooking the mist-covered Mount Fuji, Akiyama was relaxed, having left his work-related stress and anxiety in Tokyo.

"In Japan, it is common to have communal baths," he said casually. "If it does not make you and Sophie uncomfortable, we can all bathe together before dinner."

Sophie was talking to Akiko, so Blackburn was not sure if she heard Akiyama. He downed his vodka and tonic, shrugged his shoulders, and smiled.

"I'm more than comfortable with the Japanese custom," he said. "And if you'd like, I can even sing for you in the bath, given enough sake."

Akiyama laughed. "Oh, yes, Blackburn-san, I almost forgot. You're already practically Japanese. Funny *gaijin*, remember?"

"But let me ask Sophie. This is her first time in Japan."

"Ask Sophie what?" Sophie overheard and turned her attention to them.

"It is accepted custom in Japan to bathe together. Would you feel comfortable if we all took a bath together before dinner?"

She was taken by surprise, and looked to Akiko, who sat there smiling.

"Why not?" she said at last. "When in Rome, right?"

"Right."

They had a few more drinks and headed for the bathhouse. Sophie and Akiko took the last two faucets to wash, while the men washed a respectable distance away, at the beginning of the row of faucets. The men went into the pool first. Akiko and Sophie followed, tiptoeing carefully on the slippery marble floor, and sat down next to their husbands. In a few minutes, they all had their eyes shut, allowing the intense heat to penetrate their bodies and slow every physical and mental activity to almost a complete halt.

The following day they went for a tour of the surroundings. Akiyama drove them up to the first station on Mount Fuji, where they had a light lunch. Sophie and Akiko went for a walk in the gardens of the small restaurant, mesmerized by the view of the Gora hills and the chilly mountain air. The men stayed behind, smoking.

"This is a true Meaning of Life moment, Akiyama-san," said Blackburn, and told him about the plumber's commercial, his organization of PCG, and his general approach to life and work.

"You remember when I mentioned in Tokyo that Miyazaki-san was the ultimate 'Meaning of Life' type? This is what I meant."

"Well, Blackburn-san, for whatever it's worth, I hate dealing with Leaky Faucets too; but unfortunately, in my job at Idemitsu, I do not have the luxury of refusing to deal with them. You are lucky if you have been able to delegate Leaky Faucets to others."

Early Monday morning Akiyama and Akiko departed for Tokyo. Blackburn and Sophie had one more day at the resort, then a week in Kyoto, before heading back to Washington.

On their last night at the resort, Sophie got sentimental. It occurred to her that everything she had with Blackburn was unique: No one else could have arranged a honeymoon like this; no one else could have proposed like he did; no one else could have furthered her career like he did. No one else could have opened the world to her, and her eyes to the world, like he did. This was uniquely Blackburn.

"Jim," she said, not trying to hide her emotion or her tears, "we're just starting as a married couple, but this has already been a wonderful journey with you."

"Hey, come here ..." and he held her in his arms, as he knew she liked to be held. "It's been an amazing journey for me too, love. And I want nothing more than to continue the journey with you, Sophie. Absolutely nothing more."

XXXI

The Last Act

Almost overnight, or so it seemed to the public, the president turned into a hawk. His famous assertion, "This will not stand," spread through every news network both in the United States and across the world, and, more importantly, became the unambiguous signal to all involved government agencies to prepare for war.

At Central Command in Tampa, Florida, the generals who participated in the Maine War Games dusted off the old plan. Operation Desert Storm was ready to be launched, awaiting the order from the White House.

Diplomatic efforts to convince Iraq to withdraw from Kuwait had failed. Aside from all the futile intra-Arab efforts, a meeting in Geneva between the U.S. secretary of state and the foreign minister of Iraq ended with no progress, with the two men talking past each other. Soon after the failed talks in Geneva, the U.S. Congress passed a resolution, with close margins, authorizing the use of military force to push Iraq out of Kuwait.

Less than a week later, the air war against Iraq started.

Iraq's retaliation was swift, daring, and desperate—firing SCUD missiles at Israel, blowing up Kuwaiti oil fields, dumping millions of gallons of crude oil in the Persian Gulf, and invading the Saudi Arabian town of Khafji.

Blackburn watched the inferno in the Kuwaiti oil fields with disbelief. The fires seemed unstoppable, bursting with such force from the wells that it seemed impossible to even approach them. Over 700 fields had been set afire by explosive charges. Experts estimated that, if left alone, the fires would burn for several years, not only consuming billions of barrels of oil, but also causing enormous environmental damage. A U.S. firm was brought in to fight the fires, and Blackburn followed the fire-fighting efforts every day with captivation.

The land war, planned in excruciating detail during the War Games, had not even begun yet, but it was clear that Iraq was already in retreat. Coalition forces drove Iraq out of Khafji, Saudi Arabia, before the major land offensive began.

A final ultimatum was given to Iraq by the U.S. president: withdraw from Kuwait before the United States launches a ground offensive. Two days later, the ground war began. It took another two days before Iraq announced and then started its withdrawal. But this would not be a peaceful withdrawal. The retreating Iraqi forces were subjected to massive airstrikes, destroying every vehicle on the highway between Kuwait City and the border of Iraq, which later was dubbed the Highway of Death.

As Blackburn watched the news, he was astonished by the ferocity of the attack on the retreating Iraqi troops. He could not help calling Theiss.

"The retreat may not have been as peaceful as the news makes it out to be," said Theiss in his characteristic cool tone. "They were firing back at our aircraft."

"Firing back makes it not peaceful?"

"Well, we do not have a formal surrender yet. We're still at war."

"So even if they had not fired back, we would have continued the airstrikes?"

"Probably. But I do not want to speculate, Jim. The fact is, they did fire back."

"Gene, what did we achieve?"

"We destroyed some 10,000 Iraqi troops. That's where the media gets the phrase 'Highway of Death.' There was no point in driving Iraq out of Kuwait but leaving its military intact to pose another threat again. It's as simple as that."

Twenty-four hours later, the U.S. Marines entered Kuwait City. A day after that, the U.S. president announced a cease-fire, and declared Kuwait liberated from Iraqi occupation.

Epilogue
Spring 2016

James Blackburn sat in his large leather armchair on the back terrace of his house in the Forest Hills section of Washington, DC, and lit his cigar. It was midafternoon. A light rain was falling so quietly that he could not hear a single drop hit the ground. A couple of bluebirds chirped and chased each other in the far end of the garden, oblivious to the misty rain and rising humidity.

Blackburn had stopped smoking cigarettes soon after the birth of their first child, Chelsea, twenty-four years ago. The dangers of secondhand smoke had been pounded into his head by everyone. Besides, he had been mentally ready to quit, and Chelsea's arrival was as good a prompt as any. Two years later, when their son Henry was born, one of his friends had given him a Monte Cristo torpedo to celebrate. That was when he started having a cigar once in a while, no more than twice a week, sometimes only once a week. He impounded the covered terrace and turned it into a smoking room, installing glass windows around the semicircular open space overlooking the garden, so he could heat the place in the winter and air-condition it in the summer, and open one or two panes while he smoked his cigars.

It was his twenty-sixth wedding anniversary that day and he thought a Cohiba Espléndido was called for in the afternoon. Later that evening, he would take Sophie out for a lovely dinner.

As he sank into the leather armchair enjoying the first few delectable puffs, Sophie walked out and handed him her cell phone. "It's Chelsea," she said.

"Hi Daddy. Happy anniversary. Here's to the next twenty-six years!"

"Thanks sweetheart. It's late over there; are you okay?"

"It's only 10 p.m. in Vienna, Dad. It's not late. I'm still out with the Krauses. So what have you planned for this evening?"

Blackburn loved the way Chelsea was involved in their lives. She not only wanted to be constantly in touch, but often tried to plan things for them. She had moved to Vienna a year ago to study music at the Franz Schubert Conservatory and Bianca had instantly taken her under her wing. Now Chelsea wanted to know where he was going to take her mother to dinner, what gift he had for her, and what other romantic gestures were in the works. I bet she asked the same questions of her mother, thought Blackburn, and as always he indulged her.

"Someone else wants to say hi," she said when satisfied with the evening's plans.

"Hi Jimmy. Happy anniversary!"

"Thanks, Bianca. And thanks for taking such good care of Chelsea."

"She's a delight." Then, lowering her voice, she added: "I think Anthony likes her. They've gone out a few times in the past week."

"You don't say! Now wouldn't that be something?"

"See Jimmy? They'll pick up where we left off. Isn't that cool?" And the old, enchanting, unencumbered Bianca laughter cascaded through the phone.

"I better have a good talk with that young man first," Blackburn said, sounding more serious than he wanted to. "It won't be that easy to win over my little girl."

"Come over anytime, Jimmy. But let me warn you, she's not your little girl anymore. And Anthony is a perfect gentleman."

A year earlier, when Chelsea was getting ready to leave for Vienna, Blackburn had told Sophie about Bianca. "Someone I used to date a long time ago," he had said. "I know the family well, her husband, Stefan, and son Anthony. I think they're great people for Chelsea to know if she's going to live alone in Vienna."

They had been to Vienna once since Chelsea's move, and Sophie and Bianca had met for the first time. The two families had bonded.

Blackburn's cigar afternoons were his favorite times to review the news on his iPad and reflect on both the past and the future. He measured cigars by the amount of time it took to smoke one at a leisurely pace. A Monte Cristo No. 5 lasted around twenty minutes; a Romeo Y Julieta Churchill an hour and fifteen minutes. Most of the time, when he had forty-five minutes to an hour, he picked a Hoyo de Monterrey Epicure No. 2 or Monte Cristo No. 3. A Cohiba Espléndido could be stretched for close to two hours if he had no reason to rush.

His usual "tour" of the news had three main stops: oil markets, the Middle East, and Washington. All three had been taking him to Russia frequently in the past few years, and occasionally to China, which had finally woken up as an economic power. Japan was no longer in the global limelight.

He read with some amusement various analysts' commentary on the low oil prices, citing oversupply and lackluster demand as the main causes. Crude oil prices had crashed by over 70 percent in the past eighteen months, from over $105 per barrel to the low thirties. He had not been to an OPEC meeting for years, but could practically see and hear what was going on within the organization. Nothing has changed in thirty years, he thought. This is just like the eighties—Saudi Arabia driving the high-cost producers out to secure its long-term market share, and in the process punishing political adversaries. In the last couple of years, Russia had been added to the list of the rivals, largely because of its policies in Syria, which conflicted with those of Riyadh.

The big story now was the rise of the Islamic State, which had first sprung up in Syria as an offshoot of Al-Qaeda and then rapidly moved into and terrorized parts of Northern Iraq. This was by far the most dangerous and controversial development in the past two years, with the most unlikely supporters. That, in Blackburn's mind, stretched the limits of realpolitik.

The rise of a major Sunni backlash to the fall of the Ba'ath regime in Iraq and the subsequent establishment of a Shia government in Baghdad was not the surprising part. Blackburn had predicted a Sunni comeback even before the second Gulf War was launched back in 2003, which was the last straw that had made him resign from his position as special advisor to the U.S. government. But the scale of the organization of the Islamic State, the speed with which it gathered momentum, and the seemingly unlimited material and logistical resources it appeared to command, were not only impressive, but suggested coordinated backing from a multitude of sources.

Blackburn often recalled Gene Theiss' advice to follow the "undeclared objectives" of various interests. He missed Theiss. He had passed away over ten years earlier, peacefully, in his sleep. Blackburn had felt nearly the same sense of loss as when his father died, made more difficult by the nearly unconscious re-mourning of his father's loss while grieving for Theiss. Sophie was the only person in his circle who could understand what Blackburn was going through. Both her parents had passed away too, a couple of years before Theiss, within eight months of each other. Besides, she knew what Theiss meant to Blackburn better than anyone else.

He was half an hour into his cigar when Sophie walked out with a cup of tea, and sat in the armchair next to him. In a few seconds, she got up again and opened two more windowpanes. The cigar smoke had filled the terrace.

"Sorry," said Blackburn.

"No you're not," she said, giving him a kiss before she sat back down.

Robert Russell had long passed on, and so had Mr. Wilks, but the firm Sophie now ran was still called Wilks, Russell & Co. There had been some talk of changing the name when she first took over, but she had opposed it. She wanted to see her name appear as the CEO of Wilks, Russell, not of some other company.

"Did Chelsea tell you that she's dating Anthony?" she asked.

"She said nothing to me, but Bianca mentioned it. She told you?"

"Yes, this was the second time she mentioned it this week."

Blackburn was surprised and a bit disappointed.

"She didn't mention anything to me; and I thought she told me everything."

"Honey, she knows how protective you tend to be. The first time she mentioned it to me it didn't sound serious, so I didn't tell you. Today she sounded a bit more serious. She really likes Anthony. She says he combines the best of a Viennese gentleman and an Italian ..." Sophie hesitated for a few seconds and then added, "an Italian romantic."

"Come out with it, Sophie. She did not say 'romantic,' did she? What did she say?"

"Okay," she said. "I still can't get anything past you. She said an Italian lover."

"That does it. I'm flying there next week. You want to come?"

Sophie could not tell if he was serious. Fortunately, just then Henry walked in with a bottle of champagne.

"Hey you lovebirds," he said, kissing Sophie and then hugging Blackburn. "Happy anniversary. Just stopped by to drop this off. Can't stay long."

He was a student at Georgetown University's School of Foreign Service. He had never known his grandfather, whose name he now carried, but had heard enough stories about him to wonder what it would be like to live the life of an active Foreign Service officer, engaged in world affairs like no ordinary citizen could be.

"Sit down," said Blackburn. "I haven't talked to you for a while. What's new with you?"

"Not much, other than school."

It was not easy to get Henry to talk. Blackburn had to probe about specific issues to have him open up, and even that did not always work. He worried about what type of Foreign Service Henry would join once he graduated. What maze of imponderable, undeclared objectives would he help pursue, often without even realizing what they were?

Blackburn wanted Henry to understand and appreciate the real world of foreign policymaking. But he did not want to disillusion the young man too early in the game. It was best if he discovered the basic facts of his chosen field by himself. So he talked to him carefully, remembering how Theiss sometimes broached a subject in a way that led Blackburn to the conclusions he wanted him to reach without directly stating them himself. Plant the seeds of realpolitik in the young man, and let him figure the rest out.

Yet part of him was impatient to open up to his son. Impatient to have an adult, professional discussion with him about the world and the U.S role in it; impatient to impart to him what he had learned, often the hard way. He knew exactly what drove his impatience, and that was what helped him resist it. He had waited too long to have the same adult, professional talk with his father, and now regretted that every day.

Henry did not stay long. After fifteen minutes, he took his leave, wishing his parents a wonderful evening.

Reading about the latest atrocities committed by the Islamic State, Blackburn let his mind drift back some fifteen years, to the fateful events of September 11, 2001, which had changed America and opened the floodgates for a political wave that swept through Washington and hijacked the administration of George W. Bush. The catastrophe of September 11 had given a group of policymakers the justification and the license to drive through the U.S. government the costliest and most ill-considered military adventures in American history.

He knew many members of the group, which soon became known as the neoconservatives, or neocons. He shuddered as he remembered his encounters with them back in the eighties. Aimi Kaysik, who quit the CIA two years after Blackburn did because of the same frustrations and disillusionments with the government that drove him out. At first though she had tried to convince him to stay.

"Aimi, it's all a big lie," he told her. "The claim that Iraq has weapons of mass destruction is a lie, and you know that better than I do. You've read Wilson's report. He was sent to Iraq by the CIA, wasn't he? Didn't he say the reports of Iraq's importing yellow cake from the Niger were categorically wrong? You've seen the reports of the chief UN weapons inspector. There are no weapons of mass destruction in Iraq. Besides, the entire 'preemptive' war concept embraced by the administration is illegal."

"I know," she said, fighting an inner battle to still believe her government was doing the right thing. "But what if they know something we don't know? What if this war is as necessary as the first Gulf War?"

"It is not. This war will be disastrous for U.S. interests in the region. These guys don't know anything we don't know. They have a single-minded obsession to destroy Iraq, at any cost. Any cost, Aimi. Look what they did to Valerie Plame, just because of Wilson's report and going public with the big lie. They will stop at nothing. It will cost billions of American taxpayers' dollars and thousands of American lives, with no benefit to the United States at all, but they don't care."

"But why? Jim, what is in it for them?"

"Look, Aimi, I can speculate as to why, but let me tell you this: We fought the first Gulf War to restore order in the Middle East and to defend the status quo. We reversed the illegal occupation and annexation of a country. Here we are, twelve years later, about to launch a war to *destroy* the status quo and create *disorder* in the region. Remember Theiss and his 'undeclared objectives' theory? This is it. The objective this time is to create disorder and instability. That is what they want. And they have the ultimate carte blanche because of September 11."

Blackburn had tried hard to alert the government about the dangers of another Gulf war that had no clear rationale or objective. The vice president, who remembered Blackburn from his days as secretary of defense in the early nineties, had asked to see him again. Blackburn, who had already established that neither reason nor American national interests were driving this process, was reluctant at first. But Aimi convinced him to go.

He was alarmed when he got to the vice president's office at the White House. They were not alone. The vice president had three others present, including his chief of staff, who was later convicted in the Valerie Plame case. Blackburn had no desire to discuss anything serious with such an audience. He had assumed he'd be alone with the vice president, as he had been in all his meetings with him when the man was secretary of defense. After about half an hour of generalities, Blackburn left the White House, more convinced than ever that he no longer had a role to play.

Still, he stayed on until the launch of the second Gulf War. He watched the massive U.S. airpower, through the declared "shock and awe" strategy, destroy Iraq and occupy Baghdad. His instincts as a professional forecaster of economic and political trends opened up scenarios in his mind of a world where the Middle East disintegrated into religious fundamentalism and sectarian warfare. It was like destroying a key segment of a delicate ecosystem and then watching the entire system implode.

The neocons had long moved away from center stage, but their legacy lingered. What was unleashed after the second war could not be reversed or contained with one change in the U.S. administration. Even if successive administrations tried to pursue a different foreign policy, they could not undo history. Whether they liked it or not, their policies had to react to realities on the ground, compromising their options. And if the new realities on the ground were a deeper anti-American and more hostile environment, they had to fight it and act to protect U.S. interests, even if American foreign policy had created that environment in the first place. That was the nature of the damage done by the post-September 11 fanatics in the United States: The harm they brought on the country would outlive them by decades.

A news item flashed on Blackburn's iPad, bringing him back to the present. The Islamic State had just beheaded twenty people, including six of their own, and enslaved sixty women and children from a small Kurdish village in Northern Syria.

For the thousandth time, Blackburn wondered how the world might have been different if The Symposium had succeeded, if its vision of civil society had prevailed more than twenty-five years ago. Ramzi Amin had died a couple of years ago in London, a broken man, with an unfulfilled dream. There never was any news about Karim Suliman, whose family finally gave up the search and the appeals, and settled in Switzerland. Majed Al Shammary was still in the Saudi National Guard, elevated to the rank of colonel; his dream of deposing King Fahd and bringing Crown Prince Abdulla to the throne finally materialized when King Fahd had a stroke, four years after the first Gulf War, and Abdulla was made regent. But by then The Symposium had totally disintegrated and scattered.

Blackburn watched as Islamic fundamentalist ideology became the only outlet for the many grievances The Symposium had tried to address. What if we had managed to support them, he asked himself and Aimi and Sophie. What if they had become the voice that stood in the end? What if we had let those guys shape the future of the region? What a different world we'd be living in now.

That would have been a better world from your perspective, he'd remind himself, but not from the perspective of those with the undeclared objectives. Those who orchestrated this mess are celebrating now. They had to know that this would be the outcome of our actions. They did not want to leave any viable, strong country in the region. In their minds, that would not serve the interests of the West, nor of the United States, nor of Israel. The Congressional Budget Office estimated that the cost of the second Gulf War was $2.4 trillion—an unfathomable figure even by Washington standards for a single project. Yet for those who sought the destabilization of the Middle East, it was a worthwhile and successful project.

"Hey Jim," whispered Sophie, who had been watching him as he was drawn deeper and deeper into his thoughts, "time to come back to the present. I'm not going anywhere with you unless you wash that cigar smoke off."

He looked at her so lovingly that she was moved. After all these years, he thought, she's still got it. In fact, while he, with his graying and thinning hair and expanding waistline was beginning to look like his sixty-three years, she had not changed much. She still had her slender body, youthful and sparkling eyes, and one of the kindest souls Blackburn had ever known, which miraculously metamorphosed into an effective executive as soon as she stepped into her office.

"Can you take a week off sometime soon?" he asked.

"I'm the boss, remember? Sure I can. What do you have in mind?"

"Let's do that trip to Vienna," he said, standing up to go take a shower before dinner. "Next week if you can. I hear they have some great concerts this season."

Acknowledgements

I am indebted to several individuals who helped improve this book immeasurably. My two former colleagues, Fareed Mohammedi and Raad Alkadiri enriched the description of historical events recounted in the novel. The comments and suggestions of Jane Vise Hall, Armine Hovannisian, Raffi Kassarjian, Shahan Zanoyan and Nora Salibian led to invaluable editorial and story line improvements. Lucineh Kassarjian's input in the development of some of the characters was vital. I am indebted also to Natsuko Kitani for translating the Japanese song, and to my old friend and associate, Kohei Hara, for introducing me to the many Japanese institutions described in this book, not least among which the executive resort in Gora. Many thanks are due to my editor, Kathrin Seitz, who, aside from editing the manuscript, put up with some of my stylistic idiosyncrasies. Finally, I owe a debt of gratitude to my wife, Charlotte, who not only suffered through early versions of the manuscript, but also endured many lonely months while I was consumed by writing this book.

About the Author

Vahan Zanoyan has previously published two novels based on a chance encounter with a sex-trafficking survivor: *A Place Far Away* and *The Doves of Ohanavank*. His third novel, *The Sacred Sands*, reflects his own experience as an international energy consultant.

Before he retired, Zanoyan served as an advisor to governments, private organizations, and other major players in the fossil fuel industry. He currently divides his time between Southern California, Armenia, and the Middle East.

CPSIA information can be obtained
at www.ICGtesting.com
Printed in the USA
LVOW13s1606300317
529063LV00012B/830/P

7